St. Dunstan in the east

Allhalows Barking

Hackney

Bridge Gate

KU-333-005

This Marlowe

Also by Michelle Butler Hallett

deluded your sailors
Sky Waves
Double-blind
The shadow side of grace

This Marlowe

MICHELLE BUTLER HALLETT

GOOSE LANE EDITIONS

Copyright © 2016 by Michelle Butler Hallett.

All rights reserved. No part of this work may be reproduced or used in any form or by any means, electronic or mechanical, including photocopying, recording, or any retrieval system, without the prior written permission of the publisher or a licence from the Canadian Copyright Licensing Agency (Access Copyright). To contact Access Copyright, visit www.accesscopyright.ca or call 1-800-893-5777.

Edited by Bethany Gibson.
Cover and page design by Julie Scriver.
Cover illustration detailed from the *Rainbow Portrait*, c. 1600–1602, attrib. Marcus Gheeraerts the Younger (Collection of the Marquess of Salisbury, Hatfield House).
Endpaper image detailed from Visscher's view of London, 1616 (Library of Congress).
Printed in Canada.
10 9 8 7 6 5 4 3 2 1

Library and Archives Canada Cataloguing in Publication

Butler Hallett, Michelle, 1971-, author
This Marlowe / Michelle Butler Hallett.

Issued in print and electronic formats.
ISBN 978-0-86492-920-4 (bound).--ISBN 978-0-86492-925-9 (epub).--
ISBN 978-0-86492-926-6 (mobi)

1. Marlowe, Christopher, 1564-1593--Fiction. I. Title.

PS8603.U86T45 2016   C813'.6   C2015-906805-3
C2015-906806-1

We acknowledge the generous support of the Government of Canada, the Canada Council for the Arts, and the Government of New Brunswick.

Nous reconnaissons l'appui généreux du gouvernement du Canada, du Conseil des arts du Canada, et du gouvernement du Nouveau-Brunswick.

Goose Lane Editions
500 Beaverbrook Court, Suite 330
Fredericton, New Brunswick
CANADA E3B 5X4
www.gooselane.com

The woods are dark, dear, cold and somewhat thick
Like blood on a wolf's breath teeth upon your neck.
And your heart is racing it seems you've lost your way.
O lord provide me with strength enough to flee.

Will my eyes fall upon the hand that cuts your throat?

—Pipher, "The Lizard" from *Till Light*

My first acquaintance with this Marlowe rose upon his
bearing name...

—Thomas Kyd, Letter A, addressed to
Sir John Puckering

VIDEO ET TACEO

(I see, and say nothing)

– Queen Elizabeth I, ascribed

THE SIGHT OF LONDON TO MY EXILED EYES
January 1593

Coins fell on his face.

Dreaming of Tom's kisses, he twitched. *Let me sleep.*

Kit lay on his back, on a straw tick and wooden pallet, upturned palms framing his head. Coarse brown hair, threaded with grey like his beard, straggled past his shoulders from beneath a snug woollen cap, and the blue circles under his eyes reached his cheekbones. He wore clothes for winter, the fabric fraying and holed: decrepit hose and slop breeches, and, beneath a leather jerkin, three layered shirts. Sturdy shoes, buckled and shearling-lined, kept his feet warm, these shoes a gift from his father, a master cobbler, some years before. A tangerine silk kerchief covered the wind-chapped skin of his throat, and a blanket outlined his compact body: not quite middling height, and slender, sinewy. This build deceived people. Kit could move with a startling vigour and grace, winning or escaping most fights.

Ric knew it. Short and stocky, he also wore tangerine silk round his neck. He glanced at the two constables he'd hired: one each on the side of the bed as he stood at the head. The hearth lay dark and cold; the tiny window admitted scant winter light; Ric dropped another coin.

A numbing little slap: no kiss.

Eyes still shut, Kit rolled over, bunching the blankets and revealing a dagger strapped to his right thigh. His muscles felt relaxed, even heavy, a delicious sensation after months of vigilance and overwork, and his thoughts slugged like cold honey.

Ric knelt near Kit's head.

Kit rolled on his back again. *Wait.*

Flushing's winter cold reached him. So did a sudden odour of onions and meat: the sweat of a man he knew.

A warm coin on each of his closed eyes —

Kit swatted the coins away and made to stand. His legs failed. He fell back on the pallet and tick, knocking the air out of himself. Three unfriendly faces blocked his view of the ceiling.

Fucked.

Almost throwing him, the two constables hauled Kit to his feet.

Ric smiled, held out his arms. —Thou dost look utterly simian: a little monkey chained in a library.

Kit inclined his head as though acknowledging a compliment. Then he told himself to keep still as Ric approached him. Instead, he lunged away from the constables. They pulled him back, hard.

Ric stooped a bit and pressed an ear to Kit's chest. —Be not so pensive. Last night I said thy heart beat brave and true.

He looked up.

—Oh, 'tis pounding now.

Kit spat in his face.

Ric wiped his eye clean with the ends of his silk kerchief. —Save it, Marlowe. Thou'lt be thirsty.

Wrenching his neck, Kit addressed the larger constable in rapid French, expecting English would get him nowhere. —The wine. Last night. He tainted the wine.

The constable shrugged. He understood; he didn't care.

Ric faced Kit and clapped a hand on his shoulder. Voice low, he spoke in English. —If thou'dst accepted mine offer, as thou didst accept last night my gifts of dried beef and wine, thou'dst have enjoyed a sweet and heavy sleep, and, later today, a hot supper. But no. No, 'tis never easy with thee. 'Tis like the one who would steal fire, suffering then his heart to be plucked out by crows each —

—Liver, Baines.

—What?

—The punishment of Prometheus, la: liver, not heart, and eagle, not crows. For Christ's love, hast thou read nothing? Prometheus languished, aye, chained to a rock, and each dawn, an eagle tore out his liver. Scrap by scrap. Smoke rose from that blood-drizzled beak. Wounds burn, Baines. Stolen fire *burns*. As the stars etched their maps on the charred sky, the liver of Prometheus did swell. It grew back. Relentless dawn and the eagle's truth: wings interrupted the light and so defined themselves as the light shone around them, indifferent. Recognition: with or without it, the agony plays anew. Now, thine agony, Baines, how shall it come? Oh...Aye, a starling. Small.

Squinting, Ric looked to the constables, then at Kit. He found no clarity. —I do humbly thank thee for the lesson, good master tutor —

—Good master poet.

—But I beg thee, say: how earned Prometheus his punishment?

Kit smirked. —The question is: how earned Prometheus his justice?

—Ah, le garçon.

Ric was pointing. Kit looked. So did the constables.

A boy of maybe eleven now stood in the doorway, darkness obscuring his face.

Still speaking French, Ric asked the boy if he recognized Kit.

—Oh, oui, monsieur.

The boy sounded eager to help.

Then he added that Kit had used him as a catamite the night before.

The two constables dragged Kit to a wall, the shorter one snarling in his ear. —I've got a son that age.

As Ric paid the boy, adding that he felt, thinking on the boy's pain, such a stab of sorrow, Kit struggled and almost got loose. The boy ran off, footfall light and fast on the stairs, as a constable seized Kit's hair and hauled back his head

—Leave off! I've never seen that boy before!

A coin smacked his cheek.

Ric gestured to the floor. —These brazen counterfeits, aye, these artless fakes.

He waited.

The constables said nothing.

Kit said nothing.

Ric shifted his weight from foot to foot, gave a little snort, and then glared at the taller constable.

Recalling his cue, the taller constable nodded. —Oh. Oh. So, ah, counterfeiting and corrupting a boy. Be that all?

Head still craned back, Kit rolled his eyes. —Sufficeth not?

Ric switched to English. —'Tis all a gift from Tony Bacon,

in gracious response to thy refusal, thy refusal so bitter and rude.

—Baines, I'll see thee fucked with a tide-pole for this!

Ric made a little gesture with his fingers, and the constables threw Kit to the floor, one aiming a kick at his face. Kit jerked away and rolled toward the wall. Trapped, he yelled as the shorter constable ground his heel into his left wrist and got in a few good kicks at his ribs. Something cracked.

Sweet Christ Jesus, get me out —

A rapid descent over stairs smelling of the piss of every cat in Christendom: icy drizzle on his face, and a memory of Robin Poley's voice: *Rein thy pain and fear before they rein thee.* Kit started to ask for his cloak, left behind; speech demanded air and so refused him. Gasping, getting deeper breaths, he opened his eyes and blinked away tears. Low clouds promised snow. The offended father-constable on his right smiled, a man enjoying his work; Kit took note of his pewter ring and of the mole just left of his mouth. *Marks to make thee easy to find later.* He smirked at the thought. The constable noticed, and he broke stride. Avoiding the gutter, Kit stumbled. The constable shoved him; Kit staggered for balance. Then the constable backhanded Kit in the face, pewter ring to the eye, as gutter-mess flooded Kit's shoes. Waiting, Ric and the other constable fogged the air with their breath in little clouds that dissipated long before they reached the sky.

Stunned with pain, Kit sagged against the father-constable. *Get word to Governor Sidney.*

The English administered Flushing — owned it, they said — and Sidney knew about Kit and his work.

The coded message, the pseudonym, then just wait it out…

Another good shove, and he fell blind, shoulder and face hitting the ground first. Ice and rocks and muck: his body jerked into a ball, knees to his chest, arms over his face. He imagined the excuse they'd later give: *the prisoner did several times resist arrest.* Death, Kit believed, would hardly be clean or comfortable, not for him, but to be kicked to it, so far from home? To freeze to the ground of another country in a puddle of his own blood?

I deserve better.

He braced for a storm of boots and shoes.

The tiny cell got some daylight, however stunted, from being on the ground floor and near the main doors. It also boasted the wild luxury of a little wooden stool. No bed, though, nor a bench.

Despite his anger and fear, his expectation of another blow any moment, Kit leaned forward on the stool and kept quite still. He'd found the angle of least pain, and he intended to keep it.

Least pain: ribs, back, and face stabbing, throbbing burning. Eyes weeping.

Oh, this is tedious. Why in Hell…? What is't? The idea of England? The glory of defying Rome?

The glory of broken bones.

Nine-and-twenty next birthday.

Tom is right: leave it behind.

Oh, aye, just strut free, right out of this gaol.

Horse piss and fuckery.

The beatings played out in his mind, over and over, in brilliant tableaux. Tiring of this, he worked to think instead about his visit to Government House, many months ago. He'd stood before Robert Sidney as the governor leaned his elbows on his big desk, laced his fingers together and tapped his joined hands against his chin. Kit had studied the fading tapestry behind Sidney, one showing Diana standing naked within a circle of handmaidens and pointing at an intruder as stag horns sprouted from Actaeon's temples, as Sidney had murmured of the need to infiltrate networks of exiled English Catholics and disrupt the trafficking of Jesuits back to England. Though Sidney knew the man's true name, he addressed Kit by his pseudonym, Stephen Loman. Kit had decided on the pseudonym himself and thought it clever.

Loosening the silk kerchief round his neck, irritating his ribs, he grunted. *Must everything hurt? Every little thing?* He rubbed the kerchief between his fingers: tangerine silk, like the one Ric Baines wore, and a gift the night before. Kit felt stupid. And small. *Greeks bearing gifts, la.* He dipped the silk into the cup of ale given earlier with a piece of bread, wrung it out, and, thinking of his sister, pressed the cool cloth to his swollen eye.

Manna.

He clicked his tongue.

What, thou'lt only remember her when th'art bruised?

His sister's name was Mary. Infant Kit, saying his first words, had pronounced it Manna: *Manna, wait! Manna, wait!* She'd looked after all her younger brothers, but she took especial care with Kit, closest to her in age and, it seemed, blind to

danger. She'd called him Clever Kitten and Little Troublesome
One. As adults, the siblings still used those pet names, the rare
time they saw each other. Echoing Manna, Kit would call
himself Clever Kitten in his thoughts — in rebuke.

So, Clever Kitten, what woe this time?

As a child, Kit had collided with trouble so often it became
expected: water, mud, people, animals, holes. Inscrutable fortune spared him, over and over. Canterbury boys fell in the
River Stour and drowned, and Canterbury boys sickened with
measles, fevers, catarrh and died. Kit fell in the river, and Kit
got sick, and Kit always recovered. His mother or sister would
turn and discover him in the doorway, dirty or wet or bloodied, and help him clean up and dry off. Sometimes he'd stand
naked before the hearth, eyes heavenward as Manna examined
his latest folly in great detail. Once clean and clothed, he must
report to his father in his workshop, interrupt John Marlowe
crafting some new pair of shoes, and submit to punishment.
These beatings, though brief, hurt. What hurt more, as Kit
got older: the fear in John Marlowe's eyes, the panic edging
his voice. *Kit, Kit, when wilt thou learn?*

The day Kit fell into the hole beneath a dead and collapsing
oak he felt he'd fallen into some terrible truth. Spitting out
mud and a milk tooth, he looked up. Matted roots obscured
the sky. Should the tree shift either way and complete a descent, it might disturb loose soil and seal the hole. Kit scrabbled
and slipped, begged and yelled; the soil permitted no ascent.
Near dusk, Manna found Kit's shoes. He'd tossed them as
high as he could, once his voice gave out. Recognizing her
father's work, Manna knelt. Then she peered at the hole yawning nearby; her brother, hands and face just visible, waved her

away, warned her off. Manna sat near the shoes, waiting for a searching adult to wander within earshot, telling Kit stories as he fretted the damp earth, as he crushed worms and bugs with his nails. A rope got him out, a rope hauled by his father in desperate vigour. Kit got no beating that time, John Marlowe crying too hard even to look at him.

Kit sometimes dreamt of that tree, of its cracked roots shedding dirt and pointing to the sky.

Charm, Catherine Marlowe said of her son, the boy can sing birds down from trees, tickle Lucifer until he laughs, and persuade the Angel of Death to visit some other day. Kit talked well; he also listened well. He would tilt his head to one side and almost stroke the speaker with his alert, sometimes kind, eyes. People relaxed with Kit, not always recognizing they did so. He neither flattered nor fawned, not beyond the needs of social standing, yet he made others feel important, feel their ideas and desires mattered to him. Doing this, he'd coaxed useful information from Manna, schoolteachers, singing masters, Cambridge professors, Church of England priests, and, lately, a secret Jesuit in Flushing.

Cull. Ben Cull.

Kit took the kerchief from his eye — it had done no good — and knotted it round his neck again, disturbing the loop of wool hanging there. He checked the wool, made sure the knot held and the threaded key remained. Then he resumed his counting of stones. For each stone in the walls and floor, he would recite either a verse from Ovid or from the Bible in Latin and then translate it. Such tasks calmed his thoughts and even slowed the beating of his heart — something else Robin Poley had taught him.

Dread frays thy thinking, Marlowe. Fight it. Make compartments in thy mind.

The gaol's great doors opened, and the English clerk accepted a delivery: objects this time, not prisoners. Kit glanced through the bars as the clerk passed by, bearing a heavy armload of shrouds.

Shrouds for anyone who died in this gaol.

Kit let out a long breath.

A racket then, as the great doors opened once more, and an irritated voice, deep and expectant with tones of power, deplored the empty desk and bellowed for the clerk. Still bearing some shrouds, the thin fabric flapping out around him, the clerk ran back to his desk and greeted his visitor. Kit wondered at the voice and told himself he must be mistaken. Still, he got to his feet.

Governor Robert Sidney, dark hair and beard trimmed, brilliant white ruff pinned in place over billowing wool and silk, long cloak keeping him warm, strode down the corridor. The clerk at his side, Sidney stared into the dim cell until he discerned the shape of a man. Then he scowled.

—Clerk: lock those main doors, and then busy thyself far from me.

Kit waited until the clerk left before giving a bow. The pain of it made him dizzy.

Sidney got close to the bars and spat on the floor. —Thou art an embarrassment and a disgrace.

—Governor —

—Already I've got a letter from no less than Stanley on my desk, taunting me about thee and thy matters. Aye, *Stanley,* the exiled English Catholic officer. How knows he, hey? And I assure thee, he asks me not of Loman but Marlowe.

Kit shut his eyes. *Exposed. Boy-fucking Judas. All those months; all that work: ruint.*

Sidney gripped the bars near his face, as though himself the prisoner. —Sir Robert Cecil assured me thou'dst cause no trouble. What folly, then: *counterfeiting*?

—I touched no coin.

—And the boy?

—Nor him!

Sidney looked up and down the corridor, found only darkness and a desk.

—Governor, came this arrest on your orders?

—If it had, would I be here?

—Maybe not.

—Thy tone, Marlowe: for a man supplicating aid, thou dost presume too much.

—Forgive me, Governor. The light is dim, and my mind is fuddled. I woke up to a beating.

—Woke up to it?

—Ric Baines informed you of the charges against me, no?

—He speaks, too, of his fears thou'st gone Catholic on us.

Kit rubbed his forehead. —Oh, excellent. Baines gave me beef and wine, beef preserved with salt to roughen my thirst, and wine tainted with a sleeping draught. Oh, I'm pleased it amuses you.

—And why would he do that?

Kit stepped closer to the bars. —Alongside these gifts, he offered me the patronage of a new master.

Robert Devereux, the Earl of Essex, and tangerine silk is his standard.

—Patronage? Marlowe, th'art not here to write poetry.

—Employment, then. Another man would give the Queen foreign intelligence when she already receives it from Sir Robert Cecil and, before him, his father, Lord Burghley. This other man has now got the means to hire agents, and, so I am told, his foreign intelligence now rivals and sometimes surpasses that of Sir Robert. This will cause only rancour and waste.

—Sir Robert and Lord Burghley, crook-backed Young Fox and dying Old Fox: aye, they rely on the likes of thee. In the end, thou dost serve the Queen.

—Of course I serve the Queen, but I report to Sir Robert.

—Th'art perched on a slippery riverbank here, Marlowe. Only a man of position and means could so interfere with England's intelligence.

—Aye, Governor.

Not that either of us dares to name him.

—Then heed this, my caution, Marlowe. Is't thy right, thy place, to darken the name, or even question the motives, of such a great and powerful man?

Kit considered the tones of Sidney's voice: insult, anger, fear. He rubbed his arms, warming them. —I believe it may be my duty, Governor.

Sidney said nothing.

Then Kit noticed the kerchief tucked in the gorgeous ruffled cuff of Sidney's right sleeve: tangerine silk.

Dread rose. Kit grasped a bar to keep his balance and almost laughed. *And, Governor, your brother's widow is his wife.*

For Christ's love, Sir Robert, you might have told me I must keep an eye on Sidney, too.

Sidney looked Kit up and down. —I'm deporting thee.

What? —Sir, what mean you?

—I mean, I am deporting thee. Th'art Sir Robert's problem now. My only question is which of thy names to use.

—Governor, I beseech you: reconsider.

—A sad waste. Still, 'tis out of my hands.

Aye, policy. —Would you condescend to compose a short explanation to Sir Robert explaining my return? Maybe write *Look you to it*?

—Oh, like Pilate? Marlowe, thine impudence mounts like fever and shit. Wilt thou presume to command me?

Kit clasped his hands behind his back and studied the floor: a posture of humility. *Christ's love, my ribs.* —Governor, would you wipe a slick and anxious brow with your tangerine silk? Kin before crown?

Sidney reached through the bars and hooked his fingers beneath the kerchief around Kit's neck, yanked him closer.

Their noses touched.

—Marlowe, I'll take no rebuke from the likes of thee.

Kit stared into Sidney's eyes.

Sidney looked away first. Letting Kit go, he stepped back from the bars. —The very next English ship, Marlowe. I care not if 'tis a salt-cod scow. Clerk! And as for deportation's paperwork: aye, thy real name. Clerk, I say! And they can chain thee in the hold, counterfeiter.

Sidney's departing footfall joined the clerk's, and daylight flooded the gaol a moment as Sidney left through the great doors.

Kit sat back on the little stool, considering displays of power and nuances of treachery to distract himself from considering how damned cold he felt.

Not a salt-cod scow but a seventy-foot cargo ship carrying food, trade, correspondence, and men back and forth across the English Channel: *Peace of Lethe*. Kit rolled his eyes when he saw the name, or rather, the shadow of it, the lettering beaten away by salt water. Yesterday Ben Cull had expected to return to England on board *Peace of Lethe*. He'd presented himself to the watch officer, as arranged, and Flemish constables had arrested him, as arranged.

Arranged by Kit.

Grateful to be out of the cutting winter wind, ribs, back, and wrist aching, Kit followed the boatswain and another sailor belowdecks. The march from the gaol to the docks in the spitting snow in his jerkin and shirtsleeves had reduced him to shaking chills. His mind, worn now with pain, hunger, and cold, told him comforting lies: he'd be expected to work his passage back to England, or he'd be confined in a room belowdecks, perhaps ousting the first mate. Either way, he'd get warm.

Bilge stink thickened as they entered the cargo hold.

Sidney meant it?

The boatswain lit a slush lamp, a tiny well of spent cooking fats and grease; the illumination reached his lined and melancholy face.

Kit cleared his throat. —I believe the governor spoke of me and the cargo hold in jest. I'll offer ye some consideration for changing this arrangement.

The sailor nudged him. —How much?

Kit patted his belt, felt the cut purse tab, patted again, patted his jerkin just in case, grunted in disgust. *Which constable, la?*

Breath making clouds, the sailor laughed. —The old tale, is't? Someone just cut thy purse from thy belt.

I could die in here. —For Christ's love! No, wait.

The boatswain pressed his hands on Kit's shoulders. —Sit down, by the bolt.

Shivering, Kit did so, and the boatswain took down from the wall a set of shackles. He clicked his tongue, annoyed, and ordered the other sailor to run to his locker and fetch a set of keys. The sailor left, Kit's view of his departure framed by a shackle cuff.

The boatswain got behind Kit and tapped him on the shoulder. —Not one word.

He wrapped his cloak around Kit and fastened it. Mystified, Kit sat still as the leftover body heat sank into his skin. Then he looked over his shoulder and asked the boatswain why.

—Hush, I said. Wrists behind thee.

Iron clinked as the boatswain threaded the shackle chain through the bolt, fastened the cuffs on Kit. Lumpy and pocked with rust, the cuffs would scratch and gall. Then the boatswain adjusted the cloak once more, closing it. The sailor returned, squinting, breathing hard, feeling his way. He apologized; he'd found nothing. The boatswain stood up, explaining he'd discovered his keys on the wrong loop of his belt and would be above in a moment. Satisfied, the sailor retreated to better light and climbed back up to the deck, where his footfall joined the general racket. The boatswain checked the cargo, the lashings, said nothing. Kit said nothing. Then the boatswain left, bolting the door behind him.

Kit tugged on the shackles: tight, and fast. Panic, then: the hole beneath the tree — the Newgate Hole, solitary confinement and the bargain for release — struggles and shouts, then, all of it futile — these attacks a parting gift of Newgate, fought off in the Flushing gaol but swooping now, swooping and crying —

Settle thyself, Kitten, and just breathe, breathe.

Breathe.

God, sweet God above, if Thou'lt not save my freedom, wilt Thou condescend to save my sight?

Craning his face toward the slush lamp, Kit managed to open his swollen eye.

A slit: crates and barrels, low light, swift tails of rats.

He smirked. —One prayer answered.

The slush lamp sputtered.

The light expired.

PURGING OF THE REALM OF SUCH A PLAGUE

The man at the end of the corridor...

Robert Cecil stared into darkness.

What woke me?

Reason and memory told him the curtains around his bed, sheltering him from London's deadly night air, hung in place. Sight told him nothing existed.

Propped on extra pillows to ease the ache in his spine, he

considered his dream: the Queen insulting him while a man at the end of the corridor, leaning against the wall, arms crossed, face shadowed, watched. Sometimes, dreaming, Robert presumed the man was Essex. Sometimes he thought perhaps his father watched him, though William Cecil never crossed his arms like that. The dream hardly felt like a dream — more a memory. The Queen enjoyed describing, even mocking Robert's body to her courtiers. *All hail our pygmy amphibian,* she'd say, *our acting secretary, aye: Young Fox himself, Sir Robert Cecil. See how he squats before us, his brain sticky and webbed with fear, his face ugly as unrecognized sin. Approach us, Sir Pygmy.* Robert would bow to the Queen's wit. Later, she would bow to his advice.

The man at the end of the corridor. I almost saw his face.

Nearly thirty, Robert looked at once older and much younger than his age. His hooded eyes, dark blue, seemed to be witnesses to every depravity, every deceit, and some dim paths to peace. He cultivated this impression, though he'd not seen every deceit, not yet. His skin remained smooth. Heredity and bad food, too much salt and too many work-eaten nights, puffed his eyelids. The globular eyes themselves: normal eyes in a narrow head. Death-pale face: fair skin and poor health. Crooked back: scoliosis. All as much an accident, a whim of God's, as some cobbler's son getting to Cambridge.

A recent sketch for a portrait of himself and his father standing shoulder to shoulder had startled him. *Am I really so ugly?* Robert hardly cared to reach the answer.

Not long after knighting Robert, Queen Elizabeth acknowledged the staunch work done by Sir Francis Walsingham and Robert's father, William Cecil, Lord Burghley. *That we have our peace, that we still sit on the throne, that we are not seized and murdered a hundred times over, that England burns not, is due to Sir Francis, and thy father. They grow old. They need thee, Robert. They need thy dedication, and thy subtlety of mind. We need thee.* Robert had travelled in Europe for Sir Francis, for intelligence work called diplomacy. The task had pried open Robert's mind and roughed up his health. Sir Francis decided to keep Robert in England after that, to teach him not agency but mastery. Still, Sir Francis, like Lord Burghley, lamented Robert's spine. *Travel taxes thee, and running eludes thee. Thy bent back, Robert: 'tis a wretched leash.*

Robert had needed to take a deep breath. *'Tis but a crooked back, your honour.*

The deformity had appeared in infancy, blamed on a clumsy nurse dropping him. People believed in physical manifestations of a corrupted soul, taking ugliness as a merciful warning, a token of God's grace: monstrous body, monstrous mind. Robert, long dismissing the nurse's failure as a tidy fiction, accepted the bend in his spine as a thing inborn, something as inescapable as the need for air. The hunch made walking difficult some days and running, as Sir Francis noted, almost impossible. Robert often waddled. When he hurried, his feet pattered and slapped like wind-driven rain. His affliction reminded far too many people of the stories of treacherous Richard III, and Robert saw the comparison play in other people's eyes, as he saw blue sky on a fine day.

His posture worsened; his pain grew; his face, he believed, looked mild and unconcerned.

Wine helped.

Some nights he wondered just how closely Richard III's

stories travelled to Richard's truth. He did not ask this question aloud, such rashness long trained out of him. Instead, he aspired to the safety of the Queen's motto, *video et taceo*: I see, and say nothing.

Robert sipped some of the wine he kept at his bedside table. He wanted to padfoot down the hall, check on his wife and infant son, but they lived outside London in a grand house called Theobalds. Robert had grown up in Theobalds, and he much preferred it to Cecil House, his father's London home on the Strand. Robert stayed in Cecil House during the week, as it kept him close to the Queen. It also kept him close to Essex House. Essex, like Robert, took visitors at odd hours via the servants' entrance: agents, messengers, and informers — low men, often. Robert often wished he might instead accept his visits from sneaking agents at Sir Francis's old house on Seething Lane, within sight of that excellent reminder to take great care, the Tower of London.

Several rooms away, William Cecil coughed and wheezed. Robert winced. A second son, by the second marriage, Robert had made William proud, and William had long groomed Robert to succeed him in statesmanship. Allies and enemies both referred to William and Robert as a unit, as a pair: Old Fox and Young Fox. Allies and enemies both wondered just who ruled England these days: the Queen, or the Foxes. Old Fox had barely hauled himself past Christmas, fighting heavy catarrh, a severe ague, and then pneumonia. The Queen, distressed, and, in her fashion, fond of William, demanded frequent reports on his health from his son. Robert hardly knew what to tell her, at once resenting her interruptions and fearing she might collapse before the truth. He emphasized the frailty of his father's lungs and said he prayed for the easing of all symptoms. William, meanwhile, had suffered more than a pneumonia. He behaved as one bashed in the head and then abandoned to the hot sun. Some days, sitting up beneath blankets and robes, he sounded quite his old self, asking complex questions and offering ready intervention. Other days he sounded distant as a spice island, asking Robert incomplete questions several times a night. Robert, tired, often in pain, drinking wine while making notes and writing letters, would answer them, several times a night.

The Queen peered at Robert sometimes. *Thou dost work too hard. Smile.*

He'd smile.

Years before, Sir Francis Walsingham, then secretary of the Privy Council and, alongside Robert's father, the Queen's closest adviser, had said to Robert: *Thou shalt fail me. Thou dost care not too little for thy work, but too much.*

Your honour, our agents are men of England, as much as we. I care for my work, and I also care for these men.

Why? Consider the word agent. *It means tool. If a blacksmith breaks his hammer while forging something greater, stops he his work? Mourns he the hammer, or finds he another? Heed me on agents and messengers and recall that, despite our fragile religious settlement at home, abroad we remain at the smoking edge of wars against the papist kingdoms, wars we may not win. Agents and messengers, Robert: use them well; cherish them not.*

Cherish. He'd heard his parents use that word. *The children are not to be cherished.* Housed, fed, educated, guided towards duty and discipline, but not cherished: such indulgence ruined a child. William Cecil, as master of the wards, housed young noblemen and supervised their education; he observed, and worked to combat, the malignant effects of cherishing. These boys feared William's power, and they shunned Robert. Forced solitudes in a racket of voices left Robert starved for friendship and prone to accosting any stray adults for conversation. He numbed his loneliness with extra schoolwork.

At age twelve, Robert became, by necessity, a keen student of rivalry. Robert Devereux, the second Earl of Essex, came to Theobalds as a ward. William hoped that Essex, slightly younger than his Robert, would become a firm friend and ally for his son. He thought this over one evening as he studied the little earl sitting at table beside his Robert. *I see here, in my house, in these two boys, the very future of England.* Then Essex walked across the room balancing a book on his head; enchanted, William admonished Robert for the defects in his posture.

Chaos infested the house after Essex arrived. Acts of vandalism, deceit, and theft, first petty, then blatant, confused everyone. William explained to his irritated wife that they must show patience. *His mother cherished him, and he knows not the meaning of discipline of the self. We shall ignore his excess, and he shall settle.* William then commanded Robert also to show patience, to make certain young Essex felt welcome at all times.

Robert obeyed. Many nights, Robert heard sleepless Essex pacing his bedchamber. Twice Robert visited him, and then listened for hours, saying almost nothing, as Essex ruminated on his anger at his parents. *A ward? I'm abandoned here!*

After the second night like this, Essex discovered he hated Robert. He decided Robert had come hunting sadness, had drawn out confessions of loneliness and fear. So, one Friday dinnertime, after the morning's geography discussion of Newfoundland's promising fishery, sneaking ahead to the table, to the places where he and Robert would sit, Essex tainted a jug of wine. He used his own sleeping powders, a departing gift from his mother for his troublesome insomnia, adding three good measures to the jug he and Robert would share. Throughout the meal, Essex made certain to keep Robert's wine cup filled, in the manner of a caring brother, as William taught all his wards, and he even added precious salt to Robert's dish. Surprised by this courtesy, wondering if Essex had warmed to him at last, Robert enjoyed his dinner. Thirsty, he also enjoyed his wine. Essex pretended to sip his. Afterwards, in class, parched Essex watched stupefied Robert nod and doze, and he alerted the tutor: *Good master, I fear Robert may be sleeping.* To the earl's lasting disappointment, the furious tutor made no complaint to Lord Burghley.

A few days after the wine, Essex saw another chance. He sat with the other wards, enduring a lesson in astronomy. The students leaned back their heads, imagining, as the tutor instructed, the night sky splayed out on the ceiling. *Stars so close, young gentlemen, so close that you delude yourselves and believe you may pluck them from the pitchy sky and imprison them in your hands.* Essex got bored. He claimed a need to visit the jakes. Instead, he sneaked into Robert's bedchamber. *The house so quiet*, Essex marvelled, *the room so small, and the theft so easy.* Knowing where to look, Essex raided Robert's few treasures until he found the dancing wooden man on strings. This poppet, artful and expensive, made in Venice, had been a gift to Robert from his father, against the wishes of his mother, and it wore silk — motley, but silk. An artist of great skill had painted the face. The delicate mouth smirked, and one brown eye winked. William had made this poppet dance for Essex on the boy's first night at Theobalds, as a welcome, as a comfort, and Essex had smeared away tears with his fist. Now, in Robert's room, Essex grabbed the poppet beneath the armpits, crammed the works of wood and string down his doublet, and scurried to his own room, where he hid the poppet beneath some outgrown nightclothes in his locking truck. After supper that evening, Essex begged Lord Burghley to round out the visit to his wards by making Robert's poppet dance, *under your masterful guidance, good my lord.* Demurring, for his hands ached, William said he doubted he could give the young men a good show that night. Then he relented and told his son to fetch the poppet. Robert returned empty-handed, pale in his failure, and he took a beating for it, one triply shameful for Robert's being nearly thirteen, the blows being hard, and the many wards not being deaf.

Years later, Robert asked his father about the incident, and William shook his head, closing his eyes in shame. *I see it now: Essex stole that poppet and entrapped thee. 'Tis nonsense, Robert, but 'tis the only answer: that young man, with his title and rank, and all his privilege and promise, envied hunchbacked little thee. He envies thee still, and it galls him like a poison. I confess, I know not why.* Robert laid his hand over William's. *He envies my having a good father, sir.*

Not long after the business with the poppet, William sent twelve-year-old Essex on to Cambridge. He argued that the young noble's intellectual and political precocity begged the tempering discipline of firm study. Robert soon followed him there, varying his studies, declining to take a degree. Essex earned his MA. Both young men returned to London, Robert to learn diplomacy and intelligence from Sir Francis Walsingham, Essex to learn social nuance and politics in Queen Elizabeth's court.

Robert's appearance did not improve with age. He remained short and frail, and his fingers got long. Like his father, he often wore dark colours — to disguise his hunched spine, Essex claimed, adding that the dark colours helped not, alas, nothing did. *Robert, thou art so ugly, that I marvel at thy resilience, marvel thou art tempted not to commit the grievous sin of suicide. Thou dost inspire me to steel mine own resolve against tumbling adversity. Thou art a terrible accident of birthing and blood: sweet God in Heaven, what monstrosity frightened thy mother?*

Essex shot up to a height of six feet and, at last, coaxed out a beard. Like his mother, he knew how to dress with beauty and grace. He spent on clothing as he spent on everything else: well beyond his means, his father having left him only the title and a reckoning of appalling debt, and his stepfather only guiding him to an excellent tailor. His exquisite clothes, and, especially, his red hair, reminded everyone of his kinswoman the Queen and how she'd looked before smallpox, age, and wigs, before loss of flesh. The moody adolescent Essex practised smiling in a looking glass until he perfected technique, and that smile devastated hearts. He also learned how to make his brown eyes hint at deep and furious mysteries, wretched heartaches that needed only a woman's tender and patient love to soothe them. It worked.

As Robert had continued to assist Sir Francis, Essex had

continued to lift skirts in the dark, make an ass of himself on the battlefield, and flirt with the Queen in a long, improvised, and potent performance that both enjoyed and neither, it seemed, understood. Robert dreaded this flirting, this strange loving banter between Queen and favourite. Elizabeth, when not teasing, rebuking, or cosseting Essex, liked to study him, just watch him move. Compared to her other trusted advisers — greybeards all, except Robert with his bent back and strange eyes — well, the young earl looked very fine. Robert only smiled at gossip of liaisons and love between Essex and the Queen. He knew better. *Love?* Essex infested the woman's heart, curled up there like some worm, for he saw her as a woman, a conquest, a poppet. He would coddle her neglected emotions, and, holding them in his hands, rule England. Sometimes Robert thought the Queen saw this and played along to amuse herself. Sometimes Robert feared she saw nothing.

Whatever subtle dementing effect Essex might have on the Queen's heart, Robert could still speak to her mind, providing domestic and foreign intelligence as Sir Francis Walsingham had done, providing advice. Essex would usurp that, too. Sniffing the threat, Robert fought back. He offered his agents better compensation. As Lord Burghley also served as Lord High Treasurer, Robert could make such promises. Still, payments got delayed, tangled in the endless little snarls of bureaucracy, and, Robert suspected, in interference from Essex. Meanwhile, Essex paid his own agents quite well.

Reaching now for the canopy surrounding his bed, Robert petitioned a ghost. He needed the wisdom of old Sir Francis Walsingham, needed his cynicism. One of their last conversations often burrowed its way into Robert's busy dreams.

History, Robert? 'Tis as useful as a litter of mewling kittens. The present looms, a most fragile peace, and thou wouldst fuss over days gone to dust?

Days of explanation, Sir Francis. The past tells me the why of the present.

I see in thee the same ice and fire that doth freeze and burn my best agents.

Aye, they are men of England, just as you and I.

Robert, heed, for even cold abandonment may not suffice.

Your honour?

Thy hardest test, the one giving thee greatest truth, will be not merely to send thy best man to his death, but to leave him there.

I know, I know: use them well; cherish them not. Be assured, Sir Francis: if so tasked, I will make, and I will keep, this country's peace.

Let proof speak.

I know the minds and hearts of our enemies, know them with an intimacy that fouls me. I may —

Know'st thou the minds and hearts of thine agents? Aye, thy jaw gapes now.

The question still bothered Robert.

He thought of his man in Flushing. *Too long now without a coded letter.*

God's own wounds, 'tis so cold.

Robert imagined a map of Scotland, and, with a fingernail, he traced the map's outline on the soft underside of his left forearm. *Scotland — aye, succession, the dire need, the unspoken word, a childless queen, and her delicate religious settlement, the conditional peace that might die with her.* Queen Elizabeth had survived a desperate childhood and adolescence, the violence done to her more emotional than physical, though just as potent. Once on the throne, she endured plots against her life — countless plots, according to Sir Francis in his more passionate moments — and even smallpox. Her long life only strengthened her fear of death, and she tolerated no mention of succession. She had refused key marriages, exasperating her advisers no end. Considered quite old now at almost sixty, the Queen might still marry — marry Essex, some rumours said — but she would give no children, no heirs. The question of who ruled England once Death sank his claws into Queen Elizabeth's bones: not her concern. One of Robert's inherited problems, one that ambushed his thoughts at night: the conditional peace of Elizabeth's reign, the wretched delicacy to it. On her death, would England collapse? Into chaos, civil war, foreign rule? Suffer invasion by a Catholic country, English Jesuits leading the charge? Robert rubbed his forearm; the skin seemed to burn. Scotland. He needed to send a good man to Scotland, quite soon. He needed cartography — maps of roads, maps of minds, maps and legends — and his best agent worked a task far away, in Flushing.

My best agent, this Marlowe, or just my favourite?

Kit meant hope to Robert, hope that a fine mind given every opportunity for education in this new England might carry out the filthy and intricate work of peace and emerge intact, crackling with light. Kit's energy, his vigour and brilliance, got him noticed at Cambridge, despite the upstart folly of his presence on a last-minute divinity scholarship. What, a *cobbler's* son? Well, we must get our priests somewhere. His studies and residency came financed with a promise: he would take holy orders in the struggling Church of England. Old for an undergraduate, already seventeen when boys might start university at age eleven or twelve, Kit read books at Cambridge as a starving man might eat at a banquet. Some observers thought his passion must be old English chronicles and Latin poetry — a mistake, as much as assuming Kit's slender build meant frailty. Kit's true study: power, people seeking power and the lies they told, hypocrisies great and small. Eyes up from books and scrolls, he watched people, considered motives, and learned to read secret hearts.

A fellow student, Thomas Walsingham, came to admire Kit. Walsingham told his uncle, Sir Francis, about this cobbler's son happy to show off his freakish memory, happy to manipulate others' frailties until they revealed secrets. Another student, Izaak Pindar, Walsingham added, shared some of these traits. Sir Francis listened. He needed such men for intelligence work, for the security of the state, and he laboured within a scarcity of useful and experienced agents. Such men must be started young, and groomed in the field. Fearing, like many, that the Reformation had not gone far enough, and fearing, with reason, that Oxford sheltered Catholics, Sir Francis looked to Cambridge. He sought men of the once-ignorant classes, ambitious sons ready to claw past their fathers' occupations. He sought minds blazing with intellect, intellect fused with cunning and even brutality, minds perhaps even capable of understanding the warp and woof of religious settlement and reasonable peace, minds that recognized power and craved purpose.

In Christopher Marlowe, he found one. Sir Francis studied him, questioned him, recruited him, even liked him, though he'd not admit it. He reviewed this student's record: undergraduate divine, aspiring playwright, translator of troublesome poems, and reader of histories better left lost. Then he codenamed him Lucifer. Deciding to test this Lucifer for sinew and speed, Sir Francis tasked Kit to play-act the blood-weeping Catholic and infiltrate the Jesuits at Rheims.

I need thee, Sir Francis said to Kit once at his house on Seething Lane, comfortable before the fire burning in the hearth, Lord Burghley nodding, Robert Cecil watching them all. *I need thee to serve the laws and needs of England.*

The servant's plays? Sir Francis waved them away. Robert considered them a delightful side benefit, a bonus, a grace. These plays, Robert felt, admiring the language, the honesty, dared one — to do what, precisely, Robert could not say. *Jew of Malta* slapped one's face, and Robert squirmed as he considered his common hatred of Jewry and yet his loathing of the Christian characters' hypocrisies. None looked good in *Jew of Malta*. The sly wit of *Doctor Faustus* infected him with a terror reaching far past men dressed as demons — more a terror of the dim looking glass, Robert felt. *Tamburlaine* did go on a bit long, its startling though repetitive bombast reminding Robert of Privy Council meetings. He caught a performance whenever he could. After all, he must learn the mind and heart of his agent.

When younger, Robert would go to the playhouses in disguise, a ragged old hooded cloak and a walking stick, until his father took him aside one day and instructed him in the truths of fooling no one. The Queen attended the playhouses without disguise, or with a disguise so thin as to be laughable: royal privilege. Essex attended with his finery intact. Some playhouses, being so near the whorehouses, male and female, made the enterprise of playgoing risky to one's social standing, yet the playhouses did good business. Once at a performance of *Jew of Malta* by the Admiral's Men, the troupe which owned Marlowe's plays, Robert had felt certain that a young woman, not a boy, performed Ithamore. Such an act would not only muck up all manner of expectation over role but also break a law. Question and thrill jumped through the audience that afternoon, a contagion: a woman, or a boy? The actor taking the final bow as Ithamore, wig in hand, grinned and stroked his strong and shadowed jaw. Yet Ithamore that day had a shorter jaw, the gentler line padded by a round cheek.

Robert shook his head whenever he thought of it. The master of the revels, Edmund Tilney, already harassed the Admiral's Men, delaying or even denying licences to perform, saying he disliked their choice of plays — meaning one author: the danger of him; the charm, and the danger.

Aye, too long in Flushing without a coded letter.

The Rheims divine, the Catholic agitator: Kit played the roles well.

Too well.

God's own wounds: where is he?

Approaching his office in Westminster and feeling hollow from his lost sleep, Robert met his paper-laden clerk, Izaak Pindar. Gaunt and dressed in sober black and grey, Izaak wore his brown hair brushed back from his forehead and his long beard squared off at his Adam's apple. His grey eyes often considered the world asquint, and he'd got ambition, telling Robert he wished to serve England as an interrogator, a master examiner. Robert had nodded at this and bade his clerk be patient, for such work would come. Old Sir Francis had thought he detected a latent examiner in Izaak. *Not a man suited to gathering intelligence in the field*, Sir Francis had said to Robert, *too obedient, too timorous, in the end, but instead equipped to force terrible intimacies and pluck information from a trapped man's mind. Remember this, Robert, and use him well.* Sometimes Robert loaned Izaak out to master interrogators, both to give these men assistance in their difficult tasks and to afford Izaak some practise. The work seemed to poison some men, to brutalize them, even crack them. They became quarrelsome, tyrannous. Izaak Pindar appeared unchanged. His gentle voice, which made Robert doubt his strength sometimes, soothed the ears.

Many days, Izaak reminded Robert of Chaucer's clerk on the road to Canterbury: *Sownyne in moral vertu was his speche, And gladly wolde he lerne and gladly teche.* This morning, Robert said so.

Izaak bowed. —All I might do is strive to be worthy to be your clerk.

Robert nodded, acknowledging the deference, and his own distant but no less dangerous allusion to Thomas Becket. Neither of them would name Becket aloud, and neither of them would comment further on the old Canterbury pilgrimage. Their queen's father, King Henry VIII, in breaking the monasteries, made the pilgrimage and any veneration of Becket illegal. The name — the idea — of Becket remained dangerous. Fiery.

—Thou'st done well, Mr. Pindar. The reports to me on thine assistance with examination, thy questioning and use of the implements of same, are quite satisfactory.

Izaak blinked and blushed at this sudden praise. —I thank your honour.

Robert smiled. When not lending him out, Robert kept Izaak close to him, trusting him to take notes during Privy Council meetings, notes to supplement his own. After a meeting, Robert would study the two sets of notes and from them weave acceptable minutes. Izaak, Robert decided, had no real understanding of how much he eased Robert's burden as acting secretary, and Robert had no intention of ever telling him.

Izaak placed his tottering burden of papers on Robert's desk. Then he plucked out a letter from near the top of the pile and handed it to Robert.

Robert broke the seal. *Government House in Flushing.* —Whence?

—The ship *Peace of Lethe*, direct from Flushing, with two Englishmen on board. Deported, your honour.

At once relieved, exasperated, and concerned, Robert clicked his tongue. *Marlowe?*

Izaak continued. —One is released. The other remains imprisoned on board, claiming he is known unto you, your honour, as . . . I know not what this means: Marsyas the messenger? And this Marsyas is also known unto Lord Strange. Your honour, what folly is this?

Code. Marlowe's. A needful call for help. —And the one released?

—Bail already posted, your honour, for one Richard Baines, by some other office.

—Ric Baines? That mountebank?

—So I am told, your honour.

—Bail from Essex House?

—I was not told that, your honour.

Robert grunted. Then he read Sidney's letter in silence. Many literate people murmured words as they read. Robert's father had taught him this strange habit of silent reading, both men finding it useful. Done, scowling, Robert resisted the urge to crumple the paper and instead laid it with care in a correspondence box, which he then locked.

—Pindar, do this: post bail for the remaining prisoner and advance him coin for a Thames wherry. Mark it in thy ledger as Queen's business. Send the dark errand boy, for I trust him the more, and send him soon, for this bailing shall take hours yet. Thou dost need find a scrivener willing to visit the Deptford dockyards, for a start. What else?

—I must complete the agenda for today's Privy Council meeting, your honour.

—Omit any mention of the two deported from Flushing, for 'tis a trivial matter, unworthy of the good councillors' time. I shall require thy last set of notes prepared for my review by eleven o'clock, and neglect not...Hellfire!

Robert Cecil's final affliction: megrim. He worked hard, late, and often hungry. He worked past the deceptive walls of fatigue, and the red-hot bursts of pain in his spine, but megrim crippled him. At twelve, new to this weird plague, Robert decided these sparks of agony demanded a reason, a story. So he'd imagined Hephaestus exiled within his skull, where, in fierce and sullen anger, he forged stunted lightning. Now, visions of Hephaestus no comfort, Robert grasped his desk and suffered the prelude. Light shimmered. Great black Zs scarred the air, parting for a vision of a long corridor, random torches lighting white arches, and he thought of his dream: one dark figure waiting at the end. Papers scattered. Bile burnt a path up Robert's throat, and Izaak Pindar's arms supported him until he got to his chair. Soon: pain. Robert preferred the pain, its honesty, to the pathetic limbo of the warning.

Izaak drew the heavy drapes on the window and lit two candles. That light forced shadows from the spray of dried borage on the wall, borage for courage, and darkened the eye sockets of the memento mori — a human skull, a child's — serving as a paperweight on Robert's desk. The skull belonged to a set of two, the set once the possession of Sir Francis Walsingham and split, on his death, between Robert and Thomas Walsingham. Ignoring the skull, Robert shoved aside sketches, maps, and unfinished tallies until he found a packet of dried chamomile and knitbone blended with hellebore. This he gave to Izaak, who left to find hot water and wine for steeping the herbs. Robert questioned the potency of hellebore. It never seemed to lift his melancholy. Nor did it ease his pain. Still, he feared a lack of it.

—What ho, Wee Robbie?

A deep and silky voice: Robert's head throbbed all the harder. *Bloody-handed, play-acting, savage little princeling. My good father, God preserve him, pronounced to me last Sunday, gravy in his beard, how he especially pitied thee as a ward — pitied, I say — for thy mother's vigour in touring the countryside of men's beds. That, I long to share.*

—My lord of Essex. You surprise me, and grace me with your presence.

Essex smiled, one snaggletooth giving fault and thereby beauty. He wore warm hose and, beneath his woollen cloak, several shirts, silk and linen. A blued ruff topped his woollen doublet, this doublet decked with dozens of tiny buttons.

—Assistance is a matter of perch, good Sir Robert, unless you would speak to me of secure weirs on the rivers of intelligence.

Speak to thee, who wouldst batter and rape the intelligence service and then complain she declined to fix thy favourite dainties for thy supper? —Good my lord, I know not what to say. The Queen's agents and messengers labour for the protection of England, and Her Majesty.

—Agents and messengers overseen by you, their information filtered through you.

—What of it? I beg you, pardon my blunt tone.

Essex gave his most intimate smile and claimed his right to address Robert, in mixed tones of friendship and superiority, as *thou*. —Only this, Robbie: thy work is difficult, and it comes with such scant reward that I wonder how thou dost bear it.

—My reward comes each night, when I rest my head on the knowledge that Her Majesty is safe on her throne and no man burns for his beliefs, not even the foul Jesuit.

Essex pulled up a chair and sat across it, his long legs

dangling. —Aye, hang, draw and quarter them instead. Excellent deterrent. Excellent show.

—I confess I find it difficult to watch.

—Thou'st always been delicate, Robbie.

Robert wanted to agree with Essex because the man's beauty and charm pressed him to agree. The pain in his head forced tears. —Good my lord, I should caution you: I hear rumours.

—Of?

—Rumours you would take your tax profits from that recent gift to you from Her Majesty and with those profits purchase all needed assistance and expertise to set up an intelligence agency of your own, for your own use.

—Only to keep the Queen informed and advised.

—An agency to rival that already established, and already informing and advising the Queen.

—Oh, Robbie. Where would I find such agents, those men with rare skills, unless they rollick about in discontent? All men with such expertise work for thee, surely.

—In your place, I would tread this galliard with the greatest of care. The Queen giveth; the Queen taketh away.

Essex swung his legs around and leaned forward. —I offer Her Majesty the small service of mine advice, and I offer gainful employment to men unable to work elsewhere.

—Then you admit to stealing my men.

—Something of an agent's work sticks to a man, a taint, a stench, like shit to wool. I merely pay my servants well.

The jagged light of Robert's aura settled on his rival's shoulders.

Essex stood up. —How doth Sidney with the Flushing governance?

—Sidney your kinsman, my lord?

—Only by marriage. Even that is a stretch, as he doth re-mind me.

—I believe the appointment draws out his best talents.

Essex fingered the dried borage on the wall, then turned around. —I understand Sidney just deported two Englishmen. Our fellow privy councillor, Sir John Puckering, begs me to ask if the matter shall be discussed in meeting today. I assured Sir John — thine eyes. Dost thou weep?

—Megrim.

—Not again.

—Good my lord, if I felt stronger, I would offer to instruct you in the neglected art of subtlety. Studying it teaches the eager pupil the diverse needs for intricate covers, intricate covers which must remain undisturbed. Thoughtless, even reckless, exposure endangers not just individual men, but the work of the Privy Council, and thereby the life of our sovereign.

Essex lost his grin. —I see.

—I pray that you do, for a brazen insistence —

—One of those deported: Marlon? Morley?

Ah, subtlety. —Marlowe.

Essex touched the borage again; some of it fell to the floor. —Marlowe, aye, a Christopher. Playwright, is he not? Would he bear the Christ-child across a raging river?

—I doubt it.

—I'm told he's a felon.

—Felony being a standard reason for deportation.

—Counterfeiting, the rumour goes, Robbie: counterfeiting, and trafficking with papists. Employ'st thou such a man?

—My lord...

Essex placed a fresh kerchief in Robert's hand. —Here, 'tis Canterbury silk. Thou wouldst instruct me? Let me inform thee. 'Tis murmured by those who would know that this counterfeiter, this Marlowe, is thy best man.

—So says the arrogant Marlowe himself? I've not.

—He travels well, speaks honey, charms his way past Cerberus to the darkest chambers of the heart?

—He is competent. I'll give him that.

—Here, thy quill has fallen. I would question that competence. Counterfeiting smacks of a private folly.

Ashamed of how much he enjoyed the touch of the silk, Robert continued to dab his face. Apart from what his father must wear to please the Queen, his mother had forbidden soft and pretty fabrics, calling them a corrupting indulgence. Even his sister's wedding dress — she just fifteen — had been rough, sober, and spare. *Sad foreshadowing of her miserable marriage,* Robert thought.

—I agree, my lord.

—What?

—Deported, an utter disgrace, forced to leave another country beneath a cloud of dark suspicion. Alongside Richard Baines. In your employ, I believe.

—Oh, aye, Tricksy Ric. He's done me limited service, though I must enquire of my controller who gave Baines means and leave to go to Flushing.

—To rid you of a turbulent priest?

Chuckling, Essex sat down again. —If he's papist, aye. Wouldst thou not do the same?

—I desire only peace, my lord of Essex, peace being a matter of complexity and depth. I labour each day to maintain it.

—To peace, then. Peace, and poetry. I should like to become a patron. A literary man. A poet.

Robert adjusted his ruff. —Poets misbehave.

—I would teach him obedience.

—Easier to teach a whore to fly, my lord.

—Would you call that subtlety, Sir Robert?

—Reality.

Snorting, Essex got up to leave.

—Reality with gravy, good my lord.

Essex slammed the door, and Robert, despite his throbbing pain, and doubting Sir Francis would approve, laughed.

Londoners blamed the south fog for all manner of confusion and disease. Standing and waiting on *Lethe*'s deck, the tiny ship now moored in Deptford, Kit could see why. Heavy and foul, the south fog choked off sound and sight. Voices bounced, and even the tiny *Peace of Lethe* disappeared in the billows, Kit not able to see to the end of her. Holding a single coin in his fingers, still wearing the boatswain's cloak, Kit reasoned his bearings. Here: the dockyards, the warehouses, and, a short walk from the Thames, the Bulls' boarding house, the one Robin Poley liked to use, now run, last Kit heard, by Mistress Bull alone after her husband's death. Behind, north and west: the Strand, where he must go report to Sir Robert at Cecil House after dark, and some of the prisons — Newgate, the Fleet, Bridewell — and Old Jewry Street, where Tom lived. South lay the Kent Road, which would take Kit home, if he stayed the path, Deptford being a station on the old pilgrimage from London to Canterbury.

London: 'tis home now.

The reeking Thames, when I would see Canterbury's Great Stour?

London be fucked.

Sweet Christ Jesus, I'm so tired.

Bones aching, muscles stiff, Kit caught sight of the boatswain, met his eye, and made to shrug off the cloak; the boatswain jerked his face once to the left, once to the right, and returned to the rigging. He'd moved Kit to the mess about halfway through the first watch, suggesting to *Lethe*'s captain that Governor Sidney's prisoner there in the cargo hold might well freeze to death, it being January and all, and should they risk offending the governor so? The captain had relented: *Aye, death complicates everything.* Warmer, Kit had waited out the rest of his crossing seated on a bench in a corner, hands chained in front this time. He'd dozed in fits, vomited up most of what he ate, and obeyed an order to keep silent. He'd known Ric Baines also sailed on board but caught no glimpse of him. The mystery of the boatswain's mercies persisted.

The Thames fog, at least, carried no ice, promised none of Flushing's harsher cold.

Sir Robert's errand boy and *Lethe*'s captain exchanged letters and finished their conversation. The errand boy then gestured to the ladder dangling over *Lethe*'s starboard side, bowed, and stood back so Kit might descend first. Gripping the ladder hard, not trusting his wrists, Kit climbed down towards the waiting wherry. Waves snatched the little boat away from *Lethe* then gave it back. Leaning his cheek against a rung, Kit hesitated: a Godly game of keep-away, or just the indifferent motions of water and wind? He let go the ladder and took the small leap. Awkward from bruises and confinement, he clattered into the wherry, falling onto his left hip against a seat and earning the waterman's snort. Kit watched the boy then, ready to catch him. Instead, the boy jumped from the ladder with an experience that lent him grace. His moment of descent, arms outstretched, dark hair crows' wings, made Kit think of singing boys and the swift departures of their beautiful gifts. The boy landed in the wherry on his feet, hips rocking to take the shock of impact, and he sat down, composed, ready, and in no need of Kit's assistance.

The waterman looked to Kit for payment and instruction. Handing over the coin the errand boy had not long handed to him, Kit asked the waterman to row first to Cousin Gate Steps. This detour meant delaying the errand boy's return to his waiting master. The boy made no objection, and Kit, first telling himself he cared not one mote for the boy's tasks, decided he should later mention this to Sir Robert, and compliment the boy's discretion.

The errand boy looked at the water; Kit looked at the fog; the waterman looked to his rowing. None spoke.

At Cousin Gate Steps, Kit clambered up to the street. Cursing his perception of heaving land, he picked his way to the low stone building he wanted, to the little door marked with a sign of a songbird: the Starling, a favourite alehouse. Inside, a good two dozen men drank and talked. The Starling's owners had whitewashed the walls and varnished the woodwork since his last visit, so Kit made certain to compliment the landlady. She settled him at a corner table, near a struggling fire. Kit slouched in his chair like some apprentice determined to look defiant after a beating, murmuring he felt thirsty as spiced sand, his head being swamped with phlegm, would the good mistress open a reckoning? Charmed as ever, and inspired to maternal fussing, the landlady agreed, apologizing she'd only got bread, cheese, and some bacon. Kit ate what she offered and drank from a jug of ale, tasting nothing.

His cough, now a wet and rattling wheeze, disgusted other patrons. As on *Lethe*, none shared his table. Pleased, Kit in turn ignored the other men. *Just another few hours. Report to Sir Robert, then sleep.*

Somewhere.

Tom's?

Tom.

Gone how many months, Clever Kitten?

No, no letters from another country. I dared not. I intercept letters myself; 'tis too easy. He'll understand, la.

If he says no, and me with not one fucked coin to my name...

I could beg the landlady for a bed for the night, offer to wash the dishes yet.

Ah, Crimm.

Chin tucked into his cloak, bony face fit to cut the air around it, horse courser Lee Crimm ducked into the Starling. Kit studied him as he took off his floppy hat and exposed his dark hair. *'Tis black and blue and hot-iron red, la*, Kit had disputed with him once, *like a raven's feathers*. A raven in winter, now, caught in little frosts: new white hairs glittered on Lee's crown as he bowed to the landlady. Spotting Kit, Lee ordered a second drink and asked the landlady to bring over a game.

Kit grinned. *Excellent timing, Crimm, if thy timing it is.*

People Kit needed often just appeared, ready to assist, or so it had seemed to Robin Poley some years ago. *Oh, my Christopherus*, Robin liked to say, *ever the gods' darling*.

Lee and Kit, conversation sounding easy and casual, would now barter information. Lee dealt in horses and so observed much coming and going, and Kit, whenever he needed to travel, made certain to hire a horse from Lee. Kit had been gone from London so long that he expected Lee's information to be the more useful, much more than his own knowledge of Flushing might be to Lee. Etiquette demanded that the man more in need of information bought the food and drink, but Lee had already offered. Yawning, Kit discovered he cared very little right then for information.

Lee shoved ale at Kit, and the two men clapped each other on the shoulders. The landlady placed the tables set — the board, tokens, and dice — between them. In another country, the game might be called backgammon. Illegal, considered sinful, pagan, and a form of gambling, the game of tables flourished in certain pockets of England. Robin Poley had taught Kit how to play it, arguing that tables, with strategies upset by dice, developed skills and thinking that would only help a man in the field, much more than logic-bound and stately chess. Kit had come to agree.

Lee took a good look at him. —Pax, Marlowe. I'd say 'tis good to see thee, but thine eye is angry swoll, and thy skull wants to break thy skin. When didst thou last eat a good meal: Easter? And in the name of all that's good and pure, keep a little distance. I like not thy wheeze.

—Oh, excellent advice. And which cheated customer knocked out that eyetooth for thee, la?

—Dost thou notice every little thing?

—'Tis what I'm here for.

Lee made a show of picking up and putting down Kit's empty jug. —Thirsty?

—I've still got some in my cup. Didst thou miss me? Aye, confess it: missed me, la.

—I told anyone who slithered by with questions of thee that for all I knew or cared thou'st been dragged screaming into Hell.

—And I thank thee for it.

—I've got gifts for thee: brothers. Two Catholics just come down from Oxford.

—Brothers?

—Hast thou got brothers, Marlowe?

—They'd piss on my corpse and then kick it in the street.

—What? Why?

—Names?

—Donne: Hal and Jack. Hot in the head, they are. Jack Donne wears a cross around his neck. *Outside* his shirt.

Kit grinned. —Ready to fight, is he?

—Something else.

Nodding, coughing again, Kit tried not to spit the ale.

—Papists distract thee, Marlowe. Look to the reformers and precisionists, the younger ones: very hard.

—Puritans? They're on our side. Old Sir Francis Walsingham would have dragged us all the way to Reformation's new-found-land had the Queen not tethered him. Besides, most of them are too busy disputing doctrine to cause any harm outside their own little circles.

—Dispute it with violence yet. Why let the papists take all the fun?

—By their own shabby reasoning, Crimm, they've not got the free will to commit violence.

—Violent mayhem is pre-destined, then. Easy justification.

Kit frowned. —A comforting thought.

Lee swallowed some ale. —Any man willing to die for conscience and faith holds the pitch and flame that could burn us all. My parents told me stories of the burnings under Queen Mary.

—Mine, too.

—Then let us drink to no such fires.

Raising his cup to Lee, Kit considered the puritans he'd met at Cambridge, some of them plodding, a few of them quite bright, many older than average and on scholarship, like himself. Had they kept the promise, taken the orders? Did they now minister to a parish? Why else would one study divinity? Kit remembered how he'd particularly offended one of them by designing his own studies to follow as he pleased on his own time, scarce as it was. That had been Izaak Pindar, gaunt with melancholy and dried up somehow, even desiccated with...what? Envy? Kit snorted. *Izaak Pindar: I've not thought of him for years.* When Izaak and some others protested to Kit about his personal studying, his extra reading, Kit announced: *I dare to think for myself, la. Whom shall the rest of ye allow to govern your minds?* While the others turned their backs, grumbling, Izaak just stared at him. Three different times after that, Kit approached Izaak, asked if he needed help, or even just something to eat; three times Izaak rebuffed him. A loss, really:

Izaak possessed a robust streak of dispute, beaten down but not out, and Kit longed to spar with him. Two of Izaak's rebuffs came after Kit had left Cambridge for a few terms to infiltrate the Catholic university at Rheims. Rumours of Kit's travels reached Cambridge; nearly every student affected to despise him once he returned. They did this, Izaak explained to Kit's friends Walsingham and Nashe, to punish this Marlowe, to teach him some humility. When Cambridge decided to withhold Kit's MA, citing the student's wayward absences and insufficient explanation for same, even Thomas Nashe fell away, flitting back in later years as occasion suited him. Only Thomas Walsingham stood by Kit. Stunned by these betrayals, and no small bit hurt, Kit had turned then on Walsingham, using his pet name for him, testing him: *Dost thou love me, Walls, or dost thou love the danger of me?* Walsingham had clasped his hand: *I promised thee a patronage, should I ever come to money. My promise stands pure; I am thy friend.*

Coughing, Kit turned away from Lee, and then spat phlegm into the fire. *Pure.* He wished the flames' heat would reach his bones. Pale, he faced Lee again. —Noisy puritans: very good. For that warning, Crimm, I owe thee a drink, but hast thou got names?

—Only faces yet. And thou'lt buy me nothing, not tonight. Thou'st look not to have a farthing to thy name. And the missus asked if I'd be buying this or adding it to thy reckoning. Which I've already paid off.

—Pardon me?

—'Twas little. And keep thy gratitude, for now I'd beat thee at tables.

Playing the game, they kept a silence. Kit lost the round, lost it badly, the movement of tokens up and down the painted spikes as real, as immediate to him as the existence of a manticore. *Fog, 'tis all fog, and coughing.* Delighted with the rare win, Lee finished the dregs of his drink and wished Kit well. Watching Lee depart, Kit wanted very much to call him back, just to spend more companionable time with him, time free of squalid little facts, and money.

He shuddered; he coughed.

Swaying as he stood up, Kit felt like a broken rush caught in a graceful current. The landlady smiled at him as he left, and he smiled back, chin tucked down, brushing the hair from his eyes and glancing up. Outside, the sun had long set and drizzle fell. Bladder full, Kit fumbled with his clothes, surprised by how much strength this simple motion demanded. Breath and urine steamed in the cold air. He sneezed, tucked his clothes, then set himself on a path to the Strand, to Cecil House.

How must I pay out my freedom this time?

And when got my feet so heavy?

Robert's megrims might last a few hours, the sun's entire showing, or well past midnight. Once, a megrim pounded him for three days until his father shoved him into bed and commanded the servants to whisper and go unshod. A spent megrim's stain, its echo, might daze Robert for hours more. Today's megrim had sputtered out around four o'clock, and now Robert's head felt too large for his body, some floating sack tied to his chest. Alone, hunched at the dining room table in Cecil House, supper ignored and long gone cold, Robert picked through paperwork and cursed his frailties. The Privy Council meeting had nearly slipped from his control, Essex and Sir John Puckering allied against him — allied in all courtesy, of course, seeking only clarity. *About these two Englishmen booted out of Flushing, Sir Robert. Shall this disgrace compromise our intelligence operations?* Robert had come home from that encounter in the foulest humour. His father, out of bed for a change, knew to avoid him, well understanding the statesman's need for a few minutes of peace. When strained, William Cecil preferred to stroll in his garden. He would remove his robes of state and place them on a chair with the instruction *There, Lord Treasurer, you may sit,* and then examine the state of his roses and ghillie flowers, remarking at length on fruitfulness, thorns, and decay. Years before, Robert would join his father, sometimes by command. He found neither peace nor joy in a garden. Bees and wasps harassed him, and the sun burnt his pale face. So Robert stayed inside, chasing off his melancholy with the deep and dire pleasures of gambling at cards and appreciating fine wine. Over this past year, Robert drank more and more in solitude. His father saw this, and he said nothing. Besides, the servants gambled, too, and their stakes included the prize of *not* having to attend Sir Robert.

The latest loser knocked on the dining room door, knuckles just glancing the wood.

Robert lifted his eyes from his papers. —'Tis but short moments home, no time even to breathe the wine, and thou'dst pound my door with a mailed fist? Unless there rages blood, fire, or plague, sirrah, begone.

Fear muffled the servant's voice. —An't please your honour, a visitor, by the servants' entrance.

—Blessed him his mother with a name?

—He says he is a messenger, one called Marsyas, your honour.

—Show him to my study. And bring wine.

Robert snatched his papers and a candle and tottered down a separate back corridor. Agent and servant would discover him already busy at his desk.

Thinking of the child's singing game *How many miles to Babylon*, of the line *Can I get there by candlelight*, Kit followed the nervous servant to Sir Robert's study. He knew this little walk, and he knew rocking thrill, the happiness and dread of standing in that study, being admitted to a strange intimacy with a man he respected. Kit had told himself he found meaning in that study, purpose: uphold and defend... something.

He thought of a ciphered letter Robin Poley had written him from gaol, after Kit had turned over that list. Kit had broken the code without much trouble, not that Robin's message surprised him: *Perhaps next time thou'lt find the courage to betray not thy friends but thy shimmering ideals, mine own little ferret. Whenever thou dost think of me, think first of the times I rescued thee.*

Fatigue and pain weaving misery, Kit hoped Sir Robert had a good fire going.

A map seemed to command all of Robert's attention. The chill in the room, the freshened fire, and the bare wine cups, told Kit that Robert had just arrived. *Sloppy, your honour.*

Robert looked up, and he frowned. When he'd first met Kit, the university student had a rounded face, like that of a well-fed boy, and he'd chuckled at the decrepit witticisms of Sir Francis Walsingham. Now, even in poor light, Kit looked worn and hungry, planed to hard angles. Robert wondered when the man had last laughed.

Robert pointed to a high-backed chair near the fire. —Sit down, Marlowe. Evicted from Hell?

Kit removed the boatswain's cloak and hung it on the back of the chair. —Deported from Flushing, your honour. Hell being not flames but salt water, the result is much the same. I get seasick.

Shirtsleeves? Robert kept his voice stern. —Get warm. Then explain to me thy sodden failures.

Shivering before the fire, Kit bit back his first answer. —An't please your honour, I beg you: treat me justly.

—Shall I be haunted thus? I gave thee surfeit of *justly* when I paid thy bail. And what disgrace is this? Deported?

—Your honour, I was exposed —

—Aye, thine arse must be wind-chapped. And coining? How am I to obscure that? Didst thou consider, for just one shred of thy self-wormed time, sirrah, the weight of thy work?

—*Sirrah?* Oh, I'll stand not for that.

—Thou'lt stand for whatever I throw at thee.

Oh, for Christ's love. —Then la, your honour, here I stand. Must I kneel?

—Speak not so brazen to me!

—I crossed the Channel in chains!

—Aye, 'tis so, and I've harsh words for Governor Sidney on the matter, but hear me: so long as I draw breath, I will make, and I will *keep*, this country's peace. If to keep that peace I must haul cords that silence and strangle thee and then order thy corpse be lobbed in the Fleet Ditch, this I shall do and thereafter suffer neither guilt nor concern.

Kit's mouth tightened into a thin line. —So long as I know my place.

—Aye. So long as thou dost. Now, hast thou come to prate, or to give report?

The candles and the fire burned brighter now, and the light shone on the injuries on Kit's face and the glaze in Kit's eyes. Robert considered asking the man if he felt well when Kit unknotted something from around his neck and gave it over.

Robert rubbed the silk between his fingers. *Fever hot.* He took up a candle and held the flame near Kit's face. —Sidney permitted this?

—I'm not certain he knew of the beating, your honour. Nor am I certain of his loyalties.

—*What?* Dost thou know what thou sayest?

—I must speak freely on this matter, or not at all.

Robert glanced at the silk again. He knew what to expect. —Speak, then.

Kit murmured. —Essex stuffs his nest with hairs plucked from your head.

—Aye, but this shall not last. It smacks of ill will to Her Majesty, and his lordship cannot privilege his head.

—Maybe. How many men have we lost to Essex this year?

—Ric Baines is no loss.

—He stupefied me with tainted drink.

Robert looked up from pouring wine. —Tainted?

—Why is't no one believes me?

—Oh, I believe. 'Twas done to me, once. What else?

Kit accepted the cup — fine glass, not dull metal or old wood. He inclined his head in thanks, took a sip, then made a show of casting his eyes to Heaven. —Let me see if I remember it all: counterfeiting, turning Catholic, oh, and shagging a boy. Christ's love, I was busy. 'Tis all punishment, your honour. Baines himself said 'twas a gift from Tony Bacon.

Bacon, my bitter kinsman. —He is now private secretary to Essex. What is thy quarrel with Bacon?

—'Tis Bacon who quarrels with me.

Robert raised his eyebrows, impatient.

—I mocked him in his misfortune, your honour. He took offence.

Of course. How silly of me to ask. —How long has thou coughed so vile? Sit down, before thou dost fall over. 'Tis a sticky wheeze I like not — *sit down*, I say. And drink. Th'art parched, no? 'Tis tainted only with sugar, I promise thee.

Believing for a moment that a Flemish constable gave him orders, Kit sat and sipped the wine. Robert spoke some more; Kit missed it all. Robert asked Kit's opinion and then divined his agent had heard nothing. Despite the rising heat from the fire, Kit's teeth rattled again, and he'd never so wanted to lie down and sleep.

Robert stood up, lifted Kit's matted hair away from his neck, and pressed his fingers to a carotid. —A serrated pulse, and th'art damp to thy linens. Hast thou any others? I thought not. What, what else pains thee?

—Dragged halfway across Flushing, your honour, and kicked in the ribs.

Robert rang a bell to summon a servant, wondering at himself as he gave orders for the servant to fetch clean hose, underlinens, and a woollen shirt from the livery cupboard, and stiff cloth for binding a man's ribs. A knight of the realm, clothing a servant, a man accused of crimes?

Use them well; cherish them not.

Yet I'd see a sweating horse blanketed, watered, and fed.

And I freed him from Newgate. Hiding behind letters and messages, but I freed him.

One waited for a trial and a likely sentence of death in Newgate. Kit had been trapped in there nearly two weeks — a most brief imprisonment, given how a man might wait years just to hear the precise charge against him — accused of killing a man in the street. The Newgate clerk had noted much confusion over this death: which provocation, which man, which knife. The arresting constables already knew Kit from other encounters, already smarted from his elegant verbal abuse, and for that reason, to make him answer for past disturbances, swore out a warrant and hauled him in — or so Kit told it. There remained the trouble of the corpse. And the trouble of the Toms. Some witnesses had described Kit drinking that night with Tom Kyd, the poet and playwright, while others said Tom Watson, another poet and playwright, and still others said no, Thomas Walsingham, who liked poets and playwrights. Robert knew — hoped — he could strike Walsingham from the list. The early autumn weather had cooled quite a bit during that fortnight, and Kit, chilled and miserable, had sat in this same high-backed chair, eyes red, skin pale, explaining himself, explaining a death. *Oh, this is tedious. Self-defence, as before, when — the one dead, Bradley, had disputed with my friend earlier in the evening, over some mindless mistake, he insisting my friend owed his master a debt.*

'Twas not so. I persuaded him to leave us. We drank and departed, having forgotten Bradley. A little ways outside, I stepped into a shadow to piss, and the one Bradley attacked my friend from behind, grieving his head with his dagger. Bradley, the ape, outweighed me by a good three stone, and he would use that bulk to pin me to the wall and there stab me. I darted la and la, surprising him with my left hand and offering him cuts until once more I persuaded him to leave us. He snarled, walked away two steps, then fell on my friend again, kicking him, my friend still pained on the ground. I leapt on Bradley's back, for he would slaughter a man in the street. And for what? For all of poxed-up what? I would prevent a murder. My friend staggered up, and he got Bradley's dagger — Christ's love, he knows not hilt from blade — and — it can happen so fast — in the struggle, in the dark, one of us stabbed Bradley in the neck.

Whenever he thought of the incident, Robert congratulated himself for showing such broad charity in rescuing a troubled prisoner, such specific wisdom in freeing the useful Marlowe, and such subtle mercy in declining to interrogate him. *As before, he says: what means he? And he protects someone. Love, then?*

A knock on the study door: the servant returned with the kitchen maid. Kit thought they carried shrouds; he gave his head a shake and got to his feet. Neither servant spoke, and neither of them looked at Kit's face. Kit, however, studied the kitchen maid. Maybe the same age as Manna, she'd once been much plumper: loose skin sagged at her neck. Smallpox had ravaged her face and scalp, leaving her scarred and half bald.

She asked to see his ribs.

Kit took off his shirts, and Robert clicked his tongue at the bruising. The kitchen maid drew salve across Kit's bruises, gentle, as though treating burns on a child. Then she applied a poultice, slimy and cold, to the worst bruising on his ribs, and wrapped his chest in burlap. Sickened by the poultice and the pain, Kit scowled, but then he smiled at her. This strange woman's touch, unexpected, and kind...

—Mistress, my thanks.

She said nothing.

Once the servants left, Robert turned his back, instructing Kit to change into the dry clothes. Kit felt confused, even a bit lost. *Cold and naked before Sir Robert Cecil?* Burlap chafed. *Which way to Father's workshop?*

Straightening some papers on his desk, Robert looked at his agent again.

— Governor Sidney tells me thou didst disrupt the Wilmot brothers' network.

Kit snorted. —The Wilmots.

—Tiresome company?

—Cowards. Stalking them one night, I had to hide in shadows as the younger Wilmot beat a whore insensible.

—She was but a whore.

—She was working to feed herself! And for Christ's love, he must have outweighed her by four stone, she flat in the chest, not twelve years old.

Robert took a breath to reply, to rebuke; instead he pointed to his desk. —I need thy report. Sit, and write.

Kit tugged his left shirt sleeve, exposing his galled and swollen wrist. —So please your honour: stomped by an angry Flemish constable. Left, not right. Were I cynical, I might guess 'twas not accident but design, la, to prevent my using a knife. Or a quill.

'Tis a thorough job done on thee. —Then say thy report. I shall play secretary. I do it well.

Kit recited the tawdry and predictable story of the Wilmot brothers. Staunch Catholic family. Sons educated at home by a Jesuit tutor until he disappeared, then at Oxford, though neither brother would swear the Oath of Supremacy and so obtain a degree. Pooled savings, some inheritance, and money collected from Catholic kin got them to Flushing, where they would set up a network of sympathizers and smuggle Jesuits back home to England. A fight, a purpose: service to God. Standing in Flushing, looking around at buildings similar to buildings in England yet so different, and hearing languages they did not speak well, both Wilmots recognized that they had no idea how to proceed. Enter Stephen Loman, older, experienced, protective of his new little brothers in Christ, and seeking if not martyrdom then some shade of meaning to his own life and so ready to risk all, ready to book passage for a Jesuit. Kit helped the Wilmot brothers set up their contacts, taught them enough coherent French and Dutch pronunciation that they might buy food, and witnessed their passions and depravities, great and small. He stalked, contacted, and befriended an English Jesuit for them to traffic back to England, and la, done.

Robert chased details, asking questions built on questions, about Ric Baines and Governor Sidney, then the Wilmots and their connections again. Kit answered him, sometimes coughing, sometimes dozing, as Robert ciphered the long replies.

After a few hours of this work, Robert put down his quill. —Tell me more of thy Jesuit.

—Your honour?

Robert gave Kit the last of the wine. —Thou'st not once named him.

Telling himself he felt stupefied by the heat, Kit held his cup with both hands.

—Pardon me, your honour. Cull. Benjamin Cull.

—And what said he to make thine eyes go so dark?

—I am feverish, your honour, and my thoughts grow slippery. I beg leave —

—No. Speak.

I am too tired to hide.

—He said 'tis more than ideas. We spoke of the one question with two horns: how dare even a God-appointed sovereign tell a man how to pray; and how dare Rome snatch a man's faith and plait it into a driving whip. 'Tis agony, when one gets to it.

Robert stared at him. *God's own wounds, no. Not him. Not gone Catholic.*

—Marlowe, no more play-acting. As thou wouldst shake off thy pretense of ties to Rome, shake off thy ties to Cull.

—Wait. I mean, your honour…

—Didst thou strike thy head and brain thyself on the doors to Canterbury Cathedral?

Very pale now, Kit flinched as though Robert had shouted.

—Marlowe, if 'tis sympathy for Catholics I hear, for *Jesuits*, God help us, then I must… Wilt thou draw patterns in blood and design a pretty martyrdom, when thy mind, once made obedient — no, hush. I know the strains of this work, and I know thou art tired, tired beyond even the reach of thy mighty words to explain. So I grant thee a moment of thought towards a careful answer. I grant thee mercy. Choose, and then tell me: whom, and what, shalt thou obey?

Kit made it sound like a curse. —Cold salt air, your honour.

Robert waited.

—Cold salt air. It writhed through the cracks in the wall, my little room in Flushing — well, Stephen Loman's little room, now, was't not? — and sleet battered the window. I kept looking at the glass, afraid it would break. And Cull — my Jesuit — he said, 'Tis more than ideas, more than being. 'Tis gasping after near drowning. 'Tis accepting purpose. I want my days to mean something, Stephen. We'd reached the intimacy of Christian names. I envied his layers and layers of warm clothes. Mine own — holes, holes, holes. In a Low Countries winter. Mine allowance, my budgeted funds: near spent. I'd got just enough left for passage home, for the moment I got word that I might come home. Ben, for all his warm clothes, got afflicted with lice of the head. Agonies of itch, blood crusting the roots of his blond hair: he begged me to pick out what I could. I sat in a chair, and he knelt before me. Bow thine head, I told him, and — the room dark, the fire sullen, I'd coaxed almost nothing in the hearth, and I'd got just the one candle; I was so tired, your honour; all my work, every task taking longer than expected — Ben, I said, thou'st got a village of nits and lice, la. That gave it away, the *la* falling out my loose mouth. Not that he'd got a chance of escape. He might puzzle out and get it right all he pleased, but he'd not got a chance. I'd set it up. The one task that went right, arranging his arrest. And there, in the dark, by the fire, I picked his lice. He told me of a man he knew from

Canterbury who said *la*, as some did from out that way, picking it up, he thought, from the Huguenot refugees. Then he told a story he'd heard of an English student at Rheims, some years before, an English student with a Canterbury voice. 'Tis my failure, right there: I spoke true.

Expecting rebuke, Kit shut his eyes.

Robert said nothing.

—At dawn, your honour, he presented himself to *Peace of Lethe*, and, as I watched, constables arrested him. Beat him. Hauled him off. I know not where.

—He'll come to Bridewell, once Sidney's done with him.

Kit made a noise Robert could not decipher: another snort, perhaps.

—Marlowe?

—I cared nothing for him, your honour.

The fire crackled.

Robert tapped the edges of his papers straight. —I'm sending thee to Kent.

—Pardon me?

—Scadbury, once Sir Francis Walsingham's country house, now his nephew's. Thou dost know Sir Thomas.

Walls. —Aye, a long time. We met at Cambridge. But your honour —

—And I believe thou dost also know his good wife, Lady Audrey? Thou'st supped with them many times?

—Aye, though never at Scadbury. Your honour —

—A woman of intellect and discretion. She speaks well of thy translations of Ovid. That did surprise me, a lady reading Ovid.

Kit worked to read the message in Robert's eyes. —Your honour, when last we spoke, you would send me to Scotland.

Aye, right where Essex and Bacon would snare thee. —Kent is lovely come the spring, no? Sir Thomas will shelter thee as long as I ask.

He doubts me. —Your honour, I am . . . Think better of me.

—I think very well of thee. 'Tis why I am not sending thee to gaol for coining or papism. Now, Marsyas the Messenger, so light and swift in saddle, I am sure thou can'st ride in the morning.

With a stomped wrist and kicked ribs? Sweet Christ Jesus. —Once I get some sleep, maybe. Your honour.

'Tis not safe for thee in London, not until that magpie Essex gets distracted by something else that shines. And I need thee tucked away until I sound thy heart. —Come back here by seven o'clock and thou'lt receive coin for a horse, and we might get thy sorry self to Scadbury. Understand me, Marlowe: Scadbury, else I know thee not. Am I clear?

Wheezing, Kit fastened the boatswain's cloak. —Clear, your honour.

Robert clapped Kit on the shoulder, forgetting about the bruise there. —Thou'st got rough nights coming with that cough. This audience is finished.

Robert escorted Kit to the servants' entrance and watched him walk into the darkness. Stooping, he returned to his study, and sat in the high-backed chair and rested his eyes, for just a moment.

The miserable servant knocked once more. —An't please you, your honour . . .

—Show him in.

Eyes still closed, Robert knew whom to expect: another agent, face dirty, clothes dull, both wrinkled. Smaller than Marlowe, plainer, this one faked out a living as an everyman. Sometimes he used the name Parrot. When younger, and less able to resist drama and myth, he'd coded himself Prometheus. Accents fluid and plausible, dagger swift, mind a woodland of springes and snares: Robin Poley, a most experienced man.

In 1586, Robin infiltrated the Babington plot, pretending friendship, his especial gift, to Catholic traitors Anthony Babington and Chidiock Tichborne, and thereby saving Queen Elizabeth's life. Or so Robin said to Sir Francis Walsingham. Babington's version cast Robin as a traitor to all. Sir Francis wondered. After speaking to Babington and Tichborne, with and without torture, Sir Francis wondered some more. Robin, in the meantime, schooled new agents in the field, teaching them the arts of question, surveillance, cipher, and knife, taking particular care with one called Marlowe. Sir Francis came to suspect Robin of unfaithful dealings, of leanings most mercenary, and gaoled him. Despite days of questioning, nothing came to the proof, and Robin walked free, later boasting he made Sir Francis grin like a dog. Not quite a year after that, Kit turned over that ciphered list in Robin's handwriting. Kit had solved the cipher, and solved it with speed, impressing both Sir Francis and, in the end, Robin Poley. Even as the constables informed him of his arrest, Robin felt some pride. *Mine own little ferret: I taught him well.* The list meant more gaol time. Robin, flush with money, rather enjoyed that sentence, forbidding his wife to come see him, and offering bribes, buying favours, even hosting banquets, thereby building a new network of useful contacts. An investment, he called it. He told himself he only play-acted his pleasure in all this, and he told himself fortune would offer a chance to take his revenge on Marlowe. He told himself he wanted this revenge. He did nothing to obtain it. In exchange for a reduced sentence, he'd accepted some particularly dangerous work in France, and he'd not long returned to England.

Now thirty-eight, Robin walked as though his lower back had seized. More and more, when tired, he limped. Age and privation had seamed his cheeks, though he remained fastidious about his twice-weekly shave. His eyes glittered: some hardness there, some threat. He looked like a man who could both cause and solve trouble. He looked like a man in pain. Not much useful fieldwork left in this one, Robert feared. *Yet letting him go would be a waste. If I could devise some desk work for him…* Such an arrangement could benefit them both. Except, except…Robert could list a dozen reasons why he'd not taken better care of this long-time agent. The main: like Sir Francis, Robert knew he could trust nothing about Robin Poley except the man's own self-interest.

Whatever that might be.

—Poley. What blood falls from thy lips?

Robert knew the likely answer: *Please you, good your honour, craving audience, I do but humbly beg your pardon for this, my late interruption. I followed Marlowe here this evening, and I must warn you a certain noble offers agents good money, and I also hear rumours of trouble in Flushing. Rests your honour certain of Marlowe's loyalty?*

—Please you, good your honour, I do but humbly beg your pardon for this, my late interruption; I crave an audience.

—'Tis more like thou dost crave to cut a man's throat.

—You sound pained, your honour. Megrim?

—Thy words dance.

Dripping wet, Robin glanced at the distant fire, and bowed. —Then I shall speak plain, your honour. Essex has you by the throat, and he would recruit your agents.

The rumpled silk kerchief on the desk caught Robin's eye. He knew its meaning.

Robert tucked the kerchief beneath a book. —Marlowe refused. Or so he says.

—Your honour, I followed him here this evening, and he noticed me not. Is he ill?

Robert saw no reason to deny it. —Too long alone, and in disguise.

—It wears a man, aye. Eats him alive. I would expect you, your honour, in your kindness, to allow him time to recover.

—Hast thou a report to give me?

Robin bowed again. —I've learned that Essex has a man at Scadbury. Watching things.

Walsingham's servants? Hellfire. Not by the throat but by the stones. —Who?

—I know not, your honour, and I beg pardon for it.

—Knows Sir Thomas of this?

—Again, I cannot say.

—Discover it. But do nothing, raise no alarm. Then wait until I send for thee. What, what stays thy departure?

—So please you, your honour —

—*What?*

—Rest you certain in Marlowe's loyalty to you?

Thou'st many reasons to seed doubt in my mind, Robin Poley, and not one of thy reasons is clean. —As certain as I rest in thine.

Robin bowed, stumbled, righted himself. —I humbly thank your honour.

After making certain Robin Poley had left the house, Robert resumed his paperwork. He made note of coin advanced, clothing given, and money yet owed.

The stubborn memory of Sir Francis surfaced. *Know'st thou the minds and hearts of thine agents?*

Robert rubbed his burning eyes. *And what, Sir Francis, shall such knowledge cost me?*

TELL TRUTH AND HAVE ME FOR
THY LASTING FRIEND

Drunk enough to smile at what sounded like false cheers and greetings coming from all over the Brave Lion and carrying several jugs of ale, Tom Kyd ducked a rafter. He stumbled, cursed the low ceiling and his own height, and picked his way back to the table where his father, Frank, sat with many friends. Despite being tall enough to knock his head off the ceiling, and despite being thirty-five, Tom felt like a child as he approached these familiar men. Beards showing grey and white now, they remained figures of maturity and certainty, men who not only accepted but also understood and benefited from their places in the order of creation.

Tom set the jugs on the table and himself on the far edge of the bench, not wanting to jostle anyone and not being a part of the conversation. The man closest to him hunched up his shoulder and turned his hips towards Frank, shunning Tom.

Frank, grinning and quite drunk, saw none of it. —Might a man not celebrate his birthday every night?

The others at the table cheered; Tom smiled. He only visited the Brave Lion, an alehouse preferred by scriveners and clerks, with his father. Though Tom had all the qualifications to work as a scrivener, he'd never joined the Worshipful Company of Scriveners, never become a guildsman. Frank, by contrast, had served a term as the company warden. Father and son resembled each other: tall men with strong pointed chins, blue eyes, fair hair and beards, Frank's mostly white now. Each man tied his hair back in a loose tail. Frank kept his beard well-barbered; Tom's beard reached halfway to his collarbone.

Another of Frank's friends approached the table, cheering Frank's birthday and his brief respite from the imprisonment of his marriage. Both Frank and Tom laughed a little too hard. Frank's wife, Agnes, would have much to say about the smells on Frank's breath later, and about the company he'd kept. Agnes Kyd maintained she knew a good man when she saw one, and in these dark days, a man must take great care about whom he called friend.

A scrivener Tom's age, Geoffrey Morgan, smiled and waved from across the room. They'd attended school together and sometimes shared drinks or supper. Tom waved back.

All these men, thought Tom, *making good money, married, fathers: if not happy, then at least stable. I can't pay my rent.*

One of the men sitting closest to Frank leaned across the table and upset one of the jugs of ale. Spittle flew past his teeth as he lisped. —Then there's Tom, now, Tom, thine only son, refusing to follow in thy footsteps.

Tom sipped from his cup.

Frank gave his friend a good elbow in the ribs. —Tom doth more with his pen in one afternoon than thou or I could manage a lifetime. He's a poet and a translator, a very learned man. He also writes plays.

—Thank you, Father.

More spittle flew. This time the man lowered his head to the table and seemed to lose his body. He peered up between candles. —Poems? Plays? Fah, I could write a good murder tragedy on a Sunday afternoon. Hieronimo and Hamlet? 'Tis nothing, nothing but violence and gore. I expected better of thee, Tom, with thy good father here, and thine education.

Tom nodded. *So did I.*

—To Frank! To the best warden this Worshipful Company has ever known! Frank Kyd, gentlemen!

The conversation shifted to a common hatred for Londoners: the Low Countries refugees. Tom could predict the course of the tepid thinking and stale words: lazy foreigners soaking up moneys from the Queen's own treasury while yet stealing work, and intricate markets collapsing beneath the weight of labour gluts, the old song bound by its chorus of *Send them back, I say, send them back.* The man who could write a good murder tragedy in an afternoon warned of riots in the streets yet if the Privy Council refused to get these foreigners under control. His fellows hushed him; even drunk, even passionate, one must take great care with words.

The conversation changed to women, their fickleness, vanity, and charms.

Tom shifted his weight on the bench and, on a long sigh, blew some stray hair from his eyes. *At least another hour before I might start bringing Father home.*

Outside, Frank walked with his arm around Tom's shoulders, leaning on him. —A lovely night, a lovely night.

—Mind the gutter, Father.

—Some days I think 'tis true: if a man works hard and keeps honest, he *shall* prosper. Even thy mother agrees with me on that. I take much abuse, Tom, not only from her, but from other men for bowing, they say, to my wife. And why not, I say, when we bow to a queen? Peace and quiet, peace and quiet. The burnings... People, Tom, people, *burning*. Sometimes when I smell a roast of beef on the spit —

—Father...

—The sizzle of fat... Sweet Saviour, can we not just live together without screaming and blood? 'Tis cold tonight. Is thy cloak still good?

—No holes.

—And thy Kit, has thou heard of him?

Tom winced. —Not yet.

—Thy mother cares not, but I do. A long time, Tom.

—I know.

—Not a word?

—No.

—Is't true, the rumour? Is he gone abroad?

—Father, I know nothing of it.

—Aye, 'tis a kindness he does thee.

—What?

Frank sang. —It was of a maid and her heart and her hair so long, so long and tangled in the weir...

Tom nudged him. —Father, what mean you: a kindness?

—If, *if* I have guessed right from speaking with him all those Sunday afternoons... Ah, 'tis no safe conversation, this.

Wanting to snap out a reply, yet suddenly unsure what the reply should be, Tom guided his father around a collapsing refuse pile, its spreading puddle of vegetable peel, excrement, bones of fowl. *No warning. Not even a note. He knew he must leave. I can read his face like I can read a pamphlet — I can see what he wants for dinner — yet he hid this from me.*

Frank patted Tom's shoulder. —Never didst thou like puzzles.

—I love puzzles.

—No, thou'st love the solving of them. Resistant puzzles fret thy mind. And I say to thee, Tom, I see no puzzle here, only dark days and care. He tells thee nothing because he loves thee.

Tom snorted.

Frank stumbled, righted himself. —Oh, my head shall be sore come the morrow, and thy mother's voice sharp. Where in Hell are we? Call a bellman for help.

—We've nearly got you home, Father.

—Bellman! Bellman, I say!

—Father, hush, we need no bellman to light the way. Would you wake mother?

Frank shook his head. —Not for a thousand demons provoking me. Oh. Look at that. 'Tis my door. I am home. I thank thee, Tom.

Tom bowed to him. —Good night to you, Father.

Then he strode away before he might hear his mother's voice rise, before he must witness interrogation.

WILL'T NOT BE AN ODD JEST

Elbows, knees, ankles, wrists, and hips: all worked on ball joints and a complex set of strings. Essex blew dust from the poppet's face, then dug his finger in the poppet's winking eye to wipe away a smudge. While he displayed the rest of his collection of poppets behind glass on shelves in his bedchamber, Essex kept this one, this articulated wooden man stolen from Robert Cecil some seventeen years ago, stashed in his trunk. Since that theft — abduction? — the wooden man had lain, strings and joints tangled, in his oubliette. Essex peeked at the poppet a few times a year, each time feeling pleasure's thrust and adoration's visceral thrill: *I love thee, little man.* Now he grasped the poppet around the torso. Strings fell. Essex held the tangle near his face, intrigued; black mould crept over the poppet's motley silk, obscuring the pattern, and giving a stench.

Robin watched this play, feeling a bit sick.

Anthony Bacon adjusted his broad collar and tucked his curly hair behind his ears. The set of his lips seemed peevish, as if he'd trapped wasps in his mouth and now refused to free them, no matter how hard they stung. When he spoke, his voice took a nasal tone, precise consonants cutting any whine. —Poley, what dost thou make of it?

—Wisdom. Sir Robert's agent is tired and worn and shall

now enjoy a soft bed and watchful care, as might a favoured hound.

Squinting, Anthony picked up a reading stone and laid it on a piece of paper. Essex had bought him a dozen of these stones, at great cost. Anthony kept losing them.

Robin shook his head. —Bacon, I'd no idea thine eyesight was so poor.

—A vile curse from God is this, and one I warrant not. My sins, balanced against the ledgers of greater men, are small.

—Thy page, aged eleven?

Anthony looked up and scowled. —'Twas a private matter—

—And the sin was in being caught?

—The sin was in the scandal. How a man deals with his servants is his own concern. As if I am the only man ever to use a boy. I hid on the Continent for years, until my father died, running messages between adulterous couples and feuding neighbours. When I returned, I did need share lodgings with my brother and there set up a scrivenery just to pay the rent. Fah, scriveners, literate insects. Our uncle, Lord Burghley, ignored our pleas for help. To this day my cousin Robert Cecil — oh, pray, forgive me, *Sir* Robert — affects to see me not. I deserve better.

—We all do.

—The tales I hear of Marlowe's memory: true? That he solves ciphers and writes new ones? And 'tis thine opinion that if any agent knows Sir Robert's thoughts on succession, 'tis Marlowe?

Robin nodded.

—And thou'lt deliver him him to us?

—Just give me the time and the means.

Essex looked up from the poppet and studied Robin.

Anthony sighed. —Aye, time and means, thou'lt say, yet give me no details.

—He's shown defiance and taken the punishment. Leave him be, for the moment. I got a good look at his face. Blood and bruises: such waste. I deplore waste.

—Wouldst thou go gentle on him? Is this fondness for thy protégé?

—No. I'd just use my reason and my wits, *thinking* before I hired muscle, and thereby saving both money and time.

Essex strode over to them. —Poley: I want him.

—One way, or another?

Essex drew a line in the air with his ringed hand. —Intact. Body and mind. And I would harm no innocent.

—Innocent, my lord? None is innocent. We are born sinful and guilty, and besides, these are complicated times.

Holding the poppet out before him, Essex sighed. —Should Her Good Majesty die in her sleep tonight, who rules England? Sir Robert's position after the mark-for-it-shall-never-come-to-pass death of the Queen looks firm, but what of me? Where will Cock Robin be then, poor thing? Hey? A wise man will be prepared. 'Tis all I want. This, this fussing over one man... I want this done with no complications, and no assault upon my conscience. Bacon, advance him the money we discussed.

—All of it, my lord?

—Aye. All of it. Make what arrangements ye must, and trouble me no further on this matter until ye've got results.

Then Essex dropped the poppet onto Anthony's desk and strode out of the room, not caring what effect this might have on his agents.

In his bedchamber at the front of the house, facing the Thames, he gazed out the window. Wherries travelled the river, lamps lit. Feeling pent-up, irritated, as he had those first nights at Theobalds, he considered summoning his wife — an excellent match, she being the widow of Phillip Sidney, brother to Robert Sidney in Flushing, and the daughter of old Sir Francis Walsingham. Of late she made for a dull fuck, being pregnant again and complaining of nausea and fatigue. Last time she'd puked on the sheets. At least she'd managed to give him a son, a toddling little torment who got underfoot. Not caring to risk bile, Essex thought instead of his favourite mistress and took himself in hand. The wherries distracted him. Flesh still limp, he tucked his clothes and spat on the floor. *Why is't I may not have what I want? And those blurred little lights: why must they irk me so?*

TELL ME LIES AT DINNERTIME

Admitting he might be drunker than he'd first thought, Tom struggled with the lock. A sulky thing, the lock stiffened in the rain and demanded a certain jiggle of the key. Denied this pampering, the lock might seize. A neighbour, a father with a new baby, opened his door and demanded Tom cease his frequent coming and going at night, his noisome knocking and meddling with his door. The infant, head on his father's shoulder, wailed. Rain dripped from his scrivener's sign and fell on his head as Tom wished his neighbour goodnight. Inside, the darkness deep, he let out a long sigh and rolled his eyes to Heaven.

Mankind.

He made to turn the key and so lock the door behind him. The stiff lock refused to budge.

—And how in Hell shall I pay to fix that?

He took his second desk chair, the one customers used, the one Kit had sat in when sharing the desk, and propped it beneath the doorknob. Then he yanked the key free and frowned at the hearth. *Straight to bed*, he thought, groping around the food chest, where he kept his candles — or, this week, his sole remaining candle.

A snuffling then, a rustling of fabrics, and a deep cough that guttered out on the wheeze of a drowning cat.

—Blood of Christ! Kit, 'tis thee?

Another cough, another wheeze. —Aye. Candle's in the sconce. Sorry I frightened thee.

Tom strode over the two steps to the bedchamber and patted the sconce. —I know not whether to kiss thee or strike thee. Didst thou let that candle burn down?

—Oh. I —

—How many times must I —

—Well, light another, scold.

—'Twas my last one. And *scold*? Oh, thou'st heard nothing of scolding. Where in *Hell* hast thou been?

—Tom, listen —

—Everyone asking me —

The neighbour with the infant pounded on the wall as Kit sat up, tears on his face, grateful then for the dark. —Tom, please.

—I knew not if thou'dst *died*. And what, thou'lt strut up to my door, thou and thy dancing prick, and expect me to fall

to thy sweet words? Holla, thou pampered jade of Canterbury
— what rattles? Thy *teeth*?

—'Tis nothing. I am fine. Just let me rest.

Tom leaned down, clasped Kit's face in both his hands,
and pressed his lips to Kit's forehead. —Thou'st got a fever
fit to boil water. Brought me a plague, hast thou? Get under
the covers. Lie down.

—I tried to make the bed, fix the netting beneath for thee.
When I came in, I found the mattress sagging. Thou'st sleep
better when the netting's tight. My bruises, I —

—Bruises? What happened to thee?

Kit's teeth rattled again; he spoke anyway. —Piece by piece,
we carried this bed from thy father's house. The coins fell
everywhere. Christ's love, I'm cold. And he cracked those ribs.
Tom, I liked his eyes, eyes like thine as he knelt there. Lice.
Coins stick. Stink. Not pure, however forged: lead and the
alchemist. I got seasick.

—I can smell it on thy cloak. And what else stinks?

—My shoes. Gutter.

—Thy fine winter shoes? Oh, Kit. How dost thou —

—Aye, aye, how dost thou get so dirty? He'll be unhappy
with me.

—No, lie down, I said. Who shall be unhappy?

—John Marlowe, master cobbler, Canterbury. Know'st
thou what he'll say?

—Keep the covers on.

—Same as he's said to me since I learned to walk and
knock things over. *Kit, dost thou care nothing for all my work?*

Tom smoothed Kit's hair off his forehead; his fingers got

tangled. —Dost dou care nudding: I know th'art tired when thou'lt talk like that.

—Not me. My father.

—Fadder.

Kit laughed, then grunted. —Christ's love, my ribs. I've missed thee. I crave thee. Let me kiss thee, la, let me taste thy skin. I sold my comb, and I've gone too long without a barber. 'Tis a matted mess; 'tis all gone wrong. Why dost thou push me?

—Lie *down*.

—I've got errands, Tom.

—Errands which must wait till morning, now, mustn't they?

—Words and threats, and all the meanings, and I say nothing. Lock the door.

Tom poured some water from his pitcher into his bowl, then dipped a cloth into the water and wrung it out. —Here, for thy brow. No, leave it there. Like this.

—What shall we have for supper? Chardequince, aye? Plums, apples, roses, ginger, blood —

—Kit, leave the cloth; God knows, th'art enough trouble when sensible. Sit up, aye, fine, fine, now let me get in behind thee and lean back.

Tom tucked a pillow behind him, rested his back against the wall, and splayed his legs. Kit found an angle and in turn rested his back against Tom's chest. When a boy, and prone to coughs in winter, Tom had leant this way against his father, and Frank would kiss the top of his head and call him sweet son, tell him the cough would settle soon.

Frank had propped against a warm chimney wall, his burden a child.

Kit, the burning weight of thee.

The ropes beneath the mattress sagged some more.

—Fleas, Tom.

—Every bed in London's got fleas.

—Becket's martyrdom, Canterbury Cathedral, all that fuckery.

Becket? —Hush, Kit, lest the neighbours misapprehend thee.

—Becket *happened*. His meaning, all of it, 'tis the old question, la, and no king, no pope, can wipe it away. Generations of people made that pilgrimage to Becket's shrine: sacrifice and meaning, and the old question.

—What question?

—What wilt thou die for? After the blades and the blood — clotting, that moment — when the other priests dared to approach Becket's corpse — I mean the pieces of it, la, and la — and then, happy task, prepare for it burial — Becket wore a hair shirt beneath his robes — penance, aye, that gruff old peevish ascetic. Were not the draughts in that cathedral penance enough?

—Settle thyself.

—The lice frenzied out of the hair shirt, boiled up, said one witness. I told Ben that story. So the lesson of this martyrdom, O Tom, O namesake is — pass me the wine.

—I've not got any wine. Kit?

Steady breathing.

Kissing the top of Kit's head, Tom found the growing bald spot. *Th'art fire I would steal, steal and keep.*

Tom dozed. He dreamt of deadlines and copy work and some other dread, unnamed yet: his wrists in bolts, high over his head, as some giant of a man rammed him against a wall. Tom woke from this dream a few times, woke enough to tell himself the reason for it — sitting up and supporting Kit — yet each time he slipped back to sleep, the dream picked up where interrupted. It felt like a scene in which some of the actors froze while one revealed a secret.

Kit grunted and twitched. Tom let him slide down; that posture worsened his cough. Tom shoved all his bolsters beneath Kit's head; that eased the coughing but encouraged a buzzing snore. The heat from Kit's body made Tom sweat; he threw off covers and then got cold. Light changed. Outside, women compared the night's work and wished one another a good rest, and tradesmen got ready for the day. Kit muttered and wheezed. Tom frowned at him: *I could smother thee with a pillow.* Reasoning that any chance for rest had long departed, Tom decided to get up. Instead, he fell asleep.

Nothing struck his face. Nothing restrained his arms. His dagger felt heavy and useless on his thigh, and his body did not rock with the sea.

Kit felt happy. He felt defenceless.

Safe.

Not in Rheims, nor Flushing, nor am I Loman.

Tom's bed.

Start again?

He took a breath.

Oh, Christ.

Limbs like water, ribs like fire, lungs like stones: phlegm burned, shifted, and broke, and his wretched cough seized him.

Worse. No, 'tis nothing. —Tom?

Noises from the front office: in the poor winter light, Tom rustled through papers on his desk. —A moment.

—Tom.

—A moment, Kit. I'm busy.

Busy? —Tom, listen to me. I know not what I said to thee last night, but I wasn't drunk.

Tom snorted. —This time.

So many little details, once blurry in familiarity, crashed down on him: the whorls in the wooden walls, the pattern of the sconce, and the tang of Tom's sweat, something like iron in it, often reminding Kit of blood. Something of honey in it, too, deeper down. Kit hauled himself off the bed, urinated in the pot, swayed a little, and decided to sit down again. —I'm not well.

—Who's a clever mother-wit, then?

—Thou'st sound vexed.

A fist pounded on the door, and Kit, hand on his dagger, wrist aching, recognized he'd heard the noise a moment before. Threat had woken him, after all.

At his desk, Tom brushed papers to one side with the back of his hand. —I overslept, and I tidied not my desk yesterday. 'Tis Chief Constable Reynolds, who shall want his pillory sign, and I know not where I've stashed the thing. Nor have I any candle to light my way. I thank thee for that.

—Pillory signs? Has it come to this? What of thy patron?

—Speak not to me of patronage. I'd sooner see thy dagger come at me. Every single man who's cracked open an absey book and scrawls his initials in the ground with a pointed stick and thereby calls himself poet merits steady patronage whilst I starve: why is't? Playhouses closed for plague last year, no one buying scripts —

—But thou'st *got* a patron. Tedious mother-wit that he is.

Tom snorted. —I've got a beard, too, the more use to me.

Bracing himself against the wall, Kit took a few steps to the front office. —Thy scrivening, Tom, can'st thou pay thy reckonings?

Exasperation tightened Tom's voice. —Pillory sign.

Yet more knocking. Kit got to the desk.

—Kit, please, *thy* help I need not.

Kit held a paper up to the tiny window, to the scant light. —Here 'tis. *An ice-hearted slut who did fling away her still blooded babe as most despised filth, in winter. Throw cold water.* For Christ's love, Tom.

—Give me that. And get back in bed.

Kit leaned against the desk as Tom moved the chair and hauled open the door.

—Chief Constable Reynolds, good morning.

Winter morning light streamed through the door as Absalom Reynolds took a few steps in. He stood near Tom's height, chest and shoulders much bigger, jaw square, and spoke with a collegial deference, a certain formality, always addressing Tom as *you*.

—And good morning to you, Kyd. Worked your scrivener's wordy magic for me?

Tom gave him the sign. —As per orders.

Reynolds gave him some coins. —Got your next one here: wantons and harlots.

—Whores in the pillory? Slow patch, is it?

—We all got our quotas. See you Thursday.

—Right.

As Reynolds left and the office darkened again, Kit found the ale, poured himself some, sipped it. —Is he not bound to contract such work from a member of the Worshipful Company of Scriveners?

—I charge less. He pockets the difference. I was taking work from a new scrivenary set up out of Gray's Inn, Anthony Bacon. Kit, dost thou choke?

—Swallowed the wrong way. This Bacon paid well?

—Aye, on time, too, though I declined to take more work from him. He would have me copy something in cipher. I am quick with puzzles; I feared I'd solve it.

—Tom, stay Hell's distance away from Tony Bacon.

—More secrets, is't, more state and crown?

—Please!

Tom bit back the rest of his complaint. —Well, what of thee, Kit? A whole new play fit to burst out thy fingertips?

—Ah . . . I must find a place to live, first.

—Stand not on ceremony with me, thou fool. Thou'st wear a key, and that bed —

—I can't stay.

—*What?* Thou just —

—I've got an errand. I know not how long —

—Kit!

—Surfeit of thine abuse, hey? At least I'm telling thee.

—This time.

Kit wanted to turn away; he'd not got the strength.

The shifting daylight caught Kit's face. Tom's eyes opened wide. —Sweet God, Kit. Who beat thee?

—Duty —

—Blood! No, listen to me for once. Kit, this — they dangle thee like some idle plaything and then unhook thee when it suits them — what wast thou thinking, when thou didst first take this work?

—I thought 'twas good money.

—Aye. And hast thou ever been paid so well since?

Kit clicked his tongue. —No.

—And when shalt thou be paid for this task?

—On the next Quarter Day, like anyone else.

Sighing, Tom took a cloth from his pocket, dipped it in the cup of ale, and dabbed at Kit's swollen eye. —Next Quarter Day is in *March.* 'Tis only January. Keep still.

—I was drinking that.

Tom switched to the pitcher of water. —I said, keep still. Quarter Day. Last time thou didst wait till the third subsequent Quarter Day for payment. How many more delays, Kit, and how many beatings? And what of the summer's night thy master checks thy name off a list when ... Thy wrists. Wast thou *chained*?

Kit said nothing.

Gentle, Tom washed Kit's face. —Leave it behind, Kit. Please. Walk away.

—Oh, excellent advice. Walk away, because I may, with but a wave of my hand, in dumb safety —

—A sulky hog on market day is less stubborn.

—Oh, for Christ's love, Tom! How can I not know what I know? Walk away? And live on what? No, wait: I shall take up new work and, la, disguise myself as a fresh apprentice, not ten years old... Wilt thou scowl at me?

—Descant for the hangman, Kit. And thou shouldst be in bed. Thy cough —

Church bells rang the hour, and Kit stroked Tom's hair. —'Tis nothing. I'm fine.

—And when shalt thou come back? Or is that, too, a secret?

—I'll know more when I get there.

Frowning, Tom crossed his arms. Then he embraced Kit and kissed the top of his head. —Keep warm, hey? And write to me this time.

Kit leaned his face on Tom's chest. —Sweet scold.

Coughing, he made for the door.

FAIR COPY: BE NOT PENSIVE; WE ARE YOUR FRIENDS

At Cecil House, this thirtieth day of January.
Addressed to my honourable and loving friend,
Sir Thomas Walsingham at Scadbury.

Sir,

As I greet you with affection and respect, I am to plainness pressed and must express my deep gratitude for your honour's kind allowance to house a servant of Her Majesty, by extension a servant of mine, and an old friend of yours. Of this servant, Christopher Marlowe: he needs a

quiet place so he may recover from the strains of good work
and faithful dealing abroad, his affairs being of necessary
subtlety, and of high importance. Marlowe being known
unto you, from your shared time as students at Cambridge,
and from shared affection, and also to your good wife, Lady
Audrey, I need not give recommendation or even assurance
as to his character, his motives, or his deepest loyalties.
Such forces may, in the minds and hearts of lesser men,
become tangled. I fear Lord Burghley and I left him to
his work much too long. Overstrained, the strongest mind
may become delicate. On the tippy matter of delicacy, I
must caution, or perhaps remind, your honour, as you once
reminded me, of Marlowe's broad taste for the comfort of
wine, strong ale, cider, and mead. Afford him that which a
doctor orders for his recovery. Recovery is my utmost desire
as concerns him. As he gains strength, protect him, I beg
you, from excess, as such excess has, in the past, made him
quarrelsome and proud. Judiciously applied, wine might
loosen Marlowe's tongue and so reassure one who worries
over any entanglements in said mind and heart, which remain, I pray, as stout as rocks washed over by tides, as stout
as when first I encountered them. I give your honour especial thanks for your gracious kindness in lending Marlowe
shelter, food, physicke, clothing, drink, and, in anticipation
as well as care, paper, quill, and ink. I beg of your honour
one final favour in this matter: that you kindly, and by
your own hand, report to me on all matters of this servant's
health. No other of such as these servants is so cherished by
me; I would know of the slightest change, improvement, or

decline, in his strength, manner, and speech. I commit him, and you, sir, to God's protection.

> Your affectionate and assured friend,
> Ro. Cecil.

DIVERSE LEWD AND MALICIOUS LIBELS

Not long after Kit departed Tom's rooms, and not a half-mile away, on a narrow street of mud lined with crooked wooden houses, Izaak Pindar wrapped his arms round his chest and walked faster. Cold drizzle fell. *God in my heart, the weather puts me to mind of my uncle.* Memory hunted and sniffed: the trickle of water off windows and roofs, and the smell of goose fat. Izaak's robust uncle, Marcus Tilley, smeared goose fat on his chest October to May, the grey mess a potent article of faith; Marcus never suffered from cough or catarrh. In his expansive generosity, Marcus offered the orphaned Izaak a home and education, and, in later years, a surname. Izaak acknowledged but declined the gift of the name. Marcus took deep offense, and he broke out a secret: Izaak's mother had stolen the name Pindar for him, claiming some great man in London had forced a child on her. Izaak countered he'd long guessed this story and cared not: his name would remain Izaak Pindar. This one moment of defiance, the men standing shoulder to shoulder as they looked out the window, voices low, severed mercy. If Izaak would be Pindar, argued Marcus, then he would also embrace the truth of his treacherous mother, her taint still affecting her sister, Marcus's wife, Mordita. And if Izaak refused to stay the path and instead lapsed back to the old faith, why, 'twas betrayal to the very crown. Here, Izaak shouted, insisting he and Marcus agreed on far more than Marcus knew. England, like any woman, understood not her own frailties, her own need for governance. The Reformation must be led to its end. Calling himself Pindar remained a private matter, irrelevant to his purpose in life, and no insult to Marcus Tilley. After that discussion, Izaak returned to Cambridge a week early, to finish his final terms at Corpus Christi. Then he took up some parish work, giving reports to Sir Francis Walsingham on the activities and utterances, the more accidental the better, of various Church of England priests. After a few years of this, he found himself assigned to Robert Cecil. Izaak considered this a blessing, and he knew men who would chafe under all this clerkship, this endless assisting. Christopher Marlowe would never bow to it. Izaak, however, understood something prouder men missed; a trusted assistant might come to enjoy not only influence but genuine power.

Izaak had neither spoken nor written to Marcus Tilley in six years.

Hunger tore at his belly. His lodgings did not include meals, an arrangement he liked; his odd hours meant more meals would be missed than eaten. He found his own bread.

The man who smelled of goose fat passed Izaak. Memory pounced.

Twelve-year-old Izaak hurried through a Latin translation. Marcus Tilley stood up and stretched his back, and he seemed to count each raindrop on the windowpane. *A gift from God is this rain, Izaak, for it encourages contemplation of regrets, and, with fortune, the learning of lessons.*

Mordita put down her stitchery, hearing that, and she sighed. Marcus glanced at his wife, strode to her and dragged her by the arm from the room. Feet thumped and stumbled on the stairs. A door slammed. Mordita gave up no sound. Izaak conjugated his Latin verbs and wrote his Latin sentences, taking full advantage of the extra time his uncle's absence offered. He completed the lesson three times, achieving perfection. When Marcus came back, he'd find nothing to correct in Izaak. Indeed, on his return, flushed in the face, Marcus praised Izaak's diligence, and they moved to geography, to lists of England's imports and exports. Izaak, his pride in his Latin distracting him, failed to learn of Canterbury's Huguenots to his uncle's satisfaction. Truth told, Izaak cared nothing for Canterbury and how its economy tottered once the pilgrimages stopped and then adapted to the new gifts of Huguenot refugees and their silk weaving. Marcus cared. Izaak's lapse earned him a fast from supper and three hard strikes of the fire poker against his arse. Later, at table, Izaak sitting on a cushion and studying his uncle's full plate, Marcus explained the tiresome evil of women, how, decrepit with frailties, women listed towards giggling cruelties and wretched desires. *Thine aunt and thy mother both enjoyed the torment of butterflies. Aye. Catching them with their hands and mauling the wings, crippling their beauty and purpose. 'Tis the responsibility of men to protect women from themselves, or, if we fail that, to protect other men from the evil of women, to teach them governance. Thy mother, Izaak, oh, thy mother...*

The fire had glowed on the side of the pitcher, reflection bent.

Wind blew drizzle into Izaak's face, and he blinked. *London.* His favourite bakery stood before him. He smoothed his hands over his face and beard and stepped inside.

Robin Poley, also catching the scent of goose fat on that passing man, decided not to follow Sir Robert's clerk into the bakery. Instead, cursing how the dampness infested his bones and made them ache, he continued walking. A good walk, as he'd often told Kit, helped him think.

He felt possessed. Not owned: available, like farm labourers at the hiring fair, travelling craftsmen, assassins, his skills and gifts the highest bidder's spoils. He'd starved. He'd twice served out sluggish time in the Tower, and once, under another name, in the Fleet, where he paid most of his money to a visiting scrivener, himself desperate for work, for begging cards. Robin then handed the cards through grilles at street level to passersby who deigned to notice him. He'd considered those gorgeous begging cards an investment, a smarter gamble than buying bread, as bread once eaten is gone forever but the cards might lead to more bread. Begging cards, examples of beautiful lettering and compact design, had no novelty, and few Londoners bothered with mercy for the incarcerated. Most of Robin's cards — refused, ignored — fell to the wet street. Mud and slops soaked them.

Hunger and cold being excellent teachers, Robin Poley learned that freedom and imprisonment both meant suffering. *Make compartments in thy mind*, he'd taught Kit. *Control thine imprisonments and thou'lt control thy suffering.*

What did possess Robin: his own failing flesh. Already old for fieldwork, he needed to rough out a plan for the days, perhaps only fears, perhaps a promise, of when he could no longer walk. Frightening pain in his buttocks, hips, and lower spine woke him throughout the night and made the morning piss a hobbling agony. These troubles had visited before, staying perhaps a little longer each winter, blowing away each spring. This winter, his troubles worsened. Pain and stiffness in various joints might linger to midday. Getting up from a bed or a floor meant a slow struggle. A creeping fatigue tainted the hours, and a deepening pain in his right hip socket gave him visions of rotting bone. His right leg deceived him. Pretending to hang the same balanced length as the left, it shirked the ground, forcing Robin to drag the leg as he worked to smooth out his limp. Sometimes he slept in one chair with his feet propped up on a second; this hurt, but at least he could stand afterwards without toppling like a brittle tree eaten out by ravenous insects. More and more, he needed his crutch. He'd tripped over it one cold spring, several years before, while training Kit. They'd been running messages between two secret Catholics harbouring a priest, later betraying the lot of them, when Robin's dragging feet collided with a fallen branch. He'd grabbed Kit's arm to break his fall, and Kit, annoyed, had shaken him off. The branch: Nature had shown her cleverness and bent the oak so it looked like the numeral seven. The bounty: a little upstroke at the end. Robin could grasp the upstroke and then lean his forearm on the horizontal bend so that the entire seven at once lent him balance and shoved him forward. A sweet accident, first that the branch did not grow full straight, second that Robin found it. He hated to use it, as he hated his weakness. The crutch marked him.

Today, having refused his crutch, managing not to limp, he considered scriveners. Kit Marlowe had lived with a man who took work as a scrivener, between selling his plays: Tom Kyd. Scriveners, with their legal knowledge and their legible handwriting, with their copying documents for a fee: Robin looked about for a sign of a quill. He found one, and a man swinging an axe at it while another man, with dark hair and a beard and large blue eyes, quills tucked into pen loops on his belt, grabbed at the axeman's arms and yelled about raising a rent too high. Splinters flew. The man with the axe said he would claim this destruction as firewood, as a deposit on the back rent. The other man, the scrivener, Robin guessed, stood aside then, counting, it seemed, the blows of the axe. The landlord commanded the scrivener to hurry inside and take what he could carry and then be gone. Robin walked around the broken sign and caught the scrivener's name on a jagged piece of it — Gfry Morgan — just as the axe shattered the words.

Smiling, Robin waited for Geoffrey to emerge. He nodded at the scrolls and papers tucked beneath Geoffrey's arms and offered to buy some.

Geoffrey scowled at him. —Buy my scrolls? No, sir, I've great need of them for when I — I set up my new office.

—Paper. I just need some paper, and buying it from thee would save me the walk to a stationer in Paul's Yard.

Burdens slipping, Geoffrey clenched his arms tight to his body. —Oh. Aye. How much paper?

—How much canst thou spare?

—Half a ream?

Robin opened his purse and counted out twice the market rate.

Geoffrey's eyes widened. He ducked his chin and nodded at the ragged ream about to fall from beneath his elbow to the ground. Robin took the paper, and then placed the payment in Geoffrey's waiting hand. The landlord, missing this, collected his firewood. Robin and the landlord left, and Geoffrey stood in the drizzle, unable to put his money away without dropping something.

Later that evening, Robin decided to get a drink. He'd spent much of the day writing, and now, head sore, he scowled. He'd studied bucketloads of Latin poetry at Cambridge, and he enjoyed music, particularly singing in four-part harmony, so he'd not expected metre to defy him. Still, he'd managed, and now he wanted a fair copy. He wanted a scrivener. He wanted a particular scrivener: the one Geoffrey Morgan. Stepping into the Brave Lion, noticing Izaak Pindar drinking alone, Robin reasoned he'd either find Geoffrey here numbing his misery or he'd find a friend of Geoffrey's who could get a message to him.

Geoffrey sat at a table crowded by pitchers and cups. A tall man with white hair and a neat white beard stood up from the bench beside Geoffrey and clapped him on the shoulder.
—Courage, Morgan.

He slurred. —I lost all, Mr. Kyd. For the love of God, how shall I tell my wife?

—The Worshipful Company of Scriveners looks after its own. One of us will be by tomorrow.

Frank Kyd walked up to the bar, settled the reckoning, and left. Geoffrey drained the last of the ale in his cup. Then he picked up someone else's cup and drained the dregs of that, too.

Robin ordered a jug of ale and brought it to Geoffrey. —Rough night?

Geoffrey stared up at him. —Was it not a full half-ream?

—A full half-ream: 'tis thy counting? Then small wonder thou'st been evicted.

—Just my office. My house is safe. I'm only two months behind on the house.

Robin filled Geoffrey's cup, and Geoffrey gulped at the ale, spilling some. Robin topped up the cup again. —How's the wife?

—She knows none of it. She's with child; I can't distress her.

—Congratulations. First one?

—Fourth. In six years.

—I may have some work for thee.

Geoffrey pretended to write; he knocked over a cup. —I've a legible hand. My turnaround is swift.

—How much for five pages?

—Five pages of what?

—Poetry.

—Your immortality, sir, will cost you, ah ... Pardon me, my head ...

Robin suggested an amount.

Geoffrey giggled. —Five pages, or fifty?

—I'll give thee half tonight. Shall I come by tomorrow to give thee the work?

—Aye, aye. Oh — I've not got an office.

—No.

—Firewood. He broke up my sign for firewood!

—A foul injustice. Now, where shall I find thee?

Robin waited until half-past seven the following morning before he set out for Morgan's house. He reached it within the hour. After pressing his ear to the door and catching the sounds of young children's cries and pleas and demands, Robin knocked.

Inside, a woman called out. —Geoffrey! Be that the landlord again?

—Christ, I hope not.

—What?

Geoffrey's voice got closer to the door. —The landlord? Why would he come by?

Robin knocked again, and Geoffrey, eyes red, breath sour, opened the door. —Mr. Kyd sent you?

—We talked over a job last night, at the Lion.

—We did?

—I paid thee half, in advance.

Geoffrey patted his purse then turned around. —Marjory. Didst thou take money from my purse while I slept?

—Aye. How else dost thou think I made deposit on the rent and bought the bread?

A toddler, chewing on a crust, came to the door and reached up for her father's hand.

Geoffrey puzzled through words. —Marjory, what mean'st thou: landlord again?

Still hidden within the house, Marjory called out her response. —He came by while thou wast sleeping. I'd no idea we'd gotten that far behind on the rent. I couldn't look him in the eye for shame.

Geoffrey faced Robin again. —What job?

Robin gave him the poem.

Geoffrey read the first page, scanned the others, and gave the papers back. His face flushed. —Sweet God, I can't copy this. Who and what art thou? Go. Get away.

—Very good then. I'll take the advance back, and thou'lt see no more of me.

Geoffrey shut his eyes.

As one of the infants started to cry, the toddler tugged Geoffrey's hand and asked for more bread.

Robin smiled at her. —Aye, it comes down to bread.

FAIR COPY: PRACTISE MAGIC
AND CONCEALED ARTS

Sent from Scadbury this first day of February.
Addressed to my honourable and kind friend,
Sir Robert Cecil.

Having done as you asked, I now must pry time loose
from the grasp of an upset household and give you report.
Marlowe, your servant, and my friend, arrived in a poor
state, much bruised, and frail when once so vigorous, the
continuance of which prods both my humane concern and

mine individual affections with alarm and dread. Marlowe's fever is dangerous, and his breathing is troubled, being full of rales. I can get no recognition from him. I say again, for clarity: he knows me not. Nor can he name this house. When I can get any speech of him, 'tis only that he must beg Tom's forgiveness (I believe he means not me) and ride to Scadbury. In no wise will he be comforted that he has fulfilled his duties. He hath also asked for manna, and when I did read to him from Exodus, he turned away.

I sent for a doctor, and he giveth the same fearful diagnosis as doth my surgeon and even my cook. 'Tis not any contagion but a pneumonie. Death haunts the place. 'Tis now a matter of chance, or, for the man with a soul, a matter of wills not our own. We keep a watch on him, I taking my turn at the bedside.

Sir Robert, I doubt not a moment the kindness of your intentions, but I do beg leave to question your wisdom in sending him to me, all this way out to Scadbury. Or feared you losing sight of him in London? Knew you the weight of his illness? Your language is oblique, and your meanings obscured; fear you a deeper illness at work? Shall I sift for it, if he lives?

Please be assured your servant receives urgent and best care. I shall send further reports by rider.

> Your true and respectful friend,
> Thomas Walsingham.

THERE FOR HONEY BEES HAVE SOUGHT IN VAIN

A patronage I promised thee, not a deathbed.

Thomas Walsingham rubbed his brown eyes with the pads of his fingers. He'd kept vigil at the bedsides of panting and delirious patients before. The experience had yet to go well.

A new promise, then, Marlowe: die on me here, and I shall piss on thy grave.

Gideon, the household's singing boy and assistant to the cook, peeked in the doorway. He was perhaps eleven; none knew for certain. When Walsingham caught sight of him, Gideon bowed, and his sandy hair fell before his blue eyes. He offered in French to fetch anything required. Walsingham asked for wine for himself and broth for the patient. Then he gazed on Kit again, studying the marks of ageing and sickness on his face. *Just over two years since I saw thee last.* Walsingham knew from his looking glass that his own beard and hair remained brown and full; his friend looked almost a decade older.

Call me Walls. None else may use that name. Wake up and say it. Please.

Walsingham stood up, stretched his back, and paced to the window. He peered through the costly glass at his grounds, at meadow, marsh, and woods. Behind him, Kit gasped, gasped again, resumed breathing.

Dear God above, how came we to this?

Rescued from debt by this inheritance meant for his late older brother, Walsingham had taken possession of Scadbury with great pleasure. His wife, Audrey, had not seemed as happy about it. After mourning Sir Francis, and then receiving a knighthood of his own, Walsingham believed his problems erased. He made no changes in the staff of servants, explaining to Audrey the ideas of patient kindness and mercy, wondering why his instruction angered her. Audrey did come to agree that the cook, Dan Roe, earned every penny. Still, the following month, Audrey detailed the expenses of maintaining Scadbury — a long list. Custom and law demanded a clearing of books four times a year; servants and creditors expected payment each Quarter Day. The household's ongoing expenses, and Audrey's frequent travel and clothing needs — Queen Elizabeth enjoyed Audrey's company and kept her at court, allowing visits home to her husband at ragged intervals, with little notice — yawned before them, some dangerous hole. Thus far, the Walsinghams had escaped the Queen's ruinous whim to come for a summer visit. She'd inflicted this great pleasure on Lord Burghley, among others, driving the Old Fox into gagged apoplexy with the expense. Indeed, Burghley had constructed a grand house just for hosting her. In comparison, sheltering this man or employing that one seemed like smallest of favours to grant, certainly cheaper.

At Cambridge, Walsingham had promised Kit a patronage out of defiance as much as affection and respect. He'd enjoyed the strange and heady idea of becoming friends with a cobbler's son. *University*, he'd thought, *the great equalizer.* They'd been drinking that night, Kit's face rounder, Walsingham's free of lines, when Walsingham offered the shadow of a gift.

Th'art a mighty poet, Marlowe, and thou shalt have of me a mighty patronage. Count me as a friend, and thou'lt need never worry how to eat. Truly.

*Oh, excellent advice, la. And how shalt thou grant me pa-
tronage? Th'art an undergraduate second son. Patronage. Shall
I mop thy floors?*

Walsingham thought of another friend, another knight
who acted as a patron. He looked after a composer, affording
him a room in the house. Patrons might also send their funds
from a distance, while the artist found his own lodgings and
way in a city, London usually. Walsingham had never decided:
was the patronized artist who lived in the patron's house then
a servant?

Dark and stocky Dan Roe inclined his head as he entered the
sickroom, carrying broth and a spoon. He placed the tray on
the desk near the window, the desk crowded with the surgeon's
equipment, about to explain something, when Kit thrashed his
head. Walsingham and Dan strode to the bed and eased the
patient on to his left side. Sighing, Walsingham rested the backs
of his fingers on Kit's cheek as Dan stirred the broth.

A new voice spoke. —Well done, your honour.

Walsingham flinched. Nick Charing, the surgeon, stood
in the doorway. A fair man with green eyes and a long nose,
he wore his smock-of-work, a linen apron stained brown and
black: blood. Such darkness showed Nick's experience and
reliability; he'd bled many patients.

Seeing Nick, Dan clicked his tongue and scowled. He'd
already complained to Walsingham about Charing breaking
the law, offering both barbery and surgery: *At a cut rate says
he, your honour.* Walsingham winked at this economy, and
Dan had resigned himself to counting this arrogant hack as
a fellow servant.

Nick gave a little bow. —An't please your honour, I've known patients to survive harsh crisis only to succumb to ravenous bedsore. He must be moved several times each day. 'Tis a good sign he tried to move himself.

Dan waved away steam. —And 'tis also a good sign he takes the broth.

Walsingham stood up. —Charing. Comes it thy turn already?

—Not for another hour or so, your honour, but I shall take the turn if you so need.

—No, no. I lose sight of the moments. Hath a messenger come today?

Nick glanced at Dan before answering. Nick had taken over the task of talking with the messengers from Dan, and the Dan felt this change an insult, all the more so when Nick had demanded to know which other servants could read and write. Dan could not.

Nick bowed again, then strode to the sickbed. —No, your honour, no letters yet today. See, he twitches again when I touch his forehead.

—And thou didst say 'tis a good sign?

—'Tis excellent. He may know we are here. Still, I would recommend feeding him by clyster.

Dan snorted in disgust. —What need? He can swallow; he's drinking the broth.

—He loses flesh.

Dan walked to the other side of the bed. —And what else but my broth would you shove into a clyster, surgeon? Leave him be.

Gideon entered the room, laid the wine on the desk, and waited for his next command. Dan nodded to him, and Gideon gave a little smile.

Sweat broke out on Kit's face, and Walsingham dabbed it away. —He burns still, Charing.

—He shall burn until healing or death. I would bleed him again, your honour, if you'll permit it.

—No! Thou'st scarred his arm enough.

—Is he dear to you, your honour?

Walsingham said nothing.

—Your honour, I must repeat: let me bleed him. Excess of blood causes inflammation, and inflammation leads to fever. Breathing a vein may ease his fever and quiet him, so he might rest.

—Do it.

Nick and Walsingham shifted Kit onto his back, and Nick lashed a tourniquet round Kit's upper arm. Then he strode to the nearby desk and considered his collection of fleams.

Dan grunted. —Not that one. 'Tis a fleam good for a calf. What, would you bleed him to death?

—Oh, folly.

Walsingham gave Dan a tired look. —Roe, please, let the surgeon work.

—He would lecture me on broth, your honour; I would question his butchery.

Walsingham let out a long breath, and Dan inclined his head to the master of the house. Nick, now carrying a folding set of smaller fleams attached to one handle, returned to the bedside. Behind the surgeon, and seen only by Dan, Gideon made a rude face. Dan smirked, then shook his head at the boy. Nick asked Gideon to fetch the bloodletting rack from the corner. This wooden rack looked like one that might hold drying clothes; straps and buckles pointed to other purpose. As Gideon unfolded the rack and Nick unfolded the fleams, Walsingham peered out the window. Kit had a birthday coming, he recalled: three weeks and a day, such a distant prize for a man so sick. *Th'art not yet nine-and-twenty. Live, and I will give thee gifts for a lifetime. Just live.*

Kit opened his eyes, glanced about. No one saw this.

Looking up at Gideon, Nick buckled Kit's arm into place and smiled. —Well, boy, hast thou considered becoming a surgeon's apprentice?

Gideon backed away from him and bumped into Dan.

Annoyed, Kit tugged his arm, got nowhere. —Leave off.

Walsingham turned. A parched voice, cracking — still, a voice. *No tricks, God. Play me fair.* He strode to the bed, leaned his ear close to Kit's mouth. —Marlowe? Dost thou know me?

—Walls. Wait, mine arm.

Laughing now, Walsingham held his cup of wine to Kit's mouth, helping him to drink it.

Kit saw the others looking down on him. —Sweet Christ Jesus, not this fuckery. I never saw that boy before. Away from me!

Nick gripped his twitching patient's arm. —Can you calm him, your honour?

—Marlowe, Marlowe, listen to me. Th'art safe here.

Kit studied Walsingham again. Then he touched his friend's hand. —Scadbury?

—Aye, Scadbury.

—What o'clock is it?

—What day, more like.

—Day? Mine arm. Leave off, I say.

Nick finished buckling. —Aye, make a fist. Your honour, he must be still.

Walsingham pressed Kit's shoulders. —Obey him.

—Why?

—He is the surgeon whose medical care hath likely saved thee.

Dan snorted.

Ignoring the cook, Nick stroked a swelling vein in Kit's forearm. —I serve the needs of the patient: emetics, purgatives, and the letting of blood.

Puckers, scabs, and cuts: Kit looked at his left arm, then back at Walsingham.

—Whither should I fly? Stars, Walls. Stars.

—Drink some more.

—God, the rain, the rain. I kept Crimm's gelding to a walk — my ribs — and the plod, the rhythm, rocked me to sleep. Stars in that ceiling, la, the whole night sky, and I've heard the sweetest voice —

—Gideon. He found thee. 'Tis him there, by the desk. Thou'dst fallen from thy horse, ankle caught in the stirrup. In the pouring rain. I wonder thou didst not drown in a puddle on my marshy lawn.

Nick positioned the fleam. —He was in more danger of drowning on Roe's broth.

—Christ's love!

—Ah, a good vein.

Gideon paled as he watched Kit's blood flow. Dan sent him back to the kitchen, telling him to be careful on the stairs.

Walsingham took Kit's right hand again and kept him from reaching for the buckles. —Keep still.

—Burns— *burns* —

Nick gauged the weight of the bowl. —Nearly done. Ah. 'Tis but the healing swoon, your honour, and a desired effect. He shall rest in quiet now.

Walsingham sat back, looked at the ceiling, and gave a pressed and rapid prayer. Then he thanked the surgeon for his patience and skill, asked to be called when Kit woke again, and left the room.

As Nick freed Kit's cold arm, Dan peered at the darkness in the bowl. —Thou'dst need an entire pint of him?

—Use it in thy soup.

Then Nick retrieved a book from the desk, sat next to the bed, and, murmuring words, began to read.

Dan picked up the bowl of hot blood. The odours of iron and spice did make him think of soup, and sausages, and all manner of dishes of meat. Animal blood he might feed to his turnspit dog. A man's blood? A sacred mess. He would dump it outside when next he needed to shit.

Weeks of receding yet stubborn fevers, of painful coughing, of plasters on his chest and hot cups on his back, of maddening weakness, proved for Kit the truth of an idea suggested by Nick Charing: physicke exacted a fee from the patient as much as the sickness it treated, if not one greater. Kit imagined

Manna's response to this: *Now, Clever Kitten, be grateful thou'st got a surgeon's ready care, and be grateful thou'st no worries of how to pay him.* He remembered being stuck in bed at maybe age four, racked with the chin-cough, paroxysms making him vomit, and hitting Manna with his fist when she, coughing herself, had hushed his complaints. Kit had wanted their mother and considered Manna a poor substitute. He did not understand until years later that their baby sister had also caught the chin-cough and could not suckle.

Aye, no surgeon then. Just a sexton.

Resenting the weight of sickness, resenting his own frailty, Kit defied Nick's simplest and most sensible advice. Twice, despite being told he lacked the strength to stand, he got out of bed and then fell in a clattering heap to the floor. The second time he told Walsingham his feet had tangled in the sheets. Walsingham remained dubious and, like Nick, exasperated. Walsingham accused Kit of causing needless trouble for Nick and taking pleasure in it. Kit, thinking on his occasional awakenings to Nick sitting at his bedside and sketching by candlelight — fever dreams, or truth? — conceded Walsingham might be right.

He woke from a doze late one morning, feeling much more like himself; he'd dreamt of fucking. Considering such a dream, and his body's response to it, a sign of returning health, he laughed. He finished, laughing again, then swung his legs over the edge of the bed. A tray of food sat on the nearby chair: some herbs steeped in diluted wine, and a froize, a bundle of scrambled eggs wrapped in bacon and then fried. It had gone cold; he did not care. Devouring the froize, he decided to write a letter to Tom. *Aye, get a letter out, before thou'st lose count of any more days.* He sipped from the cup and nearly spat. *Knitbone.* Scowling, he knocked back the drink in a few big swallows, reminding himself that bitter knitbone possessed a potency not to be scoffed. Then he took up the mouthwash and unguent Dan Roe had given him. *Rosemary,* Dan had said, *I swear by rosemary. The unguent's good for treating the armpits and the scalp.* Kit thought that the mouthwash, rosemary steeped in vinegar, might be good for burning holes.

He swished and spat as Miriam, the laundress, knocked on his partly open door. She gave a little curtsy before kneeling to pick up his dirty linens from the hamper. Kit considered asking her to change his bedsheets when she leaned on the desk, green patches showing on her pale face.

—Girl, art thou sick?

Eyes wet and guilty, she turned away. Her breasts pushed at her kirtle as she retched.

—Please, take the pot. 'Tis almost clean. I just spit in it. 'Tis nothing. I'll say nothing. No, wait —

Green bile, a thick ribbon of it, landed on his bundled linens. Misery distorted her face as she curtsied again.

—Not to me, girl; I am not thy better. Go and rest.

Miriam shook her head. —Go and rest? I thank you, sir, but 'tis clear you've never been a laundress.

Stubborn girl. Where, then? Thou'lt share a room if not a bed with another woman-servant. Who got thee in the corner of a hallway, la? Who pinned thee to a wall and planted a bastard?

Observant and nosy, and sibling to many, many lost as infants, Kit had learned in childhood how to spot signs of pregnancy. John Marlowe had cherished his wife in that condition, doting on Catherine, fetching cold cloths, helping her to rest and get her feet up, celebrating every swell, every little kick. Birth merited joy and cakes. Neither parent said much about the funerals, the tiny coffins. *Ruth to the chincough. Sarah. Richard. Simon.* Kit had taken turns with Manna and Catherine, rocking a cradle, encouraging a fussy one to get some sleep, not always with a good grace. *Hush, brat. Shut it. Th'art making Mother sad and giving me a headache.* Sometimes Kit and Manna had stayed with a neighbour when Catherine laboured; sometimes they'd heard every sound. Once he understood the meanings of blood, cries, and coffins, Kit had come to prefer the noises of his mother's labours to the noises of his parents' griefs.

Two younger brothers had survived to adulthood. They treated Kit with a disdain that only sharpened after the debacle with Cambridge. He returned the courtesy.

Sleet rattled the Scadbury window, and Kit wondered how much that glass had cost. He thought a moment of Flushing and Ben Cull, then of Miriam and her sickness.

Sleet. Mother heavy on me, in such a miserable month?

The Marlowes had celebrated birthdays with vigour, and, Kit saw now, some sad determination. Once darkness fell, the birthday child would sit in John's big chair while Catherine presented a sweet ginger cake and a rush light, a stalk of bulrush dipped several times in tallow. If celebrating a winter's child, John Marlowe would block the hearth with a screen and snuff the candles, save one. Then John would take the rush light and light it at both ends. Bright flames raced to meet each other, illuminating the child's face. A rush light burned fast, so fast — sudden, almost violent change from dark to light and dark again. Everyone would laugh, and then chant the child's name in defiance and joy. John Marlowe would light candles anew, stoke and feed the fire, and shout a prayer of thanksgiving. At three, understanding the rush light for the first time, Kit had clapped his hands and begged for more. Before his parents could reason with him, say anything close to no, Kit offered to trade his cake, to trade all his cakes ever after, for more light. *Light again, light again!*

As Manna liked to point out, he got more light.

He got the cake, too.

How is it they loved me? I am nothing but failures and disappointments —

Two men dead, by my hand. Who loved them?

Tom.

He sat at the desk.

A letter, a letter.

A vision of Ben Cull interrupted: the beauty of Ben's face in candlelight, and his London voice like Tom's, clipped and precise, almost brittle, as he believed, or pretended to believe, Kit's mask.

Who art thou, Stephen?

Kit's eyes burned. *We'd both leave Flushing in chains. I am the man who got mercy.*

He flinched: someone near the door.

Walsingham entered the room, smiling as if holding some sweet mystery. —No surgeon here?

—Gory smock thrown over the rack, la: the leech hath oozed away. Maybe he repents his hot cups on my back. Maybe he got bored of watching me sleep.

—God keep thee from another such illness.

Kit rubbed at his eyes, drying the tears. —God keep me from surgeons.

Walsingham sat down on the edge of the bed. —He's kept thee for something. Perhaps to teach thee patience and humility?

—Oh, this is tedious. Walls —

—Happy birthday.

Kit stared at him.

—The usual response, Marlowe, is one of grateful acknowledgement. I've gifts for thee.

—Gifts?

—First, thy supper shall be pie of chardequince.

—I've not eaten chardequince since... The wayward tastes of the fruit, Walls, like ginger and strawberries and apples, contrasting flesh, and the pastry coffin... Wait. Quince is not in season.

—Preserved. Imported from Spain.

Kit imagined the expense. —I...I thank thee.

—At last, he thanks me. Oh, one more item: seeing as thou hast been so kind as to refrain from dying in my spare bed, I should like to make good on an old promise. Poet, thou hast a patron.

Afraid to risk belief, Kit shook his head. —Hast thou discussed this with Sir Robert?

Walls looked away for a moment. —Thou mayest yet need to travel for Sir Robert, once th'art stronger, but it shall be solely for duty, not for bread. My patronage stands. Thou mayest always, always, live in this house and write. Hey?

They clasped hands.

Walsingham chuckled. —I got thee speechless; by God, I shall mark this date and celebrate it each year.

—Couldst thou fetch me something else?

—Not satisfied yet?

—Quills, paper, and ink.

—I'll see what I might do. And I shall send the surgeon. Th'art bearded to the eyebrows. Creatures with sharp teeth shall take up residence in that bush. A shave, hey?

Naked before a roaring fire, Kit watched water sluice down his legs and go grey as it reached the tops of his feet. The hairy skin of his belly and thighs hung slack, some pelt assumed for a costume.

I look like a starved goat.

Nick stood by, watching, ready to assist. —The blisters on your back doth heal well. I've wanted to ask: is't a saint's key hanging from your neck? Or is't just for a door?

Remembering Robin Poley's necklace, the iron charm dangling from it, Kit grunted in response. The strength he'd felt in the morning: almost spent. Nick made a joke about catching Kit this time, if he fell; Kit feared he might have to test the offer.

—Hand me the clothes. I must sit down.

Sorry to leave the flames, Kit tugged on cleaner night-clothes and sat in the armchair. Nick tucked blankets around him, muttering of fatal chills and invalids, and Kit felt so passive, so separate from himself. He thought of the happiness from his dream in the morning. Sleet fell again, shattering against the window, sliding down the glass and collecting in little piles of debris. As Nick lifted sections of Kit's matted hair and examined his scalp, Kit explained he'd long ago sold his comb to buy food. He remembered explaining that to Tom while trying to explain something else. He remembered dried blood on Ben Cull's scalp.

—Charing, dost thou ever compare hair to sin?

—Sin? Well, no. Hair's a nuisance sometimes, but the nuisance of it buys my bread. Yours is free of lice, that I can see.

—Small mercies. Cut it.

—'Tis bad here, tangled at the neck. I shall have to bring it level with your jaw.

—Cut it, I say.

Nick picked up a pair of scissors, changed his mind, put them down. —Bow thy head.

Kit did this, gripping the chair arms as Nick gathered his hair at the nape of his neck and drew the razor through tangles and mats. He dropped the clumps of hair onto a towel, then cleaned the razor. —Now, the beard?

—Mow it.

Nick chuckled. —I've not got a scythe.

Kit stared at him, eyes wide, hearing the flap of shrouds as the Flushing goal clerk ran by. His left wrist ached; he'd reached for his dagger.

Which he did not have.

Breathe, breathe.

The sounds of stropping reached him. So did Nick's question about sudden sweating.

Kit shook his head. —'Tis nothing. I am fine. Clean my throat, bring the beard to the jawline, let the moustache join it.

—We shall hardly recognize you.

Nick's touch seemed more certain than before, harder. He cut at the longer bits of the beard with scissors, then massaged an unguent into the rest. It smelled of honey.

Sleet rattled.

Nick laid a hot towel on Kit's face, and Kit told himself to relax, to enjoy the heat. Instead the fibres of the fabric rasped his eyelids. He thought again of waking up in sickness, of Nick at his bedside, sketching something.

Kit yanked the towel from his face.

No threat: just a barber with his razor, waiting.

—Marlowe, relent. I cannot shave a man so tense.

Kit took a deep breath. —I apologize, Charing. I am not my best self.

Later, as Kit was sitting up in bed, reading, Walsingham looked in. —Th'art looking better. Aye, much less the monkey.

Kit smiled and inclined his head. *Little monkey chained in a library?*

Alone again, he glanced about his bedchamber.

Nine-and-twenty, and spoiled with gifts.

Why?

On Sunday morning, the house empty but for him, Kit emerged for the first time from his bedchamber and walked barefoot down the hall, barefoot because Walsingham had ordered his winter shoes burnt. When Kit objected to this, long after the fact, adding in tones of great insult that those shoes had been shearling-lined and the finest work of a master cobbler, Walsingham gave him the saved buckles and promised to make him the travelling cobbler's first priority. *A travelling cobbler*, Kit had thought, rolling his eyes. *What, is his work so poor he must keep running away?* Dan Roe had offered Kit his better pair of boots, but Nick intervened, telling Walsingham he'd not be responsible if the patient took a chill from walking to church in this unreasonably cold winter. So Kit stayed behind, his boyish thrill at sneaking out a free Sunday morning hollowed by a longing.

Convalescence felt more like deceit.

Church attendance being a matter of law as well as personal need or desire, Kit had not missed many Sundays in his life. He'd begun questioning it all when still a child, earning smacks from his parents. *Driven like beasts to the fair: worship? Head on a spike for the manner of one's prayers?* His father beat him for his questions one day, embracing Kit afterwards and wiping his tears away: *'Tis not a matter of prayers, Kit, but a matter of kings and queens. Now hush.* During his divinity studies Kit had choked on some doctrine, and in his thoughts he'd fought with Saint Paul, imagining the apostle to have a shrill voice. *Thy dislike for Paul excuses thee from nothing, Clever Kitten. 'Tis but a nuisance, la, no true impediment.* In a church, or the ruins of one, Kit might sense something bigger than him, bigger than all the bickering men in England, bigger than fires and wars on the Continent: a presence, or even galling absence, an absence that reassured even as it pained. He might feel that presence brush him, nudge him, breathe down his neck as it passed him by, or that absence chill him. Dispute and defy: gifted and skilled, he did that well. Still, he would not, could not, ignore what felt sacred, before which all the fighting, sneaking, hiding, burning, starving, and killing fell, squalid natures and truths exposed: childish toys. He sought that contact — the breath and the nudge — craved it, prayed for it. In a church, he fell silent.

England: Protestant services, still smelling of Reformation's fire. Stern and bare, sometimes, fearful of some terrible excess, terrible because the Word must suffice.

Rheims: the Mass, incense, pageant, all so sensual...

Catherine windows, a labyrinth designed in the floor, even a Smiling Angel statue, aye, so much beauty.

Yet it sufficeth not.

Whom, and what, shalt thou obey?

He looked around. Behind him: two closed doors — bed-chambers, he reasoned, one for Walsingham, one for Audrey. Before him: the main staircase, and down the hall, a set of double doors and, as he got closer, scents of paper and calfskin, as at Ed Blount's bookstall in Paul's Yard, only much stronger.

He smirked.

Crossing the threshold, he discovered a large room, fitted with two big windows, a wide hearth, two reclining couches facing the fire, a grand desk bearing an inkwell and a tiny skull, and bookshelves, floor to ceiling, lining three of the four walls. Bookshelves, bookshelves. Full. Crammed. Books shoved in sidewise and lying atop others. Books piled on the floor.

Kit stared at it all. He'd never seen such a library belonging to one man.

He remembered arguing with Thomas Nashe at Cambridge that ancient Alexandria had the right idea, demanding a harbour fee of books and scrolls from every visiting ship, books and scrolls to then be deposited in the Great Library. *Books,*

Nashe. Every little thing we are and might be: 'tis already in a book. Find it.

He laughed. —Sweet Christ Jesus, so many books!

Then he caught sight of a laughing man's face.

A looking glass. It hung on the wall where a set of bookshelves ended, and it gave back a dull reflection on a warp that made the face within seem quite some distance off. Kit touched the frown lines near his mouth, drew his thumb and finger down the paths, and watched the reflected self do the same. While still at Cambridge, he'd commissioned a portrait. He'd paid too much for it, in the end, and for the beautiful doublet he'd worn: silk, indigo silk, slashed to reveal russet silk beneath, and bedecked with brass buttons which the painter had rendered almost as large as Kit's mouth. The arms hadn't turned out quite right, either, nor the shoulders, some mistake of perspective. And the motto: Quod me nutrit me destruit. Kit clicked his tongue and rolled his eyes, remembering his pride as he created it. *Oh, that which nourishes me destroys me, aye, who's an important Clever Kitten? Mother-wit.* The face: Walsingham felt the painter had captured Kit's face. *A tense assurance in the set of thee, truly, Marlowe. And thine eyes: thine eyes look so skeptical yet gentle there, even kind, depending on the angle of view. What wast thou thinking of?* Now a parody of that face stared back from the blurred looking glass: the cheeks sunken, the eyes dull, and — Kit patted the growing bald spot on the top of his head — the hair thinner.

Mine eyes: gentle and kind?

Ben had said that, too. *Though thou'dst hide it, thine eyes betray a sweet kindness to thee.*

Tom liked to tease him about the colour of his eyes. *How is't something so dark shines so bright? And they change afterwards, Kit. Aye, they do so, lighten to honey and bronze. I've never seen the like.*

Snorting, Kit turned away from the looking glass and chose a book. A grammar, a schoolboy's textbook, inscribed in fading ink with a name, the handwriting spiked and shattered like broken twigs: *Francis Walsingham.*

Kit dropped the book on the desk, knocking over the memento mori.

Duty. Christ's love, in a schoolbook? Even here?

And if I said no? If I dared…

He righted the little skull.

So, Clever Kitten: who and what art thou?

How shall I sound thy heart when thy body's got so thin?

Walsingham finished drawing a blanket over Kit, who lay dozing on the couch, a book on his chest. Then he stoked the fire.

Waking to the hiss of sparks, Kit rubbed his forehead; his Canterbury Cathedral dream thinned out. —Walls?

—I'm sorry I woke thee.

—I shouldn't be asleep. Christ, I'm so tired of sleeping. And I shall break the confines of this house next week, even if I must crawl. How was the sermon?

—Thou'dst have mocked it as *filthily written*, and I'd have paid to hear thee.

Kit chuckled. —So bad?

—Dost thou ever regret not taking holy orders? Perhaps thou'dst have a big parish by now.

Transfiguration Sunday. Kit sat up, tugging the blanket with him. —What lessons?

—Thou'st remind me of my father, quizzing me. Ah, Corinthians, chapter 4.

—For I know nothing by myself, yet am I not thereby justified: but he that judgeth me, is the Lord. Therefore judge nothing before the time, until the Lord come, who will lighten things that are hid in darkness, and make the counsels of the hearts manifest: and then shall every man have praise of God.

Leaning against his big desk, Walsingham nodded. —Thy glittering memory. Psalm 131, Isaiah 49, I recall not the verse numbers, and Matthew, chapter 6, verses 8 to 16.

—No man can serve two masters: for either he shall hate the one, and love the other, or else he shall lean to the one, and despise the other. Ye cannot serve God and riches. Therefore I say unto you, be not careful for your life, what ye shall eat, or what ye shall drink: nor yet for your body, what ye shall put on. Is not the life more worth than meat, and the body than raiment? I see.

—See what?

—That you doubt me.

—Use *thou*. We are alone.

—No, Sir Thomas Walsingham: you doubt me, and you could not have chosen better lessons to fling at me.

Walsingham frowned. —Perhaps thou dost fling them at thyself. And 'tis the Book of Common Prayer orders such things, not I.

—And not Sir Robert Cecil?

Walsingham sat down on the other couch. —Strains,

Marlowe. As I would heal thy lungs, so I would heal thy strained mind. A man near death —

—A man near death for crossing the Channel in chains. In January! Never should I —

—No, never should'st thou have been so treated. Nor should'st thou have been left so long in Flushing alone, yet thou wast. And now, thou'st just darted free of death. I've seen men newly reckon their lives and desires after grave illness. Such experience may change a man, deepen, or even curdle, his thoughts and his heart.

Kit's cheeks flushed. —I'll give you the Isaiah you feign to forget. Thou mayest raise up the earth, and obtain the inheritance of the desolate heritages: that thou mayest say to the prisoners, go forth: and to them that are in darkness, show yourselves! La? Wilt thou, no, will *you* make me a prisoner in this fine house?

—*What?* And where else might'st thou have gone, thou who wast too feverish to sit up in a saddle?

—Oh, pardon me, for mine imposition on thy kindness, on this, thy grace-and-favour house, to which I was *commanded*.

—Aye, commanded, to protect and shelter thee. And 'tis no grace and favour; I inherited this estate, as well thou knowest.

—I had a place to go! 'Twas not —

—Tom Kyd's wretched rooms?

Kit slouched. —He's got a lovely bed.

—But no surgeon. Thou would'st be dead by now and thy corpse gnawed by rats.

—I've heard that noise. In Newgate. In the Hole. No pail. No drain. No light. Stars pricked the darkness, then swooped. Skeletal Death played his bone flute and led a dance, some former boy behind him keeping time on a drum with an infant's thigh bones. Haunts me still; inspires panic and sweat. Know'st how earned I that? Refusing to kneel and suck a guard.

—Dear God above, Marlowe, why must thou speak so much of prisons?

—Because 'tis fuckery all around me! Walls, please, be even and direct with me.

Standing up, Walsingham tugged his shirts. —I must ask, and I must know, as thy master's aide, as thy patron, thy protector, and as thy friend: after thine ordeals, where lie thy heart and mind?

—You say you doubt me not, yet you would ask me that?

—Marlowe, please, remember my name.

—I do, your honour.

—For my name comes weighted – *you* again. Would'st thou hide behind ceremony with me?

—I hide nothing, for I've lost the strength to hide. My friend would know that, and so, your honour, I am forced to ask: who and what are you?

—I am Walsingham! I am nephew to Sir Francis and friend to Sir Robert Cecil and thereby, and besides, a loyal servant and subject to the Queen.

Kit studied the child's skull on Walsingham's desk. —Is there but one loyalty, one way to show it?

—This is no exercise, no discussion, nor even examination; this is law and duty and blood. I feared for thee at Cambridge: thy defiance, thy will to decide so much for thyself. I feared even then thou'dst be gaoled, or exiled, aye, banished from memory and mercy and deserving of it. I love thee, friend.

I aged a year for each day at thy sickbed. Tell me: what is't, eating at thee, gnawing thy kindness and thy heart?

Kit almost spoke.

—Is't envy, Marlowe? Dost thou envy me for my clear path to duty, because thine own way is lost?

—I have not lost my way!

Walsingham said nothing.

—The ninety, Walls. In Canterbury. Queen Mary's time, when she'd make England Catholic again. Ninety people in Canterbury refused, my father told me. He took me for a walk to see where it had happened. River mist and hearth smoke filled the air. I peered through this fog, believing I might see those ninety. God knows, I could hear them. They screamed and prayed and wept, my father told me, all for the wrong loyalty at the wrong time. Puzzle it out, Kit. Get it right.

Walsingham took a deep breath. —What concluded thee?

—I was just a boy. The walk tired me out; I fell asleep. I dreamt of screams becoming church bells. My mother's work woke me: raking embers at the hearth.

Walsingham's voice caught. —Th'art shivering. Thy fever rises. Get some rest.

—Oh, for Christ's love. I am not a child! I've got work here, Walls, the press of words, duties. Mine eyes burn; my head aches. Fine, i'faith, a fever, aye. That, or Hellfire.

—Tutor Gideon.

—*What?*

—My singing boy.

—I know who he is.

—Thou wast a singing boy once, King's Scholar. Sang sweet as the lark, I warrant.

—Sweet, but not with Gideon's gifts.

—Gifted, perhaps, but quite ignorant. A Flemish refugee.

—How came he here, to Scadbury?

Walsingham shook his head. —I would have him taught his letters and figuring. Logic. And music: teach him sight-reading.

—Anything else? 'Tis much trouble for an orphan.

Walsingham said nothing.

—Fine. Once I get some more strength back, I shall tutor the boy. A truce, la?

—A truce. Wilt thou come down for dinner?

Kit relished the heat from the blankets, and the fire.

—Leave me here.

—To fast?

—Feast. I've got all these books.

Walsingham studied him a moment, noticed the anger in his eyes. —I shall send up a plate.

Kit nodded, vision drawn to the flames.

A few weeks later, Audrey returned home, arriving, Walsingham said, with birdsong and the sweet breezes of spring. She strode into the house, calling and laughing, a maid following with various burdens and a peacock in a cage. A leather strap bound the peacock's beak shut, and the bird jutted its head between the bars of the cage, that beak still a menace. Audrey wore a green wool gown nearly the same shade as her eyes, and Kit felt that her laughter woke him after a long sleep. No one had been laughing at Scadbury. Audrey's presence — just her voice — changed the entire mood of the house. Kit studied her, noticing first how Walsingham seemed to stare in worship. *Cow-eyed*, Kit thought, smiling. Audrey stood at middling height for a woman, and, despite the harsh lines of her gown, her body showed all manner of roundness: breasts and belly and hips, plump hands, even the freckled cheeks of her face. She wore no cosmetics, leaving such decorations for the court, and she'd drawn back her brown hair and pinned it beneath her cap. Kit had not seen a cap quite like it before: black velvet, embroidered with irregular yet brilliant white beads. *If those beads are pearls…* Kit rose from his bow. *Oh, Walls, thy past debts: hast thou learned nothing?* Audrey kept touching her left jaw as she spoke. A bad tooth troubled her, she explained, and Walsingham told her, one arm around her shoulders, the other gesturing to the house, of the new surgeon he'd hired.

—He'll see to that tooth, my leman. Thou'lt need bear no pain.

Kit joined them for a late supper, not as a servant of the house, not even as the patronized poet, but as a guest and a friend. Dan had slaughtered the peacock and then roasted it with the best of the remaining winter store of vegetables. He'd also scattered early salad greens — bitter — over the plates and peacock feathers over the tablecloth. *Quite the feast during Lent*, Kit thought, and he regretted not getting a better look at the peacock while it had lived. *Iridescence, like starling feathers.* Mead, wine, and cider flowed, though Kit took great care with his cup, feeling that his first few sips of undiluted wine made him too dizzy. Audrey, delighted to see Kit again, picked up their conversation where they'd left it some years before: poetry and history. Ideas leapt, connections shone, and Kit recited verses he'd forgotten he'd ever read. Audrey, witty, observant, and a gifted mimic, gave Kit and Walsingham animated stories of other courtiers, their desires and foibles, even their voices. Laughing, coughing, laughing again, Kit sometimes forgot that he spoke with a woman. He thought of Manna and her intellect, how, when last he'd seen her, she'd still not married and hardly expected to, confessing to him a great loneliness.

Kit thanked God once more for creating him male.

As they stood up from the table, Kit picked up one of the peacock feathers and studied the eye-spot, nodding when Walsingham asked if he wanted it for a quill. Then he shook his head. He must strip the plumage to make the feather any sort of useful quill, and without the plumage, the feather meant nothing. He put it aside.

He had trouble sleeping that night. After a particularly exasperating bout of coughing, he lit a candle on the embers in his hearth, wrapped himself in blankets, and padfooted to the library. There he lit a second candle and stirred the fire. Doubting he'd get much warmth, and coughing again, he chose a book, smiled, and lay down on a couch.

The candles had lost maybe a quarter inch when he glanced up and saw Audrey standing there. Kit hurried to his feet, stirring his cough, and he hardly knew where to look. Audrey wore several layers of nightclothes which covered her chest more than her gown had earlier in the day, but she'd let down her hair. It fell over her shoulders in brown waves, signalling an intimacy, a nakedness, suited only for a husband. Not even Miriam the laundress walked about with her hair exposed to male view.

Is she drunk?

Audrey turned away for a moment and closed the double doors. Then she spoke not much above a whisper. —Thy cough sounds ghastly. My husband says 'tis better?

—Much better.

—Thou'st look so — why dost thou study my feet?

Kit pointed to his own head. —Your hair, Lady Audrey.

—Wilt thou begrudge me the lack of a nightcap?

—No, I suppose not.

She sat down on the other couch. —Good. Please, look me in the face. No more standing. Pretend we are at table, if thou must. What dost thou read?

—Cicero. *De Officiis.*

—*Of Duties.* I've not read it in some time. How dost thou find any one book in here? 'Tis such a mess — oh, this house, as cluttered and draughty as the heart of old Sir Francis. I left for court and expected on coming back to find some new windows and a ceiling leak repaired. Instead, I discover, in addition to my singing boy, a surgeon, a business manager, and now a poet. What next: a golden carriage? I shall annoy the Queen with my shiny trinkets.

Kit chuckled.

—And dost thou tutor Gideon?

—I do. In this room. 'Tis his little desk there, la. I feared he'd be a plodding slave to a second language, but he got some schooling in the Low Countries. He knew his letters. Now I've got him writing short sentences, English and French.

—Sir Robert will be pleased.

—Oh. Is that the arrangement?

—Sir Robert takes much interest in my husband's charities.

Kit said nothing.

—Marlowe, th'art not long free of sickbed and already tutoring. Is't too much?

—'Tis nothing. I am fine.

—Th'art thinned out and dark about the eyes.

—Look to the surgeon and the pints of blood he took of me.

—My husband says thou art melancholy. I gave him disbelief for *melancholy* after hearing thee laugh so much today, and then some rebuke —

—You rebuked your husband?

—Interrupt me not. I demanded he explain to me how he might label his old friend a dangerous melancholic when thou dost but struggle to recover from illness and strain.

Strain. Walsingham had used that word. So had Robin Poley, once, after the business with the St. Hubert's Key. Kit looked at the hearth, and all the pleasures of the day fell away. The conversation, the food and drink, the conviviality: a pretty distraction, even a deceit. The truth: some bare hour in a library, both the time and the place taboo — respectable Christendom slept — and the company dangerous, not because he desired her, though he could see her beauty, and perhaps not even because she desired him, though he'd dared to amuse himself with the thought, but because she could see. And he could hide nothing.

—So, Marlowe: art thou melancholy?

Robin's advice, la: make compartments in thy mind. —Ask you this for yourself, or for Sir Robert?

—Both. As thou dost know I must.

Kit's fingers tightened on the book. —You would know where lie my heart and mind?

She nodded.

—Very good, Lady Audrey. My mind: tired of Latin, of all its tricks and deceits and easy rhythms and shammed wisdom. My heart: not in Rheims, and not in Rome. Sufficeth?

—And Ben Cull?

Kit studied the grain of Cicero's binding. Tears burned. —You know of my Jesuit? Well, what of him?

—Aye. What of him?

The beauty of his neck . . . Christ's love, if I could paint, I would paint just the back of his neck. His beard rasped my leg, and he asked, Who art thou, Stephen?

Audrey's fingers stroked his hand. —Christopher —

—Touch me not!

Audrey flinched. —Thou'lt speak so, to me?

—I ask forgiveness. 'Tis . . . 'tis the glut and surfeit of seven.

—The what?

—The seven works of mercy, la. Clothe the naked, feed the hungry, visit the sick, on and on . . . Christ's love, all we've omitted is to ransom the captive and bury the dead.

—Marlowe —

—You will shove gifts at me.

—Aye. And what else? Would we take them back and leave thee on a mud road?

—Leave me there naked, for even my clothes are gifts from your husband, Sir Robert Cecil, and some boatswain from *Peace of Lethe.* 'Tis all — all — *gifts.*

—What *of* it?

—I deserve nothing!

Audrey stared at him. She'd last seen a man weep when her father scattered soil on her mother's coffin. Robert had hinted to Audrey how she, as a woman, play-acting care, might draw out this man's truth, when another man, armed with force and demands, or friendship, might fail. She'd agreed. She'd not expected tears. Nor had she expected the ferocity of her recognition that she play-acted nothing. Telling herself she must maintain some distance here, social and emotional, telling herself she must keep still, she sat next to Kit and put her arm around him.

Words came on ragged breaths as he leaned on her shoulder and shook. —I led a man who trusted me a merry dance to his torment and death. *That* is — months in a strange city — the Wilmot brothers — oh, the Wilmots be fucked, but this Ben Cull — I…I've lost time to Newgate, la, time, dignity, light. Bailed out, aye, and the murder charge against me dismissed, daggers in the dark, most convenient, make my bargains, sign my contracts, charms in the fire, homo, fuge — but time in there: 'tis a forge, a forge to burn and beat a man's mind into some instrument of no good use. I *know* this. And 'twas Newgate for me, not even Bridewell. 'Tis Bridewell for Cull, as sure as dry wood ignites.

Audrey kissed the top of his head. —He wanted martyrdom. Had it not come by thee, then by another man.

—Maybe. Maybe Ben would have got to England and been arrested at mooring in Deptford. Maybe he'd be saying Mass in secret for years. Maybe he'd have drowned in the Channel. But *I* betrayed him. I did this. The least of my brethren.

Audrey's arm twitched. —He is a Jesuit, Marlowe, thine enemy, not Christ Himself.

Kit swallowed, cleared his throat.

—Dost thou love him?

—'Tis enough that I know what I've done to him. How can I not know what I know? And for what? For all of poxed-up *what*? 'Tis no faith I've fouled my soul for. The good work of princes — 'tis excuses and deceits. It shames me. And I would leave it behind, la. No more. No more of these demented hypocrisies. Yet what else am I good for?

Audrey said nothing.

It shames me, and I no longer know what I believe. Kit stood up, his back to her, straightened his nightclothes, and wiped his face. —I've done you grave abuse.

—How?

—Saying all this. Am I not a traitor?

She didn't answer right away. —Hast thou gone Catholic?

—'Tis not that simple.

—Hast thou gone Catholic: aye, or no?

—No.

—Then I see no traitor.

Kit turned to face her. —You must tell your husband what I said when he asks. And he will ask. Laws great and small: you swore to obey him.

—Laws? Like pretending I know not how Charing the surgeon breaks a law? Surgeons are not permitted to barber.

—That is a law most trivial.

—To thee. Matters it not to those who'd obey it? Shall we pick and choose which laws to obey? Or shall we just make new ones?

Like bloated King Henry? —Sir Robert has asked me: whom, and what, shalt thou obey? How answer you, Lady Audrey?

—I obey mine own conscience. And right now that conscience instructs me to keep silent, as befits a woman, no?

He thought her eyes looked both bitter and sad.

She stood up. —We may not get a chance to speak like this again. Thy doubts, Marlowe: thy doubts ignite thee, and thou dost illuminate...Please understand me: I am thy friend. And there is much else I will betray before I betray a friend.

Kit recalled Robin's note: *Perhaps next time thou'lt find the courage to betray not thy friends but thy shimmering ideals, mine own little ferret.* —I deserve no such mercy.

—None of us does.

Smiling, she touched his cheek with the backs of her fingers. Then she winced.

—You should let Charing pull that tooth.

She answered in an excellent imitation of Kit's own voice. —He touches me not.

Kit laughed, setting off yet more coughing. Audrey wished him a good night and left, closing the doors again behind her.

Once his cough settled, Kit lay down again, heart pounding. Neither of them got any sleep.

Managing not to think of his conversation with Audrey, Kit sat behind Walsingham's big desk and watched Gideon complete his English grammar lesson. The boy kept brushing his sandy hair from his eyes — Kit told him he should let Nick Charing cut it, perhaps in a shorter fringe across his forehead — and the eyes themselves, a cold blue flecked with warmer light green, widened and stared as he learned. *A strange collision of colour*, Kit thought, *like the edges of ice in the Flushing harbour.* This student's promise had forced Kit to raid Walsingham's bookshelves until he found primers, grammars, and algerismes, botanies, histories, and astronomies. Kit took particular pride in the boy's progress in speaking English — and *sounding* English as he did so. Gideon still lapsed into French, and Kit pretended to indulge it. In truth, Kit wanted the practice. He could read and write in French, considering it Latin's rougher cousin, and he spoke it well; he'd heard it from Huguenot refugees in Canterbury and then studied it in school. His abilities in French had released a flood of conversation from Gideon, conversation and trust. Kit decided to teach Gideon to read and write in both languages at the same time, and then start him on Latin, as a service both to Gideon himself, and to Sir Robert. *If we've marked this boy for espionage, then we owe him more than barest preparation. Well, Gideon, shall Sir Robert start thee as an errand boy?*

At the lesson's end, Kit handed Gideon a sealed letter addressed to Tom. —Give this to Mr. Charing, and tell him I would have it sent by messenger.

—Shall we have astronomy today?

—If th'art quick with my letter, aye.

Dan Roe, missing Gideon's help in the kitchen, sometimes gave Kit a piercing look — not accusation, not even suspicion, but curiosity. *Who and what are you?* Kit took to spending some time in the kitchen, first to learn how else Gideon worked, then to talk with Dan. Tutor and cook discussed food, Dan teaching Kit as much about cooking as Kit taught Gideon about reading. Kit rediscovered his joy in eating well and gained back some lost flesh.

He wrote, hours and hours, working on a long poem and a play. Words tumbled and roared in a fever heat, while ideas for revisions and metre ate up his sleep. He also wrote, burnt, and wrote again a letter to Manna, a letter of explanation. At this, he failed.

Gideon came to haunt his tutor's steps, so much that Kit had to ask Walsingham to remind the boy that when Mr. Marlowe closed his chamber door, Gideon must not interrupt.

Gideon blushed at the reprimand. —Oh. Why?

—He writes.

—Writes what?

—Thou'lt say: what writes he, your honour.

Gideon bowed. —What writes he, your honour?

Aye. What writes he? And what burns he?

At the bottom of the servants' staircase, squirming in his baggy clothes, and fresh from a dispute with Walsingham over wearing his dagger in the house, Kit pried off his new shoes. *My heels are chafed to bleeding. For Christ's love, that cobbler couldn't measure a foot if it kicked him in the face.*

He ascended in stocking feet, heading for his bedchamber. He knew how to walk in quiet and did so out of habit. A poem gnawed him, demanded release.

Nick stood at Kit's desk. He held up some papers, reading them — papers Kit had tucked away in a drawer. Nick seemed absorbed in his task, and Kit, almost amused, leaned on the door jamb and crossed his arms. Nick read another page. Then he rustled through some more manuscript, seeking something.

—Charing, I must apologize for the strain on thine eyes. My handwriting is poor.

Nick dropped the papers and whirled around. He studied Kit, took in his posture, his shoes in his hands, his dagger. —You're looking well.

—I am no patient now. Out.

—I should —

—*Out.*

Nick left, eyes down, almost brushing Kit in the doorway.

Very quiet, Kit shut his door. Then he strode to his desk, examined the damage.

Nothing stolen, then.

He fingered the pommel of his dagger. Tilney, master of the revels, had once threatened the Admiral's Men with a raid, demanding they turn over all copies of Kit's plays. *I shall burn them*, Tilney had said. Kit had laughed, hearing this story, laughed and said *Oh, I shall make a difficult fire.*

He snorted: a younger man's certainty.

Plays I can sell but once? Plays be fucked.

Aye, Clever Kitten, and thy mind teems with them.

Now, who set Chary-Nick on me?

He peered out the window over his desk. Gideon walked the grounds outside, practising a new song he would perform for the household after evening prayers. Kit had taught him the song, one by John Dowland, first writing out the notes from his own memory. Kit had bought a copy of the song in likely pilfered manuscript just before he left for Flushing, and he expected that the paper, left behind with his cloak, had been long since burnt as kindling. He'd spoken with John Dowland twice, and quite liked him, so he kept a distance. While Dowland obeyed church attendance laws, he remained in his heart a Catholic and would, if asked, say so.

His defiance peeked out from beneath the protection of nobles who enjoyed his music and patronized his gifts. Kit feared he'd be set on Dowland one day, tasked to follow the composer's movements and eavesdrop on his words. Against this, Kit had suggested to Sir Robert Cecil that he recruit Dowland as an agent; a musician and composer in demand had good reason to travel. Doing this, Sir Robert could obtain intelligence and keep this Catholic on a leash. Robert had said nothing to the idea. Meantime, Kit had learned the song, a beautiful tangle of words and melody and meanings knotting and falling loose and knotting again.

Now, he smiled as Gideon's voice reached him, as Gideon practised the song on his own.

Walking the grounds and feeling his hair stick to his face, Gideon enjoyed the fog. It played with sound, and he believed he could hear better in fog. At least, the fog seemed to take his voice from him and place it up high. He sang the third verse, which kept tricking him.

> Great gifts are guiles
> and looks for gifts again.
> My trifles come,
> as treasures from my mind.
> It is a precious jewel to be plain.
> Sometimes in shells
> the Orient's pearls we find.
> Of others take a sheaf,
> of me a grain, of me a grain,
> of me a grain.

Waiting near some tall oaks for a meeting arranged by letter,
irked he could not tell where the boy stood at any one moment
as the fog played its tricks, Robin Poley heard him, too.

FOUL PAPERS: WHERE WORDS PREVAIL NOT

Parish of St. Mary Colechurch, London
Old Jewry Street, Sign of the Quill.

Kit, thine absence gnaws me like a hidden sore.

At my last speaking with thee, thou wast ill, and with more,
I fear, than catarrh and cough. Now, many weeks later, still
denied any word of thee, in those brief moments I allow
myself to think on affections, affections tangled, I worry.
Perhaps I grow tedious? My folly: writing to thee when I've
not the means to send this letter, neither coin nor address,
when I know not if the one I cherish still cares, or lives, to
read it, or to write to me. This ninth day of February first
day of March tenth day of March twenty-fifth day of March
Lady Day and the start of the new year (hast thou been
paid?) the second day of April twenty-sixth of April and a
dreary Thursday 1593.

(I see, and say nothing)

FEAR'ST THOU THY PERSON?
THOU SHALT HAVE A GUARD.

Bones, thought Tom, fastening his loose breeches, *must weep as much as flesh, and in secret. I've lost a good stone and a half since this time last year.*

Tom had not slept well, the previous day's conversation with his landlord about unpaid rent infesting his dreams. Copying work waited on his desk: a contract, one of dubious legality, which would bind the signatory to high compound interest payments on a loan. Tom doubted the signatory understood *compound*, and he'd worked out the final tally on separate sheet of paper. The amount made him wince.

His stomach growled. He'd last eaten well on Sunday, at his parents' house. Most Sundays he walked to their more respectable parish to join them for church, and then for dinner. Only foul weather or illness changed this plan. When Kit had lived with him, they'd both visited Tom's parents on Sundays, earning dark looks and harsh questions from Tom's mother, Agnes. Kit, loathing the woman, had endured this abuse for Tom's sake. Sometimes, once Agnes left the table, Frank would make an apologetic noise and change the subject to plays and poetry.

Tom tied back his hair and splashed water on his face, ignoring, with some effort, the bugs on his floor. He blamed his neighbours for this, and his landlord, though in truth Tom had not kept up with refreshing the rushes on his own floors. Rushes cost money he could not spare. He loathed bugs: the crawling, the wriggling, and worst, the shining, that dark hardness reflecting back candlelight. *Iridescent, sometimes.*

Such beauty from such ugliness vexed him even more than the sight of many legs, than the thought of dozens, perhaps hundreds of bugs hiding in his walls. Feeling imaginary bugs crawling over him, he rubbed his arms to chase the sensation away.

Fleas in the bed — he could do nothing about fleas in the bed. The day he and Kit had hired a cart and then lugged that bed from his parents' house, piece by piece, had felt like a numb triumph. *A marriage bed*, Tom's mother kept saying, *'tis a marriage bed*. Tom had found he could not look his mother in the eye. Kit, often goaded to silent fury by Agnes Kyd, had bowed, given his most charming smile, and said *'Tis but a bed, Mistress Kyd*. Then he'd murmured to Tom: *And so much softer on the back than a wall, la*. Tom had nearly choked with suppressed laughter while Frank decided to suffer one his periodic bouts of strategic deafness. Working to a method, Frank broke down the bed, instructing Tom and Kit in how to put it back together and how to tighten the netting of rope beneath the mattress each morning. Then Frank had looked to his son: *There may be some fleas in the mattress*. Tom had nodded. *Every bed in London's got fleas*.

Deciding his new poem would not pay the rent, Tom pushed his manuscript aside and took up the loan agreement. Around the phrase per annum to the power of the twelve-month, not thirty seconds later, he balled up his copy and threw it at his food chest. He imagined Kit's reaction to such a mess — either *Oh, this is tedious* or *This contract be fucked* — smiled, and strode outside.

Neighbourhood children played, and church bells rang the quarter-hour. Locking his door behind him as best he could, the lock stiff, the hinges weak, and the landlord demanding back-rent before repairs, he made for Ed Blount's bookstall at Paul's Yard.

A combination of market, meeting place and business offices, of booksellers and stationers, lawyers, merchants, criminals, constables, and churchgoers, Paul's Yard, more formally, St. Paul's Churchyard, seemed to draw all London to it. After King Henry broke the monasteries, Paul's became a place more of business than worship, though worship still occurred, and men might line up to preach sermons at Paul's Cross. Men seeking work checked postings on the Si Quis Wall, so named for how the notices often began: si quis, if anyone. Tom made fair copies of Si Quis notices; they earned him very little money. Voices rose and fell and echoed up and down Paul's Walk, as various men of various stations in life discussed shipping, politics, religion, finance, schemes, duty, law, love, women, what to eat for dinner. Cutpurses worked the crowd. Tom wondered how visitors to London felt when they first encountered the famous Paul's.

And see the moneylenders in the temple?

Disappointed, I expect.

Sometimes people mentioned the spire, or rather the absence of it. Lightning had struck the spire when Tom was about three years old. He recalled how his mother had spoken of it for days, certain to teach her son how this destruction betokened God's wrath, God's disgust with those who would deviate from the path of righteousness. When Tom asked which path, and how he would know it, Agnes smacked his hand. Tom accepted this understanding of the spire until he got to school and overheard some of the other boys saying that Catholics took the wreck of the spire as a sign of God's anger with Queen Elizabeth and Protestants. Many years later, over supper in a noisy ordinary, Tom asked Kit what he thought of the loss of the spire. Tom had just finished giving a splenetic dismissal of a poem by Chidiock Tichborne, one of the conspirators in the Babington Plot: *I care not if 'tis thought dangerous; I will speak of this.* Kit, frowning a little, had asked Tom of the beauty in the poem, this elegy on facing death by execution, and Tom had dismissed that, too. *Beauty, in stupidity?* Kit had finished eating, saying nothing else. Then Tom mentioned the spire, the lightning. *What of it?* Kit asked. Tom gave him an exasperated look: *What dost thou think it might mean?* Kit snorted, muttered something about Paul on the road and how it was Lucifer who'd borne light and then asked for the reckoning so he might pay it. Not certain Kit understood him, Tom let the subject drop.

Now, approaching Paul's Yard, Tom looked at the crumbling stonework. In his grandfather's childhood, the yard had honoured the idea of the invincibility of God. Today, stripped and dented and worn by a king's orders and subsequent neglect, and echoing with men and coins, Paul's Yard proved nothing to Tom. If God interfered with printers, stationers, authors, and scriveners, he knew none of it.

Not catching sight of Geoffrey Morgan squirming in the crowd before the Si Quis Wall, Geoffrey looking hungry and vigilant, and reading a notice that Bridewell required a gaol clerk, Tom made for Ed Blount's bookstall, at the sign of the bear. Ed himself, beard and hair dark and tufty, thin cheeks puffed, waved at Tom and sat back in his chair, propping his feet on a bookshelf. Ed had lost many of his teeth, and he softened his food — bread and cheese mostly, sometimes well-stewed fowl — in the sides of his mouth before gumming it to a paste he might swallow.

Ed held up his hand a moment, covered his mouth with his other hand, swallowed, and spoke. —Tom Kyd. I'm glad to see thee. Anything new for me to publish? That long poem, aye?

—Still working it.

—Let me know when. I always have a spot for thee in my queue. And if thou'st dare go to any other publisher —

Tom smiled. —Blount, so long as thou'st got ink and press, I am thine. 'Tis difficult to finish any of it when I know not how I am eating dinner tomorrow.

Ed nodded, and the bone of his jaw, sharper than before, defined itself against skin and beard. —Oh, here. I've got four new books in from France, histories. Thou'st need more in thy library than Cicero.

—I am not sure that I do.

—Stories, Kyd, adaptation: there's thy task, and thy grace. 'Tis thou who might take the most obscure and bitter story and make a play of it.

—Well, I'm not alone in that.

—No, but thou art the one who showed the others how 'tis done. Hieronimo and Hamlet: characters for the ages.

Smiling at that, tempted to believe it, Tom duly admired the offered books and wished he could buy them all. He said he'd take the one by a man called Garnier, the tragedy *Cornelia*. —But, ah, on account.

Ed rolled his eyes. —Thou, and everyone else. And how am I to pay my yard rent, I wish to know: on account?

Yet Ed took out his ledger, made the entry, had Tom initial

it, and handed over *Cornelia*. They talked some more, Ed passing on some gossip about other writers, expecting, Tom knew, something similar in return: news about Kit, ideally. Tom just shook his head at the stories Ed told: other writers backbiting, rumour mongering, even brawling. When in Hell these men got time to write, Tom could not guess. He liked to think his own days of anger and dispute lay behind him. Long feuds with Robert Greene and Thomas Watson had only ended with those men's deaths. He still preferred not to speak to Thomas Nashe. Tom had a gift for harsh words and bitter tones, a certain recklessness with his speech, and when angered, he sounded, to his shame, like his mother.

Strolling the yard a while more, Tom observed the mannerisms of other men, and he eavesdropped, more out of interest in rhythm and diction than in meaning. The contract nagged him, and, promising himself supper at an ordinary once he got the contract copied, he headed home.

His doorknob hung askew.

He punched the door aside, strode in, and slammed the door shut behind him. The landlord, no doubt, come harassing him again. Tom just asked himself why the landlord would damage his own property when something knocked him back against the door: a large man, taller than Tom and much broader. The man tried to pry Tom aside, shove him out of the way; Tom stood his ground and shoved back. They wrestled, the stranger inch by inch forcing advantage until he chose brutal simplicity and grasped Tom's stones — hauled, twisted, wrenched. Yelling, Tom fell to the floor and curled into a ball. The man then kicked Tom in the small of the back, as though booting away some lame and useless animal.

Centipedes scurried and writhed into cracks in the wall.

The man peered down at him. —Stay there.

Tom watched him rush to the bookshelf and pluck out a small volume, bound in oxblood leather, quite expensive and a gift from Kit: Cicero's *De Officiis*.

—Blood of Christ, what dost thou *want*?

The man glanced at the book and shrugged. —Proof.

He left.

Staring at the sunlight leaking in around the closed door, Tom shook. He worked to stand, stone pain gone pulpy now, still sickening. He hobbled to his desk, eyed his belongings: beyond the bookshelf, nothing else seemed disturbed.

Tom cried out as a rat ran across the floor and back to the food chest. It stood up on its hind legs — a female, teats wobbling — and seemed to study Tom, seemed to wait for him to act. Knocking over his ink, Tom hurled *Cornelia* at the rat. He missed. The rat leapt back into the food chest. Tom screamed in fury, earning a rapid thudding of a neighbour's fist on the wall. That noise, in turn, woke the other neighbour's sickly infant, who now wailed, snuffled, and whined in a racket that might yet continue for hours.

Defeated, Tom got himself to his bed. He lay on his back, the fabric of his breeches suddenly rough against his scrotum, able to think only of shock and pain, of a centipede's many legs.

I need a reason. Proof of what?

The infant's cries settled; the daylight changed. Feeling the breadth of the bed, the empty space beside him, Tom sat up and stared down the little set of steps to his desk.

Work unfinished. Reckonings unpaid.

Belly empty.

FOUL PAPERS: IN ONE SELF PLACE

Addressed to my sister, Mary, who called me Little Trouble-some One, and Clever Kitten, and who hates me yet for the times I made her laugh in church, and who, despite her better judgment, doth cherish me, as I do her, on the twenty-sixth of April.

My dear Mary, my Manna, my Manna-of-May, this is my fifth attempt to write thee a letter. 'Tis piece after piece, draft after draft, until I've got glut and surfeit of foul papers to burn. I should, aye, have written thee long before now, and for that I am sorry, beyond mine ability to say. My work barred me. Rebuke me, for 'tis thy right (and thy gift), but before thou dost, answer me this: what rebuke shalt thou make to mine arrogance when 'twas thy skirts I clutched as I learned to walk, when 'twas thy name and thy love what reasoned my first words?

Manna, wait.

I rest at a house called Scadbury. 'Tis owned by my friend from Cambridge, Sir Thomas Walsingham, and it sits far enough from London but yet too far from Canterbury. London, 'tis all mud and filthy rivers, Fleet and Thames: a dire famine of beauty. I never did make good my promise to one day live on London Bridge, though many people do, roofs and jakes spanning the water. At the south end, traitors' drizzling heads might look down from high pikes, interrupting one's view of the sky. The old Canterbury pilgrimage started on London Bridge, first stones the command of a guilty king in his penitence. Lately I travelled abroad and witnessed worse. Scadbury is a delight, with its fields and streams and trees and fine food (the cook, Dan Roe, is an artist) and a soft bed and aye, melodious birds singing madrigals. Confinement within beauty remains confinement. Oh, this is tedious, Manna. I feel penned in like some prize beast at the fair. I've been ill. A pneumonia took me. 'Tis past, but it, and the necessary physicke of hot cups, plasters, and bloodletting, have left me weak. Mine affections murmur, and I should much like to see thee and perhaps beseech thy

When lost I first thy kind regard? The priest's visit, was't that day? Pity John Marlowe the cobbler, no doubt made nervous when he came home and found a clergyman waiting for him

The priest dandled me on his knee and stroked my hair as I recited from Matthew

I believe Father saw none of it, his eyes at the moment adjusting to the different light, but never did I ask. He looked irritated, maybe exasperated? Ashamed

I doubt not he wished the clergyman sought only a new pair of shoes. Each man then explained his delicate point to the other, and each man thought he won. Dost thou remember, Manna, for I would swear thou didst hide in the kitchen and listen. Our father pointed out that, learned as a king or stunned as a rock, I stood in this world but a cobbler's son. Said our father, *He already reads and writes better than I do: sufficeth not? He sings well, but his figuring's poor. I*

should like to see him split and tally a reckoning. Scholarship to
Cambridge? Dance him to the Devil first. And King's School,
la. How would I pay for King's School when I've got three other
children, and two of them boys? The clergyman laid his hands
on my shoulders and pushed me forward, merchant and
poppet we were, and he reminded Father how every man,
woman, and child in the county needed shoes at one time
or another, so unless England suffered a barefoot delusion,
he could pay the school fees: *Mr. Marlowe, the boy teems*
with promise. Our father disagreed: *No, he teems with piss*
and pride, in glut and surfeit. The clergyman leant his head
on my shoulder, and his beard tickled my cheek. *In these*
days, the Church of England pleads for finely trained minds,
and Cambridge offers that scholarship to excellent students who
promise to take holy orders after commencement. Send him to
King's School first.

Manna, did I never tell thee I near missed that scholarship,
only receiving it when the boy ahead of me, the true winner,
died? Odds and fortune. Nothing I touch seems the least
coloured by

Thou didst punch me on the arm after the priest left. Thou
didst hear him call me clever and sweet, hear him say he
tickled me, and thou didst envy it

Teaching thee at home, after school, paying thee back for
thy shared dame-school lessons, I forgot the weight of the
promise, giving not one thought to holy orders until my
voice broke. Examinations. Cambridge damp and cold, cold

as thou didst become when I refused to teach thee all I'd
got from university. In a few weeks? With thy shaky Latin?
Keep pace how, Manna? Thou didst task me to wipe thy
spit from my face when I confided I would sidestep the holy
orders. If a woman might transform herself into a dragon
of conflagration, char-brilliant and stinking of brimstone
against the night sky, such a woman would I call sister. I do.
*Conditions of the scholarship and plans long made: obligations,
Kit, thine obligations.* My teaching failed thee once more
as I explained I'd taken up other work. Ever subtle, thou
didst spit again, at my feet this time, and asked if mine
other work dripped from the Privy Council. *The same Privy
Council, Kit, who did need write instruction to Cambridge
to award thee that degree, after thou didst miss two terms? I
heard the rumours, even out here, and I answered questions,
and I swore on my beating heart thou'dst never turn Catholic.
The danger thou didst drag to thy parents' doorstep: how
couldst thou shove our faces into such menace? Never Catholic,
no, worse: agency. Dirty, dirty work. Dost thou know many
fine and good agents, Kit, any who've lived past thirty, any
whom thou'dst acknowledge in the street?* I countered with
bare truth: thou'dst hooked hope into me, thinking thou
might'st hold thine head high as the cathedral because thy
brother took holy orders and did discuss with thee matters
of theology, thereby proving thou didst somehow matter in
God's blank mystery plays. I struck true and hard with that;
I regret it still. Crying, thou didst tell me I'd cheated the
university, the clergy, and God Himself. Tired, Manna, I
felt so tired when I gagged thee with more truth: *No, shrew.
I've cheated thee. And that is why thou dost weep.*

Till now, it all came so easily, and till now, the work never worried me. Manna, I would bargain with God

I never turned Catholic. 'Twas ever a ruse. I can tell thee no more. 'Tis dangerous. Our younger brothers: shall they ever understand this? Or shall they continue to pretend that suspicion of my prayer is why they despise me?

The priest smelled of incense and sweat, and his long fingers

Tell me of our parents, and tell me if I've neglected to meet nieces and nephews; are new ones born? I must beg leave to come see ye. I beseech thee, say nothing to Mother and Father of mine illness, but instead assure them I travel and work in good health and think on them often.

Manna, how came I to this? In forbidden *Everyman*, 'tis Death's warning: *And look thou, be sure of thy reckoning.* I cannot trust, for I have lost my truth and would be resolved of all ambiguities. Dost thou laugh there? I would. I kneel at the hearth, chanting a hope that flame will reveal a more complete honesty, but there, leaning on the same words to tell the same stories, I fail the flame and perhaps burn this letter, too. So much blocks my way, and something vital runs short. I know not how I may get this letter to thee. I am sorry. I am sorry.

 I am sorry.

     I remain
     thy loving brother.

(I see, and say nothing)

FAIR COPY: HOMO, FUGE

Addressed from Scadbury this 26th day of April.
To my friend, Sir Robert Cecil.

Your honour,
    By mine own hand, then, I give you further report,
though I doubt 'tis the report you desire. Your servant, and
my friend, being some parts recovered from his pneumonie,
doth rise readily from bed to eat and to work. He attends
church each Sunday, and he tutors my Flemish singing boy,
the orphan of whom I've written to you before, thinking
he may with pruning come to be of great use, and this
education being a long task which keeps both pupil and
teacher out of trouble. Marlowe writes much, which I
suppose should come as no surprise but which alarms me
nonetheless, for he is secretive. At Cambridge, he showed
me every word. I would assure you, Sir Robert, that worry
for your servant's heart and mind is unnecessary, but I
cannot. The man is restless and sad. His appetite is good.
He is now friends with my cook and hath charmed him, as
he doth charm us all, and we now eat variations on pie of
chardequince so often that I make threat to cut down my
quince trees and so deny us the coming harvest, my stock of
quince preserves being exhausted, too. I am not altogether
in jest. While your servant doth gain stamina and strength,
I still would hesitate to give him any heavy or meaningful
task, for he tires easily. I write that after some dark consideration as, left to my solitary desires in this matter, some days
I would gladly watch his back grow small in the distance.

I feel guilty, in this my surveillance of him, when instead I would embrace him. Your needs task me. I regret I can offer you nothing but mine affectionate fear.

In all matters, your loyal friend,
Tho. Walsingham.

GIVE IT ME; I'LL HAVE IT PUBLISHED
IN THE STREET

On the tenth of May, Robin Poley felt God smack him upside the head. Robin had prayed that his channel crossing back to London might go gentle. It did not. Sick, pained, and chilled, and in a mood of restrained fury, he lurched and slipped and puked, astonished at the violence of what the sailors called a petty swell. Balancing demanded a sophisticated dance of hips and knees, a dance he could not perform. He'd left his crutch on board on the way over, when sailing to Flushing to finish the ruin of the Wilmot brothers. Hard limping, and a harder disguise of that limping, had worn him more than he wanted to admit. He leant on his crutch now, the ball of his right hip giving fiery agony. Fatigue pressed him to lie down in a useless slumber — no rest in it, just a painful rolling from side to side, eyes burning. Lying down also meant throwing up, so Robin hauled himself on deck to fix his eyes on the horizon, or at least on where the horizon, or God's elusive mercy, might be. After dark, he gave in and faced the struggle of climbing into a hammock. He fell, twice.

His long sojourns, his trips back and forth to Flushing,

annoyed Essex and Anthony Bacon. Robin made his pleas: he bought his bread by piecework, hiring himself to the gaols for arrests when money got particularly tight — John Deyos at Bridewell liked to deal with him — and to the great men, Essex and Sir Robert Cecil. Sir Robert believed him to be a loyal agent, and so he must obey Sir Robert and carry out his tasks. Besides, Marlowe was yet too ill for any use, though the time to approach him again had come.

Considering this, how best to tickle and please Kit's fiery mind, Robin dug into his satchel. He always carried it, and he called it his bag of works. Kit had called it his bag of trouble. Rightly weighted, the bag helped Robin balance as he walked, and its contents — scraps of wood and leather, ropes, rags, feathers, bones, awls, and a few teeth — kept his hands busy and his thoughts clear during the idle tedium of travel and surveillance. *Ferreting with thy fingers*, Kit had said. Most often, Robin carved faces into wood, his wrist giving delicate flicks. He did this work with a smaller knife, reserving his dagger for professional tasks. The sharp faces frowned.

Robin sometimes felt guided to a particular place, as though someone peered over his shoulder and then whispered in his ear: check that tree; tip that barrel; visit that cobbler. He obeyed this voice, even when he needed to hush a protesting pup agent to do so. Beside that tree he'd found his crutch. Within that barrel, he'd found a dry cloak, packed in straw. At the cobbler's, he'd found two pieces of hard leather meant for a thick sole but sliced too small, some accident, some embarrassment the cobbler would not explain. As Kit looked around the cobbler's workshop, intrigued, Robin placed an order for shoes and got the pieces of leather as a bonus. Now, in his quiet moments, Robin worked the leather with his awls and his little knife, his darkness lit by a vision.

When Robin was about seven, his mother, Jane Poley, berating his father and uncle for sloth, complaining of how much her stiff back hurt and how much the men fouled the house, earned herself a branking. Robin understood his role in the punishment: her child must be too ashamed to look on her. Except he did look on her. As Jane sat at the table, head bowed with the weight of the iron muzzle, bleeding from the mouth, weeping, Robin studied the mechanism: a cage for the head attached to a tongue-flattening gag. Vigorous metaphor and good design: ever after, Robin cultivated a taste for them, and he came especially to admire the sight of chained books — chained against theft, of course. On the second morning of the branking, Jane several times grasped her throat and mimed drinking. The cup knocked against the bars of the branks; no liquid reached her mouth. She moaned a little, but only a little, as even that slight vibration of her mouth shoved her tongue against the spike in the gag. Robin hadn't seen the spike and knew nothing of it until the removal of the branks. His uncle, relenting, had gone to the alderman, but on his walk back, sore head and thirst for more wine distracting him, lost the key. Jane lurched round the house, prying at the branks; she collapsed on the floor near her bed. Her husband and brother-in-law hauled on the bars; Robin sat at the table, back to this scene, listening. The alderman's eldest daughter stood in the open doorway, her little shape dark against the sunlight; she bore the key, secure now in a folded rag. Robin took it, walked to the cursing men and mute woman, knelt, and, struggling with the aged lock, released his mother. Robin's father and uncle yanked the cage off Jane's limp head, dragging the spike on the gag through her mouth, mauling tongue and lips, and finishing the ruin. Jane's wounds abscessed and swelled and stank; she took a fever and died, hearing the angry curses of her husband as he accused her of most foolish negligence and hoped by God she felt satisfied, for now the boy had no mother. The boy saw this, and he said nothing.

Robin could not explain, even to himself, his compulsion, his need to design and fashion this gag. As he'd trusted the cobbler, the barrel, the tree, he trusted these pieces of sole. He'd never used a gag in his work, wondering now why not: silence could save blood. Robin himself had accepted into his mouth a piece of oak branch once; a trusted friend had wedged it between his teeth so he might bite down as the friend then treated a painful wound. A necessity, that, a kindness: no gag. Robin's idea: the gag itself would pick at the mind of the silenced one, too; Robin thought of several instances when such pressure would have been useful. Knowing how his own invisible and unexplained impediments galled him, knowing the tiresome and cumulative truth of *crippled*, Robin considered speech and silence, and the pragmatics of crippling a mouth. The branks, the scold's bridle: a punishment for women. Would a gag not only stun but also insult a man, then, emasculate as well as silence? Robin spat on a knot and tugged it taut. And who would do this? Robin considered himself above the rough tasks of beating and restraint, above and yet below: *I get too weak.* He seldom bothered even with threats these days, instead hiring Ingram Frizer or, if pressed for time, striking a mouth or a pair of stones with a swiftness that made him proud. In most people, Robin found, a good smack or two elicited compliance, and he need not lose his breath. Those too stupid, or too stubborn, to learn the lesson might require a more thorough beating. Even breathless, even strained, Robin smiled over such work. He recognized that the trouble for men like himself and Ingram Frizer came when reason and discipline wore thin, allowing a taste for violence to intoxicate thought. Ingram got giddy on the simplicity of his strength and, too often, relied on brutality instead of his reason — a shame, Robin felt, as Ingram might devise a scheme cunning and fierce enough to rob a church and then trick the priest into thanking him. Robin, for his part, enjoyed his accessories, and he enjoyed his own sense of style: his scabbard studded with nail heads, his dagger topped with a pommel shaped like a human ear. Decorations and symbols: he must apply them with subtlety and care, balanced against risk. Too many mouths in this current and quite delicate enterprise, none of them women's, thank Christ, but the wisdom of the branks must not go ignored. Or forgotten. Handiwork then, pliable leather laces, the points of his awls, and the hard bits of sole: a gag. Not quite the comedic terror of the branks, but easier to carry in his bag of works.

Peace of Lethe moored at the Deptford docks. Looking around, waiting for permission to leave the ship, Robin felt that all creation sneered at him. He sneered back. Once cleared, limping and parched, he started his walk to Widow Bull's rooming house. He got there in time to hear Ingram Frizer assuring the Widow Bull that Mr. Poley would look to his reckoning, just another few days, good mistress. Widow Bull caught sight of Robin over Ingram's shoulder, and Ingram, his dark hair falling into his eyes, turned to see who'd come in, precisely as Robin had taught him not to do.

Subtlety, Frizer, learn subtlety.

Robin ignored Ingram and instead limped to a table, where he lost hold of his crutch. Ingram crossed the dim room and knelt down to retrieve it. None of the other patrons paid them the least mind.

The wayward light beneath the low ceiling exposed the lines mapping Robin's face into separate territories. Surprised, Ingram tilted his head to one side. —Cracks and crevices.

—What?

—Are you pained, Poley?

—Only for the lack of thy report. Say on.

—Not got you a drink yet.

—Likely to need one, am I?

Ingram returned with something boggy and meadish. Robin held the drink nearer to a dusty beam of sunlight and regretted it. —So. Didst thou get my proof?

Ingram looked at his drink, the table, the floor. —Aye, right away, no delays.

—Eyes on me. And deceive me not.

Ingram reached into his own satchel and retrieved a book. —I got it. I got it.

Flipping pages, Robin checked Tom's copy of *De Officiis* for any concealed treasure. —Edifying.

—Oh, we paid a visit to the Marlowes' house, there in Canterbury. His parents.

Careful, gentle, Robin placed the book back on the table. —I cannot have rightly heard thee.

—I took the reckoning of a situation and charged forth. Anthony Bacon —

—*What?*

Ingram shrugged. —Anthony Bacon did contact Ric Baines and me, saying he required papers with Marlowe's handwriting on them. You weren't here to ask. And Bacon paid well.

Robin wanted to throw something. *Oh, the great manager, Tony Bacon: I know not how he manages a piss-pot. Would he just leave me alone to work?* —Frizer, these papers: what didst thou do? Precisely?

—Me and Baines, we rode to Canterbury. But she told me nothing, and she'd got no papers, either.

—She?

Exasperated, Ingram sighed. —Marlowe's sister. Mary, I think. A right shrew, she is, too. 'Tis easier to silence a river. She even tricked Scadbury out of me.

Flapping their gums in Canterbury for something we need not? How am I to keep it subtle now?

—Poley, you're gone very pale.

—God save me! I never should have left this reckoning to ye.

—Right, you remind me: Widow Bull wants the account paid.

Robin kicked him under the table. Hard.

—Hey!

Ignoring the rest of Ingram's protest, Robin glared into his drink. Racket flared from another table as someone lost at dice and hauled out his dagger. Startling Ingram again, Robin smiled. —Oh, gentle Frizer, I would set thee to parsing thy failures. Think, and when I come back, explain to me how thou didst snarl my day.

Leaving Ingram behind to mouth *gentle* in question and pleasure, Robin settled the reckoning with Widow Bull. Then he paid her in advance for several more weeks on Ingram's room, adding that Frizer might have intermittent company, himself or another man called Nick. Smiling, Robin offered the widow a little extra for her discretion and patience in this matter, a sign of his humblest gratitude, and a recognition of her difficulties in getting by in this mad and sinful world without a husband. Widow Bull smiled back as she accepted the money, and Robin wondered how best to push her, if need be. Kit, Robin knew, played the lost lamb well, plucking maternal strings in landladies' hearts; Robin had more luck uttering innuendoes about little deaths and big rods. He hardly knew if he could bring innuendo to the proof these days, such pain and seizing in his hips and lower back, but a little imagination hurt no one. He glanced at Widow Bull's chest. Her hardened nipples poked the clinging fabric of her dress. *Ah. 'Tis not my limping charms then but the racket of coins.* Even so, Robin treated her to a quick but most appreciative look up and down.

She laughed — not in pleasure, as Robin told himself, but disdain.

Ingram watched Robin return to the table, recognizing in the man, despite the limp, despite the pain, a clarity of purpose. A certainty. *Reasons, tasks, and results*, Ingram thought. Then he recalled his dead wife, the brutal speed of her sickness, the chair paining his arse as he sat by her bed for thirteen hours, desperate to witness the moment of meaning — recovery, or death — desperate for certainty. Perhaps he'd dozed. He'd missed the moment, only recognizing the absence of her difficult breathing, the absence of her life, after relishing the quiet. The loss pained him, the grief, but worse: the stunned paralysis before blank chaos. His wife in good health one day, dead the next. Why?

Why?

Robin had visited Ingram not long after the funeral: called on him, recruited him.

Poley saved me. 'Tis reasons, tasks, and results now.

Ingram stood up, and bowed to Robin.

Robin's expectation of difficulty at Essex House did little to soothe the gall of Anthony Bacon shouting at him. The added humiliation of Essex listening to this, slouched in a chair, legs stretched out, infuriated him.

—I need time! *Time*, Bacon, and no interference.

—Interference? No, I merely took up the slack.

—Ingram Frizer and Ric Baines terrorized those people, for no good need. 'Tis *waste*. I deplore waste.

—Thou'st delivered nothing! Thy failures mount, and —

—Look at me! Dost thou think I delay for myself? Each day 'tis harder to walk. My hip seizes, and my spine burns. 'Tis like I've been poisoned. I want this solved as much as thee, but we can solve nothing by sending men to Canterbury. Tell me, Bacon: beating a man's sister, which gentle art of persuasion is that? Relent.

Essex spoke up. —That libel, that poem: is't ready?

Thinking of Geoffrey Morgan, Robin bowed. —Aye, my lord, and I've had it ready for months, in a scrivener-quality fair copy. And 'tis designed not to entrap, for that would be too easy, but to raise suspicion and threat.

Anthony rolled his eyes to Heaven. —I should hope 'tis designed for more than that. Thy boasts, Poley: this libel would snare another man and so give us leverage? Other libels already appear, little notes of hatred blaming the refugees for every ill. 'Tis good timing, now.

Robin recalled Essex declaring he would harm no innocent, and his own flippant response. He stifled a sigh. —I shall deliver. Without the libel. I only ask a little patience.

Essex shook his head. —Post the libel. Now.

—My lord, I beg leave to explain. I am not convinced —

—What, what, what: have patience, my lord? Yet more? Our man's been ill, aye, but he lives and breathes, and soon he shall surely be well enough to travel. I want him over to me before Sir Robert sends him to Scotland. 'Tis May-month. Poley, thou'lt recall the date I gave thee, which thou'st ignored.

—My lord —

—May-month, I say again, and the Queen may be that much closer to death, each day a plod and a thud in her mortal galliard, hey? My patience frays. Post the libel.

Robin bowed. —Aye, my lord.

—Bacon, give him every assistance.

—Aye, my lord.

—Oh, and Poley?

—My lord?

Essex smiled. His eyes shone. —Show him mercy. Once he understands, let him come to me. I am pleased to have thee for this difficult work.

Knees weak, Robin smiled back. —I thank you, my lord. 'Tis what I am here for.

Escorted out the servants' door, the pleasure of Essex

and his smile falling away, Robin felt trapped, betrayed: *I, who would play Essex and Sir Robert against each other and be masterless?* He blamed this feeling on Bacon, and then on Marlowe, but as he limped to the house where he rented a room, he acknowledged the frailty of his rhetoric. He lit a candle from the large one near the door and asked his landlady for a pitcher of water. In his room, he poured the water into a bowl so he might wash his face.

Reflections of man and candlelight shimmered on the water; Robin ruined that with his hands.

EXCEED THE REST IN LEWDNESS

Megrim, insomnia, wine, and three agony-burnt vertebrae just between the shoulder blades, where the worst of his hunch seemed to be crumbling, fused into a splendid backdrop of pain for Robert's morning crisis. Doublet twisted, legs sullen, he slouched towards an emergency meeting of the Privy Council in Westminster Palace.

Izaak Pindar followed him. —Your honour, your honour, your ruff, your honour. Oh, your doublet. An't please your honour, stand still a moment.

Robert kept walking. *I'd just drifted off to sleep, elusive, blessed sleep, when the messenger good as beat his way through my door. Merchants surrounding Cecil House, so brazen, so bold, singing and chanting: Toad-Cecil, Toad-Cecil, hop to it and show your face! Men standing on the docks as I got out of the wherry, pointing and laughing — I thought they'd press on me, all as one — then some gibberish about cutting throats in temples and the Paris massacre — God's own wounds broiling in the midday sun, another libel posted on the Dutch Church, some maniacal fool possessing ink and pen and his abseys but lacking the good sense God gave a louse…*

He spoke over his shoulder. —Pindar, 'tis the third libel this month. Threatening murder and fire… Should we fail to make an example, the Queen shall slice and fry us like pigs for dinner. I know God tests us, Pindar, but some days I think He's abandoned England. Have a care!

Working to leave the pinned ruff undisturbed, Izaak only worsened the doublet's snarl. —Your honour, if I may: the merchants of London starve, their commerce ruined, and they blame the interlopers from the Low Countries. Men London-born, London-raised, and London-taxed feel betrayed that the Privy Council spends scant funds housing newcomers.

A stunted cry: Robert reached behind him and plucked two long ruff pins free of his neck. —The Low Countries refugees supply us with valuable intelligence of Catholic activities on the Continent, and they often speak against their own kin. Such action deserves reward. And if these objecting London-born men stuck their faces past their own dirty alleys — oh, far edges of the world — then they might blink in the strange shared sun and be stunned at how more than London lives, how more than London bleeds. If they'd prick their consciences and trouble themselves to voyage even as far as the Low Countries and there witness, as have I, burnt earth, and mud huts of princes, then these London men would invite the refugees to table and beg the privilege to anoint their feet.

—Unemployment wells high, your honour.

—England's not got tits! One fire, Pindar, one refugee's lodgings set alight, and all of wooden London burns by dawn. *All* of it. How shalt thou explain to a burnt child the Hellish death of his parents? We needs find an author for this verse, put a stop to this — God, fire? Find the author. Harrow him. Barbaric and short-sighted, I know, but we lack time.

Izaak smoothed Robert's sleeves. —Punishing criminals is not barbaric.

The timing: 'tis slick. Essex? —Leave it yet. Do this: a proclamation, to all London. Promise dire punishment for the next man who is so foolish as to set intemperate pen to paper. Promise Bridewell. And get me a copy of that libel, with all speed, for I would know the words and voice. We — oh, God's own wounds...

Sir John Puckering strode toward him. —Sir Robert, at last.

—Good morning, Sir John.

—Good morning, you say? When we've got rioting in the streets?

—'Tis hardly rioting, Sir John. A nuisance to keep a watch on, aye.

Puckering squinted at Robert. —The Queen's messenger waits in the Star Chamber.

—Her Majesty wastes no time.

—And the messenger would run to her with the Privy Council's answer, for she is much pained by our delay in smothering this libel at the Dutch Church.

—Which was posted but last night. Aye, terrible sloth on our part.

—Sir Robert, I must ask: treat you this with the gravity it merits?

Robert looked into Puckering's eyes. —I remain bound to the same laws of time and duty as you. Even so, I thought just moments ago how the Queen might fry us like pigs once she heard of the libel and the men in the street. Indeed: I smell bacon.

Puckering glanced away.

—Sir John, I do this not only to assure you, but I shall yet ask you to pay heed, and mark what I now say. Mr. Pindar: see to it we arrest the libel's author. Soon. Write the warning — and include that brainless ass, the lord mayor of London — so I may present it to the council. Then thou shalt see it posted and return here to await my pleasure. I shall write the letter appointing thee to oversee the interrogation of the libeller. Thou shalt need to give the Privy Council regular reports. Thou'st assisted such examinations; now I'll have thee take one on thyself. As always, look to Keeper John Deyos for advice, but be ready to flex and improvise, as a master examiner would. Go.

Izaak bowed. —Your honour.

Puckering inclined his head. —Sir Robert, I apologize.

—My tender feelings count for nothing. Now, we must see to the Queen's messenger.

Izaak watched the privy councillors walk down the corridor, tall Sir John Puckering on his even stride, Sir Robert on his hunched waddle, Puckering reminding Robert of the need to consider the obnoxious weirs on the River Trent, and Robert murmuring polite acknowledgement. Noises fell away as Izaak noticed intricate cracks in the wall, as he smelled the flowers in the arms of a passing lady of the court. Izaak had seen her before but had hardly dared look her in the face; today he took note of her freckles and green eyes. Then he stepped aside to give Lady Audrey Walsingham room to continue on her errand, and he bowed, certain she not only noticed him in return but also studied him.

I matter. Today I matter.

Obeisance made, he hurried back to Sir Robert's office to write the warning.

FAIR COPY: ANY WAY SUSPECTED

At the Star Chamber on Friday, being eleventh of May, 1593.

There have been of late diverse lewd and malicious libels set up within the City of London, among the which there is some set upon the wall of the Dutch Churchyard that doth exceed the rest in lewdness, and for the discovery of the author and publisher thereof Her Majesty's pleasure is that some extraordinary pains and care be taken by the Commissioners appointed by the Lord Mayor for the examining of such persons as may be in this case any way suspected. This shall be therefore to require and authorize you to make search and apprehend every person so to be suspected, and for that purpose to enter into all houses and places where any such may be remaining, and open their apprehension to make like search in any of the chambers, studies, chests, or other like places for all manner of writings or papers that may give you light for the discovery of the libellers. And after you shall have examined the persons, if you shall find them duly to be suspected and they shall refuse to confess the truth, you shall by the authority hereof put them to the torture in Bridewell, and by the extremity thereof, to be used at such times and as often as you shall think fit, draw them to discover their knowledge concerning the said libels. We pray you herein to use your uttermost travel and endeavour, to the end the author of these seditious libels may be known and they punished according to their desserts, and this shall be your sufficient warrant.

FAIR COPY: PER TAMBURLAINE

Ye strangers that do inhabit in this land
Note this same writing do it understand
Conceit it well for safeguard of your lives
Your goods, your children, and your dearest wives
Your Machiavellian Merchant spoils the state,
 Your usury doth leave us all for dead
Your Artifex and craftsman works our fate,
And like the Jews, you eat us up as bread
The Merchant doth engross all kind of wares
 Forestalls the markets, whereso'ere he goes
Sends forth his wares, by peddlers to the fairs,
 Retails at home, and with his horrible shows:
Undoeth thousands.
In Baskets your wares trot up and down

Carried the streets by the country nation,
You are intelligencers to the state and crown
    And in your hearts do wish an alteration,
You transport goods, and bring us God's good store
    Our Lead, our Vittaly, our Ordinance and what not
That Egypt's plagues, vexed not the Egyptians more
    Then you do us; then death shall be your lot
No prize comes in but you make claim thereto
    And every merchant hath three trades at least,
And cutthroat-like in selling you undo
    us all, and with our store continually you feast:
We cannot suffer long.
Our poor artificers do starve and die
    For that they cannot now be set on work
And for your work more curious to the eye.
    In Chambers, twenty in one house will lurk,
Raising of rents, was never known before
    Living far better than at native home
And our poor souls, are clean thrust out of door
    And to the wars are sent abroad to roam,
To fight it out for France and Belgia,
    And die like dogs as sacrifice for you
Expect you therefore such a fatal day
    Shortly on you, and yours for to ensue
as never was seen.
Since words nor threats nor any other thing
    can make you to avoid this certain ill
We'll cut your throats, in your temples praying
    Not Paris Massacre so much blood did spill
As we will do just vengeance on you all

In counterfeiting religion for your flight
When 'tis well known, you are loath, for to be thrall
   your coin, and you as country's cause to flight
With Spanish gold, you all are infected
   And with that gold our Nobles wink at feats
Nobles said I? nay men to be rejected,
   Upstarts that enjoy the noblest seats
That wound their Country's breast, for lucre's sake
   And wrong our gracious Queen and Subjects good
By letting strangers make our hearts to ache
   For which our swords are whet, to shed their blood
And for a truth let it be understood.
Fly, fly, and never return.
Per Tamburlaine

TO THE END THE AUTHOR

Ed Blount waved Tom over to his bookstall. —Not seen thee for a while, Kyd. What, dost thou find better quills from someone else?

—I'd not bother to look. How now, Blount?

—I do well as I can in these times, I thank thee. Didst thou ever discover the name or reason of the stranger in thy house?

Tom wished he'd not told Ed about that. —No. Nor shall I. Some mistake, I expect.

—And Marlowe, how doth he?

—I wouldn't know.

—Oh.

—No, no, 'tis no quarrel. I've just not seen him since — so long. Late January?

—So he's not here? In London?

—What? If he is, I shall be the very last to know, when at some dark hour he comes bedraggled to my door. May I get four goose quills and half a ream of paper?

Tom tallied the likely cost in his head. These coins would be better spent on a few decent suppers, but then how might he take copy work if he lacked paper and quills?

—Kyd, listen to me. That new libel today, posted on the door of the Dutch Church. Another one. 'Tis signed *Tamburlaine*.

Tom stared at him a moment before answering. —No, no, no. Blount, show reason. Kit Marlowe's got no desire to threaten people.

—He loves threatening people.

—Unsettling them, aye, in jest, but —

—He is my friend, too, and I love him, but I fear for him. He's got no sense of limits, Kyd, pressing, pressing with his words. Some argue — not me, but some — that the man who can sink Barabbas into a cauldron and drag John Faustus into Hell is capable of, well, selling his soul, whatever that doth mean.

Tom rubbed the back of neck. —He's not... What says this libel?

—I'll sing it for thee.

—*Sing* it?

—Three different composers gave it a tune. Three I know of. Like this: Ye strangers that do inhabit in this land, note this same writing, and do it understand. Conceit it well, for safeguard of your lives, your goods, your children, and your dearest wives.

—A schoolboy's crippled metre. And th'art out of key.

Ed eased himself over his counter and stood next to Tom, shoulder to shoulder, almost touching him. Murmuring, he retrieved some papers from within his shirts. —I paid too much for this copy, and I should burn it before I'm arrested on suspicion of being its author. Read. And keep thy voice low.

Tom did. His stones ached. *Proof? My stolen book?* —Aye. Burn it.

—Then 'tis not him. I knew it.

—No. 'Tis not his words. But 'tis most foul and dangerous. A man could hang for this. And, in turns of phrase, I allow, in turns of phrase, it doth sound like him.

Ed whispered. —Who would mock Marlowe's voice for shit like this?

—Blount, I beg thee: say nothing more of it. I —

Another customer strode up to the counter, announcing himself as though doing all in earshot a great favour. Tom recognized the voice on the first syllable: Thomas Nashe.

Ed turned around to greet him, and Nashe held out his arms, all happy demands. —Blounty, Blounty, talk to me. Secrets with the scrivener? O, Noverint! How dost thou?

Tom nodded acknowledgement. —Nashe.

—Blounty, thou'dst keep thy back to me. Dost thou hate me anew?

—Still. Thy reckoning with me is half a mile long. Any chance thou'lt pay me today?

Smirking because he had cash this time, those pillory signs good for something, Tom made a little show of counting his coins. —Blount, I'll take four goose quills and half a ream.

Ed gave Tom his goods and change. —I hope to see thee again soon.

Tom counted the change, twice; Ed had increased his prices again.

Giving Ed a friendly nod, Tom left. He heard, by design, Nashe's questions: —Got a pinch in his spleen for lack of a good thrust up the arse from his lord and master, has he? And speaking of, hast thou heard of that new libel from the Dutch Church?

Tom stopped at his regular bakery and got some day-old bread and some cheese, deciding at the last moment to put it on account. The sunshine, so bright earlier after several days of rain, seemed to surrender a little, to retreat. Tom considered walking to his parents' house and asking his father to come out for a drink. Tonight, this night, Tom might allow Frank to persuade him to join the Worshipful Company and so be guaranteed better work. *'Tis not failure*, Tom told himself, *nor surrender, but reality.* Plague, plague again: last year, closing the playhouses had thrown many people out of work, and this spring, parish death tallies mounting, already promised worse. The air gave a troubling softness — dampness, rivers, rats.

Tom reached his parents' house. Voices leaked past the windows: Agnes, certain and disgusted, Frank pleading for peace. Thinking Joan would welcome a visit from her uncle, would welcome any interruption of her grandparents' quarrel, Tom made to knock on the door. As he raised his knuckles,

Agnes in mid-complaint spat out her son's name in a tone of such derision that Tom took a step back. He glanced around, to see if any neighbours had spied him there, and, guilty again, asking himself, as Agnes had asked on many occasions, just why God had created him to be such a constant and galling disappointment to his mother, he strode away.

Back in his rooms, Tom ate some of the bread and then took up his penknife. His quills needed sharpening. *Per Tamburlaine. Even a line about intelligencers for state and crown.* Tom smiled, remembering the night a strange bellman stopped him and Kit in the street, on their way home. The bellman had demanded of each of them name, address, and occupation: *Who and what art thou?* Then, sneering, he'd asked drunken Kit about his *Doctor Faustus*, asked Kit if he worshipped the Devil. *Aye*, Kit had said, *kissed his arse, too. Save thy soul and kiss mine, la.* Only a hefty bribe to help that bellman forget the conversation had allowed Tom to get Kit home that night.

When they'd lived together, Kit and Tom had shared Tom's large desk. While they both had room to work, the arrangement demanded a patience, and an intimacy, that neither man found easy to give. Sometimes Tom would just sit back and watch Kit work. He wrote hunched over, hair falling into his eyes, right arm shielding his paper, left hand swooping the quill in heavy downstrokes. *Guilty*, Tom thought, *guilty for his left hand.* When Tom had first teased Kit with the nickname Sinistra, Kit had studied his hand. *Mine own brothers say the left hand is yet one more sign the Devil's got me. A schoolmaster once beat my hand so hard that it bled and swelled up, and I could write nothing for days. None of the little cuts suppurated, thank Christ. Feel each cut, he said to me, and remember, and so learn when to train thy memory, when to still thy tongue, and when to obey thy betters. My parents said only I must learn to submit, but my sister — fury itself. Manna stood there, her mouth all crammed together, until she let loose a full riot of anger. 'Tis but thy hand, she screeched, and thou canst no more choose which hand than thou canst choose the colour of thine eyes. She even promised revenge, and her tears got in the cuts, la and la. That hurt.*

With regular sharpening and care, a quill might last a week. Kit's quills might give two or three days. Tom liked to keep a good supply of ready quills on hand, and he dressed them with a penknife most nights. One afternoon in 1591, watching Kit's stubborn and dangerous fumbling, Tom had rolled his eyes: *Give me that penknife before thou dost nick a vein.* After hearing the story of Kit's battered left hand, Tom had experimented with dressing nibs at different angles, giving Kit a sampler set of six differently carved quills for his birthday. Kit had come to favour two of the nibs, and Tom got plenty of practice in carving them, for Kit revised, revised, and revised some more, pressing hard. For a Twelfth Night gift that year, Kit had given Tom an unusual penknife, the little blade at the end of the long handle slightly curved. *A very Scythian scimitar*, Kit had pronounced, smile breaking through the smirk. Then he'd handed Tom a clutch of new quills. *Dress these for me?*

Tom used that penknife now, and he caught himself shaping a nib for Kit. He threw the quill onto his desk, and slumped in his chair, hearing in memory Ed Blount sing the Dutch Church Libel. He picked up his poem and soothed his worries with intricate work until twilight played against his little window. Looking up, Tom considered the beauty of swift change: twilight to dusk to night. The shadows of men interrupted. As Tom took a breath and glanced at his door, the lock still broken, the door itself not yet blocked for the night with a chair, someone kicked it in.

—Blood of Christ!

Tom's chair scraped hard against the floor as he scrambled to stand up.

Chief Constable Absalom Reynolds strode inside, and he pointed at Tom. —Stay where thou art.

Absalom's sudden *thou* — disparaging, contemptuous, accusing — felt like a kick in the gut. He clipped out orders to his hired constables, and two of them strode to Tom and took hold of his arms. A third constable, blocking the doorway, waited for a cue in this scripted chaos. He got it when Reynolds, first checking the back room for anyone else, gave a nod and a wink. The third constable then stood at a smart new angle to the damaged door, which he held open for a small man, who leant on a crutch.

He limped towards Tom.

The crutch taps seemed very loud.

—Thomas Kyd?

—Aye. What in Hell is this? Reynolds?

Absalom looked at Tom in disappointment and regret.

The limping man's face reminded Tom of Kit: lined at the eyes and mouth, as if from long sessions of squinting and scowling, only older, harder. He wore a satchel, the strap across his chest, and a baldric crosswise to that, dagger hanging from it in a scabbard studded with nail heads. Despite the limp, he moved with a hard confidence, glancing around the office in a dull way, as though he'd visited many times before, as though he'd got every right. Then he looked up into Tom's eyes — a steady gaze, not menacing but enchanting, and plain with meaning: *I see each secret thou'st ever wanted to keep.*

Anger rising in him, Tom twisted free of the constables. Absalom shook his head. The constables grabbed Tom again, held him harder, and, as his heart pounded and his hearing keened, the truth of the scene soaked into him. Such theatre as this demanded strict attention.

The man with the crutch picked up the quills, examined the nibs and tested their fresh cuts with his thumb. Then he limped round behind Tom and plucked the penknife loose from his hand. —Hidden weapons, too? How else art thou armed against these gentlemen of the law?

—Hired constables are gentlemen now? Upright hounds who could work at nothing else to save their lives. And I was not armed. 'Tis but a penknife.

The limping man drew the handle of the penknife up and down Tom's spine.

—Hieronimo stabs men to death with a penknife. Hast thou not seen that play? Constables, bind his hands, for he doth offer violence and resist rightful arrest.

As the constables tied his wrists together, Tom struggled to understand this prying open of time. His arrest seemed to unfold like some poisonous plant in a bog, leaf by bitter leaf, yet he would swear his heart had given up not one hundred beats. The long and scratchy fibres of the rope — rough cordage suited to binding the joins of a fence or to restraining animals — distracted him. Tom had seen baited dogs and bears tormented by such rope, throats chafed to blood and lymph and pus.

The two constables shoved him down into his chair, pressing his shoulders and leaning their weight into their hands. The limping man sat on the food trunk, facing Tom. He tilted his head to one side and seemed to expect an answer.

Tom only stared back.

Then the limping man rapped his crutch on the floor and hopped down from the trunk. —Right. Thomas Kyd, we arrest thee in Her Majesty's name. Thou —

—Wait. *Why?*

The limping man looked to the ceiling, then back at Tom. —The seditious libel lately posted on the door of the Dutch Church, said libel charring good Londoners' eyes in a scrivener's trained and fair hand, said church standing not ten minutes' walk from here. Thou shalt now, by orders of the Privy Council, suffer thine apprehension to be opened. I do like that phrase.

—I wrote no libel!

—Oh, but thou dost know what it is.

—It means nothing, my knowing. I wrote it not.

—The lone scrivener sitting up late, quite innocent: aye, 'tis possible, but 'tis a matter for an examiner to decide. I am but acting as an agent of the Privy Council and so bound to the councillors' good pleasure. My orders are clear. If I find thee duly to be suspected, and thou shalt refuse to confess the truth, then I must deliver thee to Bridewell.

Silence.

Tom remembered his mother's command when he was four and reluctant to speak.

Such laziness, Tom. Use thy words. God gave them thee.
Words weigh too much.
Words are all thou'st got.

Words stumbled out his dry mouth. —Search my rooms.

—Hmm? I heard thee not.

—Search, I say. Look wherever you wish. I hide nothing.

Absalom Reynolds made a little noise, a grunt of confused protest.

The limping man placed Tom's penknife between the papers and the quills. Then he opened the desk drawers. He found a hammer, some nails, and a tidy stack of fresh paper. Then he ordered the constables to prevent Tom from following him as he took the little steps to the bedchamber. Fabrics rustled as the limping man shoved around bedding, underlinens, and shirts. He returned, holding a small book, papers protruding from it.

A book bound in oxblood leather.

Tom paled. —Where found you that?

—Hidden in thy clothes.

—That book was stolen from me.

The limping man plucked out the papers, held them to the candlelight. Then he showed them to Tom. One sheet: words in stylized letters, in the scrivener's hand called chancery, words he'd read on the sheet Ed hid beneath his shirt, words he'd heard Ed Blount sing. Another sheet, blurring as it passed Tom's eyes, bore what looked like Kit's handwriting.

—Oh, my God.

The limping man signalled to the constables to step back. Then he leaned in close to Tom. —Something thou'st wish to tell me?

Tom whispered back. —Intelligencers to the state and crown?

The limping man smiled and shook his head, as if he and Tom shared a joke. —I thought thee innocent of the knowledge.

Kit, who is this? Tom got his voice up to a murmur. —I wrote no libel, and by thine eyes, I'd say thou'st know it. My stolen book: didst enjoy Cicero?

—Too many words.

The limping man struck Tom across the mouth.

Blinded for a moment, by shock more than pain yet, Tom leaned sideways over his desk and spat out blood. The limping man shoved an object at his face — into his mouth — and a hard tab forced Tom's tongue back to the top of his throat. He choked, then got his tongue under the tab so he could breathe. Leather mashed his lips, dug into his cheeks and the skin behind his ears, and the limping man tied knots, whispering of reckless words, of courage and cunning, of truth being misplaced.

Absalom Reynolds looked to the floor. Witnessing the exposure of evil men: a sad part of his work, and, he told himself, one of the reasons he drank. The evil man's subsequent arrest soothed the gall, restoring to Absalom some sense of balance, of correction. Still, the demands of his work made him sigh, made him nigh-on weep some nights. Knowing the evil man in question, having worked with him, spoken with him several times a week? Harsh betrayal and bitter taint. —Kyd, I never expected this of thee. Dear God.

The limping man gestured to the constables and moved out from behind Tom, coming to stand next to Absalom. He patted the chief constable on the arm, reassuring him, and then he spoke in a loud voice, an actor's voice. —Thomas Kyd, th'art duly suspected of writing and posting that libel on the Dutch Church, acts thou dost deny, and further thou dost resist arrest. 'Tis Bridewell for thee. Thy purse and thy God, scrivener: pray to them both.

TIMERE BONUM EST

('Tis good to fear the worst)

– CHRISTOPHER MARLOWE, *Edward II*

A DARKSOME PLACE AND DANGEROUS TO PASS

Izaak Pindar studied his mother. She stood much aged: skin sagging, back bent, hair lank and white. Her clothing, filthy, and so worn as to admit light, hung off her in folds, and her eyes, grey like his, stared a hard warning. Some heavy responsibility hung in the air, and she waited for Izaak to recognize it.

A man's fist beat the door. Izaak sat up in bed. Downstairs, a messenger called for Pindar, Izaak Pindar, in the Privy Council's name. The landlady, annoyed, alarmed, shouted up the stairs herself. The children woke, calling for their mother; she only hushed them and shouted for Izaak again. Straightening his clothes, surprised he'd fallen asleep when he'd only lain down for a moment, Izaak opened his bedchamber door and called back acknowledgement.

The landlady watched him descend the stairs. —The messenger said you're needed at Bridewell, Mr. Pindar.

She sounded afraid.

Izaak smiled and bade her good night. Outside, he counted some of the stars in the darkening sky.

Bridewell Prison had not long ago stood as a new palace, one of King Henry's. Before Henry built there, residents quenched their thirst and eased their maladies with the healing water of Bride's Well. The intended palace soon became a hospital, where such illnesses as laziness, defiance, and madness might be cured by the imposition of hard work and good suffering. Then Bridewell became a holding pen for beggars, prostitutes, and thieves cleansed from the streets. Corruption seeped — or perhaps justice, depending on whom one asked — and Bridewell came to serve another purpose.

Equipped with tiny cells, flogging posts, and a rack, adding to the cost-effective methods of manacling and starvation, Bridewell provided great assistance to the Privy Council's pursuit of the more dangerous civil and political cases. None drank from the well.

At Bridewell's watergate, Izaak patted his purse, a copy of his letter of authorization from Sir Robert within, and called out for the night's keeper. Torchlight: a stocky man, wealthy with keys and wearing them on his chest and sleeves as a nobleman might wear gold buttons, asked to see Izaak's warrant. Izaak gave him the letter through the bars. The keyed man read it aloud, shone his torch near Izaak's face, gave the letter back, and hauled open the gate.

Izaak set up the tired joke. —So easy to get in, Keeper Deyos?

Laughing, John Deyos passed Izaak the torch to hold as he locked up. —Easy as sin, Mr. Pindar. Getting out? Another matter. Give back the light, so please you, and follow me.

Fighting temptation to touch the keeper's keys, Izaak reminded himself of vows he'd made in the dark. Pregnant England cried out for guidance. Social flux writhed, soon, many feared, to thrash in riot and fire. The very language flowed in cross-currents and riptides, each sentence, each word, chosen to act as layered nuance within intricate Latinate rhetorics for different possible meanings. Better days must come, would come: a cleansing. Brittle monarchy and all its corruption would fall — such violence, but all to a purpose, all for a reason. Finish the Reformation and nurse the kicking newborn state. A pure government, a state, elected, aye, clearer of purpose and closer to God: men who would govern by virtue, not birth. Simple, really.

Simple, perhaps, but not swift. Izaak understood subtleties about power. One such subtlety: a man could change nothing, seize nothing, until he had learned readiness. That readiness fed on capabilities. The seed in the soil, reaching for light, tore itself apart. Izaak would, like the farmer, indeed, like the surgeon, guide buried men — guide England — through their ordeals of ascension. Such was the trouble with meaningful political change: the pain of it. Men resisted growth, fearing pain, and chose stasis and even squalor before risking health. And as behaved men, so behaved England. Physicke, medicine, sunlight: in that metaphor, Izaak saw his task, his service to England and God. His readiness, his capabilities for the coming days of struggle and change: as the sunlight broke a seed, so he must break a man.

He needed practice.

And so, while serving the Privy Council, he sought out and studied the art of examination. Tonight, tasked to examine a criminal, a man who'd written out threats to burn, murder, and terrify, tasked to examine the Dutch Church Libeller, Izaak Pindar came to Bridewell, placed and ready.

God, grant me the strength to hold fast.

He pinched his forearm. A little dart of pain, anticipated, controlled, assured him this night was no dream. He'd pinched himself like this while studying after dark and falling asleep at Cambridge. He'd incurred debt for candles — debt, when that one Marlowe received packet after packet of candles, gifts from home. So bright…

Izaak followed Keeper Deyos. Ensconced torches, flickering on cold stones, lit the way.

John Deyos, Izaak knew, took no savage pleasure in his work, just a pragmatic pride in tasks difficult, scheduled, and, given the sad failings of mankind's corrupt nature, necessary. As they walked past the treadmills, where felons paced or ran, their efforts sometimes grinding grain, Izaak recalled his first visit to Bridewell as assistant to another examiner. He'd been pleased Keeper Deyos felt the need to explain Bridewell's workings to him, pleased the keeper showed him such respect. *Jack Felon's got to keep walking, all day and all night if I tell him, but at least he might pay us back for the trouble of housing him by milling flour for his own bread. Mind, Jack's the common sort. Be different with the other lot that comes through here, the ones the Privy Council eyeballs, your papists and traitors and fallen spies. That crowd needs drawing.*

—And you're the chief examiner for this case, Mr. Pindar? Congratulations. 'Tis a fine promotion, and a sign your masters trust and honour you. I'd rather truck with you than Richard Topcliffe any day. He performs good service to Her Majesty, I know, but he craves more than service. He doth love punishment, and sometimes, in the heat of his zeal, I fear he doth forget the reason for his harsh work. There must be reason. But 'tis not my place to question great men. Here be Geoffrey Morgan, my new junior clerk. He's a scrivener, very tidy handwriting. My last two juniors died within a week of each other. The tower of paperwork, oh, 'twas unfit.

They'd ascended a staircase and now walked into a hallway, leading to big doors, where they discovered a clerk writing at a desk. He could be any clerk at any desk, maybe even one who lived in a country free of Topcliffes and tortures. Leaning his head in his hand, he stared into the distance.

John clicked his tongue. —Morgan!

Geoffrey got to his feet. —Keeper Deyos.

—This is Examiner Pindar, Morgan.

—God be even to you, sir.

Izaak nodded to him.

A heavy door clanged shut, and voices called for Keeper Deyos.

As John left, Izaak, hands clasped behind his back, paced about, looking at walls and ceilings. Geoffrey sat back down, opened his ledger and, taking great care, reviewed some entries.

John Deyos returned with an arrest party: one prisoner, two constables, a chief constable, and a man on a crutch. Grinning, John called out instruction. —All rise for his lordship, our new Earl of Chains. Morgan, the registration.

Geoffrey still studied his ledger. —Name?

Stepping back into a shadow, Izaak studied the prisoner: a tall man, fair in colouring, blue-eyed, those eyes open very wide. His hair, greying blond, and drawn back in a tail, needed cutting. So did his beard. He'd been gagged, a detail that made Izaak look again. He'd never seen a man treated so. As the prisoner stooped to let a man on a crutch unfasten the thing, Izaak felt a little chill.

God in my heart.

Geoffrey, seeing none of this, repeated his question. —Name? The prisoner's name?

Spitting first: —Thou'st know me.

Startled, Geoffrey looked up.

—Morgan, I've done nothing. 'Tis some error. Just vouch for me. Dost thou hear me?

Geoffrey glanced at Robin, then back down at his ledger. —Name?

—Thomas Kyd!

Geoffrey wrote. —Occupation?

—Thou know'st. Poet, playwright, and scrivener.

Robin stepped closer to the desk. —Dutch Church Libel.

Izaak emerged from a shadow and folded his arms. —The Dutch Church Libel?

—I wrote no libel!

John rolled his eyes. —I see why he came to us gagged.

Sniffing, as though his nose ran, Geoffrey wrote some more. His voice seemed hard, glazed over. —Evidence?

Robin handed over the book and the papers. —I found this in his rooms: a copy of the libel in a scrivener's handwriting.

Tom's voice cracked. —Not mine! The handwriting. The book is mine. Stolen from me.

Shaking his head, Izaak took papers from the desk, read the first page over and then showed it to Geoffrey. —Morgan, th'art a scrivener, no? These Hellish words: copied in a scrivener's hand?

—Aye. 'Tis the chancery lettering, common used.

—Blood of Christ, I wrote no such thing! I am not one for terror. 'Tis some snare, some policy's snare. That book was *stolen*, I say. Morgan, vouch for me.

Clicking his tongue, John looked to his clerk. —Morgan, wilt thou speak for him, or not?

Geoffrey met Tom's gaze and felt surprised. No bald plea in Tom's eyes, just agitated expectation because, in another moment, this ghastly folly, this wretched play, would end. *Get on with it.*

Recalling the copy work, Geoffrey glanced at Robin, who mouthed the word *children.*

Vouch for me.

Geoffrey looked down at his ledger. —I know him, Keeper, but I cannot speak for him.

Closing his eyes, Tom seemed to shrink a little in height.

John addressed his own guards, come now to take the prisoner from the arresting constables. —Right, show him a room. Solitary, upper floor. North corner's free. I'll look in later. Mr. Pindar, I'll show you to your chamber now, for your use during your visits, and then I shall meet with you there again shortly before six. Fine work, all. Her Majesty thanks ye. Poley, come with us. That gag: where got you that? I could use a few of those in here. I've asked over and over for a proper branks, but 'tis a fierce expense, and that budget bars me in.

Alone again, Geoffrey ran his fingers over his open ledger. Space for several more entries yawned blank beneath Tom's name. Calling on God for the strength to keep quiet, Geoffrey turned to a clean page. He shook.

Tom also called on God, begging for strength to speak.

The Bridewell guards cut the rope around Tom's wrists and charged him a fee for it, due at once. He paid it. The guards then picked up ceremonial spears from a bracket, and, faces harassed yet certain, like those of butchers' assistants driving a pig to market, escorted Tom up shadowed stairs. Tom knew from Kit's scarce stories of time in Newgate that constables and guards expected a new prisoner to babble, roar, bargain, and beg, and they would likely ignore whatever Tom said unless he offered money — *grace*, in gaol talk. Grace bought better food and drink, regular emptying of the slops bucket, clean bedding, ink and paper, visitors, priests, prostitutes... Tom had no idea what the going rates might be.

Noises flowed: voices in quarrel, despair, and drunken laughter; clanks and clatters and splashes and bangs; curses and songs and prayers and commands. Smells of excrement and sweat thinned out, and so did the noise. They'd reached the solitary cells.

A chain clinked; a man groaned.

The guards unlocked the door to the north corner cell, charging Tom for that, too. The corridor torches illuminated some of the cell floor and walls, and a useless slit of a window — just a crack between stones, a stab wound.

No bed, not even a bench.

A guard nudged Tom with a spear. —Keep moving.

Tom's feet scuffed on something rough: dirty straw. Fleas leapt from it, drawn by light and flesh.

The guards locked the door, and Tom struggled to ignore them.

Reason, reason. Deep breaths, and keep thy reason.

Tom walked to the little sill. Air leaked through the slit, smelling of the rivers. He walked away from it, telling himself to keep vigilant for... what? He stood a while. Then he examined the sill again. If he leant hard against the wall, one hip might fit on the sill. He perched. He slipped. Perched again, slipped again, several times, until he got the angle. His mind felt as bruised as his throbbing mouth.

I was sitting at home. I was —

He glanced down at the straw again, then up at the wall, at some protrusion near the ceiling: a large iron staple.

And what should hang from that?

Oh, my God.

Shaking, he wept.

TO COMFORT YOU, AND BRING YOU JOYFUL NEWS

Navigation for another country, and I've got no map.

Itching from flea bites, back propped against a wall, Tom sat on the floor of his cell. His arrest on Saturday night already felt distant, otherworldly. Now, Monday morning, he felt corroded. Fear had eaten him out. Disgust followed, disgust and loathing: the grime and filth of the cell, the population of crawling animals, some of which Tom had never seen before. Frustration, then boredom, followed. One guard, saying nothing, had brought him a pitcher of diluted wine and a hunk of bread sometime Sunday morning. Nothing else. Two other men down the hall called out from time to time, but when Tom answered them, offering his name and his willingness to listen, one man fell silent, while the other chattered about thirst and threats. Later, between five and six o'clock, that man had screamed. There followed a strange smacking noise, a shatter muted by something moist, and then a body's fall. Tom had moved as far from his cell door as he could, curling into a corner; the second man muttered prayers.

Now, on Monday morning, amazed he'd slept at all, Tom took up the wine and bread as the second man called for a woman.

—Kateryn, oh Kateryn, Kat Kat Kat.

The bread had gone hard; Tom tore off a piece, dipped it in the wine, and ate it. Hunger and thirst roared at him then, and he devoured what remained. Wiping his face with his hands, catching the sound of footsteps, he peered into the darkness.

Torchlight blinded him, then played across his eyelids. Turning his face aside, squinting, Tom forced himself to look. A gaunt man stood there, holding the torch before him, illuminating the prisoner for study. The gaunt man looked maybe a few years younger than Tom; his squared-off beard showed only brown. Dressed in grey and black, he squinted. Tom could not discern the colour of his eyes, only some of the emotion therein: curiosity, intent, shame. Then Tom recognized him: the one who'd asked Geoffrey Morgan if the libel's lettering was not in a scrivener's hand.

—Wait, wait, I would speak with you!

The gaunt man's footsteps thinned out as he descended the stairs.

Christ, can I get no answer in here?

Tom kicked more straw to the far corner and urinated. Thirsty still, he leant his face against the bars of the cell door and peered down the dark corridor. One ensconced torch burned, dim and low, only worsening the dark surrounding it. Tom sighed, walked round the tiny cell a hundred times clockwise, then a hundred times widdershins.

He'd done this six times on Sunday.

Torches flickered; water dripped.

Other footsteps: approaching guards. The man who'd prayed and called on Kateryn now spoke to the guards, begging for something to drink. The craven desperation in his voice made Tom sneer, and he promised himself never to sound like that. The guards, each wearing a dagger and carrying a spear, ignored the man and instead worked on Tom's door.

Tom's voice snapped with command. —Where is your keeper? I would speak with him.

Both guards smirked, and the taller one answered. —We be not the ones kept. And thou dost need to take care with thy tone.

—What o'clock is it? Who was the man looking on me earlier? I speak to the pair of ye. Say: who was the man looking in on me earlier?

The shorter guard jiggled the key in the lock, frowning. —Mangy bastard.

The lock released. Tom stepped toward the corridor, but the taller guard lowered his spear. —When told.

—When told?

—Aye. Come out, now.

Tom felt his jaw tighten. —Who looked in on me?

—No one. We two be the first on the floor this morning.

—Some dream, then?

—Thou'lt not dream much in here.

Glancing about for some place to run, knowing he'd not find one, Tom walked behind the shorter guard while the taller guard walked behind him. Tom had written scenes with abductions, ransoms, imprisonments, and he'd shown characters fearing and desiring tortures. The worst always happened offstage.

I'm offstage.

He studied the walls and stairs, the sounds and smells, tucking images away for later use; he'd never seen the inside of a prison before. He thought again of Kit giving only scant details on his fortnight in Newgate, his muttered advice to heed words and threats from guards, and to be most careful giving one's real name to other prisoners. This reluctance to tell a story, this verbal restraint, Tom now recognized, had been quite out of character for Kit. At the time, hungry for details, for emotional connection, Tom had pressed Kit to speak more of it. Kit had sliced his hand across the air, ending the conversation: *Oh, this is tedious. Tom, shut it. Just stop thy mouth.* Then Kit had kissed him, in some sort of apology: *Christ's love, my sweet scold, thou know'st not hilt from blade.*

Tom and his guards descended a floor, turned corners, and passed through corridors a bonfire would fail to brighten, until they discovered a little office-chamber. A torch burnt on each of the four walls, and daylight shone through a greasy window. The stocky keeper, arms crossed, fists behind his biceps, leant beneath the window, watching Tom's entrance, while the gaunt man who'd looked at Tom earlier sat at the desk, studying two sets of notes between a pitcher and cups, and an inkwell.

Tom admired the staging.

He stepped towards the chair before the desk, to face the gaunt man, but the guards grabbed hold of his arms. The gaunt man, not looking up from his notes, pointed to the chair, and the guards walked Tom to it.

Jaw clenched, Tom sat down. Then he noticed another object on the desk: the oxblood Cicero.

John Deyos ordered the taller guard to stay outside the door and the shorter one to another task, and then turned to the gaunt man. —All set, Mr. Pindar?

Tom almost smirked. *Pindar's odes?*

Pouring dark wine into a wooden cup, Izaak nodded. —My thanks.

John clinked and jingled out, locking the door behind him. Izaak offered Tom the wooden cup. Tom took it, and he sipped; the wine burned the cuts in his mouth. The cup leaked.

Calming, Tom finished the wine and placed the cup on the desk. —There: 'tis my book. 'Twas stolen from me.

Izaak picked the book up, passed it to Tom. His voice sounded gentle. —Thine?

Tom opened it and pointed to the title page, to the message inscribed there with a date, though no name. The message read *With love.* —Aye, 'tis mine.

Izaak took the book back and placed it on the floor behind his desk. Then he balanced the tip of his quill over the inkwell. —My task is to examine thee on the charge of writing and posting the Dutch Church Libel.

—Then where were you yesterday as I waited here?

—Break my Sabbath for the likes of thee?

Tom stared at him.

—I keep mine own schedule, Kyd. If that doth inconvenience thee, then look to thy guilt.

—I am the wrong man. And I wish to make several complaints about the manner of mine arrest. I was undeserved bound, then gagged like some scolding woman. I offered only compliance and yet received a rough —

—Th'art facing dire trouble, and thou'lt whinge and mewl about a few shoves? The possible charges here: resisting arrest, inciting riot and terror, sedition. Should a refugee die over this libel, some woman with child perhaps, some small boy still speaking French, thou may yet be charged with murder.

—No, I —

—We hang for murder.

—My mouth —

—Her Majesty's officers of the law make no arrests and lay no charges without good reason, for doing so is a waste of money and time. Better to waste priceless saffron. Now, thou'lt tell me thou art the wrong man. The clerk, Geoffrey Morgan —

—He knows me!

—Yet he'll not speak for thee. Why is that?

Tom shook his head. —I know nothing here.

—He hath prepared these notes for my review. Thomas Kyd, occupation: scrivener?

Tom found he was sitting on the edge of his chair and leaning forward. He shifted himself back and squared his shoulders. —Aye.

—The order was to arrest one Thomas Kyd, scrivener and playwright. Sounds like the right man to me. Thy title: scrivener, yet thy name decorates no ledger of membership of the Worshipful Company of Scriveners?

—I never joined. 'Tis a formality. I've tutored. I write, too, poems and plays. Pamphlets.

Izaak poured some wine for himself. —Stories of violence, blood, and murder, like thy plays, Hamlet and Hieronimo?

—Mr. Pindar —

—Examiner Pindar.

—*Examiner* Pindar, because I write of bloodshed means not I am capable of it.

—May we at least agree on the truth that thou didst write them?

—Well, aye. Why would I deny writing my pamphlets and plays?

Izaak sipped more wine. —Thou'st just told me thou art a scrivener yet not of the Worshipful Company. How is it thou mayest take a scrivener's work without the blessings and dues of the Worshipful Company?

—'Tis a formality, I say. My father is a former warden. He will vouch for me.

—Aye, Frank Kyd, known and respected throughout London as a good and lawful man: shall we spare him, and thy good mother, the shame of their only son's arrest, for the moment?

Tom nodded. *How know you all this of me?*

—Kyd, who else might confirm thy claims?

Tom gave the names of playwrights, actors, repeat customers, and Edward Blount. Izaak took careful notes. Tom read the list upside-down, and he felt ill.

Izaak counted the names. —Thirteen. How fortunate thou art, to draw on the favour of so many men. None else?

You would have me squawk the name Christopher Marlowe. Why?

—Kyd?

—Chief Constable Absalom Reynolds.

—The man who arrested thee?

—Aye, he was there, but —

Shaking this head, as if disappointed, Izaak drew his finger down the right hand margin of his copy of the libel. —*Our poor artificers do starve and die* — artificers being you playwrights — *for that they cannot now be set on work*. 'Tis troublesome for thee, the playhouses being closed some of last year for plague, and now again this season? Aye, by the lord mayor's orders. Didst thou hear not? Now, of playwrights: know'st thou the one Christopher Marlowe?

—We shared rooms.

—The libel mentions his plays. Aye, *Tamburlaine*. Good show, *Tamburlaine*. I always enjoy it.

'Tis chatter to madden. —Part one, or part two? Together that mess runs near four hours long.

Izaak made a note. —When didst thou last sell a new play, Kyd?

Tom snorted.

—I see. How sweet his company, then, that thou'lt share a room with an upstart competitor.

—'Tis not so.

—Not sweet company?

—No, I mean —

—May I not march to these thirteen men, many more besides, and ask them: is Marlowe troublesome? When drinking, is he not outrageous? And shall they not all agree?

Tom sighed. —Likely.

—So, a troublesome upstart competitor whom thou dost hate, understandably.

—What? No, I love him.

—Then why didst thou foul him with that libel?

—I did no such thing. I would die for him.

I wonder. —Thou'st love him?

—Aye, we —

—In what manner?

Ah. —In the manner of Christian friendship.

—The sodomy laws, winked at as they are, still carry penalty of death.

Tom inclined his head.

—A copy of that libel was found in thy book of Cicero, the same book thou didst identify as thine before I asked. Explain to me how a poem riddled with sly hints of thy bedfellow came to paper, and then the door of the Dutch Church, and a copy of it in thy cherished book.

My bedfellow, and my cherished book. Tom closed his eyes, knowing he looked guilty. The examiner had laid his snares, and that with no great subtlety. *I should just cut out my heart and offer it now and thereby save us both much time.* —The book was stolen from me, I say. In April, I found a man in my rooms —

—The book was stolen?

—Aye!

—Yet found in thy bedchamber, holding a copy of the libel? We talk in circles.

Tom's deep voice crumbled. —What is it you want?

After a moment, Izaak leaned forward. —Confirmation.

The pocked iron of the staple scraped the backs of the fingers on Tom's left hand. He stood on a bench maybe half a yard high, and John Deyos, stretching, up on his toes, facing Tom, looped a short length of chain over the staple. The chain ended in eye-shaped cuffs; John locked one of these on Tom's left wrist.

—Keeper, please.

John reached across Tom's face. —Right hand up. And done. Keys thudded and clinked as John jumped down off the bench. He counted to three, and he and the guard yanked the bench out from beneath Tom's feet.

The short fall wrenched Tom's shoulders and tore open the skin of his wrists.

Inches —

Sidestepping the bench, John looked him over. —I advise thee to give careful thought to thy speech, and to thy truth. Look to the libel.

Tom wiggled his fingers; the motion shot pain from his hands to his waist.

—Aye, 'tis real. Thou'lt play the tapestry until something snaps: sinew, thought, either one. I shall know when. Thou mayest try yapping to God, as most men do, but know that Our Father which art in Heaven touches no keys in this life. And know that I can read thee. Emotions tread thy face like grey actors on some rotten stage, right familiar and dull. Now, thou'dst tell thyself the worst of thy pain is done, that initial drop, and that 'tis not so bad, hanging here.

The guard gave Tom a little shove, set him swinging.

John clicked his tongue at this and caught Tom's legs, held him still. Muttering of pacing and escalation, he sent the guard on to other duties. Then he looked up at Tom again. —'Tis almost sweet, the way a man believes the fall itself to be the very worst part. What galls is time, and the weight of thy truth. I'd guess thine to be, what, taller man like thee, twelve, twelve and a half stone?

—Blood of Christ. Please. Let me down.

John cupped Tom's purse in his palm, balanced it there, weighed it. —Thou'st bribe me to go against my orders?

Tom nodded, refusing to cry out at the pain this caused in his shoulders and neck.

John let go the empty purse. —Thou'st not got the grace.

I WILL REQUITE IT WHEN I COME TO AGE

—*Why?*

Turning away from the library window, and from Walsingham, Kit leaned on the closer couch. His eyes burned. *What woe is this, Clever Kitten: tears like a thwarted child's?* The intensity — worse, the speed — of his emotions frightened him. His old self, tough and precise, seemed lost.

Is't Flushing? Still?

He took a breath. —Why may I not ride to Canterbury, Walls?

Walsingham drew hard on his pipe. Audrey had returned to London; Kit irritated him more each day; tobacco calmed him. —Because thou art *frail*. Dozing at the dinner table is not a reliable sign of robust good health.

—I slept from boredom. Salt cod is a most tedious dish.

—Th'art no Erasmus; thou'lt get no dispensation to avoid it.

—'Tis only twice a week by law for fish days. Thou'dst command it every meal?

—As an antidote to chardequince. I indulge thee as 'tis. Thou dost go armed with thy dagger when no other servant —

—Servant?

—What else, then? I — thy hand. Whence those cuts?

—Sharpening quills.

Walsingham smiled. —Aye, the penknife, thy bitter enemy. How often dressed I quills for thee at Cambridge? Easier days, believing an examination or enchiridion to be —

—Oh, for Christ's love. Walls, th'art hearing me not. 'Tis the fifteenth of *May*. Surely —

—Sayeth he, coughing.

—'Tis thy foul tobacco.

—Marlowe, th'art not well.

—*Not well* be fucked.

Walsingham patted Kit on the back. —A mature and considered response.

Is't sickness, my prison? Kit blew smoke away from his friend. —I must lean on thee further.

—I'd grant thee whatever I've the power to grant. Thou know'st that.

—As I cannot ride, I need to send a letter.

—Give thy letter to Charing. He deals with the messengers.

—No.

Walsingham sighed. —Is there some quarrel between ye?

—I caught him at desk, reading my papers.

—Oh. Well. 'Tis disagreeable.

—Let *disagreeable* argue with the back of my hand.

—A bit much?

—At my desk, I say, opening drawers and rooting about.

—'Tis out of character for him.

Kit snorted. —'Tis no such thing, Walls. He is sly. I returned the favour.

—What? Didst thou sneak about my house and enter another man's room?

—Listen to me: he sketches. Bodies. Bodies stretched taut. Never faces.

—He is a surgeon, a student of anatomy.

—Walls, just — wilt thou pay the messenger for me?

—Aye, of course

Kit retrieved the sealed letter to Manna from within his doublet and gave it over. —I promised Gideon lessons outside this afternoon. We shall be out in the meadow and the woods.

—Aye, 'tis too long between fine days. Keep clear of the marsh, for 'tis very treacherous after a few rains. Dan Roe's own father drowned there. See thee at supper.

—Not if 'tis fish again.

They both laughed.

Out in the hallway, Kit remembered he still carried the pipe; he darted back to the library to return it.

Walsingham slid his thumbs beneath the sealed flap of Kit's letter.

Kit ran at him, feinted on his left, then snatched back the letter on his right.

—What — Marlowe, art thou four years old?

—By what right would'st thou read my correspondence?

—By the right of the one who oversees thy convalescence, and the right of the master of this house who pays the messenger. Besides, what hast thou got to hide from me?

—Walls!

—Give me the letter.

—Not until thou'st promise to leave the seal. A thumb-print, thou'lt notice; I stole not thy signet.

—Dear God above, I — to whom would'st thou write?

—My *sister*. In Canterbury. Forget the letter. I shall pay thee for the wax I used. Weigh what's left and send me a reckoning.

—Just give me the letter. I shall —

Kit tossed his pipe onto Walsingham's desk. —Will that be all, your honour? May I be dismissed?

—How is it thou'st make *your honour* sound so much the insult?

Descending the servants' stairs, noticing the low ceiling, the narrow way, telling himself when next he argued with Walls to use the main stairs instead and so annoy him further, Kit shouted for Gideon. The boy appeared — like a summoned ghost, Kit told himself, smiling — happy to leave behind one or another dull kitchen task, and Kit announced they'd take afternoon lessons outside this fine spring day. In the kitchen, Kit asked Dan to gather pupil and tutor some bread and cheese. A growth spurt had seized Gideon, and he ate whenever and whatever he could, leaving nothing on his plate. Fair down covered his upper lip and jaws now, coming in overnight it seemed, and this morning he wore a much-darned shirt belonging to Dan, sloppy and loose but at least long enough in the sleeves. Kit smiled again. Then sighed. The parish priest, on Kit's suggestion, now had Gideon singing on Sundays for the congregation, and everyone loved to hear him. None knew the boy's age. *How much longer until the wobble and the crack? Four years? One? 'Tis what makes the singing so beautiful, the knowledge that the voice cannot last. Must I do this? Prepare him for intelligence work, teach him sneaking and lies? Can he not just keep singing?* As Dan and Gideon busied themselves with the food, Gideon asking once more permission to take the turnspit dog with him, Dan once more saying no, Kit knelt at the hearth and flicked his letter to Manna onto the fire. Flame quickened; wax melted; paper charred — the letter surrendered. Neither Gideon nor Dan saw it.

Tutor and pupil wandered the grounds for about an hour, Kit demanding recitation from this lesson or that, Gideon chattering questions about birds and weather and constellations. As they neared the woods, Kit noticed a little shelter of shadows near a diseased oak. *A man might hide there, la, and so watch the estate. A man, or Nick Charing.*

Nick emerged from the shadows of the oak and gave Kit a look of humble sorrow.

Kit passed his student the last of the cheese, glancing up at the sky. Clouds had thickened, bringing mist. —Gideon, we shall study botany. Run ahead, and find me posies, and some strawberry blossoms. Quick, now, before rain soaks it all.

Gideon bowed and obeyed.

Kit noticed deceit in Gideon's eyes, a brief glitter he'd seen before. Seen when Nick Charing came near.

Kit turned to the surgeon. —What dost thou want? Hey?

—I would make good for the regrettable business at your desk and do you a service.

—Thy service be fucked.

—I shall be visiting family in London and so have permission to leave the estate.

Kit considered that. —Walk with me? And use *thou*.

They strolled a few moments, Nick glancing at Kit sidelong. —I should trim thy beard again.

—Make me presentable?

—We shall hardly recognize thee.

Kit sat down on a dryer patch of ground and gestured to Nick to sit next to him. —Thou mayest get leave. Very good. But why should I trust thee?

—Because I am ashamed.

Kit moved a little closer to him.

Nick kept still.

—Thy fee, Charing?

—No fee. 'Tis a simple favour, and that atop another proposition that may please thee. If th'art so lonely as I.

Kit made his voice gentle, even kind. —Is that it?

Blushing, Nick looked to the ground.

Kit knelt behind Nick and laid his chin on Nick's shoulder.

—Thy beard tickles my face

Kit stroked Nick's hair. —What gave it away?

—I...

—Give thy proposition, then. I may be tempted.

—A master who shall respond with kindness, not abuse, and who shall pay thee well and on time.

—Ah, but I am choosy, and I must know: who?

—I hesitate to name so great a man.

—And this great man's work?

Nick closed his eyes, and the tense muscles in his neck relaxed as Kit kissed him there. —The same what as thou dost for stingy foxes. And, in the end, still for the Queen. God, thy fingers... 'Tis not a matter of conscience but comfort. He is most highly placed and hath what yet even the Young Fox sometimes lacks: Her Majesty's ear, though thou'lt need not nibble hers. Shall I ride to London and tell him thou'st agreed? And deliver thy letter?

Kit wrapped his arms around Nick, kissed his cheek. —I'll let a crocodile suck me first.

Nick lunged, got nowhere, and Kit threw all his weight onto Nick's back, forcing him to the ground. Face in a puddle, Nick thrashed until Kit hauled him by the hair. —Thy great man: Essex? Tell me!

—Aye!

—Then — *Christ* —

A coughing fit.

Nick fought Kit off and shoved him into some mud. Breathing hard, wiping puddle-water from his face, he got to his feet. —Goat! How is it thou'st not yet come by self-loathing to suicide?

Kit spat phlegm. —A longing for hallowed ground.

Then he dodged Nick's foot, grabbing it and so making Nick stumble and fall.

—Nick, Nick, Nick, do get some practice in. A winded man already down can best thee so easy?

—I've already let it be known I've witnessed thee using Gideon.

—Bay and bark. Gideon will deny it, for thou'st witnessed only thine own desires made shadows in thine eyes. Aye, in thine eyes: I see it. I *see* it. Which boy's body hast thou sketched, la, sketched all contorted? Tell thy masters this: I am no man's toy. Now be done with speech to me. Away.

Nick looked from Kit to the puddle and back to Kit again. —Thou…Thine arse is planted in the mud, and thou dost hug thine own ribs for fear they'll crack anew, and thou'lt dare to command me?

—Oh, I dare.

—I say this whole tiresome mess be fucked.

—I did try, Nick.

—God almighty!

Kit blew him a kiss.

Nick strode off.

Wincing, panting, Kit stood up and watched Nick head back to the house. Then he turned to face the meadow and called for Gideon. His voice failed; tall grasses waved. He took a deep breath, coughed, cursed, called again. Some distance off, a head poked above the grass. Kit beckoned, and Gideon ran to him, carrying a sturdy twig. As Gideon got closer, Kit noticed a caterpillar clinging to the wood.

—My thanks for being so quick, Gideon. 'Tis a fine caterpillar.

—Aye, all spiked and green and fat. He twists and winds himself around sharpness on the twig. Gall-bitter if I kill him, think you?

—I do, so no killing.

—But —

Kit swatted Gideon upside the head. —Mother-wit. Gideon, think: what need hast thou for killing a caterpillar? Leave him be, la.

Gideon knelt, placing the twig on the ground.

—Very good. Now attend. Hast thou seen Mr. Charing speak with any visitors? Aye, 'tis writ plain across thy face. Wait, come here. I'll not hurt thee, but mark: deceive me not.

Gideon looked at the mud on his new shoes. He spoke in French. —The stranger swore he'd cut out my tongue if I spoke of him.

Sweet Christ Jesus. —He'd not dare harm the finest voice

in Kent. Why, who should sing against the darkness then?

—He said my singing burnt his ears.

—The poxy whoreson. The tone-deaf hairy little philistine. Describe him.

—I never meant to hear him and the surgeon. The fog, fog that day... He grabbed me —

Kit took Gideon by the shoulders. —Look at me when I speak to thee. Now. Describe him.

—Seams in both cheeks. A limping cripple who needs a crutch. His scabbard: nailheads.

Kit said nothing.

—Doth that please you? The cripple said you'd make me your catamite if I displeased you.

—Pardon me?

Gideon gave a sickly smile. —I played the catamite in London. When first I came from the Low Countries, with my brother. Our mother was English. She brought us here. She died. We worked the sleuths, the baited animals. We cleaned the dung. One night my brother did not come back to me, and the weather changed, winter coming, and the sleuths closing down, and I got so hungry. I ate from the gutter. Then the man from one of the stews told me to come in from the rain, and he fed me. I worked it back. One night, this tall man with a long beard and very fine clothes, and a new hat, arrived like a king, like a king. He said he'd come only to hear the master repent for allowing men to use me. The kiss of a boy, he said, poisons like the bite of a spider, and my venomous tongue rotted souls. I knew then he wanted to buy me. Longbeard took me home, showed me to his friends, and they used me. I sang to distract myself. Why? Why is it they keep picking me out? How is it they know this of me? A scent? Is't something of my face?

When Kit answered, his voice sounded small. —Thine eyes.

—My eyes?

—Has it happened here? At Scadbury?

—No.

Thank Christ. —The cripple lied to thee; I shall never hurt thee like that. English now. Hast thou found my blossoms?

—Wait here.

Gideon ran off before Kit could remind him of protocol, of how a pupil must not presume to command his tutor. Kit knelt where Gideon had released the caterpillar; the creature still clung to the twig. *Nailheads stud the scabbard: Robin Poley. How art thou tangled up with Essex? And how hast thou entangled me? Revenge for the list — no, never that simple, not with thee. 'Tis more than...*

Kit recalled Robin's lessons in espionage, his harsh laugh, his fond names — *Oh, my Christopherus, mine own little ferret* — his rescues — *Hast not thou not one grain, one fleck, of sense* — and his strange warning once, after too much wine. *Concern thyself with the task, and not the morality of the task. 'Tis beyond thee, the morality of it all, for th'art one pawn. Be ready to kill for thy task. I pray thou'lt never come to that. And be ready die for it. I pray thou'lt duck that, too.*

Kit flinched at Gideon's footfall: so close.

Chest heaving, Gideon held out folded paper. —From Mr. Charing's room, next to mine. Here, this name, when I sound it out, Mar-lo: 'tis yours.

—How much dost thou see, la?

—'Tis tricksy, getting into his room. Both a chambermaid and the laundress —

—So each woman keeps a rival's constant watch on the door? A houseful of spies. Ah, country life.

Keeping silent, Kit read the letter.

Fucked.

I need help. I need Sir Robert.

—Mr. Marlowe, are you unwell?

He tucked the letter into a slit he'd cut inside his doublet.

—Gideon, I...I am sorry. I must taint thee. Lie.

—Could I not just kneel?

—What? No! Not *lie* that way. Oh, sweet Christ Jesus. Listen. Deception, la, tell a lie. Thou canst tell a lie for me?

—Oh! Ten lies. Plague carried off the cook today, sir.

Kit took Gideon by the shoulders and shook him. —Too happy. Lies need fear.

—You're hurting me.

—Didst thou see me after we left the house for a walk? Th'art a nest of deceit, boy: lie.

—I know not where Mr. Marlowe is.

Kit shook him again. —Lie!

—He sent me for blossoms, a botany lesson. I never saw him after that. I know not where he is!

Kit brushed away Gideon's tears with the backs of his fingers. —Shall I call thee mine own little ferret? Th'art born to the trade. Now go find me those damned blossoms. Go, I say!

Gideon ran into the meadow.

—And stay away from the marsh!

Gideon turned and waved, acknowledging the warning.

Kit patted his dagger. Face calm, heart pounding, purse empty, he strolled toward the stable.

FAIR COPY: SO SOON HE PROFITS IN DIVINITY

House of John Marlowe, Master Cobbler, Canterbury,
being from Mary Marlowe and
addressed to Christopher Marlowe, at Scadbury.

My brother: or, shall I call thee my Little Troublesome One? I should call thee worse to thy face, if thou didst dare show it me. Lacking thy company, I came to miss it until thine absence numbed my heart. I remain where I began: our parents' firstborn, caring now for them as they once cared for me, and thee, and the others.

Two pilgrims came to Canterbury, strangers, lost in the quiet streets: Ingram Frizer and Richard Baines. Pieter Duchemin, the Huguenot, visited me first, coming with a warning, he said, for he'd recognized the one Baines who was asking for the house of the cobbler Marlowe, had seen him in Flushing and thought him dangerous. Easier to carry flame in my bare hands than to know what to do with such a warning.

Baines and Frizer sought thee. 'Twas clear they sought thee for no conversation, as they claimed, but to hurt and press thee; I know not why, and I hope I never learn, for fear they will return to press thee further by pressing us.

It happened like a roof falling in. Our nephew, Ned, whom thou'st not met, and who is just learning to walk

(he holdeth my skirts), was visiting Mother and Father and
me, when Baines and Frizer thieved entry and presence:
no knock on the door. The one Baines assured us he was
once thy very good friend. This brute Frizer did take little
Ned and pick him up and tickle him till he screamed, then
pretending he would throw the boy against the ceiling.
He instead placed little Ned on the table. The one Baines
explained th'art gone criminal, counterfeiting, and Mother,
in the shame and fear of it, though disbelieving in her
habitual desperation to love and welcome thee, hid in the
kitchen. I did shout how these men might come no further,
whereon the one Frizer struck me, and crowed about thee
lying three-quarters dead at the estate called Scadbury, and
whereon the one Baines menaced Father with a dagger.
Frizer did rifle through all my books, first hauling me along
with him by my wrists in his one hand. He sought papers,
Kit, thy papers, but found none, there being none here, and
thou not being a man who saves his papers.

The back of Frizer's hand shadows my face yet, and little
Ned wakes up these past nights screaming, something he's
never done before. Ned's father, our brother, curses thee
anew. Though Father waits with his agreeable anxiousness
to see thee, and hath made thee a very fine pair of summer
shoes, delicate in look, like thee, yet tough for autumn, in,
I think, some faint hope yet of thy wedding day, though he
so waits, and though Mother recites to me the proverb of
the prodigal son, and though I dearly miss thee, my Clever
Kitten, I dread the sight of thy face. Menace follows thee, in
glut and surfeit. I charge thee: if thou dost love and honour
thy parents, return *not* to their home.

And I beg thee, Little Troublesome One: take care.
Write to me.

    Thy loving sister,
    Manna.

MOCK ON, HERE'S THY WARRANT

In his Bridewell office, late on Tuesday afternoon, Izaak read Geoffrey Morgan's notes: *Mon 14 May: Libeller manacled three hours. Confessed to crime. Taken down, left alone.* An odd footfall approached his open door. He looked up.

A man on a crutch stood there.

—Examiner Izaak Pindar?

—Aye. Who and what — oh, thou wast a constable arresting the Dutch Church Libeller.

Robin closed the door and then limped towards Izaak's desk. —I shit better than what makes up a constable.

Izaak squinted at him. —Sit down. What is't, laming thee?

—Stung by a locust of Abaddon. I've got information about your Dutch Church Libeller.

—Say on.

Robin smiled. —'Tis doubted by those who would know, and who take a deep interest in this matter, that Thomas Kyd wrote that libel.

Know? —And who are these men?

—Those who wish to see you advance. England has sore need of good examiners. They also believe your prisoner knows who *did* write the libel. Even if he knows not, he knows.

Izaak wanted to reply *I see.* He saw nothing.

He felt a little thrill, though, a sweet tickling of his mind: a chance here, a chance to inflict some misery on a man he despised? The question of authorship twisted and disappeared, some little current in a river. —These knowledgeable men: would they interfere with justice?

—God save me, no. No. They would only ease the path. And they would recognize your hard work in this matter, for 'tis no pleasant task, examining a man.

—Thomas Kyd knows who wrote it?

—He knows. The question is: how shall you draw him to speak of it?

Sighing, Izaak sat back in his chair, shut his eyes, and pinched the bridge of his nose.

—Examiner Pindar, 'tis no wound on your conscience. You interrogated the prisoner on good faith. You trusted in having the right man. Instead, you've got the next-best to the right man, and through him, you shall carry out justice.

Something clinked. Izaak opened his eyes: a purse on the desk.

—To soothe your troubled mind.

—My mind —

—Count it.

Izaak did so: enough to keep him in food and lodgings for a year, beyond what Sir Robert paid him. —My duty here is to bring the libeller to justice.

My duty is to learn the art of interrogation for greater purpose. These squabbles touch me not.

All those candles Marlowe had, burning bright —

Sodomites. Kyd and Marlowe. 'Tis only God's righteous punishment I mete out.

Robin watched Izaak hook the purse onto his belt.

Then Izaak shifted his weight on his chair. —The libel sounds nothing like him.

—Not even a little?

—'Tis written to ensnare. My last suspicion for the author was Marlowe himself. But now I must ask again. Per Tamburlaine? Can it be so easy?

So delicious?

Robin nodded.

—I always expected Marlowe would collide with early death, perhaps enrage some powerful man, but this squalid piece of terror? Not even that arrogant little —

—So you know him, then.

—Aye, Cambridge. I've not seen him for years.

—I'm a university man myself.

—Thou?

—A sizar, serving meals and making beds to pay my way. Writing bad poetry in secret. Before your time.

Digressions irritated Izaak; he ignored this one. —To the libel: Thomas Kyd hath confessed to it.

—Already? And you would say my ideas are too easy. Take you pride in your work, Examiner? Too much?

Men who would know. Men of power, then. —I should go at him again?

—Aye, why not? 'Tis raining, after all.

—I've already sent for him, for questioning.

Leaning much of his weight on his crutch, Robin stood up. —I shall see you anon.

As Robin left, Izaak recognized that his inferior had petitioned no favour but given commands.

♣

Guards escorting him down a corridor — dragging him, his body too pained for steady walking — Tom squinted and peered. The sound of a crutch thinned out; the dark corridor yielded only the tease of light leaking from Examiner Pindar's office.

Izaak dismissed the guards and told Tom to stand before the desk. He watched Tom's progress from the door: a careful picking, each step planned yet clumsy and rough, some drunkard's navigation.

Tom looked his examiner in the eye.

Izaak didn't bother hiding his surprise. —Defiance?

Tom said nothing.

—Sit down.

Stiff, slow, Tom lowered his body into the chair. His swollen hands, numb and tingling, fell into his lap.

—Wine?

—No.

—Thou shalt address me as *Examiner*.

Tom let out a long sigh. —No, Examiner, for I would drop the cup.

—Hast thou eaten or drunk anything this morning?

—How, Examiner?

—To business, then. Yesterday, thou didst confess to writing the Dutch Church Libel. How didst thou go unseen?

—When, Examiner?

—When thou didst post the libel. For 'tis thy work, and thou didst freely confess.

—I —

—Rain fell when thou didst post the libel?

Tom glanced at his hands. —Examiner, there was dew in the morning.

—There is dew every morning. What time marked the bells as thou didst elude the watchful bellman?

—Two.

—Thou'dst swear to it?

—Three?

—I admire thee.

Tom's teeth chattered.

—I admire thee, Thomas Kyd, and I shall confess it, for something of the air in this place liberates my heart and loosens my tongue. Th'art shivering, yet 'tis not cold here. Keeper Deyos calls this pain-chills. He assures me 'tis an excellent sign. I say 'tis a decoy.

Feeling he might fall, Tom grasped the edge of the desk. The tingling in his hands hardened: a burning.

Izaak dipped his quill, and he shook it. Ink spattered Tom's hands and sleeves. —Inkstains: proof that now I write thy days. These sentences may flow like a river in spate, freeing thee, or they may deceive like grass in a marsh, entangling thee — which one, depends on thy words. An hour from now, ask thyself of dreams.

Tom let go the desk, shut his eyes.

—Let us begin with the libel. Thou didst confess the writing and posting of it, yet thou can'st tell me nothing of the night. I know the reason: because thou didst sleep through that night. Thou didst neither write nor post the libel.

Thoughts colliding, words failing, Tom stuttered. —What...? I mean, when? I...Manacled for this?

—Truth now, truth free of press and pain: didst thou write or post the libel?

—But... No.

Izaak's voice grew quiet, and his grey eyes looked sad.
—Then who did?

—Blood of Christ.

—Give up the name.

Tom's voice shook. —I posted it. Please.

Izaak nodded. *'Tis fear for a loved one. He protects another. The cripple spoke true.* —One name, Kyd, and I may look to thy going free.

—Free?

—Like the starling.

Tom took a deep a breath. This pained him. He spoke.

He accused no one, he told himself; he described men he knew. He mentioned several other writers, most of them as implausible as himself. He gave the Christian names of several malcontents, their calls for change coming from the bottom of a cup and no meaningful conviction. And he named the two most despicable members of the Worshipful Company of Scriveners. He told a convoluted story of a feud with Thomas Nashe and how it connected to another dispute with dead Robert Greene, and of a bitter argument with a young and brilliant actor called Gabriel Spenser. Some of his pain receded. His eyelids got heavy, and his stories meandered. Never accusations, just names and anecdotes, information any man who knew Tom Kyd might offer up over a drink.

Names, just not Christopher Marlowe's.

Inkstains: proof that now I write thy days.

Izaak opened the chamber door and passed word for Keeper Deyos; his voice still sounded gentle. Guards hauled Tom out of the chair, and he kept studying his wrists and hands: blood and ink, blood and ink, blood and ink.

A tiny man, head bowed, knees drawn to his chest and tucked beneath his brow, writhed until he pierced the pulpy tip of the tall finger on Tom's left hand. The skin surrendered. The old inkstain split. Crouched and tumbling, eyes clenched shut, the tiny man launched forth.

A grey homunculus.

Three more followed, each different from his fellow: one tinged green, another tending to blue, the third red as a fresh burn. The blue homunculus floated before Tom's eyes, coming into sharper focus through a tear: bald head too large for the fat body. This homunculus unfolded his limbs until he hung, legs dangling and arms outstretched, in crucifixion; he bowed his head.

Tom bowed his, too, but this gesture caused pain to race up his spine and collide with the base of his skull. He threw his head back and swallowed hard, forcing bile back down his throat. The trick — oh, so many tricks to learn — the trick to easing by even the subtlest degree his drawn agony rested on a slick perfection: the pointy fulcrum of stillness. Tom had written about miseries, troubled by the details but delighted by the ease of his words. Like his audience, he relished grim comedy. His character Hieronimo, in rage and despair, cried his last words *First take my tongue, and afterwards my heart*, then bit out his tongue. Playgoers applauded and yelled and hooted their approval. Offstage, actors loved to toss the tongue about, play pranks with the bloodied prop, hiding it, kissing it, dropping it down the backs of shirts.

The grey homunculus hauled out his own little tongue and flung it away; the tongue caught on Tom's right foot.

Five hours, this time.

Hallucinated homunculi continued to burst out of his blue hands, little men and their little plays, a distracting mercy.

He screamed.

Izaak Pindar wavered into his line of sight. —Affirm he wrote it. Thou'lt come down when thou'st affirmed he wrote it.

Bargains with God, bargains with time: Tom counted.

Another thirty seconds, loose another noise.

Not yet.

—Deyos, how long —

—Each man plays out different, Mr. Pindar, as I'm after telling you —

Twenty.

—Tom, thy friends call thee Tom, and thy friends would — thy voice gives thee away, breaking at the top of thy throat like water on a rock. Though thy mind defies, thy soul would confess.

Sixteen.

—Deyos. I've a schedule —

—I cannot control how fast a man unravels. He —

Cold light.

A voice reached Tom: John Deyos. —No swoon frees thee.

Mercy fled, cold light gone: a wooden bench beneath him.

John slapped his face. —Thou'lt wake up, and thou'lt hang up. Oh, where be that guard? Tits on a bull, that one. Morgan, help me here.

—Mr. Deyos, I am no guard. I am the clerk. 'Tis not my job to manacle a prisoner.

—Sobbing mother of Christ, dost thou *see* a guard in here? No! So get thy sorry arse beside mine and help me hoist him up! Thy shoulder under his arm, like that, hold him while I take the wrist. Ah, he's swollen up. Ratchet it back. Jump down. And fret thyself not, clerk, for I alone shall remove the bench. One, two, three. Carry on, Mr. Pindar.

Thirty seconds, just thirty seconds.

—Swoons he again? Can'st thou hear me, Kyd?

Teeth clenched: —I hear you.

—See reason.

Twenty-seven. —Reason?

—From thee I need neither tears nor blood nor broken bones. I need only knowledge. The simplest facts.

Nineteen? Nineteen and hold, eighteen.

—Mercy playeth a role.

Sixteen. —'Tis rich, your mercy.

—I've harrowed the ground, and I know —

Thirteen.

A groan: Geoffrey Morgan. —Mr. Deyos, I beg leave.

—Fie on that. I need thee here.

Ten, nine.

—Tom! For Christ's love, just tell him what he wants!

Kit says Christ's love. Seven.

Geoffrey's eyes so wide: —Just tell him.

Six. Five. Almost. This thirty. Two. One.

A new homunculus shot out the index finger on Tom's right hand, and he cried out. His nose ran. A tiny lull — then all the pain roared back.

Twenty, nineteen.

—Open thine eyes and fix them on me, Kyd, for in thy life now, in what remains of it, I am God's amanuensis.

Seventeen.

—Tell me.

Stop.

—'Tis so simple. 'Tis the sweetest affirmation, and it will free thee.

Stop. Fourteen. I am nothing but the pain he makes me feel. Christ, hear me.

—Hang till thou dost rot, then.

Twelve. —What? Affirm what?

John nodded. —Good man, good man, shed thy stubbornness.

Tom peered at the back of Geoffrey's shirt as the clerk stared through the bars down the corridor. *Six. Five.* —Wrote the libel. Told you.

—Thou didst write it *not*. Thou would'st say whatever I wished to hear, but thou'lt not believe it to be truth.

Thirty. Ha. Hold fast. Twenty-nine.

—Thou'st spun me worthy tales, accusing thy friends of every depravity, some of it twice —

Father, I know nothing of it.

Aye, 'tis a kindness he does thee.

Twenty-two.

—Affirm my suspicions, Kyd. Listen well.

I am nothing but the pain he makes me feel. I am nothing but flesh. Sixteen.

Izaak recited the Dutch Church Libel. Preached it.

Tom lost count.

Nothing but the pain nothing but pain nothing pain.

—Per Tamburlaine! Is this Marlowe's work?

Ten? Nine, eight — no. —Aye! Aye, 'tis Marlowe's. Christ's love, he says Christ's love, Kit wrote it, Tamburlaine. Aye.

A misery beyond the pain took him: shame. Reduced, some mess in a pot boiled too long, not a friend, not a lover, not even a man: pain. Geoffrey eased him onto the straw, and Tom whispered promises and prayers. None noticed, instead talking over the business of concluding this matter: documents to write, reports to give. Geoffrey hugged his ledger to his chest as John held the cell door for Izaak, and they continued their conversation as they walked away.

Hearing their voices, and hearing memories of their voices, Tom sobbed numbers.

Rain beat down, churning up the mud in Paul's Yard as Ed Blount packed up his wares for the day.

—Blount, wait.

—Come back tomorrow, friend. I need my supper.

—Blount, please!

Ed turned around. —Sweet God. Marlowe?

Kit lowered the hood of the cloak he wore — too long, and dragging on the ground: Tom's. —When didst thou last see Tom Kyd?

—Just Saturday. I've heard — hast thou been ill?

Kit reached across the counter and grabbed Ed's forearm. He lowered his voice to a whisper, one difficult to hear over the rain. —Tom's neighbours say he was arrested.

—The scourge of Tamburlaine.

—*Tamburlaine?* Tom —

—'Tis not thy play but a libel. The whole city's upset, what, a week now. Where hast thou *been*?

Kit let go Ed's arm. —I crossed the Thames not one bare hour ago, only farthings to my name and them borrowed from a horse-courser, and I'm running about like a rat set alight. Blount, what fuckery is this? What libel?

—I burnt my copy, after I showed it to Kyd. The author would have us expel and deport those who've come to us from the Low Countries, but he also threatens mayhem and fire — aye, *fire* — while signing himself Tamburlaine. And alluding to thine other plays. Machiavel's there, from thy *Jew of Malta*, and the line not Paris massacre so much blood did spill.

Kit stared at him.

—This could go hard for thee, Marlowe. Thou'st dare far too much, being here at Paul's. I'm surprised thou'st not been seized on sight.

Snorting, Kit pulled up the cloak's hood; it obscured most of his face. —Fortune smiles on me and pours rain.

—The Privy Council proclamation said Bridewell.

—Sweet Christ Jesus! Tom knows not hilt from blade.

—I know.

—Bridewell?

—Marlowe. Marlowe? Marlowe, dost thou hear me? Get free of London.

—Oh, excellent advice.

—And see to that cough.

—My cough?

—I care for thee, and I would see thee treated with mercy.

—Thy mercy be fucked.

—*What?*

—Thou'st got another customer.

Kit busied himself with a pamphlet as Ed turned to look.

Squishing footsteps: a bald man, cloak straining at his shoulders, now blocked Ed's view of what lay beyond his counter.

Ed inclined his head to the man. *No good shall come of this.* —I'm on my way to supper, friend. Will you come back tomorrow?

—Oh, thou'lt help me now. I seek a poet.

Ed almost laughed. —Poets I've got. Shall we start with Seneca? Juvenal? I've some Plutarch here...No, wait: you, you sir, want to confront Cinna.

—Who?

—Cinna the Poet. Julius Caesar's time, corruption, confusion, and alarum. Concerned citizens make a terrible mistake that will damn their souls and beat a man in the street: Cinna.

—No sin. One is for the side of right, or one is against it. And aye, the poet I seek: I want his flesh, not his words.

—And I am a stationer, not a bawd.

The man grabbed Ed's forearm, as Kit had done. —The one Christopher Marlowe? Hey? Aye, I know his name. Lucifer's own little catamite, he is, scourge of God, first with his Tamburlaine and Faustus and his Guise, now saying he'll burn the city down.

—Are you a constable, sir, sent by the city? Have you warrant for this man's arrest?

—I will not stand quiet and aloof while some devil would terrorize us all — threaten *fire* — and I am far from alone. We need no warrant. Now, hast thou seen him?

—Tamburlaine? No, the playhouses are closed.

—Marlowe!

—Oh, him. No.

Elbowing aside a flap of his cloak, the man fingered his long dagger. —How looks he?

—Ill-favoured. Great lumbering redhead, nigh on six foot, tiny green eyes, and a scar on his right cheek.

—Know'st thou where to find him?

—I fear not. He's ghostly, that way.

—Get out from behind thy counter.

Ed did this, and the bulky man stepped in and knelt down. He found no one hiding there. Scowling, he gave Ed and Kit both a good shove and strode off.

Kit put the pamphlet back. He wanted to apologize for his harsh words; his shaking hands distracted him.

Taking up the pamphlet, Ed whispered. —Go. Now.

Catholic prayers cracked the voice of the other man down the hall, hanging in manacles, as Tom, sitting on the floor, his back perched against the wall, watched Geoffrey Morgan set a tray on the bench beneath the staple.

—I can't pay for that.

Geoffrey looked at Tom's twitching hands, the nails and fingers blue and grey. —Food tallies sometimes skew. Clerical errors. How clumsy I am. I even spilled some wine in it. Shall I help thee?

Wondering just how much salt water his body contained, and what to call such a rising sea, Tom flinched as Geoffrey lifted the spoon to his mouth. He took a breath, swallowed the mess: shreds of mutton, mush of parsnip, tang of wine — strong wine, and plenty of it. Tom nodded, hissing at the pain that motion caused, and took another spoonful. Racing thoughts of rage and supplication settled and some ghost of relief brushed him. *Easier if I'd break apart in pieces, easier if tough flesh would surrender before soft mind.*

Easier, too, if he could forget what he'd screamed.

Spoonful.

Spoonful.

Geoffrey murmured something about his pregnant wife, and he picked dirty straw from Tom's hair. Tom sagged to one side, and Geoffrey, ignoring Tom's *No*, telling himself the sound was a moan, eased him down to the floor.

The manacled man beseeched Christ to forgive those who now harmed him, and to forgive Stephen Loman, who had betrayed him.

PLAYED WITH A BOY SO FAIR AND KIND

When I am a man, I shall know which promises to break.

Guilty in the sunrise, Gideon knelt on the floor of his tiny bedchamber and gave himself the answers he sought, for none had come through prayer. Loyalty, protection: lies begat lies, and Gideon wished he could tell a better story. The torment of his lies had chewed up his sleep. Last night, Sir Thomas Walsingham had knelt before him, dark eyes two holes of anger and fear: *Gideon, I need thy truth. Know'st thou where Mr. Marlowe has gone? Know'st thou any reason why he might have left?* Surrendering his proof, his squashed and sweaty leaves and flowers, Gideon recited the story of the botany lesson, of running back and finding no tutor. Later, Gideon's voice wobbled when he sang, and Sir Thomas did not so much excuse him as exile him for it: *To thy room. Stay there until Mr. Roe calls thee in the morning for thy kitchen duties.*

Mr. Roe had not yet called. Gideon heard his snores through the wall.

Through the other wall, however, Gideon heard Mr. Charing's noises of getting dressed.

At Longbeard's house, Gideon had stayed in one room. He'd learned to listen.

Nick, carrying his shoes, padfooted to the kitchen. The turnspit dog snarled at him. Nick grinned at the animal, then glanced about for any stray scraps of food, thinking he'd hold them just out of the imprisoned dog's reach and watch him drool and snap. Nick had done this before, with bits from his own plate. Dan Roe kept too tidy a kitchen, food wrapped and put away, so Nick instead scooped up some ash from the hearth and blew it at the dog's face. Straining to turn away, the dog sneezed, and he set his wheel in motion.

Gideon, his bedchamber door open maybe half an inch, listened. As Mr. Charing left the house and closed the back door behind him, Gideon wondered about the dog's snuffling, the squeaking of his wheel. He counted to twenty-five, giving Mr. Charing time to tug on his shoes, or return for something forgotten, then took the silence as his cue to follow.

He murmured in French to the whimpering dog. Gideon had wanted to name the animal; Dan wouldn't hear of it. *'Tis no pet, that cur. Make him fat and happy, and 'tis thee I shall set to turning that spit.* Gideon fed the dog scraps of fat and flesh whenever he thought Mr. Roe could not see him. Dan knew all about it.

Gideon found a crumbly cheese and pried off a piece. The dog, head down, cringing, accepted the offer, licking Gideon's fingers. Gideon wondered why the dog's eyes looked so rheumy and reminded himself to tell Mr. Roe.

Outside, the rivers babbled, running fast and deep; Sir Thomas and Mr. Roe both kept warning Gideon away from the rivers, and the rising marshes. Even the grounds about the house, waterlogged, seemed to shift.

A horse whinnied — a horse not in the stable but somewhere in the woods. That alone merited investigation. Perhaps Mr. Marlowe had returned, though why would Mr. Charing meet him in the woods? The strange horse whinnied again, and Gideon felt queasy.

The cripple?

He'd not forgotten the man's threats. Confessing some of this to Mr. Marlowe had not eased Gideon's anxiety, and of course now Mr. Marlowe had run off.

'Tis so, then, thought Gideon. *I must go through this life alone.*

Alone. Whenever Mr. Charing caught Gideon alone, he offered pointed reminders of the cripple's threats. Sometimes he stuck out his tongue so that it dangled over his chin. Sometimes he grabbed Gideon's shoulders from behind, as he'd done when dragging Gideon to the cripple.

Gideon had always feared Charing the surgeon. Now he hated him.

And if I follow you, Mr. Charing, and learn something foul, something I can tell Sir Thomas, might I be rid of you?

Nick sank and slipped in the mud as he picked his way towards Robin. Still in saddle, Robin scowled and demanded that Nick help him dismount. Nick did this, relishing how the man staggered and winced.

—God save me: horseback. Every hoofbeat rattled my spine, and I thought my hips would crack. The pain of it eats me alive. Well, where is he? Still abed?

—He's gone.

—*What?*

—He missed supper last night, and his room stayed empty. It seems he took a horse from the stable. Sir Thomas Walsingham is furious.

—I expect he is. And the cook: waxes he wrathful? What of the milkmaid on the neighbouring farm?

—Poley, 'tis serious.

Gideon flinched. *I should not know his name.*

—Aye. More than thou dost know.

Robin smiled as he said that — not a happy smile — and he loosened his crutch from a saddle hook. *Mine own little ferret, wilt thou not keep still? I would explain the libel and the hostage, warn and coax thee, for thou dost love him. 'Tis what will kill thee, in the end: love. God save me.*

—Poley, heard you what I said?

—Why didst thou let him *go?*

—I am not Marlowe's keeper!

Birds chattered warnings — the calls they gave when humans were near. Gideon slowed his breathing.

Robin noticed the bird calls, too, and blamed himself and Nick for them.

Nick spoke in a lower voice. —'Tis worse, yet. I'd waylaid a letter addressed to him, a letter from his sister.

—Aye, alarum from Canterbury. I've got Baines and Frizer to thank for that.

—The letter is gone, too. Poley, I know not what —

Robin struck him: crutch on the upper arm. —Skeres, hast thou not one grain, one *fleck* of sense?

Gideon clenched his jaw. *Skeres? His name is Charing. Names. Baines, Frizer, Poley, Skeres. I should know none of it.*

Nick pointed at Robin now, looking him in the eye. —Someone stole that letter! And I will take no abuse from you or from any other man. Strike me not.

—I'll strike thee, and I'll beat thee to the ground if I must. Thou hadst but one task in this matter —

—A task? 'Twas more than that.

—Shalt thou die of a kiss?

—He...His hands —

—Ah. So 'tis thy limp promise what drove him off.

—What? No! I know not why — that hairy — that *goat* — God almighty, I'd pay him home in an instant. 'Tis all so vile.

Robin smirked. —And 'tis thy work, if I so order it. Besides, he can be quite charming.

—Well, he's charmed his way right off the estate.

Aye, but where? —If this plan frays, Skeres, I may be looking to bribe a hangman, and 'tis thy neck I shall offer first.

—Hangman? Oh, folly.

—One does not disappoint great men.

Silence.

Nick grunted something — acquiescence, perhaps — as Robin crutched towards the tree where Gideon hid.

Clothing rustled, and a urine stream spattered on the ground near Gideon's feet.

Keep still, keep still…

Done, Robin took a breath to say something else, lost his balance and grabbed at the tree, just missing Gideon's face.

Gideon cried out.

The crutch swung, scraping the top of Gideon's head as he started to run. Nick grabbed his right arm and whirled him around. Thrashing, Gideon collided with Robin, who took his other arm and hushed him as one might soothe a fussing infant. Then Gideon knew only that he could not breathe. Something had struck his belly — a rock or a fist — and he fell, eyes clenched, lungs seized.

Laughing, Nick watched Gideon writhe on the ground. Then he kicked him in the back.

—Relent, Skeres, relent. Words and threats suffice. I just want him frightened.

—And see how well frightened worked last time. Get me a length.

As Nick rolled Gideon onto his chest and straddled him, as Gideon struggled not to remember attacks in Longbeard's house, Robin dug in his satchel and passed Nick some rope. Laughing again, Nick ruffled the boy's hair and tied his wrists together. Then he stood up and hauled Gideon to his feet.

Every instinct in Gideon told him to scream. Every lesson from Longbeard's house stifled him. He cried out — a breathy squeak that made him think of mice. He bit Nick on the arm, and Nick yelled in rage. Spooked, a murmur of starlings took flight from the trees. The madness of flapping wings pressed on Gideon's ears, and he hoped someone back at the house could decipher the warning in flight. He hoped Mr. Marlowe had come back.

Robin shook his head at Nick, disgusted. —Th'art noisier than secret fucking.

—The whelp's got sharp teeth. You'd cry out, too, if your heart still pumped blood.

—Slain by thy wit, I die at thy feet. No other nature lovers out for a stroll. Hold him tight. God save me. Now. Gideon.

Robin took a deep breath, let it out, wishing he could calm his hammering pulse.

Panting, Gideon looked at he ground. —Leave me be!

Robin stroked the backs of his fingers over Gideon's cheek, fondled his left ear. —I confess, boy, thou hast surprised me, and I like it not, being surprised. What didst thou hear, mine own little ferret — oh, thou'st been called that before. I see it in thine eyes. I see many things. Now, speak.

Gideon refused.

Robin twisted Gideon's ear, hard. —Speak!

Not a sound.

Robin glanced around again, scowling, as Nick gave Gideon a shake. *Just a child — complicates everything — think think think...*

Stiff, pained, awkward with his crutch, Robin knelt before Gideon and peered into the boy's eyes.

Gideon stared back.

Robin admired this. —Sweet Gideon of the sweet voice, sweet and brave, wilt thou sing for me?

—I... What song would you have?

—I call it *Whither Marlowe?*

Gideon got quite pale. —I know not.

—Boys who lie go to Hell, Gideon, even the pretty ones.

—I've not seen him!

Robin inclined his head, as though acknowledging an opponent's superiority. —'Tis easily true. After all, he is not here to be seen. This very copse suffers a tragic lack of all things Christopher Marlowe, so much so that I must dry mine eyes for the pity of it, and…Ah. 'Twas thee who stole the letter. Thou didst sneak into the surgeon's room. Playing the spy, playing the thief — wait, who taught thee to read?

—Mr. Marlowe.

Robin nodded. *Someone's got plans for this boy.*

Gideon cleared his throat. —Mr. Roe needs me in the kitchen, so you must let me go now.

—I'm hungry. Gideon, would Mr. Roe invite me to break my fast?

—No.

—My favourite thing to eat in the morning is boiled eggs and gingerbread. Thine?

—My arms hurt.

Robin ran his fingers over the studding of his scabbard. Then he drew the dagger: pommel etched with an image of a human ear, hilt worn with subtle valleys for his fingers, blade nine inches long. He pressed the flat of his blade against Gideon's throat. —Warm it for me.

Gideon begged him in French to wait.

Nick laughed at this, but Robin laid his dagger on the ground.

Nick snorted. —Poley, lose you all purpose here?

Ignoring Nick, Robin cradled Gideon's face in his palms and kissed away some of his tears. —Sing: London, or Canterbury?

—What?

—I grow tired, boy. Has Marlowe gone to London, or to Canterbury?

Gideon stared at him. —What? I know not.

Robin studied Gideon's face. *Confusion, shame, and fear, but no deceit. He tells me truth. God save me, it should not have come to this. I —*

Gideon screamed.

Nick crammed his hand over Gideon's mouth — into it.

Biting again, Gideon spied at a bit of sky between branches. *God, why hast Thou made me so small?*

Robin dug once more in his satchel, instinct more than intellect governing him now, and he complained of how a high voice carried. He sounded as though he wished to convince someone.

The trees rustled as Gideon felt the surgeon's hand move away. He spat out the man's blood and the taste of his skin and took in another breath. Mouth pain interrupted: a hard invasion, flat, not flesh. Gideon thrashed his head; Robin fastened the gag.

Ashamed of defeat and fresh tears, Gideon closed his eyes.

Nick grasped Gideon's jaw and tipped up the boy's chin, exposing his throat.

—No!

—Poley, what *else*?

Not a command: a plea. —No. Wait. Let me *think*.

—We've come too far —

—Oh, God save me.

Gideon peeked.

Robin, mouth slack, passed Nick his dagger, then stepped aside. —I will not be stained.

LET HIM COMPLAIN UNTO THE SEE OF HELL

—Her Majesty thanks you, my lords and gentlemen of the Privy Council. This meeting for Wednesday the sixteenth of May is adjourned.

Chairs scraped and rumbled as the privy councillors got to their feet, all of them looking tired, even dazed. Robert stretched his aching back. He'd not gotten to Theobalds to visit his wife and son for weeks, and now he regarded the other men of the council with a quiet contempt of fatigue: *Must I see only these faces, hear these voices?* A four-hour meeting, two of those hours spent on just one of the six agenda items. Izaak Pindar gave a quick report on the arrest and examination of the Dutch Church Libeller, explaining how the accused had changed his confession, now darkening the name of another man, and so Izaak begged more time to discover the truth of this difficult matter. Essex gave Robert a sharp look; Robert kept his face mild; Izaak got his time. The councillors had also discussed the troubling matter of a Cheapside peacock monger, charged with attempted murder after attacking a fellow merchant, this merchant being a Low Countries refugee. The peacock monger complained of this man, a seller of brassware, stealing his customers. The deadly weapon: a flaming sack of straw. The brass merchant's stall had caught fire, and the man himself suffered serious burns. Barest chance and full rain barrels — four of them — contained the flames. Clicking his tongue, Essex asked if London's lord mayor might not be pressed upon to devise a plan for fire in the city. A line of men at the Thames, with buckets?

As the other privy councillors walked away from Robert, reminding him of how the wards would walk away from him at Theobalds, Essex approached him, looking concerned — about fire, perhaps.

—Sir Robert, a moment. And plead not to me your sore head.

—I thank you, my lord of Essex, but my head is fine.

Essex eyed the room, making sure they stood alone. He murmured. —The Dutch Church Libeller doth accuse another man.

Robert had told himself that morning to be prepared for such a remark, to develop a useful and perhaps witty answer. So far: nothing. *This libel. 'Tis no work of Marlowe, yet the defiance doth sound…And Pindar: doth he play me? Watch and wait, watch and wait.* —I wonder, my lord of Essex, if, under the strains of interrogation, the libeller sayeth that which his examiner doth wish to hear, indeed, that which his examiner guideth him to say. Sometimes truth is tardy.

And sometimes, my lord of Essex, men would interfere with the law.

Essex nodded. —How doth your faith?

—Faith in what, my lord?

—The faith one must hold against one's ears so as not to hear one's conscience crack in the night. Faith in gravy, Wee Robbie. Reality with gravy, thou didst say to me: remember now?

—My lord, have you got a point?

—I thought thou wouldst teach me subtlety, not stupidity. The Dutch Church Libeller is one Thomas Kyd, the wretched sodomite who beds with thine agent Marlowe and now accuses him. We know. We know thou wouldst protect thine agent. There is no hiding this.

Robert said nothing.

—And whatever this Thomas Kyd doth say to stop his pain, I doubt very much he wrote that libel. I am nearly certain of it. This means the wrong man screams. The wrong man, Robbie.

Robert stared up at his rival. —Know you the provenance of the libel? The author?

—The libel is but a decoration in this matter.

—If Thomas Kyd is innocent —

—Innocent? 'Tis for the examiner to decide. Dost thou remember the game we played on rainy days at Theobalds, Imagine This?

Robert heard rain trickling down Theobalds' glass and stone, felt the mansion's dampness on his skin.

—Imagine this: the wrong man languishes in Bridewell. Thou dost discover how to staunch the wrong man's wounds and calm his screams: pass the reins. Thy sad frailty of backbone, aye, thou'st never ridden well.

Robert tapped his papers against the dark table. —My lord of Essex, stand you so deluded by passion, self, and greed that you dream I've *not* explained my misgivings about you to Her Majesty?

—Hast thou run and tattled to Mother? That wigged and powdered baggage spies the wet dirt of fresh graves beneath thy nails and blows away thine envied suspicions like this much dust. To whom gives Her Majesty the gifts of money and titles, hey, Acting Secretary? When last deigned she to permit *thee* to kiss her hand? Whom doth she prefer, the crook-backed scrabbling toad who sees plots and treacheries in the shadows round a candle, or the sweet and pretty young nobleman she's fancied, oh, thirteen years now? Lean close, so I may whisper thee the truth that even now she moans to her looking glass. She longs for a gift from me, Robbie: one good bone-rattling fuck.

Robert managed to keep his voice low. —You speak of the Queen of England.

Essex grabbed Robert's shoulders. —Hear me.

—I hear. Though I'd pray for deafness, I hear.

—Give in to me, give over, and all this sad difficulty shall change to memory and vanish like a bright morning's dew. Give me thy networks. Thou mayest continue to filter and organize, act the weir on the river. I dare not dream of plucking thee from the work that best suits that knotted nest of centipedes, writhing, stuck fast and glossy in thy chest, that nest thou wouldst call thine heart. The simple difference is thou'dst act the weir for me. Leave me alone to bury my rivals at court.

—*Bury* them?

—Oh, for God's sake, Robbie, 'tis a metaphor. This is not: time. The Queen is *old*. We must work succession before the horse meets her knacker. 'Tis simple, my request: give me thy men.

—Before you steal them?

Essex inclined his head.

—Or ruin their minds by tormenting those they love?

—Not ruin: persuade.

—My lord of Essex, I thank you for this, your simplicity and honesty in your request. My answer, too, is simple and honest: no.

Essex whispered now. —Just give me this Marlowe. Let him come to me, no interference.

Robert glanced left and right at the ringed hands gripping him. —Give you a man?

Essex took his hands off Robert. —Curious, how we share a Christian name. I am the man thou hast always wanted to be.

He departed, singing one of his own compositions, lyrics tangled in rhetorics of entitlement and spite, with imagery of a melancholy knight explaining how a cold queen would soon repent her harsh ways.

Leaning against the table, considering the pragmatics of Thomas Kyd's Bridewell examination, the results of Kyd's drawn accusations of Christopher Marlowe, Robert heard the earl's song for what it was: a cry of victory.

—Mr. Marlowe. Come in out of the rain.

Kit smiled down at Joan, Tom's niece. Nine years old, Joan resembled Tom and Frank. Kit had no idea if she also took after her mother. Tom's widowed sister had died labouring on another child, come far too early. The infant had perished with her. Kit had never discovered the woman's name; Tom had spoken of her only once.

As Joan chattered, showing off her new poppet, Kit stepped inside and bowed to Tom's parents. Agnes was rubbing her knuckles, the joints swollen and red, the fingers more gnarled and twisted than before. Kit found Agnes Kyd difficult, even abusive, yet he wondered how much the pain in her hands fed the venom in her tongue. Behind her, Frank Kyd, eyes dark from a lack of sleep, smiled at Kit and invited him to sit down.

—And welcome back to London.

Kit had often commented to Tom on Frank's impeccable courtesy, his little shows of thoughtful kindness. Even so, this greeting startled Kit. —I ... I thank you, sir.

—I'm hoping thou'st come to us with news of Tom.

—Mr. Kyd, I am sorry. I was hoping you would have news for me.

Agnes scowled. —Frank, I said to thee Sunday when we saw him not, there must be trouble.

Kit nodded, recalling how Tom joined his parents for church most Sundays. He recalled, too, how he'd refused to accompany Tom that last Sunday before he left for Flushing.

Tom, just this once, let us stay home, la. Just us.

Wouldst thou avoid church?

No, thy mother. The woman hates me.

She hates what she thinks thou'st done to me.

Pardon me?

Kit, please —

Tom, I love thee. I'd go to Hell for thee. And I do: every Sunday afternoon.

I will not have thee speak ill of my mother!

Oh, but she may speak ill to me?

Agnes glared at Kit. —Trouble. I thought Tom had been late, perhaps standing in the back, some shameful dog too worried then to show his face for dinner. Then his absence inspired in me suspicions. I prayed 'twas not thee, sitting in dark corners like the happy spider, eating his bread, corrupting his heart and mind. And look, here thou art.

Frank rolled his eyes. —Still thy tongue, woman. Marlowe, I apologize for her. He's arrested, aye. What else know'st thou?

—On Saturday the twelfth, as I gather. I was not here in London. This grieves me, sir: he's in Bridewell.

Frank whispered it. —Bridewell?

—Aye. For the Dutch Church Libel.

Agnes's voice deepened, became commanding, much as Tom's did when he got angry. —Oh, my God. That... The libel? That piece of fire and fear? Thy face, Marlowe, thy guilty face: tell me how thou art to blame.

Kit's voice sounded small. —Pardon me?

Agnes, Frank, and Joan stared at him.

Kit bowed his head.

Agnes said something about Tamburlaine and knowing all along, how could Frank be so trusting, while Frank tried to hush her, and Joan asked if bad men would start fires. Then Agnes pointed at Kit, her finger crooked and bent. —Marlowe, if I could pluck thee out of time, on the day thou didst first inflict thyself upon my son, tie thee to a rock, and then heave that rock off London Bridge, this I would do, in great joy.

—Agnes!

—Mistress Kyd —

—Bridewell! When that libel mentions *thy* filthy work —

—Mistress Kyd —

—Hast thou done *nothing* for him?

Kit looked up, not caring she'd see his tears. —Mistress Kyd, while you blame me and, with some reason, despise me, you must allow, or at least guess, that Tom's arrest galls and frightens me as much as it does you.

—*I* love him.

—As do I.

Frank tugged on his cloak. —I never thought... All the clerks and scriveners I know, and I never thought to check at Bridewell. I must go register a mercy deposit. Marlowe, wilt thou come with me?

—I would, sir, but I've not been paid. I expect it soon.

Agnes took up cutlery from the table. —Frank, didst thou not tell me Geoffrey Morgan now clerks at Bridewell?

—What of it?

—I remember Geoffrey quite well. He studied at Merchant Taylors' with Tom, Marlowe. Edmund Spenser was a student there, too. 'Tis a fine school, even if it led not to a university scholarship, and I will have thee know Geoffrey Morgan's become a fine man. A moderate man. Married, and a father, making whatever sacrifice he must to look after his wife and children. They're expecting another child this summer. Why was that not good enough for Tom? No, answer me not. Thou'lt keep me rooted half the day, justifying nonsense with thy tricked-out parodies of beauty. 'Tis all trash, even what Tom writes, two steps above bear-baiting, aye, ash and dung. He hath wasted his days, bitten his thumb at every chance, playing the strumpet to the monsters in us all, those monsters better left ignored, thereby offending both man and God. Now fortune turns on him.

—Mistress Kyd, I beg you. 'Tis not just, neither you, nor the Bridewell charge. 'Tis, at best, obscene.

—*Obscene* cowers before me in fine clothes, his mouth creaking and rattling like a loose gate in a storm, deluding himself about love!

Joan ran from the room.

—Mr. Kyd, I shall take my leave.

—I'll walk with thee.

—Frank, thou shalt do no such thing.

Agnes shook as she said that.

—Agnes, if I make no deposit, then God alone knows what he might get to eat.

—Thou shalt not go! What if th'art seen? The shame of it —

She threw cutlery to the floor.

—The shame of it, Frank!

Kit shut the door behind him, as Frank took Agnes in his arms and let her cry.

At Cecil House, by candlelight, Robert squinted at the spray of borage on the wall behind his desk. He'd moved the borage from his office at Westminster; the dried leaves looked no better here. Then he glanced at a letter from his wife, the letter describing their son's sudden illness, his dangerous high fever. Reading that, feeling so helpless, so far away, Robert had cried out. A hard megrim pounded now, leaving him frantic with pain, and some new ache rumbled in the bend of his spine. Twisting, checking his spine, he peered in the looking glass.

The wrong man.

We've imprisoned the wrong man.

Essex would rule. One sad abandoned little tyrant of a boy.

Slow and subtle, aye, making men and Queen his playthings, manoeuvring this and that, but he would rule. And I stand in his way.

Robert turned away from the looking glass.

How far shall he go?

Rain fell, again — *God, this spring, this wet and miserable spring* — infesting the house with a chill uncommon for May. The low fire struggled.

Folly, folly, folly — and blood: all this fuss for one little man?

Lady Audrey swears Marlowe remains loyal to me, to state and crown. Yet now Essex would dangle love from chains and so hostage Marlowe's obedience.

So 'tis neither money nor doctrine which pries him loose from me, but love?

I've not got time for this!

Swaying, he tossed the broken borage on the flames and then filled his wine cup. He considered retiring to bed — rest in darkness, he knew, would soothe his head better than wine — and instead took a packet of dried herbs from his desk drawer. Crushing hellebore and knitbone between his fingers, dropping the herbs into his cup, he frowned at a noise: a fist beating on the servants' door.

Hellfire.

Making his way down the dark hall towards the door, Robert caught sight of a servant bearing a candle and ducked into a little alcove.

The servant opened the door. Rain got in, obscuring the caller's subdued voice. Robert stepped from the alcove and almost collided with the servant who sought him.

—Ai! Your honour.

—Who knocks?

—An't please you, your honour, a visitor humbly begs an audience.

—A desperate visitor, in this rain. Who is't?

—A messenger, he says.

—I'd guessed that much.

—Your honour. He is a muddy creature, brown eyes and angry face, and —

—*Who?*

The servant almost whimpered. —One called Marsyas.

Robert took the candle from the servant and switched to an icy courtesy. —Marsyas begs? Then, by all God's mercy, let him in.

Hearing this — by design, he knew — Kit waited until the circle of candlelight reached him. Then, dripping rainwater, he gave a beautiful bow. Robert ordered the servant to bring more wine to his study, with all speed. Following Robert to that little room, Robert's progress crooked and bent, Kit wondered if the servant had ever dared suggest that his master had drunk enough.

In the study, facing his agent, Robert shook his head. *Death kissed thee, sucked thee, and thou, who dost stand here so sharp-boned and pale, thou didst defy him.*

—Marlowe, I bade thee stay at Scadbury. I distinctly remember standing in this room, before this very hearth, bidding thee — *commanding* thee — to remain at Scadbury until such time as I sent for thee. I rest quite certain that I have *not* sent for thee.

Kit made to speak; he fell to coughing.

—I distinctly remember this, too. Sit down. I've seen lesser fools served at a banquet for dessert. Dost thou know the hour?

—Your honour, I know the hour, as much as any man, for I've marked time by London bells. What delays kept your honour busy at Westminster today? You took a late wherry home, la, and looked hunched and tired as you climbed the steps to Cecil House. Pitying you, the weights of your work, I tasked myself to wait a while and permit you to rest.

Robert's cheeks burned a deep red. —Hast thou stalked me, spy?

—I'faith your honour, 'tis what I'm here for.

—Here, in London, on a horse stolen, I doubt not, from Sir Thomas Walsingham?

—Borrowed. The mare rests with a horse-courser I know. When I get her back, she'll be in better shape than when I left her. 'Tis nothing. Besides, I had errands.

—Errands. Enlighten me.

—I visited a stationer in Paul's Yard, hoping to buy on account ink and paper of mine own, for Sir Thomas Walsingham grows stingy. Which stationer, you'd ask? Edward Blount, sign of the bear. He also stocks an excellent selection of books, should you need one.

The kitchen maid knocked, and she bore cups and wine. Robert noticed the look Kit exchanged with her. *He shows compassion for one so ugly?* Robert dismissed the woman, locking the door behind her, and poured two cups of wine. He took great care.

Kit accepted a cup and almost dropped it. *For Christ's love, so weak.* —Am I still invited to sit, your honour?

—Aye, sit. Explain why in Hell's flames thou'st come unbidden to this house. And by all thy gifts, poet, make it good.

—I thank you, your honour, for I am tired. Point the first: I fear you see not the obnoxious danger dancing before your very nose.

—Th'art sitting, not dancing.

—Point the second: an Essex man approached me at Scadbury.

—What saidst thou to him?

—The ape did affect a most incompetent attempt at *seduction* —

—How didst thou answer him? Speak!

—Your honour, if I'd said anything but no, would I be here? Would I have come to you?

Robert felt his thoughts slip on pain and wine. —Better men than thee play false. And thou'st already shown me dangerous frailty over that Jesuit.

—No, I —

—Explain, I say!

—I *would*, if your honour would condescend to let me finish a sentence!

Silence.

—Say on, Marlowe.

—Robin Poley has visited the Scadbury grounds —

—He is there as my man.

—Rest you quite certain of that, your honour?

Robert said nothing.

—Point the third: as you know, when in London, I have shared lodgings with the playwright Tom Kyd. Being in London, I would visit him. I found him not.

Robert drank some wine.

—His door hangs askew on ruined hinges, kicked in, I would guess, and his neighbours bray of arrest and Bridewell. Bridewell, your honour, for something called the Dutch Church Libel?

Robert's heavy lids hid his eyes as he plucked some sheets of paper from within a large book on his desk. He gave these papers to Kit. —A copy of the libel. Read it.

Kit did, in silence. Then he snorted. —I wonder not 'tis anonymous; the author should be ashamed to sign his name on aesthetics alone.

—And the mention of thy plays?

—Some mother-wit's jealous mockery, layered over darker purpose. Your honour, Tom Kyd knows not hilt from blade. I promise you, he no more wrote this libel than I cast coins in Flushing.

—Yet he's in Bridewell.

Scowling, Kit gave back the papers. —A hostage.

—A coincidence.

—Let coincidence argue with the blood on Tom's desk! Aye, and with a kicked door in Canterbury.

Robert looked up from his wine, eyes wide now.

—Canterbury?

Kit made his voice sweet and mellow, as if to recite a pastoral poem. —My parents' house. My sister lives with them, and she wrote to me, one Ingram Frizer having told her I rest at Scadbury — aye, how knew he so? Chew upon that, so please you.

Walsingham's business manager? —Ingram Frizer? Art thou certain?

—'Tis a hard name to mistake. And Ric Baines, la, mustn't

forget him. Baines and Frizer rode all the way out to Canterbury and terrorized my family, saying they sought papers. And now I am made to look the author of some poem threatening arson and death, while at the same time Tom is accused of writing it? Is dark night day?

—Thou'lt tell me thou'st refused Essex twice now. Is't true?

—Aye!

Megrim toyed with Robert's eyes as he glanced at the fire. The warped flames gave up strange colours: beauty. —Then I fear thou art correct: a hostage.

Kit stood up, paced about. —Your honour, look to Robin Poley. His list, that list I turned over to Sir Francis, gaoled him.

—Poley would have thee come to Essex? How is that revenge?

—'Tis not so simple. Poley would delight in the confusion. He may be playing a game with you and Essex, playing to see which of ye wins. And yet 'tis *me* whom you doubt, me whom you will confine under watch in some fine house.

—'Tis easy to doubt thee, Marlowe. 'Tis thy defiance.

Kit sat down again, elbows on his knees, hair in his face. *I am not worth this.* —Your honour, 'tis... 'tis witless. Why not just herd *me* to Bridewell?

—Break thy bones and cripple thy mind? Oh, but soft, what use art thou then?

—Madness?

Robert thought that over. —He's as sane as I am. He chooses this.

—And Tom?

—He shall be asked only of the libel.

—Oh, excellent comfort, your honour. I thank you.

—He thanks me by spitting his words.

—What expect you from me?

—Marlowe —

—Ignorance and innocence —

—That libel is copied in a scrivener's hand —

—London is rotten with scriveners!

—The process of examination —

—The evil being done to him, aye, the evil: will you dishonour yourself and just ignore it?

—I am bound by duty and law, by policy —

—Policy, your honour, when I speak of higher duty, higher law?

—Aye, policy! The nuances of which thou dost understand nothing!

—Nothing is what you have done here, and nothing shall be your deathbed comfort when God inflicts mortal pain on your body and demands a reckoning of your soul!

—Marlowe, thou'st no *right* —

—Whom, and what, shall you obey?

Robert stared at the hearth, eyes larger than Kit had ever seen them. —Am I to take rebuke from thee?

Kit waited.

Robert stood up, got his balance, waddled to the window. Rain blurred the lights of the wherries on the river. —Though the Dutch Church Libel would char thy name, I've placed some protections around thee. The Privy Council's proclamation on the libel touches thee not. 'Tis by benign remarks in council meetings after hot disputes in hallways, but I protect thee. 'Tis one reason I must, for the moment, allow the examination of Tom Kyd. We must be seen examining *someone*. He shall not be left there long, I promise thee.

Silence.

Robert beckoned him to the window, speaking once Kit stood beside him. —'Tis not safe for thee here. I may prevent thine arrest — and that only by a hair — but I can give thee no protection from angry men in the street who would seize and punish the libeller. Thy name is knotted up in that libel, and London suffers no shortage of angry men. Beaten to death, and thy corpse dumped in an alley: how shalt thou help anyone then?

Cinna the Poet. All those blurred lights. —Slink back to the poxy country and just... just wait?

—Aye. Wait. As I wait. Such are the risks of the work, Marlowe, work thou dost enjoy, and work thou hast never once refused.

Kit whirled away from the glass. —Refused? Refused *what*? When, la? How passed the night, your honour — aye, tell me the weather — when last I might have said no?

—Surfeit! Visiting me unbidden, and presuming to task *my* conscience — offend me once more, just *once* more, and thou shalt feel the protection of stone walls and iron chain! Easy, *easy* to have left thee to die last winter. Say — and in thy best blank verse, I charge thee — how thou may'st have survived that pneumonie without my trouble and care? Aye, the crush of silence. Th'art one little man, Christopher Marlowe. One. Little. Man.

Bile shot up Kit's throat as he gulped at the last of his wine. The two fluids soured together. He swallowed.

—Marlowe, attend me. I need thee safe, because I need thee in Scotland —

Staring in the cup, Kit heard Tom's voice: *Walk away.*

—And that very soon, once my scout returns, for I would trust none else with these messages. God ordains our rulers, but God also helps those who help themselves. Marlowe, I remind thee of thine oaths of secrecy. Say nothing of what we've discussed here, not even to Sir Thomas Walsingham.

Glass clinked wood as Kit placed the cup on Robert's desk. —I need no such reminder.

Robert sighed. *No, thou dost not.* —Distress shines in thine eyes. Thou would'st visit Bridewell, see thy beloved, or, if barred from seeing him, leave a mercy deposit for his food, and while there glean knowledge from the clerk. Deny it not to me. Know'st thou the word *oubliette*?

Kit met his gaze.

—Essex would use Bridewell as thine oubliette. Gaolers seize visitors; initiative or incentive, 'tis no rarity. If th'art seized in Bridewell, and if thy name is not recorded in the gaol ledger, and that of course by gravest accident, never bribery, then I... once th'art a prisoner, by whichever name, thine enemy may press on thee full weight of examination and law. I shall lose. And I shall lose thee. Christopher. Dance not into that oubliette.

My Christian name?

Robert heard his father coughing many rooms away.

—Marlowe, I will fix this. Soon. I need time. Please, take this, thy back payments for Flushing, very late, and please, accept my protection and get back to Scadbury. I shall send thee word as soon as I know of the slightest change.

Kit thought this over. Then he bowed. —Very good, your honour. I thank you.

Robert walked Kit to the door, watched him disappear into darkness.

Higher duty; higher law.

Cherish them not.

Cherish them not.

FAIR COPY: NOT OF COMPULSION OR NECESSITY

From Cecil House, night of the sixteenth of May.
Addressed to my honourable and loving friend,
Sir Thomas Walsingham, at Scadbury.

Sir,

I must once more impose upon your kindness and generosity, and I fear I may strain our mutual affection and respect. Marlowe stirs up danger by traipsing about London, danger I am not convinced he understands. I fear for him, and for what any harm to him might mean for my work. Whilst I admire and indeed derive much benefit from the man's quarrelsome mind, for it doth spur him not only to ask hard questions but seek their ugly answers, and seek them to their very end, I need him kept in one place. Sir Thomas, please understand me: I blame you not for Marlowe's stubborn presumptions of mobility, but I plead with you, even press you: *keep him at Scadbury.* I must know where he is to be found for the short-coming day when I shall sore need him, and I maintain that your estate,

however tedious Marlowe may find it, is far safer for him than
crannied London.

> Your affectionate and worried friend,
> Ro. Cecil

BY LETTING STRANGERS MAKE
OUR HEARTS TO ACHE

A restless strength rippled through the trotting mare as the
bright morning sun got in Kit's eyes. Blinded, he craned his
neck to one side. The mare broke stride and cantered, then
trotted again, testing the reins, testing him.

She wanted to run.

Kit lifted his right hand from the reins, shaded his eyes,
looked ahead at the road: puddles reflecting sunlight, Scadbury not too far off.

The mare flicked her ears back, listening.

—My girl, 'tis only my second time on thy back. May I
trust thee?

Her body pulled taut — that strength again, almost trembling — and she tugged down on the reins.

A breeze tickled the back of Kit's neck.

Grinning, he squeezed his legs tighter around her, bent
forward, and grasped her mane. He kissed the air.

She ran.

They flew.

Hooves threw mud and water to the sky. Wind buffeted
their faces. Sunlight dappled as though flung by some hand,

and colours wept. Faster, faster, faster: joy in speed, joy in light — grace. Lost in the moment, he laughed.

He coaxed her down to a trot and then a walk as they reached the estate, and they headed, with shared reluctance, for the stable. John Marlowe had taught his sons how to look after horses, and Kit, in his travels and tasks, had not only run messages on horseback but had also twice disguised himself as a stable-hand. Many people despised stablework and those who performed it. Kit, finding horses on the whole more intelligent, more noble, and certainly more compassionate than many people he'd met, considered such work a task of honour.

Dirt and dust floated in the sunbeams as he sponged the mare's legs and checked her shoes for rocks. He sang a few notes of the treble line of a madrigal he'd not attempted since his voice broke. Failure embarrassing him, he transposed down, sang again, sang better.

Tom shall walk free, la, and Manna shall recover. A matter of time, a matter of trust, a matter of powerful men working their ways. A matter of faith, maybe.

Brushing the mare's mane, Kit whispered thanks in her ear. She wrapped her head around his neck; Kit leaned there and smiled. He left her with food and water, and a promise for another run soon.

He glanced down: every inch of him spattered with mud. *My only set of clothes, too.* He thought of Manna, and he laughed again: *So, Clever Kitten, what woe this time?*

At the well, hoping he might sweet-talk Dan into heating the water for him, he reached for the bucket line — flinched. A bird swooped, speckled black plumage surrendering iridescence, greens and blues: a starling. The bird swooped again, flew a circle around Kit's head, and lighted on the far edge of the well, looking at him. Amused, Kit gave the starling a light bow.

The starling flew off, toward the woods, where it joined many more. Circling, calling.

Not just starlings. Ravens, crows, kites.

Why?

Striding across the meadow, ribs and thighs aching, Kit thought of a story from Ovid: Jupiter transforming himself to an eagle and so abducting Ganymede — talons and beak — dragging the boy into the brightest parts of the sky.

Wings beat.

Kit told himself he heard no ancient and filthy eagle. *Only songbirds.*

Yet I look up.

He slipped, discovering the marsh had crept — *Christ Jesus, that water's high* — and got to the woods. Sensing him, the birds flew up from the ground, and their racket, the beating of all those wings, sickened him. So, too, did the scent of old blood.

He crouched.

The sheltered ground showed a mess of tracks: a horse, three people — and a crutch?

He backed away from the footprints, nudged something with his heel — a tree root, perhaps, the diseased oak.

After a moment, he turned to look.

Gideon lay face down, arms tucked in at his sides.

Ravens and crows, starlings and kites: he knew.

How can I not know what I know?

Cradling the head, he turned the body over. Cried out.

Traced the air over the Gideon's throat with his finger. Took off his doublet and laid it over Gideon's face and neck.

He sat there for some time, first acknowledging that the surgeon Charing might be the better tutor for anatomy, and then explaining, as best he knew, carotid arteries and vocal cords, words and threats, and state and crown to a dead refugee.

MY REVEREND MEANING TO THE STATE

Robin shifted his weight on his crutch. Essex harangued him and Anthony Bacon both, detailing their lofty goals and their mighty falls, and this noise, and the need to be seen paying attention to the noise, made good distraction from the now quite sickening pain in his spine. As a boy, Robin had watched his father suffering the stone; the man would sweat, puke, and piss blood. Not believing simple pain sufficed to make a man vomit, Robin had reasoned instead that his father must fear the pain — who would not? — and so the fear sickened him. In his work, Robin had watched several men sweat and even turn green as they stared at his dagger and answered questions. Fear, then, its bilious results splattered at Robin's feet, as some wretch about to find his God lost his supper. That, and blood. Today, weak and queasy as fang-pierced prey dangling from a serpent's mouth, he better understood his father.

He thought he understood something of his victims, too. His fingers twitched, and his skin, it seemed, remembered knotting the gag on the singing boy. *Gideon. His name is Gideon. Was. Punched and kicked, and he could not move. Too much, too much. I begged Skeres to relent. Begged him.*

I will not be stained.

Essex smeared sweat from his forehead into his hair. His freckles seemed so dark against his pale face, and his teeth chattered. —I get so tired!

Anthony took a sharp breath as Essex turned his back to them, and Robin wondered how long Essex had suffered the quartan ague. *Squealing mosca flies eat one alive, and they breed on riverbanks, yet the greatest men in London will live on the Strand. Not that any great man would heed my advice.*

Facing a Thames-side window, Essex heard distant calls for watermen: *Oars, oars. Eastward, ho!* Physicians advised him to rest when these fevers came on him. Believing the fevers granted him clarity — vision, understanding — Essex instead stoked the heat, reading many books at once, writing poems, composing songs, conversing with friends well into the night, sometimes until he collapsed. Now, as if to examine a yawning gut wound, he bowed his head. This attitude of manly resistance and certitude, despite a blade in the belly: such beauty should have lit Bacon and Poley's mind with memory of the dead Phillip Sidney — aye, the Battle of Zutphen, sweet Phillip slain, though, truth told, a bullet to the thigh wounded sweet Phillip, and gangrene took twenty-six leisurely days to eat him out — whatsoever, sweet Phillip, whose brother governed Flushing, whose widow enjoyed the grand benevolence of being married to Essex, all this tight weaving...

Fah, 'tis wasted on these two.

Essex once more put his palm to his forehead, and his voice wavered and cracked. —I get so tired. I pray you both: hear me. A portrait of my mother, done when I was boy, shows her in a gown designed to rival the Queen's. Protective in her maternal love, she doth hold my shoulder. I stood not with her for that portrait. She had chased me from the room, for she would speak in private with the painter. Later, I stood for the painter alone. He worked his pretty artifice and set my mother and me together, so deceiving all who see the work. Yet that good woman loves me, and each time I see her, I beseech her blessing. You both consider me foolish. Deny nothing. 'Tis truth, and I desire truth: ye consider me foolish. Consider pebbles instead.

Anthony glanced at Robin, and Robin shrugged.

—Intelligence is a collection of pretty pebbles, this one plucked in a Flushing bakery, that one retrieved from a Deptford dock. The artifice comes in the arrangement, and sometimes the arrangement gives up a fact. Some truth. Something almost palpable to prop and strengthen the most gossamer workings of artifice...Tony, get my cloak, for I threw it there.

Anthony draped the cloak on the earl's shoulders. —Good my lord, warm yourself.

Essex kept still: no twitch, no fuss, no sulk. Robin thought of an actor freezing in place while another spoke lines to explain the situation on the stage. Then he thought of a man suffering a stroke. He'd almost dredged up the courage to speak when the earl strode toward him, tall, pretty, smiling.

Robin backed away. Essex took his shoulders, and Robin flinched, the earl's vigour and strength surprising him.

—Robin, sweet Robin, gentle Robin.

—My lord?

—How shalt thou bury the body?

—What mean you, my lord?

—Thou didst say 'twas clear. Clear as a boy's tears? And

'tis just one; thou mayest yet pile up the corpses higher than a Maypole. The singing boy: I would never have consented to his harm.

How knows he?

—Thou dost lose control. One of thine own men made the distressing report to Bacon, and he added his doubts of thy loyalties in this matter.

Nick Skeres. —My lord, I took not that sad task lightly. The boy had learned — he screamed, and — the noise did gall mine ears. 'Twas Nick Skeres who...I...

I let some barber command me.

I lost my way.

Essex shook his head. —I need not the ire of Sir Thomas Walsingham. Know'st thou he served gaol time for debt? I believe his economies trouble him yet. I must overlook his wife's shrewish rebuffs, aye, but this? This slaughter of an innocent? Think'st thou I've no conscience, no soul? Think'st thou nothing wakes me at night?

—Good my lord, I never wanted the boy to die. I wanted only...If you had graced me and proceeded with the plan I suggested...Oh, God, save me. What would you have me do?

—Be gaoled.

Robin's polite laugh collapsed. *Gaol? Again? Slouch in a cell and listen to my hair grow and then stare at the open door until a guard drags me through it, telling me of freedom?* —My lord, I've been gaoled.

—I know. I believe it haunts thee. And for murder? Of a child? Thou'lt host no banquets in the Marshalsea this time.

Newgate for this. I may bleat until Judgment 'twas Nick who cut the throat, but I...And now this earl's arms edge my world, and I will hang. —No, my lord. No.

—I've sworn out the warrant; I shall call the constables.

—My lord, a moment, I beseech you —

Scents of lavender and rose wafted off Essex as he stroked Robin's hair. —When I touch thine head, enough lice stick to my hand to serve as fierce judge and damning witnesses to see thee hanged, with plenty left over to stand as happy audience. Just when didst thou plan to tell me of this piddling little so-please-you-my-lord snag of Marlowe, whom thou wouldst assure me is safekept and fretted at Scadbury, thumbing his nose at me by strutting the London streets? Didst thou think I would not hear of that slave's predictable defiance? I might think thou dost somehow protect him, and so thou dost toy with me. Dost thou toy with me, Robin Poley?

Anthony got behind Robin, standing within the earl's line of sight. —Good my lord, I beg forgiveness, for I forgot that we consulted on this matter of Poley's arrest.

—Thou'st forgotten nothing, Tony. Stay here. The constables wait by the street doors.

The thud of Robin's knees hitting the floor disappeared under the racket of men marching up the stairs. Essex held open the door for the three constables, who bowed as they entered and so collided with one another.

Essex pointed to Robin. —There, that small man, mocking an attitude of prayer. Murder, I say.

The three men strode to sweating Robin but laid no hands on him, instead glancing back at the earl for a cue.

Essex applauded. —I thank you, gentlemen. My jest is played out.

Robin saw the truth of the constable's ceremonial dagger: a stage prop. Then, hurting his neck, Robin studied the actor's bearded face, one obscured by a floppy hat, but a face Robin knew by sight: the actor Gabriel Spenser.

Essex tossed each actor a small purse. —Poor, sad fellows. What is't, Spenser, playhouses closed for the season again this year?

Gabriel almost dropped his purse. —Times rich and times poor, we never refuse a performance.

—Well played, gentlemen. Bacon shall see ye out.

Anthony and the actors left, and Essex stood over Robin, still on his knees.

—Poley, I am young, as thou'lt often remind me, but, being young, I lack an older man's patient charity, so I shall speak plain. We are running an intelligence service, not St. Bart's Hospital. Thou didst promise me a man. Thou'st failed. I want him. I shall *have* him. And thou shalt deliver him unto me. Torment the hostage; kill the boys; weave the most outrageous deceits to see him charged and gaoled — aye, gaoled, so I may pluck him free — only do it in *quiet*, and so bear down on Marlowe's shoulders till my floor doth bruise *his* knees, not thine. Hey? Hey?

—I thank you, my lord, for this, your mercy.

—Leave my sight.

IN THE FEAR OF GOD, AND FREEDOM
OF MY CONSCIENCE

—Atheism?

—Atheism.

Izaak pointed to the oxblood Cicero on his desk. —And the proof: thou didst find it in this book?

Nodding, Robin retrieved a sheet of paper from his satchel. —I informed the clerk of several sheets of paper. Did he record it not?

—I must check. And didst thou keep hold of evidence? 'Tis irregular.

'Tis most desperate. So am I. —By accident. Examiner Pindar, note you the writing. Is't familiar?

Nose close to the paper, Izaak studied the marks: letters crowded, downstrokes heavy. —'Tis hurried, no scrivener's hand, and 'tis part of an argument for Arianism. Subtle and obscure, no common man's dispute. I came across this at Cambridge, studying divinity.

Robin tilted his head to one side. —Divinity at Cambridge?

—But atheism?

—Those who would know —

—Oh aye, those learned men with their deep interests. I cannot keep accepting instruction.

—Examiner Pindar, if you believe Thomas Kyd would know nothing of this paper, then you must believe him innocent. If he is innocent, then why have you not released him?

Izaak traced his finger down the margin of the Arian argument.

I would learn to break a man. Is this the gift, then? Is this the tool?

—I am an examiner. I ask the questions. 'Tis my task, asking questions. Know thy masters what they say? Atheism is an outrageous charge, rejecting, even denying not only the teachings of Christ but of the very existence of God. All bad enough for private reflection, if one could keep such thinking private, but hist: rejecting God means rejecting our God-appointed Queen.

—Aye, it shames me even to think it.

—Thomas Kyd has shown no —

—Not him.

Izaak stared. —Marlowe?

Robin felt dizzy and small. —Well, whose handwriting is it?

Izaak did not answer right away. —At Corpus Christi, he knelt in prayer beside me.

—Cozy.

—Alphabetical order. Hear me. This Marlowe's a pricking torment to any soul unlucky enough to encounter him, a most arrogant and yet most fortunate sack of moral pestilence, but he's no atheist.

—Soften you?

Izaak snorted. —I've no love for the man.

—Then how know you of his faith? How know you of the secret heart of one so difficult and defiant, one who can write with such ease of a Jew he named Barabbas, of the scourge of God himself, Tamburlaine, of Faust? Only a man who loves him would know. Rumours, Pindar. Men talk. And they weave stories: busy spiders of a new truth. Atheism. Imagine

if he infected a noble with such an idea — defiance, refusal
— as say you, 'tis a short step from atheism to sedition. Such a
charge could land him in here. Perhaps you'd be his examiner.
Aye, that pleases you.

*It doth. God in my heart, it doth. And I'd foul not my hands,
for 'tis not my fault if justice snares the man. 'Tis duty.*

Izaak drummed his fingers on Cicero. —I'd only hope
he'd make easier questioning than Thomas Kyd. That man's
resilience doth baffle me.

—Free yourself of bafflement. We've not got the time.

—Thine eyes: art thou in pain?

—It comes down to this: doth the tract found in the book
suggest Marlowe's atheism? Is't in Marlowe's hand? Kyd would
know.

—Would ye have me rack him?

The examiner craves permission from a crippled messenger?
—My masters would have you get me the information I need.
How 'tis done? Not our concern.

—But the reasoning —

—Reasoning be fucked! Just get me answers!

Izaak's voice became gentle and warm, concerned. —Art
thou in any fear, any fear of thy soul?

—What? No. No, because none of what I do here is of
mine own accord. I carry out the will of greater men, and 'tis
their souls what must answer, not mine. I am but a servant.

—A bitter one, at that.

—I killed no one!

—I said nothing of killing.

God save me, that soft voice. —Then why ask you of souls,
Examiner?

Leaning back, Izaak looked up at the ceiling. —Divinity. Always the whiff of Hellfire about Marlowe, the smack of Faust. The man is corrupt, his mind abscessed. I fear for his soul, as I fear for Kyd's.

And say you this for whom, Pindar? —I shall leave you with the evidence, then.

As Robin stepped free of Bridewell, sunshine galled his eyes.

Naked, in bright light: why?

Tom glanced at his clothes, very dirty now, clothes the guards had peeled from him and thrown in a squalid heap in the corner. Annoyed, he clicked his tongue. At home, he folded his clothes when he changed, folded them, put them away. A place for everything.

Such neatness, Kit said once, *such a sweet tidiness to thee. 'Tis how thou'lt protect thyself, la, this thy bulwark against chaos.*

—Thy mind, Kyd, thy vigorous but crippled mind.

Tom ignored Izaak. He'd got other puzzles to solve. The tapers which had lit the march from his cell, for example: all the same size. Escorting someone to this little room of great reckonings, then: the tapers' only use? Guards had held those tapers and kept so quiet, walked so slow, in ceremony. And the light here, a bonfire's worth, a reeking hassle and no doubt a wretched expense, what, a dozen torches?

Kit would burn candles the same way he took breath: no thought of how to get more.

Well, light another, scold.

'Twas my last one. And scold? Oh, thou'st heard nothing of scolding.

Izaak continued. —He hath corrupted thee, first by delighting thy body, then by attacking thy heart, whispering to thee of love and defiance.

John Deyos stood by a wall, wiping sweat from his forehead. The torches above him gave off significant heat.

—Love and defiance and atheism? Roughing out his draft on thee he then took his sermon of atheism to men of power, each peer as snared by his charm as thee? That arrogant little smirk, thou'st told me, those bright brown eyes lit from within.

Memories of conversations with Kit shone, lamplight leaking past some impediment, and Tom, fearing some sudden detail that might yet be drawn out of him, wanted to shove these memories away. His memory of Kit's voice, like Kit himself, refused to settle.

Eighth scene, Tom. And thee?

Second.

Still?

Kiss my arse.

For thee, Tom, I would kiss Lucifer's arse.

Too kind.

If only to prove that I could. Question, la. Which harms a man more: torment of the body, or torment of the mind?

Oh, the body.

So quick? And if the body withstands all that's given it, what would'st thou answer then? Here, help me with the wording of a contract, o scrivener. My good doctor's signing away his soul.

—Kyd, my questions are these.

The same questions as earlier in the morning, only this time for benefit of the audience. As Tom listened to Izaak, as he answered, bored with the repetition — *Repetition drives mine art*, Examiner Pindar liked to say — Tom reviewed standard wording of common legal documents and scraps of Matthew and Luke. He considered singing, though he found himself unable to remember much beyond the one about the maid and her long, long hair all a-tangled in the weir or the song his niece liked so much, *Riddles Wisely Expounded*. What sounds louder than the lord's own horn, and what is sharper than a thorn; what is worse than a woman's curse, and what is deeper than the sea? He knew the answers — thunder, hunger, Hell, love — just not their metre.

The metre. Has all collapsed, that I've forgotten metre?

Izaak's voice reached him. —Atheism. This sheet, his handwriting, thy book...

My books. Tom meandered through memories of books he'd discussed with Kit, so many of them, until he collided with that silly reckoning tale. *Sweet God, the one about the lover and the apples. We mocked that for hours.* A young man called, ah, Simon, doth love a lady, oh, quick, what name? Kateryn, aye, for the man down the hall, Kat Kat Kat, and Simon would show her such by presenting unto her a bounty of apples. Alas, Kateryn careth not for apples. In the apples' stead Simon now risketh his freedom for his love's deepest desire: the fruit of the quince tree. Quince trees groweth in the orchards of a knight who hath of late fallen on evil days — no, evil days have fallen on him — and the knight doth keep a dog, a huge mastiff the colour of dusk, and this mastiff doth drool a foaming slather...

Izaak spoke in tones of sorrow, even regret. —Love, and defiance. I cannot even imagine what — hast thou tongued crevices? Is it all mouth? Defiance of even the most simple rules of conduct, degrading a sacred act into something bestial.

Tom kept still. He'd got no lines here, standing in this room, not entirely sure how he kept himself upright.

Then he spoke, voice calm, deep. —Atheism? A divinity scholar?

Geoffrey Morgan paused in his little walk around the large object in the middle of the room and looked at Tom.

Izaak cleared his throat. —Lapsed. He took no holy orders, I say. Master of arts? Master of deceit. Doth he summon demons?

Oh, 'tis a new one. —'Twas just a play he wrote.

—Believe'st thou not in Hell?

—Nor am I out of it. I believe. I also *know*. As he commands no demons, he preaches no atheism, converts no man. The most he's said of church matters is to complain of Saint Paul. I said I would write a poem about Paul on the road, and Marlowe mocked the story, saying I'd be better off writing about the trickery game Fast and Loose.

—Thou'st heard him mock Saint Paul?

Tom saw homunculi. —Some divine's dispute. I understood none of it. And he was hungry when he said that. He gets petulant when hungry. 'Tis like living with a child, sometimes. I must nag him to eat, even to sleep.

Izaak cut the air with his hand. —Enough of dinnertimes. Thou'lt allow him to lecture thee on his blasphemous opinions, and then, slave, pry thee open for his comforts?

—I am no slave. He loves me. And I love him.

Izaak's eyes looked dull, confused.

Feeling the heat of the torchlight on his exposed back, on

his thighs, Tom wondered again at his own calm. *Should I not be begging?*

Izaak stepped into Tom's line of sight. He reached up, touch gentle, and turned Tom's face toward the middle of the room.

A broad and sectioned table splitting over rollers, slack ropes dangling from the four corners like long tongues of overheated dogs. Geoffrey Morgan kicked one, and the heavy rope wrapped the arch of his foot before sliding away.

A rack.

Eyes wide, belly cold, Tom studied it.

A rack stretched its bound victim notch by notch. The rolling tension first strained tendons, then muscles, then bones. Joints cracked. Tissue ruptured. Will tore. The rhetorics of guilt and innocence fell away like sweat, as did ideals, and ideas, of being human. All that remained: flesh. Tough, tough flesh.

Memory refused to release Tom. He and Kit had worked up the contract wording for John Faustus, but Kit had not let go the idea of physical torment. He'd examined tools. *A rack? Keenest proof of mankind's imagination dancing two steps shy of Hell itself. We must recognize it in ourselves: evil, la.*

Kit, we are more!

Aye, 'tis what I sayeth!

A rack is amoral, in and of itself. It is what it is. How 'tis used is what matters.

Oh, for Christ's love, Tom, how else might it be used?

Izaak sounded tired. —Is not the blasphemous tract in Christopher Marlowe's handwriting? Where lieth the rest?

Across the room, the other side of the rack, John Deyos pointed at Tom. —We know th'art stubborn, and we know th'art strong. I've only seen one other man stand up so fast from a second manacling. But when that rack's done with thee, thou'lt not even remember thou'st *got* hands. Thou'lt forget thy prick till thou dost piss thyself. Thou'lt need to reason out how to chew thy food. Stronger men than thee die of thirst with the wine in easy reach, after a racking. A mercy, I suppose.

Izaak held out the paper with great care: his sacred offering. —Where lieth the rest of his atheism?

Tom closed his eyes. —So much light.

John looked up from conferring with Geoffrey. —He's ready, Mr. Pindar. I've had him fasting. We'd never get him free before he choked to death on spew.

Tom sniffed and blew, hoping to clear fresh tears and mucus from his nose, because lying flat while snotted up always made him cough.

Geoffrey strode to him, laid his hand on Tom's right shoulder. —Shalt thou be racked for another man's sins?

Izaak spoke in Tom's left ear. —Doth he love thee? Is it love?

Walls fell, ceiling flew, stones and torches and men played out as tricks of light: only this rack existed. Only the rack.

Tom knew. Knew as he knew the corrosion of forced solitude and the misery of manacles. Knew he might accuse Kit of the vilest acts, sign any affirmation, vomit beams of light, and still this Examiner Pindar would rack him. The reasons and details of his arrest — none of it mattered. The lies and the truth — none of that mattered, either. Because the examiner would draw the prisoner. Izaak Pindar would rack Tom Kyd, because he desired it. Because he could.

Tom drew in a breath, steadied his voice. —'Tis not up to me.

John signalled to the guards to go and take Tom's arms; Tom already shuffled towards the rack.

He collapsed. The guards passed their tapers to John Deyos and hauled the silent prisoner the rest of his journey.

Geoffrey bowed his head.

BUT AT HIS LOOKS, LIGHTBORN, THOU WILT RELENT

An understanding of pain, Robin decided, demanded more than intimate and immediate experience. It demanded, despite fleeting presence, despite invisibility, a belief in its own irrational existence. Examiner Pindar understood none of it, and Robin, limping along a Bridewell corridor, sneered at the examiner's back.

Izaak counted off points of his list on the tips of his fingers. —His shoulder did leave the socket, and it gave a silly noise, a pop, some grease bubble bursting in a hot pan. When John Deyos did set the joint: a scraping grind and another pop. I do marvel at it. The man's sinews, of course, cannot be reset, and they shall trouble him the rest of his days...

Robin found himself translating Latin verses into English, something he'd taught Marlowe as a calming exercise.

Examiner Pindar had reached some of the truth of pain. The little noises of suffering, not cries and groans but snorts, whines, grunts: the meanings of pain lay there. Is one still a man, loosing those craven sounds? Is one still a man when nothing louder than a pop signals the agony of a joint coming apart? And when the pain eases, leaving one to question the memory of it, that memory, like the pain itself, voracious: is one still a man when the pain, and later, the memory of it, feel like deceit?

The pain drew me, like that? I wept, like that?

An understanding of pain, Robin knew, demanded faith.

Faith, and its responsibilities.

He found faith easy these days — his faith in folly and failure, at least. His faith in interference, if not from a bored nobleman and his Bacon-toad then from eavesdropping brats. And from men like Pindar and Skeres, who craved not reason and need — the elegance of schemes — but suffering; and who caused more of it than necessary.

Necessary? Some. Unavoidable, at least. A matter of knowledge and moderation. And plans, careful plans.

Damn that boy.

Izaak slowed his stride and glanced over his shoulder. —Why dost thou want to see him like this? So many irregularities in this case. Why art thou here?

—Save your questions for other men, Examiner. I'll stand for none of it.

Robin knelt at the bars and cried out — at the pain in his hips, he told himself.

Tom lay on his back, twitching.

Tears soaked his hair as he stared at the ceiling. Against a red curtain shot through with ragged veins of black and spattered with stars, homunculi crucified one another. Above this suffering hung a solitary homunculus, shrinking, ever shrinking.

Robin reached through the bars and stroked Tom's cheek with the backs of his fingers.

Oh, my Christopherus, mine own little ferret, if thou didst see this...stubborn, stubborn, stubborn. And clever. Too clever for thine own good: I did see that in thy first task, thy very first hour with me. Th'art worth a dozen each of Ric Baines and Nick Skeres. I would halt this and rescue thee. I would.

And thou'dst trust me not.

Wise. Yet not wise enough.

Thou'st need become evil to be wise enough.

God save me, what have I done?

Izaak crouched down next to Robin.

Shuddering, Tom kept his gaze on the ceiling.

Robin made his voice low and sweet. —Dost thou know me? Gentle, gentle, thy neck is strained.

—Crutch.

—Aye, my crutch. No, ignore thine examiner. He is nothing. Eyes on me. Know'st me not from before? Our Christopherus never spoke of me and my limp? Of how agency's coin ruins us? No tales of how I taught him to use a dagger?

Tom grunted.

—Still, *still* thou'lt protect him. I thought men like thee were extinct. Would'st steal fire?

Izaak murmured something; Robin ignored him.

Grimacing against a wave of pain, Tom counted down.

—Three, two, one. So intemperate. I told Kit anger, anger would be the deadly sin to kill him — shook his head, said *Pride*.

—And thou'st know nothing of why thou'st suffer for him?

—No.

—I'd tear that Cicero, page by page, if I thought I might move thee.

—Nothing in Cicero for you. You know not what you want, or why you are here. 'Tis all slid.

Blood over fingers. —Now thou'lt speak to the purpose. Tell me of — hey. Dost thou hear me?

Shallow breaths.

—Hey. Hey!

Crutch slipping on the stones, Robin struggled to stand.

Izaak had left. No guards stood by. The corridor darkened into nothing.

—Pindar! Hey!

Oh, God save me.

Sweat broke out on Robin's face as he stared at Tom's feet — twitching, dirty, bare.

I've forgotten the way out.

Izaak stumbled into his office, seeking the pot. It looked clean; it smelled of excrement. Izaak retched, retched again. *What ague, then? I've done right. My pilgrimage: how to break a man, this man. Not pleasure: work. Duty and work.*

His mother stood before him.

Wearing the ragged clothes, as when he'd dreamt of her, aged, thinned, stooped, she kept her hands in fists before her chest.

—You.

She stared back.

A scent of goose fat rose from the wooden pot, and Izaak dropped it.

Izaak.

Far below Izaak's feet, wood clattered on stone.

—Oh, you'll speak to me now, woman?

He who laughs.

—And what means that?

She raised her arms over her head, as though manacled, in a spire. Then her neck seemed to collapse, letting her head fall back, letting her face point to the sky — to the ceiling.

—Mother, I can change nothing here!

She shoved him away.

Izaak staggered. The desk bumped his arse, and quills fell to the floor, to the same stones pressing the soles of his feet.

He looked up: ceiling, only ceiling.

FAIR COPY: AMPLIFY HIS GRIEF
WITH BITTER WORDS

Dictated by Izk Pindar. Clerked Thursday 17 May 1593 by Gfry Morgan.

This document hereunder recordeth the affirmations and testimony arising from the examination of Thomas Kyd, scrivener, of London re: proclivities and due suspicion of one Christopher Marlowe, gentleman, of Canterbury, for authorship of the Libel posted to the door of the Dutch Church in London on the eleventh of May, and atheism.

Tho. Kyd who doth claim and admit acquaintance with Chr. Marlowe, saying the two men shared rooms and worked alongside each the other writing plays and such. TK doth affirm his suspicions that CM wrote the Libel on the Dutch Church as CM is prone to cruel language. TK doth testify that papers marked with atheistic and heretical language found in his rooms doth belong to CM being in his hand, though TK cannot confirm a date for the writing of this paper beyond sometime in the last two years. After careful consideration, the examiner feels this loose timing may point to smouldering heresy in CM. TK affirms this may be so.

Tho. Kyd doth testify:

Chr. Marlowe never once named Sir Robert Cecil his master but TK guessed it and afterward CM never denied it

CM was lately abroad

CM is fond of his older sister

CM shows a tender protectiveness to those he loves and is quick to anger

CM drinks intemperately

CM blasphemes

TK and CM have lain together, many times

CM's eyes lighten from brown to bronze when he is goodly kissed

TK doth affirm:

CM is duly to be suspected of authorship of the Libel in the Dutch Church, said poem being intemperately littered with allusions to his plays, these plays being well known and even recited by the sort who would frequent playhouses

CM's reputation for quarrels and brawls

CM's copying (his handwriting being confirmed after careful perusal) a blasphemous text, and thereby CM's likely atheism

Tho. Kyd doth testify his lasting regret in this matter

Recommendations from Examiner Izk Pindar: the arrest and examination of Chr. Marlowe on suspicion of sedition and atheism

This document is a full and accurate record of the examination of Tho. Kyd

Izk Pindar

Jn Deyos

Tho. Kyd (his mark)

Gfry Morgan

PLEASING CERBERUS WITH HONEYED SPEECH

Descending the private Cecil House steps to the wherry dock, wondering what this Friday would bring him, Robert declined to acknowledge Robin Poley. He did, however, signal to Robin that he might board the same wherry. Wincing, pale, Robin sat down. Cross-currents wrinkled the waves as Robert settled against a cushion and ordered the waterman to row them to Westminster.

—Didst thou mean to see me, Poley, or didst thou get lost? 'Tis hard for thee, I know, to tell Cecil House apart from Essex House.

—An't please your honour, I come to make report.

Robert remembered dreaming that morning of the man at the end of the corridor. This time the figure leaned on a wall, arms crossed, hips cocked. *Not tall. Not Essex. Who else?* —Aye, tell me of Scadbury. Sir Thomas is quite disturbed by the death of a singing boy.

Robin shifted his weight. —I shall examine Marlowe's dagger.

The wind blew Robert's hair in and out of his heavy-lidded eyes. *I said nothing of a knife nor of a murder.* —Poley, I fear th'art growing feeble. How dost thou sleep?

—Sleep is pain-ridden and sufficeth me not.

—How sad. Hear those bells: so late o'clock? Do me a kindness, Poley, and pay the waterman when we get to Westminster. Then go find somewhere to sleep until I call thee.

Almost weeping, Robin inclined his head.

Intent on the Star Chamber, Robert bent his back to hasten his stride. Izaak Pindar followed him, murmuring report on his progress with the Dutch Church Libel, and adding something about a new and troubling matter: rumours of men's atheism. Two men rounded the corner and almost collided with them: Sir John Puckering and the Earl of Essex, also discussing, at some volume, the menace of atheism.

Essex spoke first. —Ah, Sir Robert, good morning.

Glancing first at his clerk, his look sharp and questioning, Robert inclined his head to his fellow privy councillors. —My lord of Essex, Sir John.

Puckering frowned. —Sir Robert, we are most alarmed.

—I fail in vision; I cannot see around corners.

Essex laughed. —Very good.

Puckering just blinked. —Corners? Sir Robert, please, if I may direct your attention to matters of government.

—My attention never wavers, Sir John.

—Really? Then what say you this morning to the rising trouble of atheism?

—I believe 'tis more a phantom than a trouble. We face the very palpable threats of riot and discontent and sneaking papists, or sneaking liars who would hide behind the papists and then, at night, catapult England back into the days of fire and blood. I wonder if atheism is not but one more ghost making up the fog which blocks our sight of the truth.

Izaak felt dizzy.

Robert straightened his doublet. —In the end, Sir John, what means it, this word: atheism?

Essex raised his eyebrows. —It means everything, Sir Robert, every threat, every menace, every moment of turning away from the face of God.

—How know you this, my lord?

—I will not be insulted.

—I mean no insult, my lord of Essex; I mean only to ask the necessary questions.

Puckering sounded irritated. —Sir Robert, I wonder at your hesitation. Is it your norm? I wonder, too, at your prejudices here. Is this fondness misplaced?

—Sir John, please. Discretion begs a moment —

—I am trying to be kind to you, Sir Robert, in this, your difficulty, when one of your servants is accused of a crime.

—What crime? What accusation, Sir John? What proof? *And why have I heard this not from my own clerk?*

Sorrow lengthened Puckering's face. —The charge is made by a man who knows him, and the proof will rise in the questions. Examine the accused. 'Tis what we do. If he's innocent, then he is innocent. 'Tis said, in the report Examiner Pindar giveth us from Bridewell — I've got my copy here — that your agent's, what, *paramour*, testifies your agent speaks in the ear of nobles. As if sodomy's not bad enough: preaching atheism to nobles and knights, Sir Robert, to men of wealth and power? 'Tis the very apex of defiance, and here one tips into treason. If one believes not in God, then one cannot believe in the sovereign's right to rule!

Robert reached to open the Star Chamber door. —Sir John, you forget: the man studied divinity.

Puckering leaned his arm on the door, blocking the way. —Angels fell.

—So much fuss over one little man.

Essex clicked his tongue in reproof. —Little? With those plays, those skills? That mind?

Puckering took back his arm. —Sir Robert, the Queen is old and needs her rest. I would hate to trouble Her Majesty with this matter and —

—Fine! Fine. Call for a motion for his arrest. We shall examine him in council. Mr. Pindar.

—Your honour?

Robert clenched his teeth. *Outdone.* —Make note of it.

♣

At this meeting of Her Majesty's Privy Council this Friday the eighteenth day of May, 1593.

A warrant to Henry Maunder, one of the messengers of Her Majesty's Chamber, to repair to the house of Mr. Thomas Walsingham in Kent, or to any other place where he shall understand Christopher Marlowe to be remaining, and by virtue thereof to apprehend him and bring him to the court in his company. And in case of need to require aid.

IMO EXTRA CAULAS

(Indeed outside the fold)

– Thomas Kyd, Letter A

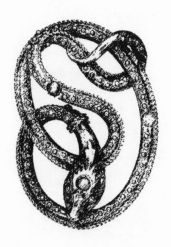

NO, BUT WASH YOUR FACE

—We must be shaved.

Kit flinched, and his quill flew from his hand. —Sweet Christ Jesus, Walls. How long hast thou stood there?

Walsingham, still wearing his nightclothes, hair sticking off in several different directions, closed the door behind him and strode to Kit's desk. He picked up the quill, gave it back. —Thy door was ajar.

—I needed ink. I took some of thine from the library.

—Writing already? 'Tis not even five.

Kit covered his yawn with the back of his right hand. Little cuts marked it. —Starved sleep. What said'st thou? At the door?

—Wast thou not listening?

—Not to thee, no.

—Guests, a few hours due, and we're both hairy as apes. We must be shaved.

—Guests and shaves be fucked.

—Marlowe —

Kit shook pounce onto his fresh ink. —Is't the Queen thy guest?

—What? *No*, thank Christ.

—Then I shall not be shaved.

Kit resumed writing.

Walsingham read over his shoulder. —*Here's channel water, as our charge is given.* Channel water?

—For Christ's love, Walls! *What?* What is't thou'st want? I am working here.

Walsingham snatched the quill from Kit's fingers and

placed it on the far edge of the desk. As Kit reached for it, knocking over the jar of pounce, Walsingham picked up Kit's papers. Kit made to take them back, missed. Eyes widening, Walsingham held the pages out of Kit's reach, and read.

—*To pierce a windpipe with a needle's point?* Young Mortimer? Thou'dst write of Edward II — Piers Gaveston and royal favourites and utter chaos in the court —

—Aye. Favourites and chaos. It makes a good play. Now give it back.

Eyes navigating ink blots and crossed-out words, Walsingham read some more. —Aye. Dangerous good, I doubt not. It shall be banned. Perhaps even burned.

—I shall be a difficult fire.

Kit almost believed himself.

—Marlowe, th'art making a fair copy; thou'st finished the writing of it. How long, what, all this spring?

—I had a patronage, Walls.

—Thou didst write this *not* in just a few months. Didst thou? Thou wast still in bed — abroad, wast thou thinking of it? Writing? How long hast thou sheltered this in thy mind?

Kit smirked.

Walsingham read some more of the scene aloud. Then he sighed. —Violence, degradation, deceit: thou dost write them well. Doth this cause thee no shame?

—I write what I *see*. History is no window but a mirror. And as for shame, Sir Thomas Walsingham: those woods, la, and the fresh and unmarked grave therein, where thou didst command me recite the order of burial — me, who took *not* holy orders — shame was my hearing thee and Dan Roe *dig* as thy good wife, concerned for my delicate lungs, forbade me the strain.

'Tis more than thy lungs. —Thou didst recite it well.

Kit snorted. —Recitation.

Walsingham waited.

—And now thou'st need me to entertain thy guests? The household poet earns his keep?

Walsingham nodded, relieved. —Prettily. I'll instruct Charing —

—The crocodile slithers back and sheds his tears: sweet Christ Jesus, how scald is he — cuts a throat and then makes leg to thee, all I thank you, your honour, for this, my chance to visit my ailing and honoured mother in London. Horse piss and fuckery! Charing touches me *not.*

—I see. And how else shalt thou be shaved?

—Why didst thou not order him to *stay* in London, la? Or didst thou fear thou'dst wake the hangman and set him staggering after the lot of us?

—I sent Charing after thee, aye, but he offered, and we were searching for Gideon, that damned marsh...Hast thou ever poked a marsh with a hooked gaff? Audrey returning the same day, and I knew nothing —

—He's —

—*Hush.* I *know* what he is. I can make no show of it. We must behave in the old peaceable manner. Sir Robert is pleading with me to keep this buried — quiet, I mean; no trumpeting of defeat, as he puts it. 'Tis for *thy* protection.

Kit whispered. —Protect thine own soul, Walls, for I merit none of it. I abandoned that boy —

—'Tis not so —

—And I would stab Charing as soon as —

—Jest not of stabbing, lest I confiscate thy dagger.

—Let jest argue with Gideon's secret grave!

—And if a magistrate saw that cut throat and decided to ask after thine absence?

Kit shoved himself back from the desk and nearly collided with Walsingham as he stood up. His whisper hardened to a mutter. —Castiglione's *sprezzatura*! Declare it a style. Holla, my lords, 'tis my new barbery: I call it the Dead Boy's Beard. See how thick and lush it comes in while yet pinched to points.

—I could strike thee.

—Aye, a perfect solution to our quarrel: I shall stay out of sight. Close my door when thou goest, la, so I may be not interrupted.

—Thou shalt *attend* me and give conversation to my guests, for no matter what friendship struggles to live between us, thou art a servant of this house. As a servant of this house, thou shalt behave as commanded, and 'tis my command that thou shalt be *shaved*.

Kit closed his eyes. —What was he to thee, Walls? What poultice to thy conscience?

—Just some man I needed to hire.

Needed? —Not Charing. Gideon.

Walsingham did not answer right away. —Not what thou'st think.

I know not what to think of thee anymore.

Walsingham rubbed his eyes with the pads of fingers. —I've seeded no bastards. Sir George Pindar, know'st thou him.

Pindar? —No. Gideon told me of a man with a long beard: 'tis him?

—Aye, a beard to his waist, and a reckoning of sins to his feet. He oversees a loose network of Catholics, and sometimes turns them over. Other times, I fear, he doth corrupt himself to name them not. On Sir Robert's behalf, I did visit Sir George one night. I'd heard rumours of him keeping a boy, and when I asked, Sir George called Gideon out, commanded him to sing, and then...offered me the use of him. I — I pretend blindness to so much that sometimes truth kicks me in the stones. I bought the boy outright. A high price, and I already swim in debt. And I fear Sir George only spent that money harming others. Still, this one — I helped one — we shared a saddle back to Scadbury, and he trembled all the way, and I sudden asked myself just what I planned to do with him. And Audrey...

—Audrey doted on him.

—She's lost three, before she felt a single kick. The midwife told her no quickening meant no life. Audrey would beg to differ. The priest told her *Bloodied rags merit no prayer.* Aye, she doted on Gideon.

Kit let out a long breath. —And now ye have guests.

Scents of cooking wafted from the kitchen.

—Very good, Walls. A shave. Only this: stay in the room while that bitter Cain holds a blade to my throat.

—He'd not dare.

—Dares' edges fray, Walls, and if his hand slipped, he'd celebrate.

Staring out the window, at the woods, at the marsh, recalling the fuss at Cambridge over Kit's degree, Walsingham nodded. *My promise stands pure; I am thy friend.* —I'll stand by thee as long as thou'st ask. Just tell me: why art thou so certain Charing would kill thee?

—Walls, please, in these few hours I have left, let me work.

Shaved down, then.

Eyes glittering, head aching, hand clutching a cup, Kit played his role. Dinner began early, about half-past eleven, and by one o'clock the party had consumed variously hot and cold fish, fowl, pork, mutton, beef, bread, puddings, three different wines, and two different meads. A promised sweet dish of eggs, sugar, cream, and nutmeg had yet to appear. Kit belched, his noise lost beneath a louder rumble from Lady Someone. *And feast our prisoner as our friendly guest — Tom — Christ — I must — I must tell Roe he's superb — glut and surfeit, take and eat, all this flesh, my bowels shall be bound for a week.* Sweat beaded his forehead as he drained his cup of dark wine. Walsingham noticed this and filled the cup with apple cider, Kit's favourite. Kit knocked it back, gulping. Thirst quenched and worry drowned, for the moment, and voice carrying, Kit gave more sparkling conversation, leashed danger nudging it: ah, poetry; ah, Latin; ah, fucking. Mine accent? Canterbury, my lady, how keen your ears. My good father is a cobbler (pause for the gasp). A scholarship, your grace, gifts and fortune (pause for the praise). Why, no, my lord, I have never asked my father if he takes pride in me. Know you the verse in *Amores* wherein — what say you, your grace? Ah, you must needs ask Sir Thomas about that.

Kit swallowed the final mouthful of cider from his cup — *my legs melt* — and so managed not to hear much of Walsingham's mumbled explanation that no, his singing boy would not grace the house with his lovely voice, for he'd not long drowned, the marsh so high, why, two cousins and the cook's own father had drowned there, treacherous ground, very sad. Then Audrey yanked the conversation from awkward grief to poetry, offering, as substitution for songs, recitation. Kit looked at her, eyes big. *Please, no.* She made a subtle gesture with her hands; he must stand. He stumbled, touched the table with outstretched fingers, got his balance. The guests, the lord and lady of the house: he looked into their eyes, each by each. Some sweet taste of Hell: they all desired it, begging by command.

Pride, lust, gluttony, sloth…

Dost thou love me, Walls, or dost thou love the danger of me?

Exquisite filth, metre nearly perfect — improvised — hovered behind his lips. He refused to give it. Instead, he recited something pastoral and quite pretty — also improvised. When asked who wrote such beautiful verse and where it might be found published, Kit only smiled, and he picked up and put down his empty cup. Bowing, he begged Lady Audrey's forgiveness as he left the table for a moment.

Passing through the kitchen on his way to the back door, smiling at the exhausted turnspit dog who now slept in his wheel, legs dangling through the slats, Kit waved to Dan. Busy with his work, Dan only nodded. Nick, lounging at the servants' table, took a letter from his satchel and started to read it. Then he got up and followed Kit.

Outside, Kit stood near a corner, opening his hose. Nick leaned against the house, facing him. He smiled.

Kit smiled back. —Ah, sweet Nick. What, didst thou not surfeit on a view of it when I lay ill? Or would'st thou suck it? Kneel, la.

—Th'art drunk.

—Angry, too, though nothing hurts any less for it.

—Thou'st speak of kneeling. Practise it more, and learn the safety of humility.

Kit tucked his clothes. —Not to thee. Not if Lucifer himself shoved me. Thine hands so steady this morning, shaving me, so very skilled. Gideon had no beard. Still, such a clean cut. Breached arteries, la, and the heart's dire pumping.

Nick bowed.

—For Christ's love, Charing!

—Lower thy voice.

—Oh, 'tis low enough.

Nick stepped closer. —Look to Robin Poley for the blood and the gag. I only followed orders.

Gag?

—Marlowe, thou'lt not kneel. Would'st thou stoop? Even with the width of a barleycorn, to spare a loved one pain?

—I've harmed no one.

—Thy refusals do. And *why?* How much more blood for thy pride? 'Tis easy. Thou'dst but report to a different master, and what care'st thou for that? They both serve the Queen.

—My master is the better man.

Nick waited a moment. —Thy Tom's in Bridewell.

—I know.

—Still so cold?

Kit's breath shuddered. —Salt water in January.

—I happened to meet the messenger this morning.

—Not a letter for me, is't?

Nick fanned himself with the letter. —Not so addressed, though it may speak of thee.

Kit leaned his forehead against the cool stone of the house. *I am a very toy.*

Nick touched Kit's beard. —Take comfort in this, my mercy.

Kit waited.

—Dire pumping, as thou sayest. Dead in minutes.

Kit wrenched round and thrust his knee at Nick's stones. He missed. Nick stumbled and slipped on the wet ground, smacking his head on the stone wall. He fell. Kit cocked his pelvis, opened his clothes, and urinated — enough to fill a pitcher, it felt like — all over Nick.

Kit sighed, in happy relief. —Cider courses right through me, la.

Grinning, Kit lurched into the kitchen. Then a rock the size of a child's skull struck the back of his left thigh. He fell to his knees and cried out, and Nick leapt on him from behind, shoving his face to the floor. Kit's teeth smashed against his lips, cutting them, and he heard two vicious smacks, one from the rock as it hit the floor in the space between his right hand and his head.

Nick rolled off him, and Kit scrabbled away and turned to face him, noticing as he did so the fine gold-leaf gilding on Audrey's shoes.

Very pretty. Father could do better. Sweet Christ Jesus, my teeth —

Audrey stood over Nick, grasping a large iron spoon. Nick clutched his mouth and jaw, whimpering. Blood leaked through his fingers.

Voice tight, Walsingham hurried into the kitchen.

—Audrey? What noise? Charing? Marlowe! Revenge for the razor, is it?

The cold of the stone floor seeped into Kit's bones as he spat blood.

Audrey passed the spoon to Dan, who accepted it without a word. Then she stooped to retrieve the rock. —Take this, husband, this, with which Charing would brain Marlowe. Charing dropped it when I struck him. Do notice the dent in the floor. The stone floor.

As Dan gave Kit and Nick rags to staunch their bleeding mouths, Walsingham almost dropped the rock. Then he lifted it as if to throw it at Nick. Dan took the rock from him and placed it on the hearth.

Audrey jabbed her finger at Nick and then at Walsingham. —I want him off this estate!

—Hush, woman!

—I will not! Give him a horse — I care not for the loss, just rid me of the sight of him!

—And send him where, Audrey?

—Send him to Hell!

Nick rose to his feet; Dan got behind him, ready to seize his arms.

—Audrey, 'tis not meet I just hurl the man at the road —

—Need we a second murder?

Nick rammed his elbow into Dan's belly and bolted. Kit and Audrey both ran after Nick and, in a drunken fumble, caught him, fell with him. Sober, and furious with pain, Nick writhed and punched and kicked, hitting Kit in the belly and Audrey twice in the face. Nick rose from the tangle spitting blood, and he lunged outside.

Sickened, fearful, Kit turned to Audrey, who lay still, her eyes clenched shut. Walsingham knelt next to her, lips and hands fluttering, while Kit removed Audrey's cap and dug his fingers deep into her thick hair. He looked up, feeling he should apologize. —Walls, her head is sound. See to her face.

Dan's final egg dish frothed and spilled over the edge of its pot, giving smoke and a harsh smell. He lugged the pot from the fire as Audrey demanded they pursue Nick. Walsingham's face looked drawn — guilty — and he smoothed back Audrey's hair. Then he embraced her, hard.

Kit ran outside. Nick had saddled the mare and now beat her with a crop, making for the road.

—Murderer! I hope she throws thee into a tree!

Cracking thy neck, so thou dost lie on cold ground for hours, unseen, able only to twitch and drool.

Feeling very drunk now, very slow, Kit lurched back to the kitchen, almost in tears. *Why? Why all of this?* Kneeling by Audrey and Walsingham again, wishing he could wipe the blood from Audrey's face — surprised by how much he wished this — Kit noticed paper on the floor: the letter Nick had been reading. Kit took it up, checked for the seal.

Cecil House.

—Walls, here. Charing spoke to me of intercepting a letter.

—The seal's broken. He's read this!

Audrey accepted a compress from Dan and held it to her face. —God, that hurts. He's knocked that bad tooth loose. Thieving *letters*? I like this not.

—No, Lady Audrey. Let me help you stand.

—Cura te ipsum, Marlowe: thine own battered self. Rest a moment.

Kit nodded. Then he smirked. —'Tis a fierce spoon you wield, Lady Audrey.

Footfalls: the dinner guests approached the kitchen. Hoofbeats: horses rounded to the back of the house.

Walsingham looked up from the letter. —Sir Robert delayed the messenger and pursuivants as long as he could, but they knew to come here. Marlowe, the Privy Council has issued a warrant for thine arrest.

No wit, no poetry: Kit just stared at the cold stone floor.

Audrey took a shaky breath as she fixed her cap. —Husband, see to our guests.

—Audrey, I . . . Who in Hell is that?

A man with fair hair and a square jaw strode through the open back door. He wore an elegant colour-blocked vest over his shirt. Keys dangled from right side of his heavy belt, manacles from the left. Three big men followed him. —A bloodied man on the road directed us here, and then we got no answer at the front door. Is this Scadbury, the house of Sir Thomas Walsingham?

Walsingham stood up. —Dear God above! What else this day, what else? Aye, this is Scadbury, and I am Walsingham. Who and what art thou?

He bowed. —I am Henry Maunder, messenger of Her Majesty's Chamber; here is my standard. I've come to serve order of arrest and apprehend one Christopher Marlowe. Is he here?

Voice quiet, steady: —I am.

—Thou? I expected someone bigger. We are to escort thee direct to London, where th'art to wait on the pleasure of the Privy Council. Th'art charged to obey mine orders and give no resistance.

Still on his knees, Kit made a show of straightening his shirt and doublet. —A pretty speech, la. And the charge?

—Atheism.

Kit looked up, eyes wide. —Pardon me?

Henry took the manacles from his belt, and the three pursuivants stopped gawking at the kitchen and fixed their hands on their daggers and their eyes on Kit. Henry cocked his head toward the horses outside. —Time, now. Marlowe: thy wrists.

—Wait...

Walsingham got between Henry and Kit and flattened his hand against Henry's chest. —Hold, sirrah! Be none of that. Thou'lt put no binding to a gentleman.

—Your honour, mine orders are clear: in case of need, to require aid. I may yet by weight of law press the entire household to assist me.

—Four of ye, to one of him?

—Not only are we told he is cunning and violent and tricky with words, your honour, but he doth resist arrest! If —

Kit raised his hands, showed his palms.

Henry nodded at this and gestured to his men. The three pursuivants returned to their horses, Audrey herded the guests back toward the dining room, and Dan stared into his ruined egg dish.

Kit looked at Henry, sighed. —May I stand?

—Stretch out thine hands, far from thy dagger.

—I thank you. And might I beg a moment's leave to collect my belongings? You've my word I shall return to you. Post men at the other doors if you doubt me.

—Be quick.

Bruised thigh and punched belly paining him, Kit bowed, then limped towards the main stairs. The Walsinghams and their confused guests parted to let him pass.

In his bedchamber, he took a quick inventory. He already wore much of his clothing. Walsingham had promised him a new cloak but had yet to give it, and the woollens and jerkin could, he hoped, wait for winter. He wiped sweat from his face then smoothed down his doublet, the fabric wrinkled still from the recent wash, some faint stains from Gideon's corpse still visible on the inner lining. He dragged his new satchel out from beneath his bed with his foot — the satchel another a gift from Walsingham — reached within a slit he'd cut beneath the mattress, and retrieved the latest draft of his letter to his sister.

Walsingham approached the door as Kit tucked the letter into his satchel. Ignoring Walsingham, Kit strode to his desk and hauled open drawers, taking out stacks and stacks of paper: revisions and revisions, the one complete and the second incomplete fair copy of his play, and a legible draft of a long and often absurd poem about love, power, and treachery, about crossing the water — not finished.

Why is't I've not burnt the most of this?

Walsingham walked to him, holding out a wide leather envelope, one that fastened shut with a loop and a piece of bone. —Here.

Kit accepted the gift, straightened his manuscripts, tucked some of them in the envelope. Then he lay his palm on the leather. —I, Christopher Marlowe, do utterly testify and declare in my conscience that the Queen's Highness is the only supreme governor of this realm, and of all other of Her

Highness's dominions and countries, as well as in all spiritual
or ecclesiastical things or causes, as temporal, and that no foreign prince, person, prelate, state, or potentate hath or ought
to have any jurisdiction, power, superiority, pre-eminence, or
authority ecclesiastical or spiritual in this realm.

—What?

—From the Oath of Supremacy. I believed it.

—Aye. We swore it to receive our degrees. What of it?

—I *believed* it. 'Tis but lines in a poxy play.

—Thou'lt mock the oath with a man like Maunder in the
house? Lower thy voice!

—Second man to say that to me today. Fine. I shall whisper. 'Tis more than ideas. 'Tis matters of faith, la. Faith, and
policy. I believed. I *served*. And I've fouled my soul.

Walsingham took a step back.

—A handsome packet, Walls.

—Calfskin. I'd thought to give it thee at Christmas. For
thy fair copies, but I see now 'tis too small. Marlowe, what
is this?

Standing at the bottom of the stairs now, Henry Maunder
called out. —I beg pardon, Sir Thomas, but we must ride.

Audrey demanded to know if Henry's mother had ever
taught him patience, or mercy. With greatest courtesy, Henry
answered that he must obey the same laws that bound them all.

Kit took the three dressed quills from his desk and tucked
them in the tiny pen-loops on his belt. Then, scowling, he
fished the leather envelope out of his satchel. —Walls, keep
this for me. I would lose it in gaol.

Walsingham reached around Kit and laid the envelope on
the desk. —Come back for it.

Descending the stairs, Kit watched where he put his feet. At the bottom, he looked up, glanced at Audrey and the darkening welts on her face, bowed to her, then inclined his head to Henry Maunder and followed him outside.

Starlings sang, and a sweet breeze stirred Kit's hair. The pursuivants stood ready, and Henry mounted fast. Kit admired the neatness of it all: four men on horseback surrounding one on foot, leaving him a wheezing mare, white on the muzzle, who might, if whipped to the bone, match the speed of a lame cow.

Eyes burning with tears, Kit laughed.

Henry and the pursuivants parted to allow Walsingham to come near. He joined Kit by the old mare and offered him a hand up. Kit mounted. He glanced down at Walsingham then, who, calm in the face, wiped his hands on his hose and reached up his cleaner right hand to clasp Kit's. Any utterance now would be memorized, perhaps mauled, and turned over as possible coded secrets, as evidence. They dared not speak. Kit leaned over and took Walsingham's hand, clasped back. Henry Maunder ordered the ride to London begin. Kit let go.

MY HEART'S SO HARDENED, I CANNOT REPENT

Striding to his office in Bridewell, Izaak shook off unhappy dreams: his uncle, Marcus Tilley, yelling of sin and stones and Latin conjugations; and Christopher Marlowe, finding Izaak collapsed from hunger on the ground. In life, Kit had offered Izaak a hand up and some supper at the buttery. In Izaak's dream, as Marlowe once more made his offers, and as

Izaak squinted to decipher the figure reaching for him, both divinity undergraduates looked like old men.

Interfering upstart, presuming he might deign to help me, showing off his money — and where got he that money?

The day Izaak collapsed, he had, for several weeks, slept only four hours a night. He'd done this because Kit could do it, and because he envied Kit all those candles from home. Beneath this regime of interrupted sleep, Izaak suffered a rapid decline. His mind seemed to numb and then hollow out, thoughts and logic dancing just out of his reach. He'd experienced visions of his dead mother, and he'd earned a miserable failing grade on an important assignment and thereby nearly lost his scholarship, shaming everyone. The university then commuted this threat to rustication: suspension for a term. Izaak must go home. Home? Sleaford, and Marcus Tilley? Home, just escaped? And what result of this disgrace? What long hours of contemplation, and punishment, might Marcus devise? Considering all this, Izaak could neither eat nor drink nor sleep. Awaiting decision one drizzling afternoon, he'd curled up against a shadowed wall. He'd gone unnoticed for hours, until Kit found him, and extended his hand. Cambridge then rescinded all punishment. Those informing Izaak of this sudden mercy cited another student's pleading intervention, a fellow divine's concerns that Izaak Pindar might be not incompetent but unwell. Izaak had never asked which fellow divine. He'd guessed. Only one was that observant, that interested in finding the innards, as he called it, finding the why.

A cobbler's son. Fah.

A cobbler's son who could point to his father.

Studying the ink stains on his desk, Izaak begged God

to let his mother appear. He got no apparition. Instead, he gnawed on a memory: eight years old, holding the hand of his young mother as she walked beside him up the long path to Marcus Tilley's house. *He is a great man, Izaak, a landlord now, my sister's husband.* Later, after dark, after hard words from Marcus, words of not welcome but requirement, Izaak had laid his head in his mother's lap. She'd smoothed his hair from his forehead and tucked it behind his ear. *Izaak, Izaak, smile. Whatever happens, Marcus shall take care of thee.*

Knuckles rapped on the door.

Mother, you abandoned me!

Izaak pinched the bridge of his nose.

God in my heart. Please, Mother, speak to me. Tell me you loved me. Tell me you wished you'd chosen me, and not Rome. Tell me how I've not always sat behind a little desk in Bridewell.

The knocking got louder, and Geoffrey Morgan presumed to enter the room. —Examiner Pindar. You asked for the presence of Keeper Deyos.

—Aye, aye, a moment. Away.

Izaak glanced round the office, sighed, and joined keeper and clerk. All three walked with a stiff-necked briskness to Tom's cell, as though on their way to a meeting they considered pointless yet wished to be seen attending.

Squinting, Izaak pointed to the heap of clothes and limbs leaning against the cell wall. —Ready him.

John unlocked the door, and Geoffrey entered, ready to perform his customary check. —Good pulse, no fever — ah, no. Keeper Deyos: the stare. I get no recognition from him.

Izaak frowned. —What means this?

John bent over, gave Tom a glance. —'Tis a little blessing,

Mr. Pindar, visited on some of the most tried ones in here. For a time, the mind crawls away.

—Haul it back.

—Why?

Beneath his anger at the keeper's defiance, Izaak had no easy answer.

—Waste not your valuable time, Mr. Pindar. Come back tomorrow.

Kneeling, Geoffrey drew his index finger back and forth before Tom's face; Tom's eyes followed the finger.

Izaak straightened his robe. —We shall achieve little in this life with such easy surrender and neglect, Deyos.

—Surrender and neglect?

—Mine examination of this man is incomplete. Your duty, Keeper —

—I need no...Want you this man broken? Be that your goal? You're three parts of four across the water now.

Geoffrey sighed, almost moaned. Three children, fourth on the way, a copied poem, and his own deep guilt, versus one man: most wretched arithmetic.

At night, Geoffrey dreamt of Hellfire.

Izaak turned his back to prisoner, keeper, and clerk. —Such foulness in here.

Geoffrey nodded. Then he caught Tom studying him, reasoning. Tom's face got calm and certain. Geoffrey had often seen Tom look like this at school: Tom Kyd, head of the class, first to part the veil on logic puzzles, first to slide to the answer of a reckoning tale.

Tom stared into Geoffrey's eyes, and Geoffrey felt guilt stain his face. *He knows my hand touched that libel.*

Izaak complained some more of the bad air and said he would depart for the day. John offered to escort him to the doors, but Izaak held up his hand, as if to dam chatter, and strode off.

John rolled his eyes. —Sobbing mother of Christ, what I haven't got to bear. Morgan, come along.

Geoffrey struggled not to speak aloud. *Blue eyes. I've known thy blue eyes since we started school. Thomas Kyd, wilt thou vouch for me?*

Flames crackled; Geoffrey looked to the floor.

—Morgan!

A meaty hand slapped Geoffrey's shoulder.

—Come along, I said.

Obedience returned him to freedoms.

PERHAPS THY SACRED PRIESTHOOD
MAKES THEE LOATH

On the quiet ride to London, tricking out a sense of calm, Kit charmed Henry Maunder into conversation — church architecture. Then Kit surprised himself further by telling Henry about his Canterbury Cathedral dream, and Henry confided he'd got a recurring nightmare of playing hide and seek in a church suddenly under attack by reformers: axes to the icons, fire up the nave. One of the constables coughed and cleared his throat at that; Kit and Henry fell silent.

In Southwark, where they left the horses with Lee Crimm's assistant, the truth of the ride afflicted Kit. His thighs ached;

his lungs caught. Weak, weak, weak: so much time, and *still* he felt unwell.

Wherry crossing done, the party now tramped north. Henry and Kit walked at the front of the group; the three constables marched behind them. They moved well away from the Strand and Cecil House.

No audience. Well, 'twas scantest hope.

Away from Bridewell, too.

Henry seemed confused, almost apologetic. —Marlowe, I cannot yet deliver thee to the council, they not being in session.

Farringdon Street. The Fleet Prison, then. —I hardly expected you would.

—'Tis some days a galling chore, escorting a man under arrest. Often he fights and frets and then settles into a surliness. Sometimes he weeps. Sometimes he tells me the long and tangled story of how he fell to my charge. Thou dost seem — resigned? Is't resigned? Accepting? Is't faith? Thou who art accused of atheism, art thou faithful?

—I am very tired.

At the Fleet's Farringdon Street grille, hands groped and voices begged.

The Fleet's gaol clerk, flanked by two bored guards, recognized Kit as a knowledgeable, nameless man who paid well when seeking information. Saying nothing of that, the clerk prepared to assign this prisoner to the master's side, where a moneyed inmate found better accommodation and food, when Henry gave him a sealed letter. The clerk opened it, read it at a whisper, and announced the arrest and arrival of one Stephen Loman, due solitary confinement.

Kit shut his eyes.

One little man, Christopher Marlowe.

One little man locked up under a false name. Is this your mercy, Sir Robert, your protection? Or a punishing reminder?

Fuckery.

The clerk confiscated Kit's dagger and satchel, and Kit tallied in his head the amount in his purse, wondering how much he must pay to get the dagger and satchel back come the morning. He'd got no doubt he'd soon need his dagger; he wanted only the satchel — the unfinished letter within it.

Henry flattened his hand over the clerk's ledger. —I shall hold his belongings until I fetch him tomorrow, at the Privy Council's pleasure.

Kit peered at him, wanting to catch his eye, signal thanks. Henry avoided looking at him. Instead he tucked Kit's dagger and scabbard into the satchel, hung the bag across his chest, and signed the clerk's ledger to confirm delivery of the prisoner, by any name. Then he left.

Kit felt as confused by this as by the boatswain back on *Peace of Lethe.*

He inclined his head to the clerk and followed the guard — *my little pilgrimage up the nave, is't?* — telling himself the darkness mattered not, for he'd slept in such darkness before.

When accused of counterfeiting coin. When accused of killing a man. When accused of raping a boy.

This deception failed. At the cell door, he noticed his shaking hands.

The guard looked Kit up and down. —Due before the Privy Council. And how'dst thou earn that?

—I bore candlelight into Hell, kissed the arse of Lucifer, and sold to him my soul.

Unlocking the door, the guard chuckled. —Keep the bill of sale? Hey, thy voice: Kent? Canterbury?

Kit stared at him.

—I lived in Canterbury a while. I feel I should recognize thee. Stand there, in the better light. No, no, thy face is strange to me.

—I had a fancy shave.

Just this morning?

The guard chuckled again. Prison wit, he decided, bravado. —Stand well back from the door now, aye, good fellow.

Kit watched the guard lock up and leave. Then he paced about.

So, Clever Kitten, what woe this time? Gaol, again.

For Christ's love: atheism? If this goes to trial, I — I'm fucked.

Breathe, breathe. Settle thyself. Ex quattuor autem locis,in quos honesti naturam vimque divisimus, primus ille, qui in veri cognitione consistit, maxime naturam attingit humanam —

He staggered then, as though shoved, and memories swooped: Ben, Tom, their voices loud yet obscured. His pounding heart drove sweat to his skin, and he heard himself teaching a student who did not exist that the proper term of respect for the Furies, the Eumenides, was the Gracious Ones, or Kindly Ones.

—Flatter them, Gideon, lest they tear thee apart. And make compartments in thy mind, where thou mayest hide.

Down the hall, voices rose: postured promises of intimate violence knotted up with fantasies of revenge on guards, wives, informers, thieves, Catholics, neighbours, landlords, whores. Entire stories streeled out in the chatter, so many voices…

Kit leaned against a wall and crossed his arms, cocking his hips to get his weight off his bruised thigh.

Any other night I'd listen.

I'll get no clarity from other men's words.

Wide-eyed in darkness, he considered endings.

HONOUR IS PURCHASED BY THE DEEDS WE DO

Rain dripped off the hood of Henry Maunder's cloak and pattered hard on the ground. —A first, this, escorting a prisoner on a Sunday morning.

Kit's aching head and body slowed his stride. *Boy-fucking Judas, how many cloaks? Mine in Flushing, then the boatswain's, then Tom's, then one promised by Walls, and today I'm in doublet and shirtsleeves and soaked to my bones.*

—Whither bound, Maunder?

Henry turned to look Kit in the eye. —Another departure: York House, on the Strand.

Kit knew York House by sight — a grace-and-favour house for whomever served as lord keeper of the great seal — and he wondered if Sir Robert ever visited Sir John Puckering there.

Kit asked to halt a moment. He tilted back his head and opened his mouth, then cupped his hands. One guard grumbled about delays; Henry watched Kit drink rain. Kit swallowed and nodded, and Henry signalled to the party to continue. —When we arrive at the house, I shall return thee thy satchel and dagger. I expect thou'dst get but a poor sleep?

For Christ's love, how much drank I yesterday? —Sore head.
—Dream of thy cathedral?

He had. Only this time he stood outside of it, ankles chained, worried about his shoes, worried he stood outside Notre-Dame de Rheims instead. He never got to the door, to the ceiling. Remembering Rheims, the labyrinth design in the floor, the Smiling Angel statue near the ceiling, he'd called out, first in Latin, then in French: *I've lost my way. The ninety who burnt. I've lost my way!* Wind blew clouds across the sky and stole his voice.

He said none of this to Henry. Rain trickled down the back of his neck.

A worried-looking woman let them in the house, leading them to a servants' corridor that connected to a grand room. The house felt cavernous, oppressive. Henry gave Kit his belongings back, and Kit took them with gratitude, noticing his papers seemed undisturbed. Strapping scabbard and dagger to his thigh, he felt less vulnerable now, less naked. His stomach churned. He'd not eaten at the Fleet, too queasy from yesterday's drinking and today's fears, and not in a mood to pay several times the market rate for slop better fed to a pig. Residual scents of eggs, bacon, gingerbread, and fowl told Kit that Sir John Puckering ate well.

I doubt his cook rivals Dan Roe.

Roe. I never thanked thee.

The men waited.

Outside, church bells rang a quarter hour, a half hour, three-quarters, the full.

Certain he'd heard someone duck out of his sight, someone who'd been watching from above, Kit looked up.

A partially open ceiling allowed a glimpse of the floor above, its railings and balustrades. No one stood there.

The bells signalled another quarter hour.

Henry shifted his weight from hip to hip. —Aye, 'tis always so: make dire haste and then wait-on-our-pleasure till thy bones crumble.

Kit nodded. *Sweet Christ Jesus, for a pipe of tobacco.*

The woman returned, pinching a folded piece of paper and holding it before her as though it smouldered. —Which of ye is Maunder?

Henry took the paper and read it. The note ordered him to Bridewell: no explanation, no clarification, just the order to go. Surprised, he discussed this with his constables in a murmur, nodded to Kit, and left.

Once more, they waited.

When they'd first arrived, York House felt like a dark shelter from the rain. Now, sun blazing outside, the house seemed to contract with stifling air. One constable had removed his doublet, but the other, like Kit, wanted to be ready to appear at any moment and so suffered the rising heat.

Kit studied the constables. *One fair, one dark, both blue-eyed, similar jaws: brothers?*

Oh, this is tedious.

The two guards sighed at the same time, lips flapping.

Kit knew they waited by design, Sir Robert calling such a delay sweating a man closer to the truth. Knowledge soothed nothing.

He coughed.

They waited.

A delicate footfall behind them: Kit refused to turn, working first to decipher the message of the shoes — something his father had taught him.

A grown man, tall, light step and so unburdened, oh, delicate shod: calfskin? Wealthy, educated.

The blond guard whispered. —Be that the Earl of Essex?

Kit and the dark-haired guard turned, and the three men bowed to their better. The motion sent blood plummeting to Kit's head, and as he straightened up, the blood fell away, leaving him dizzy and faint.

Essex, his slashed doublet of black leather laced snug over a shirt of tangerine silk, smiled. Rose, lavender, and some new spice, earthy and sweet, like the meadow at Scadbury after a rain, scented the air around him. —Good morrow to ye, gentlemen of the law. Please ye good sirs to wait some distance off, as I would speak with your prisoner.

Besotted by celebrity, stuttering, the blond guard bowed again. —An't please you, my lord, no: this one gets violent.

—He shan't. Not here. That dagger is but a decoration.

—But my lord...

Kit recognized the spice: saffron, rare and expensive.

The dark-haired guard glanced down the hall, up at the partial ceiling, at the earl's feet. —Good my lord, we dare not abandon your gentle self to menace and threat.

Essex waved the concerns away. —'Tis a Sunday morning. Your work should not drag ye from your saviour and your God. Risk not your souls for farthings. Hie ye to church.

The guards looked at each other, their questions struggling.

—I shall answer for ye. Now, I insist: to church.

The guards bowed and left, hesitating at the corridor's first turn, whispering, and then continuing on.

Kit studied this famous commander of men, this beloved royal favourite, this dancer, singer, poet.

Saffron stains his jaw and forehead, la. He tints his hair and beard. Oh, sweet God, lend me strength not to laugh.

Essex lost his smile, and his eyes seemed to flatten out. —So small. Where is thy fight now, and what assistance is thy fiery mind? Most of all, who and what art thou to stare up so bold at me? Art thou not the felon, the poppet, the demanding Alexis, and the blaspheming atheist, Christopher Marlowe?

—I am Christopher Marlowe.

—Dost thou not recognize me?

—Devereux, my lord the Earl of Essex.

—And master of the horse, and knight of the garter, and Her Majesty's privy councillor, and yet thou'lt not kneel?

Kit looked down at the earl's fine shoes. *Aye, calfskin.*

—Th'art cocky and expensive, Marlowe, but th'art not worth spilt blood.

—No, my lord, I am not.

—However, thy worst faults overlap mine own and thus inspire in me gracious mercy: I grant thee audience.

—I've petitioned none of it.

—Fury spits that. Give me thine eyes, thine hands, and thine unnatural memory that tempts me to believe in ghosts as well as God, and thy Tim — no, Tom — shall be released. Come, 'tis simple. Speak.

—I'll not —

—I need but one completed task from thee, a petty matter in Scotland. Sir Robert would send thee north, so no hardship of surprise there.

Kit heard the schoolmaster, beating his left hand: *Feel each cut. Remember, and so learn when to train thy memory, when to still thy tongue, and when to obey thy betters.*

—Should I accept your lordship's gracious offer, then I must needs accept it again, and again, crouching to peep between your fingers, and darting with prayer when guilt seizes your hand and makes it a fist. I will offer you nothing of myself, for your wage is death.

Trembling, Kit expected a blow to his head.

Essex just clicked his tongue. —Christ, 'tis like talking to a woman: reason and sense, begone. Thou wouldst utter *guilt* to me when thine own guilt rattles the cage of thy voice? Come, I would embrace thee.

Leather and silk pressed Kit's face.

—Such knotted shoulders. What, what, what? Chilled? Poor Tom's-a-cold? Hush. Let me finger the tears from thy lashes, and we shall call the halt to this mad dance. I ask, for the final time: wilt thou give me thy little self?

Kit writhed.

Essex released him.

Hair falling in his eyes, Kit heard his father's voice. *The ninety who burnt. They screamed and prayed and wept, all for the wrong loyalty at the wrong time. Puzzle it out, Kit. Get it right.*

The floor banged his knees, yet he fell, fell, fell.

Head bowed, he said it. —So please you, my lord, I am yours.

Silence.

Essex knelt, too. —I'll not have thee.

—My lord?

Essex dug his fingers into Kit's jaw and hauled up his face.
—I'd box thine ears, but I would have thee hear and remember every word, *every word*, flung at thee today. Th'art one signature from Bridewell — my signature — and there thou shalt be wrung dry. Submission comes too late.

Church bells rang. Arrivals sounded behind closed doors; Robert complained, voice pained and sharp. —God's own wounds broiling in the midday sun. A pretty sight, this empty house. Is't a sudden scarcity of watermen? I should like to start a meeting on time, for a change, yet I see not one other councillor, not even Essex, who said he'd welcome us. Pindar, check the corridor behind the dining room, past that door.

—Your honour, 'tis a servants' way.

—Check it, I say.

Essex shook Kit's face free of his grasp, stood up, and wiped his hand on his hose. Shoulders hunched, neck bent, Kit stared at his own knees. Izaak Pindar discovered them so: Christopher Marlowe kneeling in humble petition to his master's rival.

Ignoring Izaak, Essex strode into the dining room and greeted Sir Robert on this beautiful day, i'faith, how the sun streamed through the windows, oh, knew he a good glazier?

Tom —

Kit raised his head.

Izaak smiled. —Well met.

—Pindar?

—Get up, and attend. I must review protocol with thee. Address each man —

—I know thy protocol, and I smell thy policy. What role play'st thou here?

—Wilt thou not just *listen*? Address each man to his station, as your honour or my lord, or in those plurals. Should'st thy memory fail thee, sir and sirs are usually safe. Speak only when spoken to, and presume nothing. Wait here until I call — where are thy guards?

Robert bellowed. —Mr. Pindar!

Izaak hurried to his master; Kit sagged against the wall.

As Essex played with the arrangement of the chairs, two other councillors arrived, and Robert took care to greet them: the host Sir John Puckering, of course, and, rare attendant these days, shuffling, leaning on Sir John's arm, William Cecil, Lord Burghley. William looked to be having one of his distant days, such days scarcer but still a problem. His mind might snap back like a bowstring, or it might travel all day.

Robert bowed to him. —Good my lord, and my honoured father. You are looking well this morning. I apologize, sir, for I'd no idea you wished, or, indeed, felt well enough, to attend.

—Sir John Puckering did come fetch me, saying you had need and desire of my presence and advice.

Ah. Smiling his gratitude to Puckering, Robert spied Essex bearing down on him. *Shall I be haunted thus?*

Essex touched Robert's elbow and murmured in his ear. —Wee Robbie: he's mine.

Nodding, Robert pretended to study one of the shields.

As Essex strode off to take a seat, Robert turned his attention back to Puckering. —Sir John, how kind of you not only to host this meeting but to do me the great service of fetching and escorting Lord Burghley.

—My pleasure, Sir Robert. Today's agenda demands experience, wisdom, discretion, and each available vote.

—It doth. Sit you down, Father. Mr. Pindar, mark the attendance.

Izaak took a quill from behind his ear. —In attendance: his lordship William Cecil, Lord Burghley; his lordship Robert Devereux, the Earl of Essex; the honourable Sir John Puckering, Lord Keeper of the Great Seal; and the honourable Sir Robert Cecil, acting secretary.

Robert accepted a stash of papers from Izaak. —My lords and gentlemen, I must comment on today's scant attendance — make note of it, Mr. Pindar. Two days ago this council issued a warrant of arrest for one Christopher Marlowe. He's accused of atheism. He waits in the corridor.

William toyed with a button on his sleeve. —The clouds broke apart as we voyaged here, and they did remind me of some steed of war, speared, muscular neck bowing as he bled.

None spoke.

Robert nodded to Izaak, who read the cue, strode to the door, and hurled his voice like an actor projecting to reach the dead. —Enter the accused.

The accused entered.

Murky portraits and battered shields hung on the wall. Kit ignored those, instead giving a quick study to each councillor seated at the long oak table, finishing with Robert.

Not done yet, Clever Kitten.

Returning to the side of the table, Izaak named him. —My lords and gentlemen: Christopher Marlowe.

Kit bowed to the Privy Council.

Izaak dipped his quill in ink. —Where shalt thou be found in London, Marlowe?

—Parish of St. Mary Colechurch —

—Speak up.

He cleared his throat. —Parish of St. Mary Colechurch, Old Jewry Street, not far from the church, sign of the quill.

Essex pointed at Izaak. —I am still new to council, clerk, but recall I not how an accused man must also be recorded by title or task?

Robert nodded again, and Izaak bowed and gave answer. —You are quite correct, my lord, and I humbly thank you. Marlowe: title or task?

—Scholar, poet, and gentleman.

Essex raised his eyebrows; Robert read a report; Izaak wrote with care. —Gentleman.

—Doubteth me, clerk?

Not bothering to look up, Robert rapped the table with his knuckles. —The accused enjoys no leave to speak so free.

Kit bowed, all apology.

—As acting secretary, I shall open the questions. Marlowe, the truth, at once: art thou atheistic?

Essex leant back in his chair. —Oh, 'tis common known, and it doth spread like sickness. I feel grave concern for some of my peers.

—My lord of Essex?

—I blunder, Sir Robert, the new man still, and I offer the council a new man's apology. Carry on.

—I thank you. Marlowe: art thou an atheist?

—No, your honour.

—Pindar, note the — Marlowe, wilt thou *laugh*?

—Forgive me, my lords and gentlemen. I am giddy. Lately, when sleep comes at all, 'tis studded with bad dreams.

William poked Essex. —His face is wet.

Robert rapped the table again. —Order, please. Marlowe, thou art an atheist, if thine accuser be true, and . . . My lord of Essex, what paper is this you pass me?

—My memory fails, Sir Robert; I meant to give it you before. I know not the hand, but the words dance to heresy's vicious rhythms. 'Tis, some would say, atheism writ large.

Robert glanced at the writing and shot Kit a dark look.

Kit shot it back. —Sir Robert, may I ask who found and furnished that paper?

—When spoken to!

Silence.

Essex raised his hand.

—The acting secretary recognizes the Earl of Essex.

—If I may answer: Marlowe, this sheet was given over by thine accuser, after 'twas found entwined in his papers. My fellow councillors, this Marlowe must yet answer for the Dutch Church Libel, per Tamburlaine.

—The acting secretary recognizes Sir John Puckering.

—My thanks, Sir Robert. I ask the council: should not the charges be entered as two separate offences?

—The acting secretary recognizes the Earl of Essex.

—I second the Lord Keeper's motion.

Robert nodded to his rival. —So please you, my lord of Essex, the Lord Keeper made no motion. He asked a question. The acting secretary recognizes the Lord Keeper.

—My thanks. I so move to ask the council to separate and clarify the charges.

—And I second. Stall us no further, Sir Robert.

—So noted, my lord of Essex. The acting secretary calls for questions.

William placed his worried-off button on the table and advanced his swollen fingers to a ribbon. Then he poked Essex in the arm again. —How differs sedition from atheism in England? Young Devereux, I charge thee: give me good answer.

—Good my lord, I enjoyed the privilege of being a mere ward alongside your son, under your roof and most excellent guidance. I ask you now, Lord Burghley, would any learned or even conscious man not agree that the natures, manifestations, and dark dangers of sedition and atheism lie together in bitterest embrace?

—Devereux, wouldst thou flatter me?

—No, my lord: I ask your advice.

—Take this button; some man's lost it.

Kit bit the inside of his cheek. *Sweet Christ Jesus. These are the men who run England.*

Looking at Kit, Essex tossed the button high in the air, caught it, closed his fist around it. —Sir Robert, brought you a copy of the Dutch Church Libel?

—So please you, my lord of Essex, the acting secretary has not yet enjoyed the pleasure of recognizing you. The acting secretary recognizes the privy councillor signals his desire to speak in order. My lord of Essex. My lord of Essex?

—What, what, what?

—You wished to ask a question, my lord?

William hawked and spat a small glob into his ribbon to soften the knot. —For that matter, how differ sedition, atheism, and treason? A dark trinity there. Know I not this man?

Kit bowed to him, but only William saw this, as Essex and Puckering stretched their necks, trying to peek at Robert's papers.

Izaak fished a sheet from one of his bundles. —Sir Robert, a copy of the libel, so please you.

—My thanks, Mr. Pindar. The acting secretary recognizes Lord Burghley.

—For 'tis difficult, this business of trust. As I always advised my son, and such pride warms me when I think on him: be true to thine own self. No, the crookback. The pretty one's my ward.

Essex snatched the libel from Robert's hand. —Marlowe would read us this, hey? Failed divine, cobbler's son: preach us a sermon; give us a poem. Grieve us with thine high astounding terms. Come: take it.

Kit stepped closer to the table, accepted the paper. He read it, as if for the first time, murmuring.

Puckering almost shouted. —Aye, 'tis signed *Per Tamburlaine*, and it sounds the very voice of... What was't, my lord of Essex, the phrase?

—The scourge of God.

—'Tis a magnificent play, I grant, but much in love with itself, its power, or so I am led to understand. I attend not the playhouses. But 'twas writ by the very man standing before us.

Essex looked up from whispering to Izaak. —True, Sir John, and this libel doth repeatedly allude, blunt and pleased

— jigging veins of rhyming mother-wit, hey? — to some other lewd plays this Marlowe's been so good as to scribble out: the Paris massacre, and the one about the Jew. Marlowe, th'art too proud of thy works to deny their mention here. Answer me!

Holding the libel quite still, Kit looked up. —So please you, my lord, I dare say someone plays fast and loose with my lines, but this libel: 'tis *not* my work.

—Felon and brawler and even undergraduate trouble-maker: why should we believe thee?

—Simply put, my lord: I write better.

Voices rose, and Robert, disguising his smirk, rapped the table again. —Order, please. Order. To the accusation — my lord of Essex, you stand?

—By God. I shall not...I *will* not bear it. Sir Robert, how dare this — this *slave* take tone with me? Us? I'd see mine own men whipped for less.

—None doubts that.

—Sir Robert, this Marlowe comes before us a known criminal, disciplined and gaoled for fighting in the street, an incident in which another man *died*, yet now he stands there, cocked and proud, amply framing himself with habitual defiance while yet guilty of atheism, sodomy, and murder!

Puckering looked at Robert. —Sodomy again? How many laws —

Robert's eyes opened wide. —Murder, my lord of Essex?

—Aye, and counterfeiting. Marlowe, wipe the sweat from thy brow with thy trembling little hand and tell this Council, these good men and true, how thou wert deported from Flushing.

Mouth dry, Kit tried to swallow. —So please you, my lord, that was another country —

—And besides, the boy is dead?

Sweet Christ Jesus. —My lord —

Robert jumped to his feet and slapped the table with open palms. —I demand order. In the Queen's name!

Puckering cleared his throat, smoothed his clothes. Burghley tugged his beard. Kit and Izaak each studied the other. Essex hid a smirk with his fist.

Robert took a deep breath. —We must hear the accused speak to his charges, which purpose, I believe, was the *reason* for this meeting. Marlowe, what say'st thou?

—I say this: 'tis absurd. Atheism, my lords and gentlemen, when I might be ordained, and take up holy orders? I worship God, and our saviour, Christ. No dark sacraments shroud my conscience, and 'tis not me conjuring demons but John Faustus. I confess: the charges frighten me. Know I mine accuser?

Essex clasped his hands behind his head. —Biblically.

Robert sighed. —My lord of Essex?

—Hmm?

—When you are ready.

—Oh, I'm ready. Marlowe?

Kit stared at the tangerine silk. —Then I say…I am sullied and dissembled by one…My loved ones — I…

Not got the words.

Robert watched tears shine in the dark circles beneath Kit's eyes. —The acting secretary speaks for the council in recognizing the distress of the accused and grants him a moment of thought, to pause, and so make careful answer.

Kit took a breath.

He bowed his head. —So please you, my lords and gentlemen: I stand here, beaten. I await your lordships' dread pleasure.

Essex looked to Robert. —Bridewell?

Robert kept his gaze on Kit. —Mr. Pindar, make note that the secretary shall speak the council's pleasure in this matter, as must, I regret, be done, attendance so low and quorum so far away. My lord of Essex, *wait*, I beg you. Christopher Marlowe: Her Majesty's Privy Council doth command thee to keep daily attendance upon us, reporting each day at the hour instructed — *without fail* — until such time as the council doth license thee elsewise or to the contrary. Remain at thy London address for further messages of command, else face immediate arrest. Th'art dismissed.

Essex snorted. —Daily attendance when he merits gaol? 'Tis outrageous.

—I wish to keep an eye on the accused, good my lord, lest harm befall him before I digest all the implications of the serious crimes discussed here today.

—Digest me no digestions! This man —

Robert pointed to the door. —Gone deaf, Marlowe? I said, th'art dismissed.

Kit bowed and departed, closing the servants' doors behind him.

Robert stood up, and so did the others, as Izaak strained to write notes. —Her Majesty would thank you, my lords and gentlemen, and I thank you, and the clerk. My lord of Essex, I thank you for finding my father's lost button. Good my lord, you seem overcome. Is't the heat?

Essex inclined his head close and patted Robert's shoulder, demonstrating brotherly love and respect, just as Lord Burghley had taught them. —Dost thou think, wee Robbie, that I care if a man keeps his appointments?

Robert lifted his rival's hand from his shoulder and clasped it in both of his, chuckling, as if at the earl's quiet wit.

Essex pulled free. Sounding brittle, he addressed the other councillors. —Gentlemen, I beg your indulgence for mine intemperance: I am not well.

His theatrical exit, the other councillors accustomed to it, got lost in murmurs of good wishes for safe travel home, and rode any other man that leaky wherry painted with the rose, and oh, the disgraceful state of watermen these days. Robert approached Puckering, who'd made to follow Essex. —Sir John, I needs presume on your earlier kindness in bringing Lord Burghley, as I must now tend to matters with my clerk. Here, money for the wherry back to Cecil House.

Puckering frowned, nodded, gave the younger man back his coin. —I need no such assistance.

William glanced up from his sleeve. —Are we to meet again in council so soon?

—I shall keep you informed, my lord, and good father. Mr. Pindar, if you please, close the door behind Lord Burghley and Sir John, and then attend me. My thanks. Now. Thine own title and task: clerk to Her Majesty's Privy Council, is it not?

—Aye, 'tis so.

—Hast thou dropped a phrase?

—Aye, 'tis so, your honour.

Robert shook pounce on Izaak's notes. —Dost thou not also serve as my private clerk?

—That privilege is mine, so please your honour.

—So please me?

Robert blushed, scowled. *Shrewd judge of character, am I not? How much hast thou bled me, Pindar? Ridding myself of thee only trumpets my defeat to Essex. Friends close, enemies closer.*

—If thou wouldst please me, Pindar, never more make so bold and brazen a display as to be seen taking whispers from Essex, or any other councillor, in meeting!

—Your honour, I beg —

—Thou'dst *beg* nothing. Thy voice so slick — would'st thou usurp? No, surfeit of thy speech. Thy denials only foul the air. And what whispered Essex to thee?

—Only of the stains of guilt on Marlowe's face.

Robert snorted. —Hurry to sum up thy present task at Bridewell. How hast thou stained thy hands there, I wonder, so quick to manacle and rack...No, speak *not*! Speak not to me. Peer at the sky, Izaak Pindar, and seek there the peace —

Robert's voice caught.

Time and tears and blood: the waste!

—Attend me, Izaak Pindar, for the sake of thy soul.

Heart pounding, Izaak scurried to his accustomed spot, the right side of Sir Robert Cecil.

—Truth: what witnessed thou in that corridor?

—Marlowe kneeling before Essex in supplication, so please your honour.

Hellfire. —Pindar, I love thee not, so 'tis out of charity I would tell thee this and give thee some shield against the earl's whispers. His lordship's purse is deep, and his mind, I grant, is bright as flame — but steady as bog. He's as like to hire a murderer and send death stalking thee one morning as give thee recommendation to the Queen. Dost thou yet see how thy life is bound to my hand? I should order thine arrest and then forget to schedule for thee any such appearance as even Marlowe enjoyed today. I should leave thee to warming a gaol cell in winter with only thy breath. Th'art but one little man, and my work is this: while I live, I will make, and I will *keep*, this country's peace.

Robert took up the notes and ledger, shuffled to the far door and shoved it open with his shoulder. The flap of his feet echoed down the Thames-side corridor.

Izaak kicked one chair out of the way and slumped in another. —Let he who would have peace prepare for war.

—But Peter sat without in the court, and there came a servant maid, saying: Thou also was with Jesus the Galilean.

Izaak flinched, looked up.

Kit had crept back in from the servants' corridor and now tugged on his shoes. —But he denied before them all, saying: I know not what thou sayest. And as he went out of the gate, another maid saw him, and she said to them that were there: This man was also with Jesus of Nazareth. And again he denied with an oath, I know not the man. And after a little while, they came that stood by and said to Peter: Surely thou art one of them, for even thy speech doth discover thee.

—Matthew, chapter 27. What of it?

—Twenty-six. Verses 69 to 73, Douay-Rheims, and filthily written. Blush, la, for shame of thy lapsed memory, or for shame of thy tormenting an innocent man? Or dost thou lack the blood?

—What I lack not is licence. Grace, too.

Kit clasped his hands behind his back. *Shall I ask thee of Sir George Pindar?* —Bargains. The same scholarship, and the same evaded promise at its end. Here we stand.

—Is't true: thine eyes?

—Mine eyes?

—They change colour? Aye, thy turn for blushing. And the man, Bradley: didst thou stab him? 'Twas thee? Perhaps that investigation should be opened again: was't murder? Thy blush departs and leaves thee pale. Thy Tom, thy pliant Tom, hath told me so much. Thou'lt call him *sweet scold* in fond tones and say even his sweat smells of honey, and yet I must still ask: how is't he loves thee? Thou, the man before me, breath sharp with stale drink: wast thou carousing yesterday, thou who wouldst pretend to worry? And now, wouldst thou bribe me?

Kit wanted to take a step back; he stood still. —I would pray for thee.

—Desperate and thereby illegitimate prayer: oh, such wealth.

—I . . .

—Dismiss not the will of God in these matters, Marlowe. I perform my duty. Aye, duty, duty and sacrifice: strangers to thee. Something else Tom Kyd said to me, of thee: *he knows as much of sacrifice as he knows of the moon.* Thine atheism, thy turning from God: 'tis thy defiance. I saw it at Cambridge, and I see it now: thy self-serving insistence on individual responsibility and will. 'Tis not mine acts what make meaning here but my prayers. Each step, each word, each tear: all long decided, and most of us stand not free, but damned. A few, hidden and blessed, shall ascend to Heaven, regardless of sin, as both a rebuke and a proof to mankind, signs of the inexplicable workings of God. The rest is not our business.

—Horse piss! Tell me not of the greatness of the prize when thine appetites gallop. I see the pleasure in thine eyes, the love of thy bitter work. I see it!

Izaak closed his eyes, pinched the bridge of his nose. —'Tis more than thee, and thou know'st nothing of ends here. Nothing.

—I know a floor beneath my knees.

Smirking, Izaak looked away.

—Consider Peter.

—Who?

Almost falling into a chair, Kit faced Izaak. —Saint Peter, the apostle, remember him? After curling up for a nap in Gethsemane, after Judas and the kiss, Peter denied Christ. Three times. Such denial is the most grievous and galling sin we know, for it wraps the root and fuse of every other sin. Only mercy dripping from Christ's wounds... Peter, a man like me, like thee, as flawed as the sea is salt, had he died before Christ forgave his denials, his denials so craven and base, whither Peter's soul? Hell? Or dost thou think Hell's a fable?

—No fable. But thou'st missed many crucial points, divine. Peter existed solely to betray Christ and then receive Christ's forgiveness. Peter's sins and Peter's accent and Peter's death are moot, for he stands among the elect, chosen to ascend past the common agonies of cursed mankind. A schoolboy may grasp this.

Head down, Kit brushed mud from his shoes. —'Tis a schoolboy's pedagogy.

—Is there no talking to thee? God in my heart, Marlowe, thy words, even the sound of thy voice — thou art, without doubt, after mine uncle, the most vexing man I've ever met.

—Oh, pardon me.

—How shalt thou go to Christ without shame?

Kit looked up, eyes glittering.

—What is't thou would'st bray, thy little phrase, when thou'dst dispute with me about grace and argue instead of works? When thou'dst dismiss the apostle Paul?

Such a gentle voice. —The work of faith. And 'tis not grace I dispute — I *never* disputed grace — but the idea's abduction and abuse.

Izaak shook his head. —Thou dost envy Paul and his sudden sight, his clarity. Admit this.

—Or what? Thou'lt rack me til I do? Pindar, we — Izaak, Izaak, hear me. For Christ's love, we studied together. I tried befriending thee. I spoke to thy rustication, la — means this nothing to thee? No. Very good. How shall I reach thee?

—Beg.

Kit stood up from the chair, knelt on on the floor.

Jaw slack, Izaak studied the top of Kit's head, wanting to touch the bald spot.

—My knees go numb this day. La, I beg. Izaak, thy bones are on brief loan to thee, and while they shall crumble, they've *not* warped free of a Bridewell floor. They are more. *Thou* art more. And so I ask thee but this one bare mercy. Let Tom Kyd go.

—Thou'st no claim on me, Marlowe, not my time, not my mind, certainly not my soul. Away.

—The same waters choke us.

—'Tis not so, unless thou'st got a child to bear across.

—Stretch out thine hand.

Izaak waited a moment. —Sodomite.

—So learned, yet no other word?

Izaak said nothing.

—Then we shall drown.

—What? Thou'lt stand? I've not released thee.

—May God have mercy on thy soul.

Kit limped towards the servants' corridor.

—Marlowe. Bridewell stops men's hearts.

Kit walked through the door.

—Ignore me not! Marlowe!

A distant door closed.

Chilled, despite the heat, Izaak heard his uncle's voice, the memory of it not just come to life but growing into a cage. Marcus hurled accusations: dishonoured expectation, meaningless speech, failure, shame.

Once more, Izaak Pindar must concede defeat to this Christopher Marlowe.

FOR WANT OF INK, RECEIVE THIS BLOODY WRIT

After a long sleep, thirteen hours in and out, sometimes hearing bells, Kit woke up on his back, hands near his head, palms up. He remembered lying down in that position. A demented hope flickered in him, his now normal hope that he'd dreamt all this mess and Tom lay beside him. Even as daylight burned hope away, Kit reasoned it to death.

Now then, Clever Kitten, wouldst thou feel not his warmth?
I thought that I heard him laughing.

Coughing then, spitting out the night's phlegm — *and how much longer till my lungs shall clear?* — Kit knelt at the bed, rolled back the mattress, and tightened the netting's ropes.

He ate an apple and some of the bread he'd bought yesterday, the food lying next to some candles — he remembered nothing of buying food and candles — and then decided he must repair the door.

This work demanded patience, thought, and tools he'd not used for years. Tom owned a hammer and a few nails; Kit found these in a desk drawer. He also found the scimitar penknife on top of the desk. He picked it up, blew the dust off it, then tucked it in a drawer; he'd not got time or strength to consider it. Imagining his brothers' mockery — one loyal son a cobbler, the other a carpenter — Kit struggled with the hinges. Some hours later, the door better fit the jamb and closed all the way. The lock, always weak, lay far beyond his skills.

After a vigorous discussion with the neighbours about the sounds of hammering, Kit enjoyed a most illuminating, and expensive, conversation with Tom's landlord on the subject of mercy in winter. That conversation ended with Kit's insistence that two months' back rent, two of five, must suffice.

—Away from me, la. I've got an appointment.

He made his appearance, York House again. As before, he waited a long time. Then he stepped into the dining room and bowed before a much larger gathering of councillors. Most of the councillors, like Sir John Puckering, gave him a look of anxious distaste. Essex smiled. Robert studied his papers. Kit repeated his oath to remain in London, swore to his good behaviour so far this day and promised the same for tomorrow, heard his dismissal, bowed, and departed.

Is that all?

The late afternoon light beat down, fighting off clouds and rain. Walking fast, coughing, concentrating on the metre of a couplet, Kit got himself, unawares, to an alehouse called the Estuary. Much as scriveners and clerks had claimed the Brave Lion, poets and playwrights had claimed the Estuary as theirs, and if one sought such a man on the north side of the Thames, then either the bookstalls in Paul's Yard or the Estuary made good wagers for finding him. Kit had met Tom in the Estuary. Met him properly, talked with him instead of just glancing at him in a playhouse. Almost fell into his blue eyes.

Kit gave his head a shake, continued walking.

He stopped outside another tavern, small and dark, called Cry of the Kite and, recognizing no one, drank alone, drank enough to trick out a sense of confidence and calm, not quite enough to make himself obnoxious — a fine line, he knew. Silent, avoiding eye contact with any other man, he staggered back to Tom's rooms, where the different balance of the repaired door startled him. Then he got to bed, leaned his face on one of Tom's pillows, and breathed in the scent. He refused to swat at the fleas.

A memory caught up to him, memory of a voice: Robin Poley.

Parse thy failures, my own little ferret. Feel not; watch, just watch. Rein thy pain and fear before they rein thee.

Kit threw aside the covers, sat up in the bed.

Robin. What in Hell has thou done to me? And why? And where shall I find thee?

Drink pressed him into a parody of sleep, sitting there.

On Tuesday, Kit made his third appearance before the Privy Council, suffering, as on Sunday, from a sore head. He told himself he felt stronger for this bit of suffering. His face, skin pale, eyes sunken and dark, said otherwise.

Peeking from beneath his heavy eyelids, Robert noticed this, and he devoted some thought to arranging an audience. Then he gave a little snort — *Wee Robbie, he's mine* — and resumed his pretence of studying papers.

Essex sat back, scowling as Sir John Puckering asked Kit a few pointed questions about his habits.

Kit decided to lie. Just to see what might happen.

—I work translation from the Latin, so please your honour.

Essex studied Kit to gauge his response as Puckering gave a little sneer. —Poetry?

—No, your honour, though good as: Cicero.

—And doth it keep thee good and busy, well-occupied?

—It doth, your honour. May I ask, my lords and gentlemen: whither Pindar, the clerk?

Robert looked up. —No, thou mayest ask *not*.

Essex waved his ringed fingers at Robert, dismissing his concerns. —The clerk is made examiner. Today, he examines.

Kit inclined his head to Essex. —I thank you, my lord.

Shall those manacled and racked scream and thereby prove the examiner's being good and busy?

The councillors all stared at him.

Robert shook his head.

Kit bowed, backs of his fingers touching the floor. *What have I left to lose, your honour?* —I give oath to my continued good behaviour, with neither law nor custom broken by my hand. Sir Robert, shall I return tomorrow?

—Go, and await thy summons.

Once again, Kit walked for miles. He took supper in a low ordinary — low for prices, and low for company — jostling men he knew to be thieves. Robin liked to eat here. *I shan't find him, though: too easy.* Sitting near the door, Kit took up a spoon, broke the coffin of pastry over his meat pie, and poked at the parsnip and gravy beneath in search of any actual meat. Out of habit, he eavesdropped. Nothing of use came to his ears. Irritated, bored, he finished the pastry and gravy, leaving much of the bounty of parsnip, and got up to leave.

In the doorway, he collided with Ric Baines.

Ric bowed to him. —I thought thou'dst died in here. How dainty thy tastes, then, to dawdle so over thy food.

Kit shoved Ric against the door jamb, surprising them both with his strength.

Outside, he cursed. He wanted to get to Cecil House and beg an audience but knowing Ric would follow him there galled.

Ric spoke in his ear. —Be not so pensive. Never before could I sneak up on thee like this.

—Not without a sleeping draught, no.

—Walk with me.

—Why?

—To amuse me. Thou'st owe me that.

—How slack, my accounting.

Candlelight from the windows of the ordinary and the neighbouring alehouse reached them. Kit waited for Ric to speak again, to move...

Ric kept still.

Kit spat on the ground. —When I turn my back, shall it be thy knife I feel?

—Not tonight.

—Where is Poley? I would speak with him.

—He shan't be any help to thee.

—Then tell him this: I would scrape out his skull and arrange his sticky brains upon my desk and so feed crows and kites and divine a reason. For he's got a reason, no? All this hucker-mucker? Libels and Bridewell and blood?

Ric shrugged.

—Good night to thee, Baines.

—Thou'lt not compare me to a starling?

Kit spoke with cheer. —Tide pole.

Ric followed him, all the way back to Tom's rooms.

Barring the door with the chair, Kit told himself he did not care.

Lying on his belly, lying on cold and decaying ground, black leaves, silver moss — mist fell, threatened to become cold rain — stretching his left arm, reaching, reaching hard beneath the decrepit oak for his nephew's hand — Gideon's hand? — before the oak fell and sealed the hole. Fingertips brushed his.

Kit woke up gasping, and his cooling sweat left him

chilled. Thinking of Audrey saying *Cura te ipsum, Marlowe: thine own battered self,* he lit a candle, sat on his side of Tom's desk, and wrote to Manna.

So, Clever Kitten, what woe this time?

Another explanation, another draft, aye, more foul papers.

He tucked the unfinished letter in his satchel, stretched out his arms on the desk and lay his head down.

Some hours later, he received his instruction for the day's Privy Council appearance. Then he received a revision. The best assurance not to miss a revised call: stray not from this one self place. Kit took the revision in hand and slumped against the big desk. *Call it confinement and be done with it, la.* Rolling his eyes, he memorized the new appointment place and time and set out for a bakery. When he returned, a third note stuck out of the hinges.

Whom do you test and task here, Sir Robert: me, or the errand boys?

Kit served out a three-hour wait until the Privy Council decided it was ready to see him. He came prepared this time, carrying some of Tom's books in his satchel. Perched on a little stool, he read Chaucer's *Troilus and Criseyde,* admiring, as ever, Chaucer's metre and rhyme. Then he thought about *Canterbury Tales,* strange and unfinished.

All those voices.

Tom had often read to Kit in bed. The night Tom read *The Prioress's Tale,* Kit laughed so hard he wept. Appalled, Tom had put the book down.

Kit, 'tis not funny.

Her pissing little pedantic voice, the old hobgoblin stories about murderous Jews, and that slaughtered youngster wouldn't shut up…

Standing and bowing as some noble or another passed by, Kit considered why the pilgrims had told one another stories.

Competition. And the prize for the best story: a free supper on the way home.

The greatness of the prize. Well, wasn't that worth it all?

Izaak Pindar called his name.

I am not hiding.

I am waiting for darkness, so I might find Robin.

Use thy forced time well, Clever Kitten. Write something.

He refused to answer knocks and calls at Tom's door: Tom's landlord, confused and sometimes frightened customers seeking a scrivener, an errand boy on behalf of a creditor, neighbours, the landlord again…

Sweet Christ Jesus, how is't Tom gets anything done?

He barred the door with a propped chair.

Then he sat back at the desk, covered now with a mess of papers, and recognized something.

I abandon people.

Over and over. The ones I love most, I leave behind.

Ben Cull's face as constables stepped forward, the sadness in his eyes as he saw Kit watching this, sadness and knowledge — until he doubled over, winded from a punch to the gut, eyes clenched shut.

Feel not; watch, just watch.

Is that where I'll find meaning: shut eyes?

He thought of Audrey at Gideon's graveside, how they'd argued about Kit reciting the order of burial.

Sufficeth not I command it?

No, Lady Audrey, it sufficeth not. I lapsed. I am no priest. I should make it a sham.

'Tis already a sham!

Then leave it to rot! Bad enough we lie and say the boy drowned in the marsh. How much more shall we play to the darkness and deny this death any meaning, la?

'Tis the murder has no meaning, Marlowe, not this boy's death, and not this boy.

I've no power against murder done.

Oh, but thou dost. The agony here: make meaning of it.

Shall I give you couplets or a sonnet, my lady? Rhyme royal?

Honour him!

Her voice had broken there.

Someone knocked, and Kit almost threw a book at the door. The visitor knocked again and called out not to Kyd but to Marlowe. A strange voice, a man's, and he spoke to another man, mentioning the libel. Yelling now, yelling of Tamburlaine and fires, they pounded on the door. Kit listened for the neighbours, waiting for one of them to call out, to interfere. The men tried the door; iron and wood rattled and creaked; the chair held.

Muttering, the men left.

Kit eased his grip on the edge of the desk.

And which of the acts of mercy was that?

☙

Walking after dark, seeking Robin, Kit got tired and thirsty. This time, he did enter the Estuary. All the voices, the heat from the bodies: drunken laughter in poor light must make better company than a desk and a candle, than nightmares and a half-empty bed. He wove past various men, seeking faces he knew, until he reached the bar. From the chatter he picked up unwelcome news: plague had closed the playhouses. Actors, theatre owners, and playwrights found themselves out of work for a second year.

Boy-fucking Judas.

—Marlowe.

Tones of snide command, some reserve, perhaps even some fear: Thomas Nashe projected well enough to be heard over several other conversations. Heads turned.

—Marlowe, Marlowe, Marlowe bright, how many miles to London Town? Per Tamburlaine, indeed. I've been telling everyone thou'st written no libel. Even when thou'dst not show thy face, I've protected thee.

Kit forced a smile. —Nashe. Been a while.

—Not long enough, for thee, I expect, when thou'st owe me not only for the success of thy plays but wagered money.

—Pardon me?

—That card game: thou'dst call it the Knave and the Three Toms. Watson, Kyd, and me.

Kit drank from his ale. —I settled that reckoning with thee and Watson that same night.

—'Tis not what I recall.

Kit studied him. They'd been so close at Cambridge, laughing and mocking, even writing a play together, though

Kit had done most of the work. *Damned near all of it*, Kit had said afterwards. Perhaps Nashe mocked still? *No, the shine to his eyes: he chooses to forget.*

—Nashe. I paid thee. Long since. How doth thy wife?

—I've no one to back me here, 'tis true, for Tom Watson's dead.

—Aye. A loss.

—And of course, Tom Kyd's not here.

Kit placed his drink on the bar. His voice sounded small. —No, he's not.

—So 'tis my memory fighting thine. And my memory plays true: thou dost owe me money, as thou dost owe me for all thy success with thy plays. Not that thou'lt sell one this season.

Kit beckoned Nashe closer, and Nashe stepped to the bar, eyeing Kit's dagger. Kit reached for his purse, took out some coins, and offered them. He murmured. —Thou didst need only to ask. I would help thee without this staged little stunt.

Nashe looked at the walls, at the floor. Then he grabbed the coins and rammed them into his own purse. He projected again. —At last. I am heartily sorry I did need to shame thee.

Laughter rose; chatter resumed.

Oh, for Christ's love. Kit moved away from the bar. —Good night to thee, Nashe.

As Kit made his slow progress to the door, Nashe took up the children's singing game again, improvising here and there.

> Marlowe, Marlowe, Marlowe bright
> How many miles to Babylon?
> Three and three and three by fright.
> Can I get there by candlelight?

Aye, if thy spurs be sharp and bright.
But can I get there by candlelight?
Aye, if thy heels be quick as a kite...

Kit glanced back, appalled. Nashe had named him before strangers, named him when people would already punish Tamburlaine. Men crowded round Nashe now, hoping for a drink, and Kit spied that shine to Nashe's eyes again, the shine of fearful choice. He'd looked the same when he fell away from Kit at Cambridge, shunning him over the refused degree.

Shine like that till th'art rotting in the grave, Nashe. Shine like that till Judgment.

After Thursday's Privy Council appearance, again to a small committee, Kit bought sharpened quills from a Cheapside merchant, recited Psalm 39, returned to Tom's rooms, and wrote. He drafted forty-two lines, twenty-one rhyming couplets, about Hero studying her shattered reflection, her changed eye colour, in the glass pieces surrounding her dropped lamp.

Burn it.

Hearing church bells ring for six o'clock, Kit looked up from the desk. Tom's rooms, despite the tidy inventory of books and scrolls, felt so bare. Quiet. When writing, Tom worked his metre by speaking it, auditioning and discarding words until satisfied, one sentence at a time. Kit, who worked mute, would roll his eyes and sometimes snarl a demand for peace. He'd found the first week of living and working with Tom like this vexing. Then, as though something in him fell away, he felt soothed by Tom's voice, not just its tones but its constancy. Tom could no more stop talking than he could keep his emotions from playing across his face, as he and Kit learned that financially disastrous night playing cards with Watson and Nashe. Kit had come to see Tom's talking, Tom's clear face, not as weakness but honesty, and he cherished it.

I just want to hear thy voice.

He asked himself if this suspended existence must be his new normality.

A man adjusts — too easily, sometimes.

Tidying his papers revealed the bloodstain on the desk.

Who struck thee, Tom, thou who knows not hilt from blade? Thou who no doubt obeyed the slightest order?

Bridewell.

Kit stretched his arms from his sides. Then he raised his arms over his head. He saw he kept his wrists well apart, easily the width of his head. He forced them closer together, imagining manacles. Pain shot down the length of each arm. He stood up then, working to keep his wrists still, and held that stance for three counts of ninety. Nerves tingled; muscles ached. His nose ran. He cocked his pelvis and threw back his head. His mouth dried out. Joints and tendons burned, burned, burned, and he winced at the pain in his shoulders and neck as he lowered his stiff arms.

Sweet Christ Jesus, not even five minutes? And standing, not hanging?

Ben — Tom —

Feel not; watch, just — watching be fucked!

He beat the door at Cecil House, begged an audience, nodded and spat at the servant's message of refusal. Then he got to Southwark, seeking Robin. Every haunt, every spot they'd visited together, Kit asked after him, by all his names: Poley, Parrot, Prometheus.

None had seen Robin, or would admit to it.

Kit dreamt that night of the wound on Robin's chest, of hesitating when Robin ordered him to press the heated St. Hubert's Key to it. Then he dreamt of Rheims Cathedral, certain as he walked up the nave that the statue of the Smiling Angel laughed at him. His robes tangled around his legs and tripped him, and he fell to his hands and knees, looking for the design of the labyrinth in the floor. Then he dreamt of hearing voices: people he knew, just talking. Walsingham. Audrey. Gideon. Manna. Ben. Robin.

Not Tom.

For Christ's love, I go in circles!

Friday evening, weary from his long wait for the Privy Council, Kit got to the Starling, hoping to find Lee Crimm.

He thought of the dark-haired errand boy who'd leapt from *Peace of Lethe*'s ladder into the wherry. He thought of Gideon.

Lee seemed to be waiting for him. —I heard thou wast in town. That is, I heard Henry Maunder escorted one Marlowe to the Fleet.

Kit gave Lee a mug of ale. —Thou know'st Maunder?

—He's got to get his horses somewhere.

Kit smirked. Then he laughed. —Crimm, that decrepit mare —

—Slow as a rock. I save her special, just for criminals like thee.

Slurping rounded out the silence between them until Lee, shifting his weight on the bench, spoke. —Well, thou'st bought me a drink. What needs?

—Tell me of the gaol clerks. Any change in the last year?

—Aye, four of them died while thou wast abroad, leaving thee at ignorant disadvantage. Fortune, she's a bitter harpie.

—Would supper turn the harpie's head?

Lee smiled, and his tongue darted in the gap where his eyetooth had been. —I've eaten. But I also feel I owe thee, for when Maunder returned the horses in Southwark and spoke to my apprentice, before ye all crossed the Thames, I kept to the shadow. I saw thee. I saw thee, Marlowe, and I said nothing.

Kit considered this. *And what couldst thou have said?*

—And if Tamburlaine setting fires weren't enough, I've also heard thou dost char the immortal souls of this noble and that with scholarly lectures on atheism. Th'art most busy.

Ric Baines and his rumours. —Oh, 'tis nothing. In another country, I did turn Catholic, counterfeit money, and pierce the innocence of a boy. Sometimes I go about and poison wells.

At night I seek the ninety who burnt.

As both men laughed and drank, Kit worked up a rhyming couplet about the meaning of Lee's Christian name. He parted his lips to utter this when Lee asked if he'd heard the news about the Donne brothers.

—What of them?

—Jack doth fine, but Hal decided to shelter a Jesuit. At Thavies' Inn.

Kit raised his drink. —A law student, harbouring a Jesuit: brightest courage or dimmest mother-wit?

—Courage? Young fool was asking for trouble. Begging for it.

—Execution set?

—Dead already.

—What? When?

—Plague, in Newgate.

Laughing, Kit choked on his ale. —Bitter!

He thought of the remaining brother, Jack: distant, or close? Grieving, or relieved?

Hal: martyrdom, or accident?

Kit leaned forward then. —I would know who clerks at Bridewell.

—*Bridewell?*

—'Tis a gaol. Gaols have clerks.

—Christ on the Cross, Marlowe.

—What, thou knowest not?

—Oh, I know. If 'tis here in London and worth the knowing, I know it. I just question thy wisdom in asking me. Pax. I'll have no more of thy darksome grinning.

—I grin as I please. And darksome? A friend of mine enjoys Bridewell's darksome hospitality. I wish only to speak with one of the clerks away from his work and thereby sidelong register some funds to put towards my friend's comfort, those little luxuries of food and drink, aye, perhaps to the far edge of debauch, food and drink twice a day. Crimm, he'd gotten five months behind on his rent.

—Then, on top of whatever else they inflict upon him, he starves in there.

Kit nodded.

—Th'art a gentle-hearted friend, Marlowe.

—Name me a Bridewell clerk.

Lee studied him. —'Tis a simple matter of visiting the gaol and registering a mercy deposit, yet thou dare'st not approach those stones. In the name of all that's good and pure, *whom* hast thou offended? If I said I would deposit that money for thee, thou'dst ignore me, no?

—I shall find a name soon enough. Save me a few hours' work; 'tis all I ask.

—'Tis folly. I say again, let me make the deposit for thee.

—No! I will do it myself, by mine own hands. I must — there is so little I may do now. I must do *this*.

Lee frowned and sighed, but his frown seemed to mask something else: a little smile, perhaps.

—Crimm, for but the slip of the tongue that releases a clerk's name, thou mayest consider thyself forgiven of me for whatever thou didst not say at Southwark.

—Shalt thou harm him?

—Thou sayest thyself I am gentle-hearted. Some men call me kind.

—Thy kindness would light fires.

Kit stared at him, eyes interested, Lee thought, but hardly kind. Or patient. Not for the first time, Lee wished he'd never met this man.

Then again, Marlowe and his anger might be useful.

—Pax, Marlowe. I'll meet thy petition, once my stubborn thirst is quenched.

Kit stood, bowed, and left the table, returning with two big jugs.

This time it was Lee who grinned.

❧

Kit ducked into a shadow near the entrance as a tall man left the Brave Lion: Frank Kyd, angry, speaking with a friend.

—Still no word, Frank?

—Geoffrey Morgan plays me false, I am sure of it. A deposit he'll take, aye, but no visitors will he admit, and no letters will he pass. How is't a prisoner might be forbidden letters?

—Depends on the crime.

—Tom is innocent!

—Every man's son is, Frank.

Kit resisted calling out; voices and footsteps faded.

Inside, he spotted several men who fit Lee's description of the clerk — dark hair and beard, big blue eyes — but only one of them who also looked ashamed. Neck jutting, shoulders high, he drank alone.

Kit wedged in next to him at the bar, on his left. —Busy night.

Geoffrey glanced sidelong from his cup, grunted.

—I need your help.

—I'm no one to help you.

—I think you are.

Geoffrey took a better look at Kit, eyes stopping at the dagger. —Who and what are you?

—A man who would register a mercy deposit.

—Oh, for the love of God. Go to the prison, then. Look I to be at work right now? I'm just here for a drink.

—I cannot go to Bridewell, being cowardly.

—Not cowardly but wise. If your eyes burned with half of what I see in there... God, what a man won't do for payment.

Kit bought Geoffrey another drink, making sure to jingle his purse. —Keeps the wife in good linen, at least?

—'Tis a foul pittance. I had my own office, once, my own business.

—Dark days.

Geoffrey took a few good swallows. Then he turned and faced Kit. —We've conversed on this before. Only it wasn't you but a man who limped. He thought he could hide it.

—When was this?

—'Tis something of brimstone on ye both. What seek you?

—As I said: I want to register a mercy deposit, and I will gladly pay an extra fee to save my soles the wear to Bridewell. I'faith, 'twas a bungling cobbler who shod me last.

—Be plain. For whom?

—Tom Kyd.

Geoffrey slammed his cup on the bar. —Fuck your mercy. Fuck your mercy and all its prettiness. Mercy, for one accused like him? All sides of me: mercy, mercy for Tom Kyd? What of the innocent man in this, the man tangled in the weirs?

Kit almost whispered. —It galls, la. Should I offer you —

—No! Away from me! I'll have no more of strangers and their money.

—Please —

—Devil take thee and fling thee into wretched solitude. I am gone.

Mistress Kyd, is this your moderate man?

Stride long, Kit followed Geoffrey out of the Lion. —A moment, I beg you.

—Leave me, else I shall call for a bellman.

—And what good can he do, half a parish away? Morgan, just listen to me.

Geoffrey faced him. —How know'st thou my name, sirrah?

Kit shoved Geoffrey towards a wall, shoved him again into an alley. —*Sirrah?* Oh, I'll stand not for that. Now, 'tis a simple matter. I would register a deposit, clerk.

—I'll not take it, nor thy letters, nor any other comfort thou'dst give him. I can't!

—Thou'lt *take* this money —

—Bellman! Fire!

Boy-fucking Judas, if I'm arrested here…

Kit rammed his forearm across Geoffrey's neck and so pinned him. —Just keep still. Thou'lt want to breathe. No, no, still, I say, lest I crush thy windpipe…A moment, I'm using the wrong hand…Let me — there.

Money clinked into Geoffrey's purse.

Kit told him the amount. —Ten percent for thee. Register the rest for Tom Kyd. And if so much as a farthing goes wayward, clerk, I shall know of it, and our next meeting will be unpleasant.

He jerked his forearm off Geoffrey's throat, and Geoffrey slid to his hands and knees, learning to breathe again. Kit glanced at the pools of light on the street, heard no one approaching, and walked away from Geoffrey, just one more man heading home.

He'll be fine in a moment.

He stopped, padfooted a few steps back, listened.

Geoffrey coughed and spat, gasped, coughed again.

Aye, he's breathing.

Kit felt dirty. Soiled.

And stupid.

He deserved none of that. And what guarantee have I that money gets to Tom? And what emptiness is this? Aye now, Clever Kitten: did thine eyes change colour? Money and fright given, soul risked — so easy, such evil, so easy — and nothing solved. Nothing!

Walking fast, he coughed harder than he had for days.

Ordeals. God, sweet God, scrape me clean.

Star Chamber?

Saturday morning, grit-eyed from a poor sleep, Kit crumpled the newest summons from the Privy Council and threw it to the floor. Then he stooped and picked it up, smoothed it out, read it again. Westminster Palace: Star Chamber.

A cobbler's son, see the inside of Westminster Palace? Aye, why not? Royalty once trod the corridors of Bridewell. He saw Westminster, as some reprobate under escort, flanked on all sides, bound for the Star Chamber. He stumbled, and three different men grabbed his arms — not to support him but to prevent him running away. *They'd drag me, if they must. Write to thy sister of it, Clever Kitten. Make her proud of thee.*

Sweet Christ Jesus, how came I to this?

Named for its ceiling, gilded stars against darkest blue, the Star Chamber gave venue for the contrition and fear of those under darkest accusation. The Court of Star Chamber heard civil cases and tried nobles but examined the accused in secret. One so guilty, so wretched as to be hauled before a court or even just the Privy Council in the Star Chamber should stare up at this ceiling and consider his place in the mysterious workings of the universe, should learn, at last, and perhaps too late, humility.

Feeling small and warped, some reflection of himself in a puddle, not entirely aware of the councillors' voices, Kit commanded himself to defy his fear, to defy the idea of the Star Chamber.

He threw his head back and stared at the ceiling. Terrified. Then intrigued.

The whole night sky?

He wished the Admiral's Men could stage *Doctor Faustus* in the Star Chamber: *See, see, where Christ's blood streams in the firmament.*

He got dizzy.

Councillors sniffed and cleared their throats as Robert explained Kit's presence.

One little man, Christopher Marlowe. One. Little. Man.

Wanting to peek at the ceiling again, Kit swore his good behaviour and bowed at the command to obey the next summons.

And once more: nothing. No further confrontation with Essex, no audience with Sir Robert, no change from Bridewell.

Oh, this is tedious.

He strode to Tom's rooms, head down, along Cheapside, Old Jewry Street not far off, working in his head his letter to Manna, his explanations —

A rock hit him. About the size of a small apple, on the upper right arm. He turned to see where the rock had come from when another hit his collarbone, and then several more flew past his arms and shoulders. He stumbled, blocked his face with his forearms and peered between his outstretched fingers: three women, hurling stones.

Aiming for his head.

He bolted into the crowd.

The women chased him, screeching certainty and accusation: Necromancer, Devil-worshipper, Fire-starter, Tamburlaine. —'Tis him! 'Tis him! I know his face!

Kit ducked behind a vegetable stall, colliding with the merchant's legs, scrabbling beneath the cart and its little tablecloth. The three women ran by, promising justice. As their voices faded, Kit, breathing hard, glimpsed before the cart another man's muddy feet.

Ric Baines chatted with the vegetable merchant about the weather and bought some parsnips. Then he knelt, lifted the tablecloth, and peeked in, voice calm and amused. —Boo.

He dropped the cloth and walked away.

Kit got out from beneath the cart, sitting a moment on the ground by the merchant, who carried out another transaction. Kit looked up.

The merchant seemed young, maybe twenty, beard light red and sparse. Freckles dusted his nose, and his brown eyes sparkled. —Are you hurt?

—I think not. Thank you. Thank you.

The merchant laughed. —Murder's bad for business.

Standing up, wincing, Kit nodded. Then he bought an absurd amount of parsnip, a vegetable he loathed. He would boil it for dinner.

❦

A reprieve: the Privy Council would not meet on this, a Sunday, leaving the good lords and gentlemen of the council, and the accused, free to rest and consider devotions, with humblest apologies for the weight of last Sunday's duties.

Kit smirked: *Hie thee to church, damned atheist.*

One little edifice or another, shelters of wood, shelters of stone, crammed with human bodies, echoing with words: church. The nudge and the breath, the cathedral nave: *A simple thing: by law, I must go. Law which got me to university. Law built on a bloat-king's defiance. Romans 13: Therefore he that resisteth the power, resisteth the ordinance of God. And they that resist, purchase to themselves damnation. For princes are not a terror to the good work, but to the evil.*

Poxy Saint Paul.

He studied his left hand.

Perhaps the Devil had me, all this time. That long-fingered priest and his long-fingered words: Such a clever boy, such a pretty boy, I've not seen the like.

Flattery. At Cambridge, a feeling of being watched and test-ed, evaluated by those in power, those whom he must impress and whose intellects he must seduce while pretending not to know they watched him. Ability, power, sweet corruptions, little tendrils of it, tainting his loves, if these delights thy mind may move: history, poetry, fucking, and Christ. And when the sparkling drunk wore off, when the interfering sun lit up truth's chains, he found himself as trapped as Sir Robert in his wayward and demented dance with Essex, as Izaak Pindar in his Calvinist pre-destination, as Walsingham in his debts and his estate.

'Tis more than ideas.

So, Clever Kitten, Little Troublesome One: art thou a recusant? Hast thou done it at last, allowing no prince to stand between thee and thy God? Hast thou gone Catholic?

Proximities galled.

He could reach Canterbury, start by renting a horse from Lee Crimm and taking the Kent Road — and miss his appearance before the council. Ric Baines would find him, and Essex would win: *Run off? Haul him back. And Bridewell this time, as both sense and law demand. Surely, Sir Robert, you cannot object. Not now.*

He could discard thought and reason, numb his mind to think only of simple payment and go mercenary, tread Robin Poley's dream of the agent choosing his work. He'd find work in Flushing — if he could get passage, if he could arrive without Governor Sidney finding out, both most unlikely. *And Christ's love, another crossing? The stink of salt water.*

He could pray, again, for Tom's freedom. *O my God, be not slack.* Prayer felt like no comfort but a goad. Kit understood the Bridewell process for the prisoner of policy not just as an abstract checklist but as a keen and well-ordered escalation, designed to break body and mind until desired information fell loose. He'd studied this curriculum with Robin Poley, learning how even Catholics welcoming martyrdom might scream the word mercy, learning how Bridewell won. Weights: torture and time. Tom: this man's body. Anyone's body, but, no, this man's body, *Tom's* body. Hair he'd tangled his hands in. Skin he'd kissed.

Question, la. Which harms a man more: torment of the body, or torment of the mind?

Oh, the body.

So quick? And if the body withstands all that's given it?

Bridewell, Bridewell — dominating his thoughts the way both Canterbury and Rheims Cathedrals once had. *Even in a heavy south fog, I'm not free of it, for I know it stands there, and I know its meaning. I might cross the Thames a thousand times in one day and not be free of the sight of Bridewell. I might scale a spire and hurl myself in suicide but still, as I fell, glimpse Bridewell.*

How can I not know what I know?

Bells pealed, so many of them, all over London. A dozen churches stood within an easy walk of Tom's rooms alone. Bells, bells…

Neighbours shut their doors, hurried their children along.

I shall not go. I shall not go.

'Tis no atheism, no wayward Calvinism, nor even secret Catholicism what pricks.

'Tis disgust.

I shall obey no bells!

Trinity Sunday.

He rose from the desk.

Almost late, he slipped into the very back of St. Mary Colechurch and stood. He thought he recognized several congregants; he made no gesture to them, made no sound. Lessons flowed round his head, and he recited, eyes closed, whispering. The sermon struggled with the Trinity, getting lost in Latinate periodic sentences and extended metaphors of human flesh, colliding with sudden supplications for mercy from the plague.

The priest had gone pale. —I would I speak like bells and explain, but I am dumb.

Kit snorted. *Filthily written.*

Robin Poley studied him.

Kit's eyes widened. A good two dozen people stood between them, and Robin, on his crutch, moved with many others to the doors. He scowled, in pain, Kit guessed. Jostling the people surrounding him, Kit twisted and stepped and got nowhere. He craned his neck; Robin, shuffling within his own press of people, escaped his sight.

Several minutes passed before Kit could get outside.

Robin had gone.

Stride long, head bent, Kit hurried back to Tom's rooms. He prayed, hearing so much noise in his head that he hardly knew the words he uttered. He fasted. He bit off his fingernails and bit again until he tasted blood. One set of neighbours, voices clear through thin walls, discussed him, discussed the warnings delivered by a man called Baines: this Marlowe was an evil conjurer, a dark criminal, a sodomite, a predator, keep the children away. Tempted to yell some Latin, something that sounded like a magic spell, Kit instead tasked himself to keep a promise, the one made to Sir John Puckering in flippant deceit.

Aye, translation. Settle thy mind.

He looked at Tom's bookshelves, so small after Walsingham's, yet such wealth. Agnes Kyd had often complained of the money Tom spent on books. Those books required for his trade, for scrivening: she could just accept that squalid need, as she might accept a piss-pot. But the books Tom bought for pleasure? *In these dark days, Tom, what needs so many books?* Listening to this folly one Sunday afternoon, Kit had invited Agnes to come and judge, to examine Tom's books and inform them both which books must burn for heat in winter, especially the Latin, la. Agnes had fixed Kit with a look of such ferocity that he felt pinned to the wall. He'd met her gaze. He'd known, of course, that Agnes Kyd could read no Latin. She could not read at all.

I should regret humiliating her.

I don't.

Kit brushed his fingertips over book spines. *Translation, translation — sweet Christ Jesus, what an ugly poxed-up language is English. Find beauty. Find Cicero and his duty, the one every schoolboy . . .*

Where is't?

Tom so organized, so neat, and *De Officiis* not in its place?

Kit stepped back from the shelves and sought oxblood. He opened the desk drawers, shut them. He checked the food chest: crumbs and rat feces. He stood before the shelves once more, checking the books each by each. In the bedchamber he upended Tom's little pile of clothes. He patted the mattress. Back before the bookshelves: *perhaps 'tis slipped behind.* First he removed the books one by one. Then he swept shelves clear with his forearm. Books thudded to the floor; dust rose in little clouds; a long misplaced quill revealed itself.

—Where is't?

He slipped on a book, landed on his arse.

—Where!

A neighbour thudded a fist on the wall.

His movements beauty and speed, Kit got to his feet and threw a book at the sound of the fist. Then another. Another. Crying out. He threw nine books in all; his cough stopped him.

Books, Nashe. Every little thing we are and might be: 'tis already in a book. Find it.

Books at his feet.

Stepping stones, la.

Stones in a bridge. Penance and pilgrimage.

He recalled the childhood promise: *One day, Manna, I shall live on London Bridge.*

Becket's antagonist — Becket's king — had built London Bridge in penance, in contrition, in desire: a path, a path for a pilgrimage to Canterbury.

And who dared mention Becket?

Cross the water?

The dust from the books made his eyes weep, his nose run.

How many miles to Babylon?

One by one, he placed the books back on the shelves.

My glittering memory, and I've no idea how thou'dst arranged thy books, save for one I gave thee?

Tom, I am sorry.

After Monday's appearance, unaware his shirt-tail hung out, Kit loosened his doublet. His face itched where the beard grew in, and his hair had gotten just long enough to fall in his face while remaining too short to tie back. *A little monkey chained in a library.* Fasting still, very hungry, he smelled fresh bread.

He looked up: Tom's favourite bakery.

The luxury of white bread.

Inside, he stood before a wall of bread of many shapes, rougher loaves — best white behind the counter — and clasped his hands in front of him. Butter glistened on some of the loaves; others showed the patterned slashes of knives.

At Scadbury, Dan would talk to Kit while kneading bread, talk and talk of his past, delighted to have someone listening.

Kit had wanted to learn how to make bread; Dan wouldn't hear of it. *'Tis not thy place.*

I'm a servant of this house, like thee.

Oh, aye, a servant, which is why thou dost sleep on the upper floor near the master's bedchamber. No. 'Tis not thy place, I say. And th'art not strong enough yet. One go at this, and thou'lt be coughing for hours. Here, bring a piece of that heron's heart to the turnspit cur.

Considering now the rules of who made the bread, Kit heard a man enter the bakery and place an order at the counter. A tight manner of speech, consonants precise in a flat and hollow tone: Kit felt the speaker lacked the ability, or the desire, to accept the baker as another human being.

—Two small loaves of thy finest white.

Recognizing the voice now, Kit reached for a ravelled brown loaf slashed with a cross.

Coins clinked as the baker gave the customer his bread and change. —Thank you, Mr. Pindar.

Kit waited for the door to close. Then he turned around, paid for his bread, and emerged to the street, glancing around for Izaak. *How now, he who laughs, he who squints? Sweet Christ Jesus, Pindar, I could stalk thee blind; th'art leaving me a trail of breadcrumbs, la. Oh, such a stride: chin high, step even, seizing thy rights, thine equality to any great man, even as thou dost stuff thy cheeks.*

I walk like that.

He followed Izaak all the way to Southwark, discovering the man had expensive taste in not only bread but prostitutes.

Waiting outside the stew, Kit wondered if ambitious clerks made a good salary.

Not that good.

Izaak emerged from the stew, smiling a little and looking refreshed, and jostled through a crowd as a crier announced baited dogs. Izaak paid admission and strode up to the animals and keeper. Then, with strange speed, and just out of the dogs' reach, he knelt. The dogs snarled and lunged, and their keeper looked to the leashes. The bonds held. Blobs of foamy slather landed on Izaak's clothes. One of the dogs, a bitch in heat, bled as she leapt and crouched, and in her few still moments, she watched Izaak, and snarled.

Kit let out a long breath. *She smells the truth of thee, Pindar. God help thee if she slips her leash.*

I'll learn nothing else here today.

Feeling empty, and numb to the animal-baiting, entertainment he'd once enjoyed — the danger and spectacle of pained beasts that would reach past their lot — Kit made to leave. A boy, maybe eleven, barged in front of him to nail up a bill for the bear garden. The paper showed a sketch of some two-headed beast and promised, in a scrivener's tidy handwriting, O, fortunate voyagers, starved of theatre in these plaguey days, for a simple coin of the right weight, a once-in-a-season, perhaps once-in-a-lifetime show...

Kit paid admission. As he took a middle-row seat on the north side and glanced up at the sky, checking for rain, he wondered how the bear garden stayed open when the playhouses must close. *Who bribed today, when contagious death loves all? We never close the churches.* Plague would hit as plague itself desired, not as any human predicted. *Fear and despair:*

*fevered strays grimacing at lumps and sweat would run in the
streets, could they rise from their beds, and scream a prayer for
lumps and sickness to shrink, recede, or fall away, but 'tis stuck,
for it comes of a man's own flesh, and perhaps of a man's own
evil: 'tis of the man. 'Tis more than ideas.*

  'Tis random?

He murmured. —Homo, fuge.

Sunlight beat down. People jostled him, getting to their
seats; he opened his eyes and stood up to let them pass. Two
rows before him, just to his left, Izaak took a seat, squinting
at the ring, struggling for clarity.

Bear and dogs opened the show. The curs, weighing
from one to five stone, showed many teeth and ribs. The
bear, storied as a tribute and even misplaced love token to
Queen Elizabeth from Tsar Ivan himself — a very Muscovy
bear — entered on all fours, chained at the neck. His keeper
fixed the chain to a pole. Claws hauled out years ago — Kit
considered how this might be done: bindings and pincers? —
the bear reared up on his hind legs, and growled and snarled
as expected, but twice he fell silent, closing his eyes, raising
his snout to the sky. Choosing blindness, the bear struck out
at three leaping dogs and hit each one: yelps and thuds and
howls. Kit watched a keeper pucker his lips. He whistled to
his beasts, his noise unheard beneath the barks and cries of the
audience. The dogs cringed and backed away from the bear,
which roared once more, raising its forepaws as though blessing the crowd. As two out-of-work actors swept up bloodied
sawdust, the keeper led the chained bear off. Back on four legs,
the bear moved at a calm wiggle. The dogs gathered at the
legs of the whistling man. He pointed offstage, and the dogs

trotted away. The man took a look around the ring, spotted another man in a floppy hat, nodded to him, and followed the dogs.

The man in the floppy hat strode to the middle of the ring, swooped his hat to the ground and bowed, rose and bowed again, so greeting all of his encircled audience. Kit thought of Lee Crimm and his hat. This man was not Lee Crimm. He opened his mouth, exposing his beautiful teeth, and Kit recognized him: Gabriel Spenser. He'd played Zenocrate in runs of *Tamburlaine*, when he was shorter and thinner and bare of that dark beard. Kit thought him quite a good actor, in a dangerous way: fiery, manic, chaotic yet brilliant in his selfishness, onstage and off. Risk attracting him, man repelling him, Kit had written his character Ithamore with Gabriel in mind. He'd admitted that to no one but Tom. He now hoped Gabriel would play his Piers Gaveston. Gabriel had insulted Tom early in the 1591 season, and Tom had boxed his ears for it, the punishment specific: one boxed the ears of a defiant servant, or an upstart child. Gabriel, dizzy and deaf, had knocked Tom to the floor, and the other actors had hauled Gabriel away, calling him *boy* and threatening to kick him out of the company, threatening to go on tour and leave him behind, unless he showed better sense.

Kit smirked. *Gabriel, Gabriel, abridged archangel, little mother-wit: the actors made good their promise, la, and abandoned thee to London's plague.*

Gabriel introduced, in what sounded like drivel he'd written himself, the upcoming and fearsome sight, a spectacle arranged at great trouble and expense for an audience deprived of distraction from their troubles. He described, at some length, the accomplishments and reputation of these keepers of the beasts. Then, as if taking rebuke, he lowered his voice, and he sounded tired. He would attempt a description of what these fortunate Londoners would see, for he was capable, aye, capable, but words, petty words failed the task, and words fell at his feet, useless, hollow, and limp, as words must always be.

Kit snorted.

Audience members roared for the beast, the two-headed beast, roared for Gabriel to choke and be gone.

A creature stumbled into the ring: a pony and rider. The pony's ribs showed; the rider, small and hunched, wore a hooded cloak. The pony hesitated and shook its head and long mane; the rider's hands moved with the mane, not holding the pony but thrashing with it. Gabriel spoke some more, losing clarity to the audience's roars and cheers. He grinned, showing again his lovely teeth. The pony dropped its head, and the little rider stilled. Gabriel, catching some cue from offstage, nodded, raised his open palm, and this time slapped the pony's left haunch, so hard that the air seemed to crack. Neighing, showing its own teeth, the pony thrashed its head; once more the rider mimicked the pony. Then, with a swift delicacy and grace that made Kit gasp, Gabriel tugged down the rider's hood and struck his face.

Gabriel projected well. —The magot! The hairy little man!

The ape screeched and tugged his arms, which were bound to reins. As he struggled, he hauled on the bit in the pony's mouth. The pony reared, showing the rope tight across his belly, this rope tying the ape's ankles. Frightened, the ape grabbed pieces of the pony's mane, and the pony reared again.

Kit had seen sketches of magots, but he'd not known an ape's eyes could look so much like a man's. *Fear, and the intelligence to recognize that all those watching him hold the power to release him — the power, aye, but not the will.*

Izaak leaned forward, elbows on his knees, squinting hard. Many in the audience cried out in pleasure and shouted abuse. The pony bucked; the ape screeched. Keepers danced around the pony, trying to loop a rope around the animal's neck but missing, missing, first with style, then with anger. Gabriel, well out of the way, frowned, and the crowd's noise obscured the animals' cries. *Let me up. 'Tis vile, let me up.* Penned in by other bodies, by his own despair, Kit slouched down in his seat. He scowled, shut his eyes, turned away…No, no, the scene must play out, and he must watch it. Little licks of pleasure — blood, fire, and tyranny in a play: practised fakery. These agonized animals: a loose authenticity, a truth just past his reach, a mystery compelling and comic and bare.

He yelled with the crowd.

Later, he wrote to Manna by candlelight, wrote of simulacra and little apes.

He slept then until maybe half past three in the morning. Coughing, he discovered he'd drawn his dagger. He sheathed it, washed his sweaty face again, the stale water smelling of reeds and mud — *I must get more today* — and walked outside.

The sky lightened at the far edge of the east, some promise of fire, and Kit discovered what had roused him: a watchman, taunting someone at a high window. The house had been bolted shut from the outside, and the door marked with a cross and the words *God have mercy upon us.*

Kit winced. *Plague, only three doors down.*

The watchman, drunk and muttering, hobbled between the house and his vantage point. The darkness at the upper window shifted; someone peered out. That window would be the only access to the people trapped in the house, trapped until they healed — until they died. Friends and neighbours might, under a watchman's eye, place food and drink into a basket lowered from a window, and the inhabitants would then haul the basket up, desperate not to spill. The watchman must ensure no one sneaked out of the quarantined house, and he must do this with or without relief. The City of London paid well for this dire work, coin and wine; few men took it up. Kit feared sickness overtaking the few watchmen. Quid custodiet ipsos custodes? What Hell, then?

This watchman, short and stocky, swigged more wine and crossed the street to stand beneath the window. He danced, a galliard maybe, and laughed. Then he addressed the window. —Thou'dst despise me, hey? Kick me in the street? Look now! Look now! Fortune turns and grinds thee beneath her wheel. Thy bones are grist! Thou'lt die in misery, thou and thy whore wife. Thy spawn, too, thy brats: may they cry in fever as thou lieth prostrate. I dance, thinking on thee. Aye, 'tis me out here, free and happy. 'Tis me. Me!

Kites and crows and ravens called; Kit walked away. He got to the Strand and nodded at each of York House, Cecil House, and Essex House. The Thames reflected back the flames of dawn, then settled to itself, dirty and dull. Cursing his stupidity, his coming all the way to the river without a water jug, Kit glanced at London Bridge, thought a moment about the people who lived there, and wondered how a plague quarantine worked on a bridge. Hungry now, he sought a bakery.

Instead, he walked to a church. He'd no idea which one: a little stone church, low ceiling crumbling, heavy wooden doors yielding. The hinges, well oiled, only rustled. Legs heavy, chest sore, he walked towards the altar. He knelt. Nothing. He lay face down on the floor. *Help me see, help me see.* Again, nothing. He lay on his back, stones chafing his scalp, and spread his limbs, made himself an X, imagined the binding on a rack. He got up. Dust motes floated in scarce beams of light, so many motes that Kit wondered if the light was not, in fact, made of dust.

Aye, there's thy blasphemy, Clever Kitten. Thou, thou who wouldst touch the light: thou art the dust.

Some hours later, once the stationers opened for business, Kit visited Ed Blount. Startled to see Kit, Ed warned of rumours worse than the libel: atheism, Devil worship, sedition.

Shaking his head, Kit lowered his voice. —Men still seek me? Come to thee?

—Aye. Several times now, though never one who knows thee. They all demand description. I play them false.

Kit's eyes sparkled. —After how I spoke to thee?

—'Tis nothing.

'Tis far more. —I thank thee, Blount.

—Thank me by giving me a manuscript to publish. What sloth, poet?

Kit grinned. Then he looked to the ground. —Promise me something, la. Ask Tom that when thou'st see him again.

—He'll be released soon?

—Christ's love, I hope so.

Ed glanced about at the men behind Kit, checking for any menace or threat. —Marlowe, thou'st moved in high circles. Wilt thou not petition a powerful man for help?

—I'm done petitioning men. Take care, Blount.

—Aye. Take care.

As Kit turned around, some other men in the yard recognized him, their looks of cold joy disguised as looks of pity and concern. Kit ignored these men, and he ignored some alleged poet whose name he'd forgotten, some poet who raised his index finger and pointed at him, expecting Kit to submit to his interrogation. He ignored Jack Donne, who glanced at him with fear, and glanced away, pretending nothing had happened. *Misery loves company, Donne; what eats thee?* And he ignored Ric Baines, who stood at a puritan's bookstall, perusing pamphlets.

Kit strolled a while, meandered really, cutting through the filthiest lanes he could find, just to annoy Ric. Then he stopped in an expensive ordinary. The day's special: pie of chardequince, with lamb. Ravenous, mouth flooding, he took in the aroma. Earning a sneer from the proprietor, Kit asked for the oldest loaf of bread and the least expensive cheese. He left with these purchases, cheese and bread both hard as stones, and returned to Tom's rooms.

A sealed letter peeked out the hinges, another note advising him, oh, grind of fortune's wheel, of a Privy Council meeting change. Chr. Marlowe, scholar and gentleman late of the parish of St. Mary Colechurch, London, on oath to remain there, must attend the lords and gentlemen of the Privy Council and wait on their pleasure at the Star Chamber in oh, look at that, less than an hour. Kit rested his head against the door; the little thud soothed him. He smacked his head harder; that, too, soothed him. He drove his head into the door, hard enough to crack some of the rotten wood. Stunned, he stepped back and craned his neck from side to side. *Now, Clever Kit, abridge thy baneful days.* A neighbour woman emerged from her house, wondering at the racket. Kit bowed to her. Then he grinned and waved at Ric Baines. Surprised, Ric frowned, and picked his way toward him, sidestepping children, dogs, and rubbish piles. Maybe a yard away from Kit, Ric tilted his head to one side. Kit did the same. Ric took a step backward; Kit copied that, too. Kit drew his dagger and waved it in a strange line; he signed his name in the air. Ric's mouth fell open. Kit took aim and pitched his stale bread at Ric's head. The loaf bounced off Ric's cheek, and a dog lunged for it, catching it in mid-air.

Commanding her children to get inside, the neighbour woman glared at Kit. Then she called him Devil, and spat. Ric stood there, mouth open as if to ask a question. Kit bowed to him with great flourish and laughed.

He started his walk to the Star Chamber.

WHEN TO MY SORROW I HAVE BEEN ASHAMED
TO ANSWER FOR THEE

Tom had eaten twice a day, several days in a row, and his racked body worked to heal. He'd crawled and then shuffled round the edges of his cell. Sometimes he'd speak to a guard, not that any guard spoke back. Geoffrey Morgan checked on him most days, entering the cell and taking Tom's pulse, asking if he'd eaten.

Pain and fear settling, Tom grew bored. Staring at walls and ceiling maddened him. He found a shard of stone and, standing a few minutes at a time, carved marks into the wall until the shard broke apart. Then Tom pretended he held a quill and wrote in the air, his fingers long tubes of numbness shot through with pain, his letters misshapen and huge. He asked Geoffrey for a book, any book; no such treasure arrived. He devoured each meal, dreading its addition to the final reckoning, to the no doubt tidily written bill he'd get on release.

Because of thee, Kit.

And where art thou now?

Shame assaulted him, waves of it, making him shiver, making him sick: all the things he'd told Examiner Pindar, all those intimacies betrayed.

Time splayed, and a new despair rose like a stench.

I am forgotten.

And deserving of it.

Tom opened his eyes as though he'd only blinked, not fallen asleep.

Izaak Pindar crouched down before him.

Caring nothing for protocol, Tom spoke first. —Travel you by cloud of smoke?

—Pillar of fire. The keeper shall be here shortly. Th'art much recovered.

—I wobble when I stand.

—Standing? Very good. Thy voice is strong, thine eyes are wet: thy resilience, Kyd, is a marvel. I commend thee.

Tom had prepared an eloquent petition; instead he spoke with the flat boredom of exhaustion. —Your commendation be fucked.

—So thy courtesy needs work.

Tom wiped his nose. —Your commendation be fucked, Examiner. Better?

—What posturing is this?

—I've sat here for *days* with no press or question from you. Let me go.

—Mine examination is incomplete, I admit, and I am here today to sum it up. Recall, please, how I may —

—Say on, say on, say on.

Izaak reached for Tom's throat, touched his beard. —God in my heart: not yet?

Feeling cold, Tom looked away.

Izaak stood up, and his voice flowed down like spilled honey. —He is charged with atheism and must give daily attendance on the Privy Council.

—Atheism, and not imprisoned? Is there some trouble with the charge, Mr. Pindar? Sticks it not?

Izaak's eyes brightened. —Is't love, strengthening thee? Aye, thou'dst said it before: love. Love, yet thou'dst accuse him of writing blasphemies. How tough thy flesh; how tender thy heart. Love?

—'Tis strange to you.

Izaak shook his head. *See'st thou that woman, flicking in and out of truth beneath the torch? My mother. Once, she would comfort me and smooth my hair. The old faith. She chose pride and defiance before me. She abandoned me to Marcus Tilley for nothing more than how to say her prayers. I loved her. Love? I was not loved. I was betrayed.*

Tom studied Izaak, working to read the emotions on his face.

Izaak noticed this. —Stand up.

Tom obeyed. Pain shot in long lines from his neck, down his shoulders, and out his fingers: paths of the homunculi.

John and Geoffrey arrived, Geoffrey with his ledger and pencil. Both men looked irritated. The examiner's summons had interrupted some delicate accounting: the disposing of the dead.

Geoffrey pointed to a page in his ledger. —'Tis the one Ben Cull. I found him as I've drawn here, in my sketch.

—Aye, heart seizure. Mr. Pindar, I've not seen you for several days.

—I have neglected mine examination, and for your troubles, Keeper, I apologize.

—No trouble for me. His food's bought and paid for.

Tom looked up. He'd not written to his father — he couldn't — and his father had not written to him. —By whom?

Geoffrey smiled at him. —Charity, from an anonymous donor.

A dart of hope: Tom almost smiled back. *Kit?*

Izaak squinted at Geoffrey. —Clerk, why dost thou utter the word *charity* with fear in thy voice?

Geoffrey said nothing.

—Keeper Deyos, thy clerk's throat: what happened?

—Morgan, thou wast robbed, no?

—Friday night.

Face close to Geoffrey's throat, Izaak peered at the bruises, as if working to recognize handwriting. Geoffrey stepped back, and Izaak looked up at the staple. —Keeper, the manacles.

John nodded and walked down the corridor to fetch his tools.

Geoffrey threw down his ledger. —For the love of God! Mr. Pindar, why? Why torment him again? You've manacled him twice. You've *racked* him. What else may you get from him?

John returned with the manacles and bench, listening to the dispute while gesturing he'd help Tom to stand on the bench. They climbed.

Izaak looked Geoffrey up and down. —Who art thou, Clerk? I am not bound to answer thee.

—Mr. Pindar, are these measures...

—Are these measures *what*?

The bruises on Geoffrey's throat darkened. —Warranted?

—Examine I the wrong author?

Iron chain scraped iron staple.

—Keeper Deyos, I would question your clerk.

—Morgan? He's worked here since... No. No, Mr. Pindar. You do err, sir.

Izaak smiled a little. —A rebuke, from an experienced man.

John nodded at Geoffrey, who looked down at his splayed ledger and blushed.

Izaak murmured something, raising his voice as he finished. —And grant me the strength, O God, to falter not in this, Thy work. Amen. She's gone. Deyos, Morgan, attend: I represent the Privy Council, and by that, I represent the Queen. My duty remains the discovery of the Dutch Church Libeller. This I must do. Sedition stains, leaving a moist and reeking mark, as of bile, as of blood, and our enemies deny us the courtesy of plain sight. A Jesuit who wears no robe: how would one know him, in the street? A rioter who serves the very state he would tear apart: how would one know him, in the dark? The answers lie curled up and sleeping in the sad art of examination. Keeper Deyos, detain Geoffrey Morgan until such time as I may examine him.

Geoffrey knelt before his dropped ledger. —Mr. Pindar, you...You would arrest me?

I would have thee show that prisoner no more mercy. And I would have thee stop questioning me and so upsetting the order of duties. —I may yet charge thee with my suspicions of the libel's authorship. If th'art innocent, I shall know it soon enough, and this procedure shall be, at most, an inconvenience. A man with nothing to hide spends little time in a cell. If th'art guilty, or even tainted with guilt, I shall prove it. Thy choice: roar and spew in fear and so give away thy guilt, or behave as an innocent man and show the patience and forbearance taught us by our saviour. I shall get to thee.

Until then, eat thine objections, clerk, and pick them from thy filth in the morning.

Marjory. —Keeper Deyos, if you lock me with the main crowd, they'll swarm me. They will kill me.

—I know. Solitary. For thy safety. Just till we... Sobbing Mother of Christ.

Izaak watched them leave. Then he climbed up on the narrow bench and stood next to Tom. —How is it I must start again?

Tom stared straight ahead, at a particular stone. He'd stared at it many times. A thread of white ran through it, and sometimes, depending on the light, or on the tears in Tom's eyes, the thread would glitter.

—Kyd, hast thou ever accepted, or even set upon thyself, a necessary task, only to find it so difficult thou'dst abandon it, save for thy dignity?

—My dignity?

—Desire, then, desire to see the task done, whatever difficulty, whatever sacrifice.

Tom said nothing.

—It being that thy world is so small —

—We share the same world.

—Not so.

—We share this bench!

—Thy world is *small*, made of one man's mind, thine, and so 'tis corrupted. My world, broadened and deepened by mine education and now mine experience, collides with thine and envelops it. Taking thee, I use thy flesh and thy mind — thy world — for mine own tasks.

Tom's knees buckled in familiar pain. He grasped Izaak's sleeve, and his feet got purchase.

—One man or another would face the charge of writing the Dutch Church Libel. Thou, Thomas Kyd, mean almost nothing to me as Thomas Kyd. Less than the libel. And I care very little for the libel.

Finding he'd tangled his fingers in Izaak's sleeve, Tom took a breath, let go.

Izaak stepped down, fluttering his collar. —In light of these developments, I must revise the charge against thee. 'Tis atheism.

Tom felt very tall, very far from the floor. The stone floor. It would smash his face.

—Kyd, the charge shall ruin thee. Thou'lt be shunned for work and credit. Thy patron shall grow distant, and men thou didst once call friends shan't deign to see thee in the street.

—You've no evidence of atheism. How shall you make it stick?

Tom regretted his question even before he finished asking it.

—When thou'st already confessed and confirmed so much? Just watch me.

When Tom spoke again, his voice betrayed no defiance, no spite. Nor did it deepen in anger and command. It sounded flat. —Examiner Pindar, if I mean nothing to you, why ruin me so?

—Because thou dost love him.

I am so tired. —'Tis so. I love him.

Izaak wished for a moment he'd not answered so fast.

—Raise thine arms.

The manacle cuffs brushed Tom's fingers.

—Remain so.

—Examiner Pindar —

—What objection? I harm thee not. Lower thine arms.

Tom obeyed. His arms tingled and burned.

—Love? Raise thine arms.

I will not.

Yet the manacles brushed Tom's fingers again.

—And if I ask thee, Kyd, of Marlowe's atheism, his monstrous opinions?

Tom took a breath to speak. Then he clenched his jaw.

Smiling, Izaak shook his head. —Thou'st borne false witness, and that for thine own comfort, nothing more. By thy words, he doth face charges that might yet execute him. And here, in this place, this moment, thou wouldst scream defiance, while obeying my hollow commands. Yet by thy words, thou dost love him.

The thread in the stone glittered. *Why stand I here? Step down, step down.*

—Thou art craven.

Step down!

—Thomas Kyd, who could love such a one as thee?

Izaak locked the cell door behind him.

Walking away, he listened for the sounds of Tom's feet on the cell floor.

Nothing.

God in my heart, I believe I've done it.

GREAT GIFTS ARE GUILES

Rain fell as Kit walked to Cry of the Kite, looking for Robin. Apprentices filled the Cry, drinking hard and shouting threats to absent masters, clapping one another on the blue-robed shoulder and promising fidelity in defiance; tomorrow, heads sore, they would do as told. Kit recognized no one, and some of the apprentices, eyes glazed and vicious, studied him, the solitary stranger. Kit hurried through his second drink. Angry, he made for the Starling.

Lee Crimm sat facing the door, playing tables with a business partner Kit had met before, an ironmonger. Jack Donne leaned against a wall, glaring fury over the rim of his mug, considering, Kit guessed, the same trinity he'd chewed on last week in Newgate. *Cross, Crown, heart. Sweet Christ Jesus, Donne, art thou yet one-and-twenty?*

Lee stood up and now strode towards Kit, and Kit smiled, expecting pleasantries — not a shove on both his shoulders. He staggered backwards.

—Marlowe. Thou said to me thou'dst harm him not.

Kit's left hand hovered over his dagger. —Wouldst thou knock me over?

—Aye, knock thee on thine arse and kick thee. I saw those bruises, and Marjory weeping. Art thou some butcher's starving dog? If thou'dst widowed her —

—Crimm, I —

—I only wanted to give him a fright!

—Wait. Thou didst *expect* me to beat him?

—Not hard, maybe just shove him around, but…Christ on the Cross, child after child, another on the way, I just wanted to keep him off her a while.

—I will not be used as some…hammer by thee — or anyone else.

—Think, Marlowe, use thy brilliant mind. How is't I knew so well the schedule of that Bridewell clerk?

Oh, for Christ's love. —What is he to thee?

—Brother-in-law.

Kit ducked his chin, as though ashamed. Then he looked up, straight into Lee's eyes. —A cherished one, la: thou didst sell him out for two jugs of ale. Should I have bought thee another twenty-eight?

Lee stared at him. —We are finished.

—I am glad of it. Th'art too good a man to quarrel with. Buy thee supper?

—Marlowe, thou'st hear me not: we are *finished*. I'll no more of thy company, and thou'lt get no horseflesh, no names, no *help*, from me.

—Crimm —

Lee tossed his ale in Kit's face. He'd not got much left, ruining the gesture, but the intent, the insult, remained clear. Grinning, Kit shook his head; drops of ale fell from his hair. He threw himself at Lee, tackling him to the floor. Words spewed, rhythms beautiful and savage, as he struck Lee three times in the face, hearing a little pop. Jack Donne and the ironmonger hauled Kit away; he'd not got the strength left to twist free. Lee, gagging on blood, sat up. Kit started to cough, a deep and barking cough, and the men holding him dropped his arms and backed away.

Kit drew a cloth from his satchel and held it out for Lee. Arm trembling, Lee accepted it, held it to his nose and mouth. Kit knelt down, then raised his hands, palms out and well away from his dagger. —Crimm: I am sorry.

Lee held out the cloth: gone red. His nose sat at a new angle. He looked in Kit's eyes, and he spat.

Nodding, Kit got to his feet.

Jack Donne and the ironmonger stared at him in mystified accusation.

Eyes narrow, the landlady pointed to the door.

Alone, then.

Kit bowed his head, and he bolted outside.

This mist, this soaking mist.

A south fog infested every little nook. Knuckles sticky, face wet, Kit brushed people, hit walls, and trod in something foul. Then, by St. Mary-le-Bow, he collided with a bellman.

—Pardon me.

The bellman grabbed his arm. —How is't I heard thee not? Speak, thief.

—Leave off. I am no thief

—Prowling in the night: then what art thou? Retreat not from me. Keep still until I shine this light — blood on thy fingers?

Church doors hit Kit's back. —Wait —

—Wait for what? Hey?

The bellman shoved his staff at Kit. The finial of the lamp pole skimmed the side of Kit's head; the heat from the lantern warmed Kit's cheek.

The bellman's face, squinting and fierce, emerged into light, his hair and beard, grey and white, looking like threads of fog. —I know very little in these nights but the cries of the fevered sick, and the barking of plague dogs, dogs I must hunt and strangle. Against all this, criminals spree. Who and what art thou? *Speak!*

—Peace! Peace, bellman. The blood is from a fight, and the man lives.

—Thy name. Now.

—Pardon me, my heart pounds. Loman. I am Stephen Loman.

The bellman studied him. —I walk at the far edge of my parish. My light dies, and I know not thy face, so I must demand the truth.

—Aye. Dark days, Bellman.

Ask me not where I'm going. Ask me not.

—Whither goest, Loman?

Kit named a street near Old Jewry.

—Shall I walk thee there?

Acquiesce. If thou'st nothing to hide, then thou'lt not object to a bellman's escort. —My thanks. How goes it now for you?

—The nights trouble me. Give me back the cold tedium of winter. Heat stirs up more than plague. 'Tis the mass graves, the noise of bone and flesh thudding in holes — already worse than last summer — and our lord mayor's done nothing. I've not got enough watchmen for my streets. Earlier tonight, I chased a tailor, man of five-and-thirty, as he ran off like a guilty boy. Know'st thou what he carried, Loman? Know'st thou what he dropped, because he stumbled as he fled from my lawful summons?

Kit guessed, but he felt he'd no right to speak.

—A box. Within it: a child, maybe eleven, little face a

blistered mess, lying dead of plague, as dead as thou art alive. And why the secrecy, why the nighttime walk to an open grave? I'll tell thee: so we'd not bolt his door and leave there the warning mark of quarantine.

—So he might get to work tomorrow and feed his family.

The bellman stopped walking. —Art thou one to cheat the law of common good?

—I said not that I approved. I meant only that I understand.

After a silence, the bellman snorted. Then he pointed with his lamp. —Thy street.

He disappeared into the darkness and the fog.

Kit doubled back to Tom's street, counting houses, then reaching up to touch the sign of the quill. *Got it.* Promising himself bed, he lifted the key from around his neck.

Dropped it in a puddle.

—Boy-fucking Judas!

He knelt, patting the wet ground until his fingers touched the key.

Once inside, he leant against the big desk, facing the wall of books and scrolls.

Stepping stones and London Bridge, Clever Kitten? Pilgrimage, thou? In a south fog, yet? Quo vadis, Domine?

He picked up the chair, ready to prop it against the door.

Lamplight shone on the window.

Outside, one man whispered to another to wait.

A hand pushed the door, found it yielding.

Robin Poley, bearing light, crutched into the room. He eased the door shut behind him, shone the lamp about, and spoke in a murmur. —I heard thee cursing, so I know th'art here. I'll not hurt thee, mine own little ferret, not tonight. I would only speak. Where art thou? Think on the times I've...I promise...No, God save me, thou'st got no faith in me. Then listen. The atheism: I know, I know, 'tis extreme, but thou and thy defiance...and that boy upset all. Gideon and his miracle of the dew, eavesdropping early in the morning: didst thou teach him that? I know thou didst teach him to read. Was he bright, then?

Silence.

Robin crutched to the hearth, back to the desk. —I never meant...The boy forced my hand. Thy Tom is one matter, but Gideon...I've beseeched Essex. On my knees. I beg and cajole and flatter him to resume his mercies and once more let thee come to him. Sir Robert believes th'art gone to him already. Let me — oh, my Christopherus, thou wouldst fight, and for what? Thy fight is but an idea. Come, come out where I can see thee. No? Then listen well, for I am begging thee: give Essex what he wants, his delusion of command. Give him that, and stay free within the compartments in thy mind. We'll get by. We'll get by. Sufficeth?

Words and the start of a cough jammed Kit's throat.

Robin placed the lantern on the desk.

Dragged footsteps and the tap of the crutch thinned out, and the door shut again.

Beneath the desk, knees drawn to his chest, Kit watched the imprisoned lamplight play on the wall. Robin had taught him about priest holes and hidden closets and chimneys and trap doors. He'd also taught him the obvious: look under beds and desks.

Thou didst spare me just then, Robin.

Kit crawled out from beneath the desk, stood up.

A folded note peeked out from beneath the lamp, words in an old and easy cipher — the first one Robin had taught him.

Then it sufficeth not. As I expected. Come live with me, and bait the bulls; we shall discuss Prometheus and the daily visits of eagles, and the bile they spill. I'll buy thee dinner.

Kit tucked the note in his satchel. *The Bulls' rooming house in Deptford. Not been there a while.*

After he secured the chair against the door, he took up the lamp. *'Tis a lamp. Just a lamp.* Sniffing back tears, ashamed of them, he lit his way to the bedchamber. He hung the lamp from the sconce, got into bed, and lay there, staring at the little flame.

Cocky and expensive, but not worth spilt blood.

Cicero's advice: of evils, choose the least.

Stepping stones and London Bridge. How falls away the greatness of the prize when 'tis a dead man?

How many miles to Babylon?

Robin not expecting him until dinnertime, Kit strolled a while, strolled as though innocent and unburdened. He bought a fresh loaf of ravelled bread slashed with a cross and tore it in pieces, eating as he walked. He entered an expensive-looking alehouse he'd never visited, one called Cupid's Bow, where he drank two pints out of thirst, and, feeling no effect, readied his third when he noticed boys peeking around the kitchen door. Catching his eye, they ducked out of sight. The Bow's only patron, Kit sipped now, listening: hushed and high voices, Low Countries French. Huguenots. Refugees. Not finishing the ale, Kit stood up, and the landlord hastened to his table, asking what else he desired, now that he was refreshed, just name the pleasure, sir. Kit shook his head and left without speaking. Outside, he glanced around for Ric Baines so he might ask him if Tony Bacon with his taste for pageboys enjoyed visits to Cupid's Bow. He did not see Ric. That meant nothing.

He walked towards the Thames, fingers to his purse for money to pay a waterman. Glancing at London Bridge, at the distant spikes at the south end where bound heads rotted, he lifted his hand. *Ben, yet?* Then he looked towards Bridewell. *Or still inside? I' faith, Ben, I'd introduce thee and thy sweet mind to another friend of mine. Maybe you've both already met, dragged beside each other in a corridor? Hanging next to each other on a wall?* The blatant brutalities of prison and torture and execution, and the subtler brutalities of surveillance and seduction and betrayal — yet recusancy flourished.

'Tis more than ideas.

He'd got to cross the water to reach Widow Bull's. The Thames wound sharply near Deptford. Distance and lines: he'd be free of the sight of Bridewell. Deptford, a station on the Kent Road, on the old Canterbury pilgrimage, pointed the way home. *Home?* A fool's errand on foot, and a fool's errand after Manna's bruises, and Manna's plea.

Still, I may be tempted.

More than two hundred buildings perched on London Bridge, businesses and homes, their overhang creating a tunnel, a two-lane span for wheel and foot traffic. Studying people as he walked, Kit noticed the children who lived there, how well they looked, how robust. Three girls, close to Gideon's age, ran past him, clutching poppets; ribbons streamed from the toys' heads. Kit smiled. He thought of the Flushing girl the younger Wilmot had beaten and kicked. Then Kit recalled the thuds and cracks of his own injuries. *Broke he thy bones, girl, while I hid and listened and said nothing? Aye, that noise; I knew.* A vendor called to Kit then, offering meat pies. Kit stopped to admire the food. Then he apologized for wasting the vendor's time, explaining he'd made a promise for dinner. The vendor only smiled and bawled out to the next passerby.

Taken short, Kit paid for use of a jakes with a door. Done, he stood and stared down the hole at the filthy tidal waters splashing the bridge's starlings. He dug in his purse for the rest of his coins and dropped them through the hole. They plummeted, and the water puckered round them, smoothing out again in a swift moment. Then Kit reached in his satchel and crumpled up his papers — the note from the Privy Council, the note from Robin Poley, his new drafts for more of *Hero and Leander*, his report for Sir Robert on Izaak Pindar, his incomplete letter to Manna — and dropped them. The balls of paper rode on breezes as they fell, but they fell, and the river soaked them, and they sank.

He lifted the key from his neck, hesitated.

Giving a sharp tug, he broke the thread and dropped the key, too.

At the southern end of the bridge, the church of St. Saviour's, once St. Mary Overie, broke into his line of sight. The old idea: sanctuary, asylum. Queen Mary had condemned bishops to death within those walls. Once, an accused man might cry *Sanctuary* and hide within a church for forty days, until he chose surrender, or exile. Choosing exile meant giving up all worldly goods, even most of one's clothes, and then walking to a designated port while carrying a wooden cross, hoping any witnesses would leave one unmolested. It meant boarding a ship and never daring to return home. King Henry had changed all that. As he broke the monasteries, he banished sanctuary. *Even if he'd not, how might I plead for sanctuary, beg a priest's mercy when accused of atheism?*

Kit looked up.

So heavy, those heads: if not bound in place, they'd slide down the pikes.

'Tis more than ideas.

'Tis faith.

And the birds eat.

He felt a nudge and a breath. He felt light.

WE NEVER BEG, BUT USE SUCH PRAYERS AS THESE

Pie of chardequince — fowl, wings and ribs protruding from the dark sauce, bones a brilliant white — cooked and set before him by Widow Bull herself: Kit smiled his thanks, then nodded to Robin Poley. —Thou'st remember.

Studying Kit's face, noting the inky circles and sharp cheekbones beneath his eyes, Robin shoved a fork and spoon across the little table. —About thee, everything.

—All this fuckery, Robin: revenge for the list?

—At first. In truth, 'twas just a contract. I just wanted to recruit thee. Then...So much waste, in this scheme, and in the man's desires. I deplore waste.

Kit said it around a mouthful of hot food. —Shalt thou command the surgeon, or do it thyself?

—Do what?

—Kill me.

—So I'm tasked, and so I would, by mine own hand, if only to show thee my respect. His last words on thee: if I can't have him, none shall. Th'art cut loose, my Christopherus.

—I've got thee to thank for that.

Robin leaned closer, eyes merry. —Dost thou truly believe 'tis so simple? 'Tis a matter of elegant survival, and even freedom, after a fashion. Th'art making quick work of thy dinner.

—Famished.

—What, fasting and prayer?

—Want some?

Robin took a wing, sucked the sauce from it. The skin looked bumpy and pale, and a pinfeather remained. He plucked it, reminding Kit of picking lice. —I need thee, mine own little ferret. I despair of Nick Skeres — Nick Charing, to thee. He's a poor student. It comes to study and being famished, no? It comes down to bread.

—Explain, then, tutor, how and why we sit here. Give me clarity.

—Parse thy failures.

Kit bolted more food before answering. —Very good, then. Failure the first: listening to thee.

—Oh, my poor heart. Thou dost wound me. I should be offended.

—Failure the second: taking and spending the money before taking and eating the bread.

—How wilt thou buy bread without money?

—Wrong bread, Robin. Take, and eat? No? Third: not heeding the warning, however useless and absurd, of the ninety who burnt.

Robin frowned. —Burnt? I follow thee not.

Kit traced his fork through a puddle of sauce, and the tines left paths. The sauce oozed again, obscuring these marks. —Puzzle it out, my father told me, get it right. The ninety who burnt died for the wrong loyalty at the wrong time, Robin — for Christ's love, I'm not certain I understand it myself. Yet I knew the risks. Not as I know them now, but I knew. And I thought that because I am smarter than the lot of ye, shining with gifts — better, somehow — I'd escape. Dart into Hell, singe mine eyebrows, find the innards, find the why, and then slip the snares and the noose, and, Christ knows, write poxed-up *plays* about it.

—Quick and sharp as the finest knife, thy mind, and bright as Lucifer.

Kit dropped the fork; it clattered against the plate. —Bright? No: very dark. And I've done nothing that will last.

—Oh, my Christopherus. Thou'st done so much, loving the work that gnaws thee, caressing its jaws. Was that not the motto on thy portrait?

Kit smelled the paints, felt the burning of the sunlight on his left cheek. *Where is that painter now? Or that damned portrait? The money I spent.* —Quod me nutrit me destruit. Must we dawdle?

—Th'art ready?

—Almost. No. I wish I might see my sister.

—Thy Manna. Is she well?

—Thou shalt *not* use that name for her! Thou'st foul it, thou and thy bitter tongue. Thou scald — thou'dst fuck a woman with the nail of the Cross and smile as she bled!

Others in the dining room turned to look at them: one angry man on his feet, leaning across the remains of a pie of chardequince, left arm crossing his chest as he reached for his dagger; the other man leaning back, palms up, eyes wide.

Sitting down, Kit brushed a tear from his cheek; another one dripped off his beard. —Spare me thy horsepiss concern for my sister.

—Look not to me for Baines and Frizer visiting Canterbury. I was in another country. In Flushing, picking up thy loose ends. Thou'lt be pleased to know the Wilmots are —

—Flushing and the Wilmots be fucked.

Sighing, Robin crossed his arms. —Th'art in no cooperative mood.

—I'm in a mood to understand. I'd thought thee beyond any one man's commands, Robin Poley.

—So I was. But I grew fevered on a plague of pride; 'tis sickly contagious. And now, even as I'd leave Essex behind, the singing boy's blood, sticky in a springe, traps me.

Kit needed a moment before he could speak. —Thou'lt kill a *boy* —

—I killed him *not*! Nick Skeres cut that throat, Nick Skeres punched his solar plexus, Nick Skeres kicked him on the ground, and Nick Skeres tied his hands!

—Sweet Christ Jesus, Robin.

Smiling, Robin inclined his head, in respect. —Pluck the heart and then pummel the conscience until thy guilty target spills his knowledge. I taught thee well. Nick cut the throat, but I am responsible. *I* feel the guilt. Thou'st understand?

Kit nodded. —Thou'lt kill a boy, yet last night thou didst spare me. *Why?*

Robin stood up, leaning on his crutch, slipping. His knees wobbled, and he shifted his weight from hip to hip. —Because I become pathetic. I shamble and limp. I would doze half the day in a stupor if pain woke me not. I've suffered this illness before, felt it flood me and then recede.

—Aye, that cold spring, '87, thou didst limp. I'd watch thee struggle early in the mornings, and I'd wonder about pain, but thou didst seem so strong. I said nothing. It may yet recede again.

—And it may not. My joints seize. Mine eyes burn. My stamina fails. My hips and spine *rot*. I fear some day I shall freeze, bent and stooped. The *pain* of it — and if I should come to a day when I can no longer walk?

Kit nodded. *What of the day th'art seized and stifled?*

Robin leaned on both his crutch and the chair. Pain distorted his face, for just a moment, until he hid it. Then he stretched his back and arms like a man about to start a journey. —So, my Christopherus: another contract?

—Pardon me?

—I told thee: I deplore waste. Now, I shall be gone some hours.

—What, shalt thou *leave* me here? Whither bound?

Robin peered at Kit, confused. Then he beckoned Kit closer and spoke in his ear. —Essex House. Hast thou not been listening? I will beg thy life.

—'Tis thou who's not listened. Robin, I fell to my *knees*, and Essex refused me. Sir Robert knows I knelt, and now he, too, refuses me, and will grant me no audience.

—Yet Sir Robert charged thee to appear before the council each day. He would keep thee alive, at least.

Kit smirked. —I am missing that attendance right now.

—Shall I get thee anything else to eat?

Kit shook his head, licked the fork. The food had taken some of the pallor from his face, and he felt much stronger.

Not strong enough.

—Tom Kyd suffers and rots with each breath I take. I love him. Robin, please: finish this.

Speaking at a normal volume, Robin pointed to the door with his crutch. —I must walk about before my joints seize. Widow Bull does fine work with hedges and flowerbeds. Come see the garden.

Kit followed Robin outside, and the dazzling sunlight, the heavy scents of flowers in bloom, the sweet noise of bees at work, ravished them both. Kit looked at the sky: blue, all blue, miles and miles of blue. This day, this warm and brilliant day after so much cold and rain: anything might happen. Even mercy. Even life.

Even death.

Robin said something about the qualities Essex preferred in his agents and then about his plans for the next few years. —I drew him flowing charts. He likes flowing charts, as Ramus the Scholar made, so tuck that in thy godly memory. My flowing charts delineate how thy skills mayest yet play into his needs. Thou wouldst need to work under my watchful eye, and any mistake thou dost make I must answer for. I shan't try to deceive thee. Our first year or two at this station would be tiresome —

—Tom?

—What?

—Tom. Hast thou seen him?

Robin nodded.

—Is he harmed?

Robin nodded again. —But settle thyself. He'll be released once th'art decided and put to use. 'Twas always the plan. 'Twas thy pride what complicated everything. What, no epigraph? No snatch of Ovid? I am disappointed.

—Oh, pardon me.

—Wilt thou wait for me? Wilt thou stay here?

Kit peeled off his doublet, releasing a sharp savour. —And where else in poxed-up screaming Hell might I go? Besides, Ingram Frizer waits behind that hedge, set to tackle me face first into the muck.

Robin laid his hand over his heart. —Such cynicism in one so young.

—I'm a balding nine-and-twenty. And I'd got an excellent teacher.

Each man gazed at the other; Robin looked away first. —'Tis a little room, in Skeres's name. Thou'lt find there a deck of cards, the one I stole for thee back in '87, those beautiful cards thou wouldst not accept, and a tables game set comes with the room. Poor occupation for thy mighty mind, but it shall fill the hours. Behave, I implore thee. I've set firm parameters for Skeres today —

—Ah, sweet Nick.

—He would love to play thine executioner. I heard about the kisses. And the spoon. Provoke him not.

—'Tis Skeres who provokes me.

—Provoke him not!

Kit glanced at Robin's hand on his arm, reminded of the day Robin tripped over the crutch.

—Marlowe, I've no wish to cajole a fever-fucked noble who's not so much as wiped his own arse in this life and who's already threatened me with prison, only to return to find thee slain by a slack man gone petulant with hurt feelings.

Bees hovered near Kit's mouth, drawn by the quince sauce staining his teeth red.

Kit shook Robin off.

Robin sighed, looked at the hedge. —Horseback and wherries. God save me.

He crutched away.

Kit stood up from the berm and called to the hedge. —I shall be going inside now, thou great hacked-off ox.

Inside, eyes slow to adjust, Kit asked the dark shape of Widow Bull where to find Nick Skeres and ascended the stairs. The third step from the top had gone soft and creaky. Waiting for the heavier tread of Ingram Frizer, Kit raised his knuckles, ready to knock.

Oh, knock? What fine manners, Clever Kitten.

Then he just turned the knob — quiet and swift — and let the door swing open.

He discovered a crowded room: low ceiling, two large four-poster beds, a hearth, table and benches, some chairs, two windows, a washstand, and Nick, snatching his hands out of a satchel.

Startled, Nick looked up. Then he grinned. The bruising across his mouth and jaw from Audrey, eleven days old now, showed yellow and grey. Three of Nick's upper teeth, cracked off, reminded Kit of shards: stone, metal, glass.

Ingram following him, Kit strode to the bench nearest the wall and hauled it out a little ways. He sat down, stretching his arms, tucking his hands behind his head, and thudding his feet on the table.

Ingram sat down across from Kit and looked to Nick.

Nick stared at Kit and took a seat next to Ingram.

Silence.

Ingram drummed his big fingers on the table, near the deck of cards. —We've not been introduced.

—Marlowe.

—I'm Frizer. I've heard much of thee.

Nick chuckled. —Frizer, tell him how thou'st know Tom Kyd.

Kit looked into Ingram's eyes. —Aye. Tell me.

—Oh, that was weeks ago. I only saw him once.

Kit said nothing.

—I knocked him around. I needed... I stole a book from him, but thy Tom came home early, hey?

Still, Kit said nothing.

—Marlowe, 'tis not that I harmed him. I had my orders. I was part of a greater task.

Kit remembered the look in Ben's eyes just before the Flemish constable struck him.

Nick stood up, trying to shove the bench away from the table, forgetting Ingram sat there, too. —He crushed thy catamite's stones, Marlowe, and left him weeping on the floor like some beaten whore.

—Very good, then. Knee or fist, Frizer?

—Hand.

Ingram demonstrated his grip and twist on the deck of cards.

Kit nodded. —I should learn that. Oh, those cards: Robin Poley stole them from a Catholic noble, whom I shall not name, and they are worth more than the three of us combined would make in a lifetime.

Ingram pressed the bent cards with his palms, and Nick opened his mouth, closed it, opened it again. —Is that true?

—Not all of it.

Ingram lifted his hands from the cards and shot Nick a dark look, quite offended.

Nick gazed to the ceiling, as though beseeching God to force the conversation to make sense. —Marlowe, dost thou understand not? A powerful man wants thee buried and forgotten, and if we cannot forget thee, he'll ruin and blacken thy name, even after thy death. Th'art shit on his shoes.

—Needs he a cobbler? I could recommend one. I'faith, I've no quarrel with his tailor.

—Poley's already defied a command to kill thee. 'Tis maddening, seeing one's task, enjoying licence, and yet being barred from completing it.

—And thou wouldst work in espionage? Oh, sweet Nick, thou'lt need more patience than that.

Ingram nodded. —Aye, he's right.

Kit studied Ingram then, drawing a long breath and

reminding himself to keep his hands behind his head. This man who'd struck Manna, who'd tossed infant Ned at the ceiling, who'd mauled Tom's stones: huge — not just tall but solid and broad and, for all his bulk, quick and light when he moved. *And thou, Clever Kitten, art so small. Thou'lt win no fight with him. Not unless thou'st stab him first.*

Robin had always cautioned Kit against violence, even as he drilled him on dagger and fighting skills. *Thy last resort, this. A far better use of thy blood and thy mind to outwit, or outrun, but thou must also be able to outfight. Best yet is sweetest hucker-mucker. Use thy wits before thou wouldst fight, and set the scene so thine opponent's got no escape. Choose and design thy fights with greatest care, and then fight as if thy soul depended on it.*

Kit took his feet down and leaned forward, hands clasped on the table. *Mine opponent? And who, precisely, is that?* —Frizer, hath sweet Nick there told thee why he hates me so?

—No.

—I used my knee. Then, as he writhed on the ground, like, oh — aye, some beaten whore — I pissed on him.

Ingram's bubbly laugh broke free, and he patted Kit on the shoulder.

Nick whirled around. —Hey! 'Tis not funny. And 'tis not so. Marlowe missed.

Kit winked at Ingram. —I'faith, Nick may have tripped. Not to worry, for our story endeth happily: the lady of the house did but goodly smack Nick in the face with an iron spoon.

—Lady Audrey? That little butter pot?

—Backhanded.

Ingram only laughed harder.

Nick strode over to Ingram and slammed his fist down on the table. —Frizer! He's tricky about the mouth.

Kit pointed at himself. —Who, me?

—He'll persuade thee cut thine own throat, yet.

—Frizer, thou'st need not me for that when thou'st got a surgeon here to cut thy throat *for* thee. Keep an eye to his hands. Besides, Nick is still angry I'd not let him use me.

Nick blushed. —God almighty! I fuck no men, and I promise thee, no man comes near me!

Kit raised his eyebrows. —Such vigorous protest. I beg forgiveness. Boys, then.

Ingram clicked his tongue and scowled. —Oh, nothing disgusts me more. Nick, 'tis so?

Nick's groan blended with the hard knock on the door. Kit cursed himself for not hearing the creak of the step.

Nick hauled the door open. —Where'st thou been?

Light hair stuck to his head by sweat, tangerine silk ribbon tied round his upper arm, Ric Baines brushed dust from his sleeves. —Running messages for Tony Bacon. I've crissed and crossed all London this morning. He approved the expense budget, in his benevolence and might, so I opened the reckoning downstairs with Widow Bull. We'll have noise, if we need it.

Kit spat on the floor. *Robin Poley, keeper of the beasts.* —Didst thou not first check with thy leash master, Baines? Poley's not here.

Ric sneered at the dark corner where Kit sat. —Good, you've got him. Unlike thee, Marlowe — who art, what, the man's own little ferret — I owe Robin Poley *nothing.* He grows old and frail and shall be left behind, if he refuses to take care.

—Then to whom dost thou answer, poisoner?

—Come not the divine angel with me. Poisoner, he says. A sleeping draught. Thou'dst do the same unto me in a heart-beat. Besides, I was gentle with thee.

—Arriving with two other men to kick loose my shit and then drag me halfway across Flushing: aye, gentle.

Ric leaned in and patted Kit on the cheek. —I myself did tuck thee in bed that night and so left the door unlatched.

Kit nodded. *One mystery solved.*

—In truth, Marlowe, I thought the draught had failed, for thou didst talk and talk until I considered smothering thee, just for a moment's peace. One moment 'twas vigorous dispute, the next rhythmic nonsense. Good metre, though. I should have written it down. Thy sister resembles thee, only softer, not so bony. Thou wert softer, once. Hast thou not been eating?

—I had a lovely dinner.

Ingram thought a moment. —The boy looks nothing like thee at all. What is he to thee?

—A nephew.

Ric walked over to Nick, who was staring out a window. —None downstairs seems concerned. How didst thou get him here?

Nick snorted.

Kit took a card from the deck, laid it face up on the table. —I willed myself to come here, Baines, and I will myself to sit in this corner, just to make it all a little easier for ye, scald knaves that ye are. Christ knows, ye need the help.

The three men stared at him; he laid three more cards in a line. Soon they all crowded him, studying the cards, keen to decipher the message: deuce of spades, jack of hearts, five of clubs, queen of clubs.

Kit looked each man in the eye. —Gentlemen: it means nothing.

Nick swept the cards to the floor, and they pattered as they fell. —Toy not with me!

—Nick, I am the captive here. How may a captive toy with a commander?

—I — thou —

—Sweet Christ Jesus, if 'tis on the likes of the three of ye Tony Bacon depends, he shall be hanged, drawn, and quartered, and kissing his own smoking bowels, before Christmas. Were I Robin Poley, I'd beat my head off the wall for despair. And were I Essex —

Nick fell on Kit, grabbed his shoulders and shook him. —I would pay thee home this instant! 'Tis not a name to be thrown about by thee! What, thou, a great man? *Thou*, noble and graced?

—Nick, if thou dost remain in my lap, I may be tempted.

Nick smacked his head on a rafter, getting up.

Kit reached in his satchel, and Ingram grasped his wrist. Astonished, Kit kept still. *So fast. He'd break my bones to kindling.* —Frizer, I am reaching for a cloth to press to my sweating forehead. Reach in there thyself and prove my truth.

Ingram let him go.

Ric frowned then. —Marlowe, give over thy dagger.

—No.

—Skeres, what is this? He admits he is captive, yet he offers defiance?

Nick sighed. —Marlowe, just surrender it.

—Why?

Nick's eyes shone.

Fury, Kit thought. *And something else.*

Kit stood up, dropped the rag, and stretched out his arms.
—My dagger? Take it.

Nick reasoned out how to do this, finally kneeling before
Kit and unfastening the scabbard from Kit's right thigh. Kit
kept his arms still, and, as Nick glanced up, he smiled.

Not the stones: the ribs, with the pommel of his own
dagger. Kit admired the element of surprise, the way Nick
declined the cheap blow but instead struck the more intimate,
for the surgeon of Scadbury House knew this patient's body.
All that coughing, weeks of coughing: the ribs had never
healed. They cracked anew — stabbing, burning — and Kit
fell, collapsing onto the bench instead of the floor. He considered this a victory. Gasping, queasy, he grinned at Nick and
beckoned him closer.

Nick hauled Kit to his feet and started to drag him out of
the corner. Writhing first, Kit fell limp on Nick and vomited.
Bile, chardequince, and fowl hit the floor, and Nick, revolted
by the touch and smell of the fluids, added to the mess. Ric
turned away, rolling his eyes; Ingram laughed and pronounced
it better than pissing.

Kit spat pieces of food. —Thou'st owe Robin Poley for that
dinner. It cost good money.

On his hands and knees, Nick closed his eyes and snarled.
—One of ye, clean this up.

None moved.

At the washstand, Kit poured water from the jug into
the basin. He scooped up water with his cupped hands and

splashed his mouth and beard. —Strong tone of command to thy voice, Nick.

Nick scrabbled around. —Stay where I can see thee.

—Thou mayest see me washing, la.

Nick got up, snatched Kit's doublet from the bench, and threw it over the mess on the floor.

—I'faith, Nick, I just had that laundered.

Ingram and Ric laughed.

Kit laughed, too. —It got fouled covering the face of the boy thou didst murder.

Silence.

Ric and Ingram studied Nick, and Kit took a step towards him.

Nick retreated. —I told thee, thou must look to Robin Poley for that. I merely —

—Cut his throat.

Nick slipped on the doublet, got his balance. —Poley gave the order! As he should!

—*Why?*

—The boy learned our names.

—Because thou didst *say* them?

Nick turned his face away.

Rib pain worsening, vision blurring, Kit returned to the table and benches and sat down. Ingram picked up the cards from the floor, his face close to Kit's feet, and Kit considered kicking Ingram but could see nothing to be accomplished by it, except perhaps hurrying the afternoon along and getting beaten to death.

Not yet, not yet. I would come to Thee without shame, just not quite yet.

Rein thy pain and fear before they rein thee.
The birds eat, the birds eat —
Robin, where art thou?

Already close and heavy, the air soured with vomitus and sweat. Nick struggled to open one of the stiff windows. He pried some glass aside, cracking it.

Ingram pointed to a shelf near Kit's head. —A tables set behind thee. I hear th'art an excellent player. Give me a round?

Playing hard, struggling with nausea and pain, Kit lost three games of four.

Ric, who'd been lazing on one of the beds, thudded his feet on the floor. —Skeres, why delay we?

Kit smirked. —Had'st thou hoped to watch, Baines? Such intimate theatre demands patience.

Nick rifled through Robin's satchel, tucked something in his belt. —We must wait for Poley.

—No, 'tis thou who must wait for Poley. I've tasks of more weight, and more satisfaction.

Ignoring Ric, Nick walked back to the table. He congratulated Ingram for winning, then asked Kit how it felt to lose.

Kit noticed the sheen to Nick's green eyes, the quiver in his scowl, the rope over his belt.

Provoke him not.

Kit spat at him.

Again, Nick hauled him to his feet. They danced a wayward step, Kit first resisting the pull but then falling into it, even helping Nick, shuffling in the direction Nick wanted to go. Nick got Kit to the bed behind Ingram and sat him there. Coughing, Kit held up his hands. Nick hesitated. Ric scratched the skin under his beard; a cloud of scurf fluttered down onto his shirt. Nick's hands shook.

Eyes full of knowledge, Kit looked up at Nick and smirked.

Nick threw himself at Kit and pinned him to the bed. Kit told himself not to struggle, reminded himself he'd got neither strength nor air for it. He coughed; he struggled. Knowing he'd lose, he watched, almost amused, as Nick tied his right wrist to a bedpost. Quills and feathers poked his back.

Aye, quills and men and power and folly: all I lack is ink.

Nick tied his left wrist.

And a free hand.

Wheezing, Kit laughed.

Nick stared down at him. —What *is* it with thee?

Breathing shallow, Kit grinned at his tormentor. —Nick, Nick, Nick, thou didst but need to ask me nicely.

—Goat! I will finish this.

Nick wiped spittle from his chin — his teeth now caused him to spray as he spoke — stood back and glanced around the room, not quite guilty, not quite looking any man in the eye. Returning to the other bed, he picked up more rope. Kit closed his eyes, sought strength for the next round. Hearing Nick's footfall, he got ready to kick, but Nick jumped on him and straddled him. He struck Kit's face with his fist. Just a hard tap, Nick told himself, a finding of reach.

Enough for blood.

—Boy-fucking Judas! Leave off!

Nick's second and third punches fell with all the strength of a healthy man. —No more words!

Kit's mouth flooded. He turned to spit. Head too low, blood too fast, he had to swallow, and he hardly cared about Nick tying his ankles to the lower bedposts.

Ingram and Ric looked anywhere but at that bed.

Nick scowled at the doublet on the floor. Then he sat on the bench next to Ingram, watching Kit. Ingram, pinching little tokens between his big fingers, set up another round of tables.

Ric passed Nick a letter. —I'll be party to none of this. Skeres…Christ. Tell Poley I was here, and give him that. Say 'tis a map, should he forget his task and lose his way.

—Aye. Go.

Nick stood up, grabbed a chair, and hauled it to the side of the bed. He sat down and leant forward, elbows on knees, looking very much the confused but concerned surgeon studying a difficult patient.

Kit's eyes opened wide. *Bloodletting. Hot cups. Sketching at night.*

A cheer rose through the floor.

Downstairs, in the dining room, Ric bought a round for everyone present, putting it on Anthony Bacon's account. He knocked back his own ale and left the sullied inner light for the brilliance outside, for flowers and bees and a sweetness on the wind. He walked around the garden a while, asking himself why he'd always considered flowers useless when their beauty and scents provided such rich distraction.

Skeres and his games: 'tis more than needed.

Not my worry, not my task. And when I left the room, Marlowe lived and breathed.

After a while, Ric started his journey back to Essex House.

Nick also descended to the dining room, asking Widow Bull for some rags and another jug of water to clean up a small spill upstairs.

She told him to wait.

Boredom, Kit decided, copulated with fear and created a messy whelp, one strong enough to devour faith: dread. Swallowing more blood, sick with it, sick with pain, he studied Ingram's broad back.

Say nothing, say nothing…

Ingram moved the tables tokens back and forth.

Thou'st come to it, Clever Kitten. No bargains. Ask him not for help.

Dice rattled.

—Frizer.

—Mm?

Kit sighed then. His swollen mouth made his words sound feathery. —Nothing.

Ingram turned around. —No, if 'twas nothing, thou'dst speak not. So what sayest thou?

—Why must it take so long?

Ingram sounded surprised. —Th'art frightened.

Kit looked into his eyes.

Someone beat on the door: Nick, calling to Ingram. —'Tis barred! Didst thou latch it?

Glancing over his shoulder at Kit again, Ingram strode to the door and opened it. —Aye. Who else?

—God almighty, doth Marlowe laugh *again*?

—Laugh at what?

Head down, Nick sidled in. —I will not be mocked.

Ingram and Kit both watched Nick ball up Kit's soiled doublet and throw it into a far corner. He cleaned the floor as best he could with the rags from Widow Bull. Those rags followed the doublet. He picked up his own satchel, one Walsingham had give him as a bonus when Kit survived the pneumonia. First, he took out his fleams and, making sure Kit could see him, held them up to the light. He examined them, shook his head. Then he retrieved the razor.

Oh, for Christ's love.

Chin and shoulders high, mouth tight, Nick approached the bed. He opened the razor and held the blade over Kit's abdomen. —Dost thou think I'll falter?

Look not at the razor; look at his eyes. —No.

Nick moved the razor down, stopping over Kit's stones. —Shall I shave them?

—Thou'dst do it well.

—Aye, but marry, the heat: my hands sweat. The blade would slip.

Ingram scowled. —Nick: why?

—Because I hate him. Because I can.

Tugging the ropes, Kit worked to shift his weight. —I applaud thee, Nick Skeres. Or, ah, so I would.

—What trick now? Applaud me? Why?

—Because, in this moment, thou art honest.

Nick leaned in. —We shall hardly recognize thee.

A new voice spoke. —The flaying of Marsyas?

Nick yelled, and his razor clattered on the floor. Kit cried out. Ingram winced and cringed.

Scowling, Robin Poley rapped his crutch on the floor.

—Skeres, thou didst leave that door unlatched. *Anyone* could have walked in on thee!

—I...

Another cheer rose from dining room. Robin struck Ingram and Nick on their upper arms with his crutch, though not very hard. —Get me a chair, before I fall.

Ingram took Robin by the shoulders and guided him back a few steps to the bench.

Seated, Robin turned not his head but his entire upper body to look at Ingram. —Thanks, gentle Frizer.

Ingram murmured something humble.

A flicker of sadness in his eyes, Robin studied Kit, his bindings, his injuries. —Oh, my Christopherus, ever the gods' darling.

Kit smirked, hurting his face.

Robin smirked back. —Let's get thee up. Skeres, come over here.

Sitting on the farther bench, Nick stropped his razor. —No.

—What?

Ingram, hearing the anger in Robin's voice, stood up, crossed his arms.

Nick looked up. —I said no. Poley, why delay we? The orders are clear.

—Put that razor away, before thou'st cut thyself off.

—Stand up and say that to me, old man.

Robin did stand up, in pieces, it seemed, leaning on his crutch. He shuffled as he turned around to face Nick, and the pent fury in his voice, that voice coming from a small and frail man, chilled even Kit. —I say it, and more. Thou, thou art less use in this work than a poxy cunt, leaving doors ajar, announcing my name to a boy, playing little rack games. I'd bite my thumb at thee, but thou'st merit not even that gesture's wasted strength. Now: fold thy razor, and hide it in thy satchel.

Nick stared back. His master in the field, his conduit to payment and purpose: so feeble. One good knock, and he'd fall. He'd fall, and he'd struggle to rise.

Ingram took a step towards Nick and stood just behind Robin's shoulder.

Nick sneered. —What is't, Frizer? Quick to show thy servility?

Ingram took Nick's wrist and twisted it. The razor clattered onto the floor, and Nick sank to his knees. Kicking the razor away, Ingram stared down at the top of Nick's head. —'Tis called loyalty and obedience.

Robin nodded. —Frizer, get that razor out of harm's way for me.

Ingram stooped and retrieved the razor, still grasping Nick's wrist. Nick twisted and jerked but got nowhere until Ingram let him go. Then Nick took a few steps backward and watched as Ingram took up the open razor as if to throw it.

Ingram hewed the blade into a rafter.

The handle dangled.

Ingram inclined his head to Nick. —It shall need stropping.

Turning his back, Nick strode to the window, where he pressed his forehead against a warm pane of glass. He caught a faint reflection of himself: his mouth, his teeth.

Robin looked at Kit again. —He's left thee no slack.

—'Tis nothing. I am fine.

Grinning, Robin worked to loosen one of the bedpost knots. His stiff fingers slipped. Then his hair fell to one side, exposing the protruding vertebrae of his neck.

Kit whispered it. —Th'art in agony.

—'Tis not my first time rescuing thee. Frizer, help me here.

Ingram crammed his body between the bed and the wall, on Kit's right, as Robin, balancing on crutch and bedpost, drew his dagger. Concentrating on ropes and knives, none of them saw Nick approach.

Robin stumbled as Nick's foot knocked the crutch away. Grabbing the bedpost for balance, Robin dropped his dagger. Ingram, penned in, could do nothing as Nick snatched up the long knife. Smiling, Nick fingered the decoration on the pommel, the little ear.

No one spoke.

Nick looked down on Kit. —If I cut thee loose, wilt thou finally kneel?

—Not to thee.

Nick sneered at this but still caught sight of Ingram creeping back towards the bench and seized Robin from behind. —Hist, Frizer. Not another inch.

Expecting the dagger at his neck, Robin refused to struggle. Keeping still now made his body a dead weight and forced Nick to stagger for balance. Even as he reasoned how to react, Robin felt a jab of fear as Nick grabbed his jaw. Forced it up. Exposed his throat. Something delicate cracked in Robin's neck, and a hot tingling shot down his left shoulder and out his fingers, and Robin found he feared that tingling, the subsequent numbness, as much as he feared the dagger.

Nick peered at Kit and Ingram, confirmed he had their attention.

Robin spoke first. —Thou dost enjoy this.

—I've a letter for thee.

—Woulds't *thou* me, Skeres?

—I would carve *thou* in thy flesh. Clarifies that the matter?

Robin rolled his eyes. —And thine ending?

—My what?

—Hast thou sufficient coin for two corpses today?

—Well, I'd take it from thee. And in exchange, I would give thee a letter.

—Such a good little keeper of messages, thou. No boy stole this one?

Nick glanced the blade against Robin's skin and drew blood. Ice, fire: it felt like a shaving cut at the hand of an incompetent barber. —'Tis a letter from Baines. In case thou dost lose thy way.

—I know what it sayeth.

—Then when shalt thou *do* what it sayeth? Dost thou love him? Is't *love* stays thy hand?

Kit watched blood drip down Robin's throat and stain his shirt. *Such blood, from such a tiny cut?*

—No, Skeres, 'tis waste. I deplore waste.

As the bloodstain on Robin's shirt spread, Kit wondered about the cauterized wound on Robin's chest. The long lecture Robin gave on wounds and infection and the mercy of stabbing to kill, his words hissing like their weak fire in the mist as Kit dangled the St. Hubert's Key charm over the flames until it turned red, studying the flame and not the wound —

Nick spat. —Poley, th'art wasting *time*. Thy final petition failed, aye?

—My final petition clarified for Essex just whose hand cut that boy's throat. The same hand that would cut mine, had its owner the stones for it. My final petition involved my sworn and signed statement of thy guilt in the matter, and my final petition resulted in Essex believing me, not thee. I give thee points for thy treachery, Skeres, for thy getting to Essex and Bacon first, but thy version of the boy's death hath raised one excellent question: why should I kill anyone when I have servants to kill for me?

Nick turned pale, then red. —Servant? I am no servant to thee!

—In their eyes, thou art nothing more. I had to remind Essex of thy name.

Ingram shifted his weight.

Neck and jaws paining, Robin continued, and he spoke as though revealing a tender secret. —In truth, Skeres, I did need beg for *thy* life. Our great man prizes loyalty above all. As do I. And one final consideration for thee, Skeres: when thou'st killed me and knelt to steal money from my purse, what of Frizer there, standing between thee and the door? Shalt thou win a fight with him?

Nick's hold eased.

—Now, give me back my dagger.

Once Robin stood clear, Ingram strode towards Nick and punched him in the belly, hit the solar plexus. Unable to breathe, Nick fell to the floor and writhed there.

Kit felt a deep joy. *For Gideon, that. Now maul his stones, la.* Then Kit turned his face away. —Glut and surfeit. Poley, relent.

Robin shook his head. —'Tis all he understands. Frizer, get Marlowe free.

Ingram finished sawing through the ropes, leaving the ends still knotted around bedposts, ankles, and wrists. Then he helped Kit sit up. Catching sight of the razor handle above, Kit felt dizzy, and he almost snarled a question at Ingram, almost asked why he'd done nothing earlier, why he'd accepted and then ignored Nick's assumed authority. His mouth hurt too much for more words.

Feel not; watch, just watch.

Robin scowled. —Frizer, get Skeres out of here. Fresh air, ale, throw him down a well, I care not. Just get him out. I'll send for thee in a while. I'll need thy help yet.

—Anything.

—My thanks, gentle Frizer.

Ingram bowed to Robin, patted Kit on the shoulder, as if in reassurance, and then took Nick by the arm and got him to his feet. They left, and Robin latched the door behind them.

He turned to face Kit.

Still sitting on the bed, Kit said nothing.

Tangled branches, we are. —Thou'st lost thy dagger, mine own little ferret.

Kit tasted blood again when he spoke. —I let Skeres take it.

—What? Why?

—Because he had to kneel to get it.

Robin smirked. —A heavy price to pay for that one moment of satisfaction.

—Cheap. Is't for pity of a laundress thou'st let me up? Enough blood on the sheets? Or must we dance with more fuckery yet?

—I could have smothered thee, bound there. Why in Hell did I not smother thee? Oh, look not at me like that. Bright brown eyes seeing so much — thou mayest chart each lie I've ever told, no?

Kit stood up and stretched his stiff arms, looking away. —Each lie. The way I might chart stars. Sweet Christ Jesus, the stink in here.

Robin knocked him onto his belly, on the floor. Kit felt only some distant surprise — Robin's weight, so light? — as he writhed and heaved like some landed fish and threw Robin off. The dagger clattered against the floor, and Kit snatched it, running for the door, path straight and clear, as in his dreams of Canterbury Cathedral. *'Tis what it meant, all this time? So easy?* Joyful, he fumbled with the latch.

Tom.

Each lie, Robin. What promise have I got that Tom goes free if I —

—Boy-fucking Judas.

He grimaced at the floor and let the dagger fall from his hand.

Turned around.

Kicked the dagger over to Robin.

Crossed his arms and watched.

Faith, then.

Rib pain nearly buckled his knees.

Taking up the dagger, Robin got to his feet. —Battered as thou art, 'tis thou who could kill me, Marlowe. I'd hoped to surprise thee.

—I thank thee for it.

—Th'art trailing rope still.

Kit glanced down at his wrists, nodded. —Hard knots.

Racket from downstairs rose: many men's voices, talking, laughing.

Robin's eyes looked hot, feverish. —God save me. Run.

—Run *where?*

Robin looked at the windows, the door, any hole, any escape. —Essex refused even to see me. I got nowhere with my petition.

—'Tis writ plain across thy face.

—He would gaol me.

Kit sounded gentle. —I know, I know.

—I could hang yet. I —

—Robin: *finish this.*

—What?

—I'm begging thee.

After a moment, Robin tugged at his shirt and exposed his old wound.

Kit studied it: a red and black line, hairs grown over it now. A light stab wound, more of a poke, Robin had said. Over his heart. Enough to hurt. Enough to bleed. Enough to make him stagger and cry out *Not yet.* Near the scar: his charm, his St. Hubert's Key, not really a key at all but a conical piece of iron. Remembering, Kit heard the fire hissing in the mist, heard Robin panting as he leaned against a tree, felt the charm dangling from his hand.

Somewhere, behind them, the man who'd stabbed Robin lay dead, himself stabbed.

Stabbed by Kit.

Marlowe, tie my hands. We've none else to hold me down. Now, my charm must be hot enough so it burns the wound clean but sticks not. Should that iron stick to me, mine own little ferret, I shall haunt thee to thy dying day. See that branch I broke up? Take a piece of that, and get it between my teeth so I might bite — no, finish this!

Iron, blood, smoke, flesh.

Not a scream: Kit had never settled on the best word for Robin's noise.

The wound had healed clean.

Robin closed his shirt. —Like that?

Trembling, Kit nodded.

—Stand there. I'll get behind thee and tie thine hands.

Expecting a knife in the back, Kit obeyed.

—Oh, my Christopherus, th'art more trouble... How many times have I rescued thee?

—And my shimmering ideals.

—Now, wait —

—Nothing pricks thy conscience. Thou'st got thine orders.

Robin scowled. —Test that.

Tugging his arms, Kit thought of *Lethe*'s boatswain and his keys, of the slush lamp and the cloak. —Tight.

—The ache in my back... Give me a moment.

Kit stood there, looking at the door. *Without shame. I would go to Thee without shame.* Whorls and splinters in wood, little faults: his heart pounded, his vision keened. *Manna, wait —*

—Marlowe, I'm too feeble to reach.

Kit knelt.

Robin startled him then with the gag. Kit flinched, almost losing his balance, then, understanding, opened his mouth. Robin fastened the thing, stepped back. Crutch and man, crutch and man: Robin limped until he stood in front of Kit.

More than ideas.

Shaking now, Kit threw back his head, as at the Star Chamber, and looked at the ceiling. *Tom — Robin, come on...*

Nothing streamed in the firmament.

Ben saying to me: my submission to Rome, Stephen, is my submission to Christ. Thine?

He relaxed his neck and looked straight ahead.

I love him.

Robin knelt before Kit. —I need to make it look an accident. I shall be quick, Marlowe. Thine eyes so bright...Only look away. Make compartments in thy mind and look away. Look not at me, I say.

Kit refused.

—Look away!

Robin would tell himself later, parsing his failures, that he'd lost his balance, leaning on his crutch with his tingling left arm, lost his balance and tried to catch himself on Kit, that the dagger slipped in his hand and flew as he fell, slipped in his stiff and pained hand, slipped.

No slipping. The dagger struck. It struck, because one kneeling man stabbed another.

Right eye, on an angle of descent.

A quiet hiss of pierced skin — invasion — scraped bone, and a gentle yield.

Robin yanked the dagger free.

Screaming behind the gag, Kit struggled to free his arms, took his weight on his right hip, fell over. The wound collapsed, ready to knit; blood interfered.

Robin studied the blade: stained to almost eight inches. He'd ruined the eye and pierced the brain stem. He'd done this before. By his own hand, as he'd promised. Quicker than stabbing the heart, and kinder, he felt, than cutting the throat. Less messy. And Kit's breathing would catch, slow, stop. Any moment now.

He brushed the backs of his fingers over Kit's cheek. Kit seemed to nod.

Laughter and shouting rose again from downstairs, and Robin could no longer hear Kit's breathing. He checked the carotids: nothing. He leaned his ear close to Kit's face: nothing.

Make compartments in thy mind — Robin's compartments collapsed. Memories of being a child, a husband, a father, a student, a man who'd sought cleaner work and failed, collided. Staring down at a dying man — which moment? when? this corpse? — these remains of a life, this talisman of bone and flesh, a man whom, once untangled from policy and need, Robin considered a friend, he felt whole, complete: himself. The light got bright, even brilliant. He wanted to close his eyes, and he told himself the light made him weep. Blood had spattered his shirt and now, drying, it stuck the fabric to his skin. Robin had never felt so alive.

Or so gutted.

I lost...

Blood pooled and glistened and inched towards him, even as it sank into the wooden floor. Not just abstracted blood. A man's blood. It reached his knees. *Mine own little ferret: thy blood.* A message in it, too: ciphered, perhaps.

Tom Kyd suffers and rots with each breath I take. I love him.

Robin hid his face in his hands. *God save me. I've no weapon against this, no key, no charm.*

Oh, my Christopherus: thou'st won.

GOOD PENNYWORTHS, BUT MONEY CANNOT PROVE

At Essex House, Anthony Bacon shifted his wrapped foot and peered at his correspondence through a reading stone. He read the letter aloud to Essex, who, standing with his arms crossed, stared out the Thames-side window.

—Bacon, why must thou sound so petulant?

—'Tis the grief of my gouty foot, my lord.

—Oh.

—My lord, shall I light another candle?

—Another?

—It grows dim, my lord.

Scattered light: wherry lamps lamps glowed, up and down the river. Essex frowned. *The light only worsens the look of the water.* —Read me the final paragraph again.

—*And so, Sir Robert, I feel I must acknowledge a boy's behaviour, a boy who felt abandoned and lost. With humble gratitude, then, I return to you that which is yours: the poppet I stole. As the theft is old, the damage is time's. I pray you approve of the box.* Will you sign it, my lord?

Essex paid Anthony no heed, instead raising his right forearm before him, as in defence, then opening his fingers wide until he blocked the sight of the lamps.

In his office at Westminster, hungry for the supper missed hours ago, Robert prepared the agenda for tomorrow's Privy Council meeting. He considered the wording of one item, settling for: *A motion to issue a warrant of arrest for Chr. Marlowe on his brazen defiance, his failure to keep attendance on the Privy Council and await the Councillors' pleasure. In case of need, to require aid most stout and confinement close.*

Robert dipped his quill, hesitated. A necessary arrest, but where to hold him, with plague raging in the gaols? *I learn, Sir Francis, of hearts and minds, but as I would teach him obedience, I need him alive, and in reach. I would tempt him back to me. He's not worth my trust, yet I say that when I may not trust myself.*

Izaak Pindar interrupted, holding an urgent message and a small wooden box. Robert told Izaak to wait while he read the note, as it likely needed a reply. The seal: Essex House. Izaak poured wine into Robert's glass, and Robert took a good swallow. He broke the seal, unfolded the paper, and recognized the deformed handwriting of his poor-eyed cousin, Anthony Bacon. Robert sniffed the paper, caught faint scents of lavender, rose, and saffron. He read the note, drained his cup, read it again.

You write not, my lord of Essex, of any poppet.
Use them well; cherish them not.

He cleared aside his Privy Council work for the moment and wrote a letter to Sir Thomas Walsingham. Shaking pounce on the wet ink, he ordered Izaak Pindar to call a messenger for the early morning. When Izaak left, Robert folded the paper, addressed it, sealed it, left it on the edge of the desk for Izaak to retrieve. Telling himself he grieved the waste of resources, Robert bowed his head and struck it on the desk.

Bending his spine like this caused Robert great pain. He knew to expect it, and he stayed bowed like that until tears pricked. Gripping the edge of his desk, he sat up.

When Izaak returned to get the letter, Robert was sitting up, mouth tight, writing tomorrow's agenda. Izaak peeked into the pitcher of wine: nearly gone.

Robert asked Izaak several workaday questions. Izaak answered them to Robert's satisfaction.

Then Robert put down his quill. —The Dutch Church Libeller: nothing came to the proof?

—No, your honour.

—How long ago released thee thy suspect from Bridewell?

Izaak considered deceit. He filtered so much trivia before it reached busy Sir Robert, case closures and release dates. He might compile such facts on a list, and Sir Robert might only glance at it and nod.

Izaak swallowed, cleared his throat.

Robert's voice rose. —God's own wounds broiling in the midday sun: he's not still in there?

The messenger arrived at Scadbury early in the morning of May 31, and Walsingham welcomed the interruption. He stood quarrelling with Audrey over his new ability to balance the household accounts, to pay all the servants and every single debt by the next Quarter Day, June 24, and start clean. Audrey refused to accept this sudden solvency as a blank gift of fortune, demanding instead to know whence, whence this flux of cash? Eyes heavenward, Walsingham softened his angry face when Dan Roe knocked on the library door, announced the message, and gave over the letter.

The blessing of the interruption soured.

—Oh.

Audrey walked towards him. —What? What says it?

Eyes down, Walsingham folded the letter, tucked it in his shirt. —Trouble with Frizer. Business in London. I — Audrey...

—Marlowe?

He nodded.

—How murdered?

Walsingham stared at her, then tapped the letter beneath his shirt. —There's nothing here of murder.

—Silly me. Died in his sleep, then, safe in bed with some-one he loved?

—'Twas a dispute over a reckoning.

—Tally it up, pay it out, and begone, aye, nothing to see here. So thou'lt go to London, husband?

—At once. I hope to be back before dark. I've no wish to spend the night, but I know not —

—Thou'lt stay not at Cecil House?

I'd as soon burn it down. —I am due in Deptford.

—Deptford? All the filth of the river. Oh, sweet God, he deserved better. He'd earned better. He and Gideon both.

—Hush, woman. Hold thy tongue.

Audrey obeyed.

For a moment.

—Husband, I shall not be here when thou dost return.

—*What?* The Queen's sent not for thee.

—No, she hath not, and I am heartily sorry for it, but Lady Mildred hath many times pressed invitation on me to visit her and Sir William. Dost thou know where they live? Shall I draw it for thee, on a map?

—I know where they live.

—Wilt thou *say* it? Aye, back of thy hand, knuckles at thy jaw: strike me, then. Do it. Thy blow shall mark me, and I *will* explain.

He lowered his hand. —Sir William and Lady Mildred reside in Essex.

—Aye, *Essex*. Be not so dense! In London, husband, at court, Essex did loose his charm upon me, and his sweet words, and when I gave him nothing in kind, he did offer me money. Money for thy debts and obligations in exchange for the small matter of my describing to him thy business, thy charities, and any guests of this, thy grand house. I refused him, because thou hast married no whore.

Walsingham made to speak, said nothing.

—Thou, husband, dost hold a different opinion of money and flesh. How much? How much, thy wages from Essex? How much to —

—I betrayed no one. I am loyal to Her Majesty.

Audrey turned away from him. —Thou art tainted!

He grabbed her arms, whirled her around. —Dear God above: thou'lt dare accuse me and then show me thy back?

Her jaw shook, and though she wept, she did not look down.

—Tell me, Audrey. That night. Thou and Marlowe in this library. What happened between ye?

—Nothing.

—What said he?

She shook her head.

—Audrey! I heard thee walk down that hall, and I know thou didst close the doors because the racket of his cough got blunt. Speak!

Silence.

Walsingham hauled her close to him, kissed her ear, scraped his teeth over it. —How didst thou play-act the boy for him, hey, thou with thy dimpled plump arse and the butter-mounds of thy paps?

Her spit landed on his hand.

He let her go, and the sound of her rapid stride to her bedchamber filled his head.

Walsingham reached Deptford in time for the funeral, though not for the coroner's visit. The story: a fight, a tragic brawl, a dispute over who would pay the reckoning, oh, evil days. Quarrelsome Marlowe had rested on a bed behind the one Frizer, then leapt up, stole the dagger Ingram Frizer wore on his back, and attacked him, grieving Frizer's head with the blade. Frizer, being penned on either side by Skeres and Poley, could not avoid this attack, and yet he fought back against this murderous rage and, in self-defense, killed this Marlowe, stabbed him in the eye.

The coroner, his report in mealy Latin, described the

wound as one inch wide, two inches deep. He sounded the depth with a finger. He also made firm note of the dagger's market value.

Insisting, causing delays, woollen black mourning suit almost cooking him, Walsingham viewed the body just before the shrouding. Hot and rank: all was hot and rank. He said a little prayer of thanks for the wisdom and generosity of Dan Roe; the tufts of rosemary helped. Widow Bull stood there, an old sheet draped over her arm, explaining her fury and embarrassment at such a thing happening here, at her respectable rooming house, and how in the name of God would she get the blood out of the floor? Then she clicked her tongue and sighed. Walsingham ignored her. He already felt like he intruded here, in this foul little room holding some message, some secret.

So much blood.

Walsingham knelt to lift the doublet from the face.

Dost thou love me, Walls, or dost thou love the danger of me?

Walsingham's fingers touched only air. *So much blood —*

Shoving Widow Bull aside, he ran from the room. She stumbled, cursing him, warning he'd go barren of joy the rest of his days. Though he thudded his feet on the stairs, each word reached him.

Geoffrey waved the guard away and left the cell door open behind him. —Th'art released.

Tom stared at him, working to understand a language he'd lost. First, he needed to take in Geoffrey's own freedom. That idea, the apparent simplicity of it, the lack of fuss, invaded his mind and left room for little else. —What?

—Thine examination is complete, and th'art free to go. I've sent for thy father.

—Not charged?

—Cleared. As am I. Just in time, too. My wife had a son last night.

—Congratulations. I am not charged?

I named him Thomas. —No, not charged.

Leaning on Frank, Tom shambled towards his door. His arms felt too long, and his legs felt too short. A deep burning shot down his spine as his hands tingled, as his feet shuffled and dragged.

—Father, the sky should have changed.

—What? 'Tis the sky.

—I thank you for hiring the cart, but the sky should have changed. *I* have changed. Clouds look pretty, after all this? Oh, repaired you this door?

Frank followed Tom inside. —I knew not 'twas broken.

—The constables kicked it in. And the man with the crutch.

Frank said nothing.

Inside, Tom looked around. Then he leaned against his desk. *Rearranged books: a thorough search of my rooms. How kind, putting the books back, how kind.*

Frank opened the food chest, looked inside, checked the desk. —I'll go get thee some bread. Thine ink's dried up, too.

Tom shuffled into the bedroom: rumples on Kit's side of the bed, and a lamp hanging from the sconce. He turned around to ask his father a question; he'd no idea what the question should be.

Frank stood in the doorway now. —Sit down. I've bad news for thee. No, sit. Thy Kit... Sweet Saviour, Tom, what happened to thee?

Tom shook his head.

Audrey was a woman who kept her promises. Walsingham knew that. Such fidelity: one reason of many he'd fallen in love with her. Still, he hoped this time she'd break faith.

No. She'd gone.

In the library, still parched from his drinking the night before, drinking as he chased sleep, he studied the two couches, the piles of books, his desk, and the little skull atop it.

Then he shuffled toward the looking glass.

'Twas never the money. Dear God above, it got so tangled. Marlowe is — was — my friend, and I loved him. Essex recommended Skeres and Frizer to me. Sir Thomas, he said, I hear you need some servants for your house. No, no, good men and true, mine own. I regret I cannot keep them at Essex House, but I will not see them stuck, for I care about my men. May I supplement their wages, then?

'Twas never about the money.

His reflection: eyes tired, hard, accusing. The phantom in the mirror shone back disbelief.

FAIR COPY: FIRST TAKE MY TONGUE,
AND AFTERWARDS MY HEART

Addressed from London
Parish of St. Mary Colechurch
Old Jewry Street, Sign of the Quill
To Sir John Puckering, Lord Keeper of the Great Seal

At my last being with your Lordship, to entreat some
speeches from you in my favour to my patron who (though
I think he rest not doubtful of mine innocence) hath yet in
his discreeter judgment feared to offend in his retaining me
without your honour's former privity. So it is now, Right
Honourable: that the denial of that favour (to my thought
reasonable) hath moved me to conjecture some suspicion
that your Lordship holds me in, concerning atheism, a
deadly thing which I was undeserved charged withal, and
therefore have I thought it requisite, as well in duty to your
Lordship and the laws, and also in the fear of God, and
freedom of my conscience, therein to satisfy the world and
you.

The first and most (though insufficient surmise) that
ever darkened therein might be raised of me grew thus.
When I was first suspected for that Libel that concerned the
state, amongst those waste and idle papers (which I cared
not for) and which unasked I did deliver up, were found
some fragments of a disputation touching that opinion,
affirmed by Marlowe to be his, and shuffled with some of
mine (unknown to me) by some occasion of our writing in
one chamber two years since.

My first acquaintance with this Marlowe rose upon
his bearing name to serve my patron, though my patron
never knew his service but in writing for his players. For
never could my patron endure his name, or sight, when he
had heard of his conditions, nor would indeed the form of
divine prayer used duly in his Lordship my patron's house
have quadred with such reprobates.

That I should love or be familiar friend with one so
irreligious were very rare; when Cicero sayeth they in whom
rests a cause why they should be esteemed are worthy of
friendship, which neither was in him, for person, qualities,
or honesty. Besides, he was intemperate and of a cruel heart,
the very contrary to which my greatest enemies will say by
me.

It is not to be numbered among the best conditions of
men to tax or upbraid the dead when the dead cannot bite
back. But thus much have I (with your Lordship's favour)
dared in the greatest cause, which is to clear myself of being
thought an atheist, which some will swear he was.

For more assurance I was not of that vile opinion, let it
but please your Lordship to enquire of such as he conversed
withal, and some stationers in Paul's Churchyard, whom
I in no sort can accuse nor will excuse by reason of his
company, of whose consent had I even, no question but I
also should have been of their consort, for the craftsman
recognizes the craft from but the slightest trace.

Of my religion and life I have already given some
instance to the late commissioners and of my reverend
meaning to the state, although perhaps my pains and undeserved tortures felt by some would have engendered more

impatience when less by far hath driven so many indeed outside the fold which it shall never do with me.

But whatsoever I have felt, Right Honourable, this is my request not for reward but in regard of my true innocence that it would please your Lordships to think the same and me, as I may still retain the favours of my Lord and patron, whom I have served almost these six years now, in credit until now, and now am utterly undone without herein be somewhat done for my recovery. For I do know his Lordship, my patron, holds your honours and the state in that due reverence as he would no way move the least suspicion of his loves and cares both toward her sacred majesty your Lordships and the laws whereof when time shall service I shall give greater instances I have observed.

As for the libel laid unto to my charge, I am resolved with receiving of the sacrament to satisfy your Lordships and the world that I was neither agent nor consenting thereunto. Howbeit if some outcast Ishmael for want or of his own dispose to lewdness have with pretext of duty or religion, or to reduce himself to that he was born unto by any way incensed your Lordships to suspect me, I shall beseech in all humility and in the fear of God that it will please your Lordships but to censure me as I shall prove myself, and to repute them as they are in deed those who would commit the most deadly injustice and deceive while appearing to all to be good and righteous men. 'Tis the greatest injustice to rack the truth to fit the times. For doubtless even then your Lordships shall be sure to break through their lewd designs and see into the truth, when but their lives that herein have accused me shall be examined and ripped up effectually, so may I chance with Paul to live and shake the viper off my hand into the fire for which the ignorant suspect me guilty of the former shipwreck. And thus (for now I fear me I grow tedious) assuring your good Lordships that if I knew any whom I could justly accuse of that damnable offense to the awful majesty of God or of that other mutinous sedition towards the state I would as willingly reveal them as I would request your Lordships' better thoughts of me that never have offended you.

Your Lordships' most humble in all duties.

Th. Kyd

A GIFT PREVAILS WHEN
DEEP-PERSUADING ORATORY FAILS
August 1594

Tom hung the *Closed* sign on his door and locked it, doing this with some delicacy. The hinges wanted to give way, and his landlord insisted on more back rent before repairs. The August sunlight bleached the dust, though from certain angles the dust still glittered. Tom had some money, a partial payment from his new patron. He'd already thrown some of it to his landlord. Now he wanted to settle a reckoning that mattered.

Ed Blount finished speaking with another customer as Tom waited. Tom noticed his new book on display, pride of place for Ed. *My new book: a translation of another man's work.* Tom wondered how many copies of his *Cornelia* had sold. He knew better than to ask.

Then he recognized that Ed spoke to him.

—The Admiral's Men are rotten with coin this season.

Tom nodded. —I doubt it not. Two seasons with the playhouses closed: everyone's dying for a show.

—'Tis *Jew of Malta* making the money.

Homunculi. —As if I might go see it, lacking the coin, lacking the time, and lacking the peace in my head. As if death suddenly made that play safe.

Ed took a sharp breath. —What brings thee my way, friend?

—I would pay some of my debt.

Ed took out his ledger, recited the amount owing and showed it to Tom, who offered to pay half of it. Ed accepted this, wrote the amount in his ledger, and Tom initialed it.

—Kyd, th'art so pale. Art thou not well?

Tom considered how best to answer. The words he spoke invaded his mouth, drove off the words he'd thought. —Toes an inch from the floor, Blount.

—What?

—Ink and paper matter less when a man is dead. And one cannot eat ink and paper.

—I know. Thou didst love him —

Tom flinched. —What matters? He's dead. Over a year, now. And the sky changed not.

—Kyd, I am sorry.

Tom looked Ed in the eye.

Ed wished he wouldn't.

Sweat cooled on Tom's knees and chest as he got out his key. The walk back from Paul's Yard, not quite half a mile, wore him out these days. He touched the door; it swung open.

Loose and easy. As if the lock had never been fixed, as if someone else were home, keeping an eye out for customers, ready to bid them wait.

Tom crouched down to examine the lock. Scratches and cuts: someone had knifed his door.

Oh, and what to steal this time?

He'd already bickered with his landlord this week; now he must pay for damage, too. New sweat pricked out over Tom's chest, and, as he caught his breath, he felt dizzy. Inside, leaning on the desk, waiting for the spell to pass, he eyed his bookshelves.

Nothing seemed disturbed.

Clothing rustled, on the bed.

Tom shuffled to the two little stairs and peered into the bedchamber.

The little man who'd arrested him last year — bearded now, his beard mostly white — sat on the bed, head jutting forward, reading a book: Tom's translation of Garnier's *Cornelia*.

He looked up from the page. —I found this at Blount's. 'Tis a harsh story.

Tom expected fear, sought anger, found only fatigue. Emotions seemed broken: shattered, jumbled at his feet. He glared at his visitor. —Why art thou here?

—Aye, *thou*. We've come to that. A harsh story, as I say, and this thy dedication to thy new patron — a new patron for thee. How came that to thee? Thou'lt not tell me? Thy dedication, then, written here: Having no leisure (most noble lady) but such as evermore is travelled with the afflictions of the mind, than which the world affords no greater misery, it may be wondered at by some, how I durst undertake a matter of this moment: which both requireth cunning, rest, and opportunity; but chiefly, that I would attempt the dedication of so rough, unpolished a work to the survey of your so worthy self. I can see it in thine eyes. Come, sit next to me, before thou dost topple over. Closer than that; I shan't bite. Wherein, what grace that excellent Garnier hath lost by my default, I shall beseech your honour to repair with the regard of those so bitter times and privy broken passions that I endured in the writing it. Thy modesty is exemplary.

—I see not thy crutch.

—The past winter was kinder to mine afflictions. Knew I not but only fourteen months have passed since I saw thee last, I'd guess thou'st aged ten years. Thou'st fear me?

The book's messy typeface filled Tom's vision. —No. Thou dost mean nothing.

—I should be offended. Aye, my poor heart. Thou dost wound me.

—Thou didst say it thyself to me in Bridewell: the punishment, the examiner, the reasons, it all means nothing. How doth mine examiner these days? Pindar, aye: writes he any new odes?

Snorting, Robin tucked the book in his satchel. —Master Examiner Pindar doth quite well for himself. His tailor must kiss his feet. Whatsoever I said to thee in Bridewell, if it all meant nothing —

—*Nothing?* Know'st thou how my time there has ripped up my mind — know'st thou the subtlest lick of such Hellfire?

I *dream*. My nightmares plague me in the noonday sun. Phantoms setting themselves alight and parading across thy vision, not only at night but in broadest day: hast thou seen it? I walk to the baker for bread, and I smell prison air. I deliver a pillory sign to Chief Constable Reynolds, and I hear chains. I sit at my desk to work and splash ink on my skin, and, as the ink dries, I am screaming in manacles. And the... Blood of Christ, they racked me. *Racked* me, and for what? Tell me how that is nothing!

'Tis nothing, Kit had always said, *I am fine.*

Robin took a breath. —If it all meant nothing, I would not be here, catching fleas from thy bed.

Tom's voice got quieter, hollow. —Every bed in London's got fleas.

—See? Thou dost say that as though the fleas mean something.

Tom snorted.

Robin looked straight ahead. —Even when I'd not admit it to myself, he knew what I would do. I lost something when I... when he died.

—I care not.

Now Robin looked at Tom. —No. Nor should I expect any different from thee. Love, then.

—*What?*

—Love nearly destroyed me. He came to me, when he still could have run, when he knew what I must do. He came to me on a pilgrimage, because he would finish it. For love. Of thee, I suppose.

Tom said nothing.

Robin blinked a few times, licked his lips. His breath smelled of wine. —Did not his death free thee from Bridewell?

—Did not his life put me there?

—No, please. Listen —

—Away from me! Go!

—He... God save me.

Tom's chest hurt again, and his breathing caught. —I need reason.

Robin bowed his head, slid his legs off the bed. —I tried to give it thee.

—Love?

—Thou'st spit the word like poison.

—Love? He made me feel... Dost thou know happiness? Hey? When the simple presence of someone else evens out thy very pulse? When thou'dst take comfort in the comfort of another, when thou wouldst, if denied that person, pray to die? Or when thou'dst die *for* him? I'd have... I hung... Around him, all my anger, all the poisons in my heart, bit by bit, just — just eased. Settled. And when I understood he loved me, all I feared afterwards was losing that love, losing him. Know'st thou any of that?

Robin shook his head.

Tom's voice got quiet. —I was better when I was loved.

—Thou'st gone grey in the face.

—Thy presence sickens me.

—Lie down. I shall get thee something to drink.

—No redemption there.

Robin paused on the steps. —No.

He poured flat ale into a cup, carried it to Tom.

439

Tom took the cup, drank.

Then the two men studied each other for a moment, and Robin turned away again. This time, he left, struggling to close the damaged door behind him. Tom sipped more of the ale, then dropped it. Nauseous, panting, some painful weight beneath his ribs shoving him, crushing him, he lay down on the bed.

Love?

—End—

NOTES

The excerpt from the Pipher song "The Lizard" is used by permission of Pipher (Lee Thompson).

Tom's letter in "First take my tongue, and afterwards my heart" is based on a document written by Thomas Kyd called Letter A. I've modernized the spelling, adjusted some punctuation, translated the Latin, clarified that Tullie is Cicero, changed the first "Lord" to "patron" for clarity, taken a guess at the illegible words, omitted the mention of Harriot, Warner, and Roydon, and added a sentence.

Section and chapter titles come from four plays, the Acts of the Privy Council in May of 1593, a libel posted on a church, a troubled letter, an unfinished poem, a song, and perhaps a queen.

"Video et taceo" – Queen Elizabeth I, ascribed

"The sight of London to my exiled eyes" – Christopher Marlowe, *Edward II*

"purging of the realm of such a plague" – *Edward II*

"Tell truth and have me for thy lasting friend" – Thomas Kyd, *Spanish Tragedy*

"Will't not be an odd jest" – *Spanish Tragedy*, Additions

"tell me lies at dinnertime" – *Edward II*

"Be not pensive; we are your friends" – *Edward II*

"divers lewd and malicious libels" – *Acts of the Privy Council* 11 May 1593

"practise magic and concealed arts" – Christopher Marlowe, *Doctor Faustus*

"there for honey bees have sought in vain" – Christopher Marlowe, "Hero and Leander"

"Where words prevail not" – *Spanish Tragedy*

"Fear'st thou thy person? Thou shalt have a guard." – *Edward II*

"in one self place" – *Doctor Faustus*

"homo, fuge" – *Doctor Faustus*

"Give it me; I'll have it published in the streets." – *Edward II*

"exceed the rest in lewdness" – *Acts of the Privy Council* 11 May 1593

"any way suspected" – *Acts of the Privy Council* 11 May 1593
"Per Tamburlaine" – Dutch Church Libel
"to the end the author" – *Acts of the Privy Council* 11 May 1593
"timere bonum est" – *Edward II*
"A darksome place and dangerous to pass" – *Spanish Tragedy*
"To comfort you, and bring you joyful news" – *Edward II*
"I will requite it when I come to age" – *Edward II*
"So soon he profits in divinity" – *Doctor Faustus*
"Mock on, here's thy warrant" – *Spanish Tragedy*
"Played with a boy so fair and kind" – "Hero and Leander"
"Let him complain to the See of Hell!" – *Edward II*
"Not of compulsion or necessity" – *Edward II*
"By letting strangers make our hearts to ache" – Dutch Church Libel
"my reverend meaning to the state" – Thomas Kyd, Letter A to Sir John Puckering
"in the fear of God and freedom of my conscience" – Letter A
"But at his looks, Lightborn, thou wilt relent" – *Edward II*
"amplify his grief with bitter words" – *Edward II*
"pleasing Cerberus with honeyed speech" – *Spanish Tragedy*
"imo extra caulas" – Letter A
"No, but wash your face" – *Edward II*
"My heart's so hardened, I cannot repent" – *Doctor Faustus*
"Perhaps thy sacred priesthood makes thee loath" – "Hero and Leander"
"Honour is purchased by the deeds we do" – "Hero and Leander"
"For want of ink receive this bloody writ" – *Spanish Tragedy*
"When to my sorrow I have been ashamed to answer for thee" – *Spanish Tragedy*
"Great gifts are guiles" – John Dowland, "Fine Knacks for Ladies"
"We never beg, but use such prayers as these" – *Edward II*
"Good pennyworths, but money cannot prove" – "Fine Knacks for Ladies'
"First take my tongue, and afterwards my heart" – *Spanish Tragedy*
"a gift prevails / When deep persuading oratory fails" – "Hero and Leander"

ACKNOWLEDGEMENTS

I felt the thrust of this one in the spring of 1993 when reading an introduction to Thomas Kyd's *Spanish Tragedy* and learning about his arrest for the Dutch Church Libel. Not long after that, I encountered Charles Nicholls's *The Reckoning: The Murder of Christopher Marlowe*. I kept tackling this story between other projects; I never expected it to leave my desk. For a while I tried to make it a play, and in 2001 the Playwrights Atlantic Resource Centre set me up with a dramaturge. I learned a lot from that. One thing I should have learned is that I am no playwright.

As always, thanks to my husband, David, who is my first reader and staunchest support, and to my family.

Thanks to Bethany Gibson for the edit, for the conversations, and for good hard shoves.

Thanks to Joanne Soper-Cook for editing an early draft of this as a novella and for daring me to let it become a novel.

Thanks to Ian Cameron at the English Department of Carleton University, for supervising my MA work on the letters of Thomas Kyd and, almost twenty years later, reading and commenting on a draft of this novel.

Thanks to many friends for expertise, manuscript reads, and encouragement in dark days: Fiona-Jane Brown, Jeff Bursey, Robert Chafe, Richard Cumyn, Lindsey Fitzharris, Donna Francis, Anne Furlong, Natasha Gauthier, Kim Hart-Sutton, Joel Thomas Hynes, Catherine McDonald, Kieran More, Ron Ryan, Heather Stewart, Lee Thompson, TC Tuck, and Steve Zytveld.